WAR STORIES
HOME AND AWAY

SUE REID

JILL ATKINS

VINCE CROSS

While the events described and some of the characters in these books may be based on actual historical events and real people, Kitty, Sophie and Edie are fictional characters, created by the authors and their stories are works of fiction.

Scholastic Children's Books,
Euston House, 24 Eversholt Street,
London NW1 1DB, UK

A division of Scholastic Ltd
London ~ New York ~ Toronto ~ Sydney ~ Auckland
Mexico City ~ New Delhi ~ Hong Kong

First published in the UK by Scholastic Ltd, 2009
This edition published by Scholastic Ltd, 2017

War Nurse
First published in the UK by Scholastic Ltd, 2005
Text © Sue Reid, 2005

Sophie's Secret War
First published in the UK by Scholastic Ltd, 2009
Text © Jill Atkins, 2009

Blitz
First published in the UK by Scholastic Ltd, 2001
Text © Vince Cross, 2001

Cover photography © Richard Jenkins Photography

ISBN 978 1407 17864 6

Printed and bound in the UK by CPI Group (UK) Ltd, Croydon, CR0 4YY

2 4 6 8 10 9 7 5 3 1

The rights of Sue Reid, Jill Atkins and Vince Cross to be identified as the authors of this work respectively has been asserted by them in accordance with the Copyright, Designs and Patents Act, 1988.

Papers used by Scholastic Children's Books are made from wood grown in sustainable forests.

www.scholastic.co.uk

Contents

WAR
NURSE

Sue Reid

Sunday 3rd September 1939

We were all at home when the news came. It was an ordinary Sunday – just like any other Sunday in our family.

Mother was closeted in the kitchen with Cook. Father ambled out of his study, paper in one hand, pipe clamped between his teeth. Peter was bent over the wireless, fiddling with the controls. Peter's my brother, two years older and a bit of a whizz with gadgets – at least he thinks he is. I told him to stop or we'd miss the Prime Minister's broadcast – and then he told me we would anyway if he couldn't fix it and we had a bit of an argy-bargy about it.

Then at 11.15 exactly – as if by magic – the crackles stopped and the Prime Minister's sombre voice drifted into the room. Mother and Cook rushed out of the kitchen. Father slowly put down his paper and took the pipe out of his mouth.

Five minutes – that's all it took to turn our world upside down.

We were at war with Germany. That's what the Prime Minister had told us.

Deep down I don't think any of us were surprised. Under their leader, Adolf Hitler, the Germans had already marched into Austria and Czechoslovakia. Then two days ago they'd invaded Poland. This time

Hitler was given an ultimatum. If he didn't agree to withdraw his army from Poland by eleven o'clock this morning, a state of war would exist between our two countries. He hadn't.

I sat there, as if frozen. Peter's hands were motionless on the controls. Suddenly, I found myself wishing that we hadn't quarrelled. Then I heard a click as he leaned across and switched the wireless off. Somehow that seemed to wake us up again.

Mother got up first. "I'll help you pack, Kitten," she said, practical as ever. I got to my feet too then.

A week ago, I'd had a letter from the Red Cross. It said I was to report to Standhaven Military Hospital as soon as war was declared. I'd joined the Red Cross as soon as it seemed likely there'd be a war. I wanted to be a VAD – a Red Cross nurse. (We're called VADs after the Voluntary Aid Detachments which we're all members of.) Even though I'd been at school most of the time I'd managed to pass my First Aid and Home Nursing exams *and* complete my training in our local hospital. Now I'm allowed to nurse soldiers.

In my bedroom, I dragged my suitcase out from under the bed. The last time I'd packed it I'd been going back to school. All that was behind me now. But it still made me feel a bit odd.

There was a lot to go in. First, my VAD uniform.

I opened the wardrobe, where the uniform hung, and laid it out on the bed. There was an awful lot of it. Some of it – like the navy serge overcoat – I wouldn't need until winter. Then there was my nurse's uniform. Carefully I folded the grey-blue dresses and the white aprons with the big red cross on the bib. Then there were the white half-sleeves that I wear on top of my nurse's dress, and caps to go in too. When everything was packed, I put on my "outdoor" uniform – a navy serge jacket and skirt, worn with a white shirt and black tie, black cotton stockings and rubber-soled clumpy black shoes (horrid!).

Mother pinned a badge on to my sleeve. She looked terribly proud as she did it. That badge says that I'm a "mobile VAD", which means that I can be posted to an army hospital anywhere in the country. When I'm 21 – in two years' time – I'll even be able to serve abroad.

Last of all, I put on the hat. Peter roared with laughter when he saw me in it. He said I looked as if I had a pudding basin upside down on my head. "We army chaps had better look out!" he said. I felt annoyed and opened my mouth to tick him off, when something made me stop.

"We army chaps," he'd said. Only then did it dawn on me. I'd be nursing young men – boys – like him. It could even be *my* brother, lying wounded, in bed. Suddenly I felt so frightened. Peter was joining the Infantry. He looked so young – far too young to be going off to fight.

"Oh, Peter," I gasped suddenly. I flung my arms round him, burrowing my head into his shoulder, not wanting him to see that my eyes were wet. He hugged me back and then he stuck a finger under my chin and looked down into my face, all big-brotherly.

"Don't be a goose, Sis," he said, fishing in his pocket for a hanky. "I'll be all right. You'll see."

Then the phone rang. It was Anne – my best friend. Like me she'd joined the Red Cross and we'd done our training together. Unlike me, she was still waiting to be called up.

"I rang to tell you the news," she said.

"I know. War. Isn't it awful?"

There was silence down the line. Something was wrong. "I'm not coming with you," she said. She went on in a rush before I could say anything. "I've been posted to an army hospital – near Leeds! I can't think why!" She gave that throaty laugh of hers. I felt too choked to speak. When I didn't say anything Anne went on: "Kitten, look. I'm going to keep a diary. Will you keep one too? We can pretend we're writing to each other. When it's all over we can show them to each other."

"Why don't we just write to each other?" I said tearfully.

"The post's bound to be awful, Father says. It'll be fun," she urged when I didn't answer. "I will write to you too of course."

"Promise?"

"Promise."

"All right then," I said slowly, even though I wasn't sure how I felt about showing my diary to anyone – even Anne. A diary is a private thing.

And then the line crackled and Mother called to me and so sadly I said goodbye and put the phone down. Everything in my life was changing – and all of it horrid.

The rest of the morning passed in a bit of a whirl. Somehow the news had leaked out that we were off and soon it felt as if the entire village was trooping into the house. Peter and I were made to parade up and down the drawing room in our uniforms. I felt awfully embarrassed but Peter looked wonderful in his lieutenant's uniform.

Peter left first – everyone being terribly brave about it – and then it was my turn. Bert, our gardener and odd-job man, helped us pack up the car. "What have you got in here, miss?" he gasped as he heaved my suitcase into the boot. Then there was my bicycle and tennis racket – even my hockey stick – to fit in.

"Honestly, Mother, I'm not going back to school!" I protested when I saw her march up to the car with *that*, but she said you never know, it may come in handy. I don't know how we got it all in.

As we drove away I turned back. It all looked so safe and cosy, the house nestling amongst the trees, Cook and Bert standing by the door, waving.

I felt as if I was losing something precious and my eyes grew watery again. I tried to pull myself together.

The old life was over, I told myself – but the new one was about to begin. It would be an adventure.

Truth to tell, I was feeling lonely and a bit frightened. We were at war and I was going away – far away from everyone I cared about. Already I felt homesick. Who would I talk to when things were bad? Who could I tell about how I felt?

Then Anne's words floated into my mind. Her voice in my head was as clear as if she was in the car with me.

"I'm going to keep a diary. Will you keep one too?"

I haven't kept a diary since I was a child.

I'd promised her I'd do this.

I needed a friend – a friend I could say *anything* to. Maybe my diary will be that friend for me?

I was dropped off at the station. From there I had to catch a train down to the hospital.

On the platform there were a lot of girls and young women, all wearing the same uniform as me. Some of the older ones had stripes on their jackets, which told me that they'd been VADs for far longer than me. I scanned their faces, but I couldn't see anyone I knew. Where were the girls who'd trained with me?

We VADs weren't the only people waiting for the train. As I skulked on the platform, a soldier winked at me.

"Going back to school, miss?" he asked. He was grinning as he looked at my hockey stick. I blushed hotly. "None of your lip, Private," a Sergeant told him sternly.

The train drew up with a whistle and great puff of steam. Suddenly the Sergeant was by my side.

"We'll help you with that, miss." He jerked his finger at a group of soldiers. "Oy, you. Over here."

I stood back, feeling a bit dazed as the soldiers swarmed around us, heaving suitcases, rackets and bicycles up on to the train.

Inside my compartment I studied the faces opposite me. We smiled shyly at each other from under our pudding-basin hats. We didn't know each other now, but one day, I told myself, those faces would be almost as familiar to me as my own.

3rd September, 11 o'clock pm

I'm writing this under the bedclothes, my diary on my knees, torch in one hand, pencil in the other. I can't turn on the light or I might wake Nurse Mason. And in any case, there's the blackout to think about.

I've not been at the hospital for one whole day, but already I've so much to write about.

I'll begin with the hospital. It's a sprawling Victorian building, rather like St Jude's, my old school. As we drove through the grounds in the bus the army sent to meet us, I saw green lawns and tennis courts and then the hospital itself came into view, slipping in and out behind the trees.

Our sleeping quarters are in the hospital itself. Most of us are in dormitories, but I'm billeted in a small room on the second floor. I share it with one other nurse. All I know about her is that her name is Nurse Mason – and unlike me she's very tidy; there's not one thing out of place on the boxes we use as our dressing table and cupboards. I don't know how she's going to cope with sharing with me, or me with her.

The only other thing there's room for in here are our beds. My bed's awful. First of all it's tiny so that if I stretch out in it my legs hang over the end. Then there's the mattress – a horrid lumpy thing that Bunty says is called "army biscuits". I thought she was joking but Marjorie and Molly say it's true and their father's a colonel so they should know. But when you look out of the window, you can see trees and through them a scrap of shimmering silver – the sea. That almost makes up for everything else.

After we'd been dropped off we were told to assemble in the hall. Matron and a QA Sister were going to talk to us. Mostly it seemed to be about what they expected of us – and what we could expect of them.

The QAs are members of Queen Alexandra's Imperial Military Nursing Service. They're our superiors, for – unlike us – they're fully trained professional nurses. The Regular QAs are full-time army nurses. The Reserves are civilian nurses who joined up when war broke out, like us.

Last of all we had a talk from a Sergeant, who reeled off a lot of stuff that I just know I'll have trouble remembering. Army rules – there seem to be so many of them.

There's one other important person I should mention. This is the Commandant. She calls us "Members" and we call her "Madam". The Commandant's a sort of chief VAD, and she looks awfully fierce. But she says we're to go to her if ever we have a problem.

After they'd gone, I was standing in the hall feeling a bit lost and lonely again when suddenly I heard a shriek. "Kitten!"

I blushed pink. Now everyone would know my nickname!

And then I saw who it was weaving through the packed hall towards me.

"Bunty!" I cried. "Bunty!" I flew across the room and hugged her. "Where were you? I didn't see you on the train."

"Mother dropped me and the twins off," she told me. I looked up at the two girls who'd followed her across the room. They grinned at me.

"Molly! Marjorie!" I cried, hugging each of them.

"Isn't this fun," said Bunty, beaming. "The old St Jude's gang – together again."

"Where's Anne?" Molly asked me. "Didn't she come on the train with you?"

"No," I said dolefully. "The army's sent her to Leeds."

"How absolutely typical!" said Marjorie.

"But why? She joined the same detachment as us!" exclaimed Molly.

"Never mind," said Bunty, hugging me again. "You've got us."

After our "medicals" – all us new VADs have to have these – and supper in the VADs' dining room (the army calls this a "mess"!) we piled into my tiny room. I dived into my luggage, scattering stuff everywhere, hunting for my chocolates – Mother's farewell present.

"Your mother's such a darling," Bunty said, mouth full. "Remind me never to eat a meal in the hospital again."

"It wasn't that bad," said Marjorie.

Just then the door opened and we all looked round. A tall, thin girl was standing in the doorway. I saw her stare at us, all squashed up on

11

the bed together. My eyes followed hers round the room. It was an awful mess. I went pink.

"Hello," I said. "I'm Kitty Langley – you must be my roommate, Nurse Mason." I smiled and held out the chocolates. "I'm sorry about the mess," I added hastily.

She didn't smile back. She just stared at the chocolates – as if she'd never seen one before. Most peculiar.

"No, thank you," she said stiffly at last.

The door closed quietly behind her. We all stared at it.

"Not very friendly," Bunty said.

"She's probably just shy," said Molly kindly.

I shrugged. It probably wasn't going to be much fun sharing with Nurse Mason, but just then I had more important things on my mind.

Tomorrow I begin work – on a medical ward. I'm longing to start though I feel awfully nervous too, but Molly's on duty with me. That's something.

Monday 4th September

I was already awake when my alarm went at six. I had a crick in my neck from the hard army bolster, but I was too excited to care. It was my very first day as a military nurse.

I stumbled about in the semi-darkness, fumbling with the buttons on my uniform, hunting for my white sleeves and apron, while my roommate opened the blackout shutters.

I couldn't do my cap at all!

I raced down the corridor to the dorm. "Bunty!" I wailed, putting my head round the door. Bunty was still in bed.

"Go away," she mumbled.

"It's half past six!" I said, but she just groaned and pulled the sheet up over her head. I couldn't see the twins.

No time to lose. I tore back to my room. I looked at the rectangle of starched white cloth in despair – already it was crumpled from all my attempts to fold the wretched thing.

I felt like bursting into tears. My very first morning and I was going to be late.

Nurse Mason came to my rescue. "Give it to me," she said. I was so surprised that I just handed it to her. I watched as she laid the rumpled rectangle out on the bed, smoothed out the creases and expertly folded it – three neat pleats on each side. Then she pinned it on my head.

"Thank you," I mumbled, feeling awfully small. The merest glimmer of a smile flickered across my roommate's pale face.

I watched as she carefully pinned on her own cap. Unlike me, of course, she'd remembered to make it up the night before. She patted her hair. Not that she needed to – there wasn't a single strand out of place under the crease-free cap.

I just do not know what to make of Nurse Mason!

After breakfast I made my way down to the medical ward where I was to work – Ward B. I was feeling very nervous as I walked down the long corridor, my rubber-soled shoes noiseless on the lino. I'd already got lost once. Outside a pair of double doors, I stopped. Taking a deep breath, I pushed them open.

Before you reach the ward you have to pass Sister's office. There's a window in the office, so that the Sisters can look into the ward and see everything that's going on. Not that our Sister needs it, though – Sister Rook has eyes in the back of her head.

Beyond the office stretches the ward proper – two long rows of beds, one down each side of the room. I counted twenty – ten on each side – but quite a few of the beds were empty. There were screens leaning against the wall. These are pulled round the patients' beds when they need some privacy – like when they're being given a bedbath, or having a dressing changed. Most of the patients were sitting up in bed, bowls of water and shaving foam in front of them. Two men dressed identically in shapeless blue suits – the hospital "blues" worn by all patients allowed up – were playing cards at the ward table.

I'd arrived on the ward punctually at 7.30. Another VAD was already there. It was Nurse Mason.

There was one other person in Sister's office. A pair of beady eyes looked up at me from under a QA's long, flowing cap. "Another raw VAD," they seemed to say. "What *am* I to do with them?"

At 7.35 Molly appeared. I listened as she stammered out her explanation. She'd got lost, she said. Found herself on the Surgical ward.

Was sent down here. Sister nodded, as if she'd heard it all before.

"All my girls know that I will not tolerate lateness," said Sister Rook severely, when we were all assembled. Her gaze rested on Molly. I felt my toes curl inside my shoes. It could so easily have been me.

She took us through our duties. "We have our own ways of doing things here," Sister said. This, I was soon to learn, fell far short of the truth.

Top of Sister's list was cleanliness. "I expect the ward to be thoroughly cleaned. I will not tolerate dust. It's dirty and spreads disease," she announced.

The beady eyes rested on us again, as if daring us to contradict her.

"Yes, Sister," we chorused.

Untidiness was next on Sister's list. She looked at me as if she'd guessed how untidy I am. I blushed. Wish I didn't blush so easily.

Trolleys were being wheeled into the ward now, and Nurse Mason and I were sent off to give the patients their breakfast.

"Nurse Smythe, I'd like a word with you," I heard Sister say to Molly as Nurse Mason and I scuttled off. As I went from bed to bed, trying not to spill the sloppy porridge, I saw Molly shoot past us into the annexe at the end of the ward. When she came out again her eyelids were pink. I wondered what Sister had said to her. I did feel sorry for Molly then.

After the patients had finished, we darted round the beds again, removing bowls and mugs. One of the men sitting at the table winked at me – I smiled at him, hoping he couldn't tell how nervous I was feeling.

Next we had to do the cleaning. There's an awful lot of it – and we VADs have to do it all – every day. I was quite surprised when I discovered this. In the civilian hospital where I'd done my training the cleaning was done by wardmaids. In a military hospital, Molly told me, it's usually done by orderlies of the Royal Army Medical Corps (RAMC). But most of ours have gone out to France.

Before we could start we had to pull out all the beds – awfully heavy, as most had patients still in them. After that out came all the lockers.

Now we had to sweep up all the fluff.

I went over to the annexe where I'd been told the cleaning things were kept. I looked around helplessly. Over by the wall, I could see an odd long-handled thing and a large tin of polish. I couldn't see anything else.

I poked my head out of the annexe. Sister was nowhere to be seen.

Very well then – I'd improvise. I ran some water into a sink – it was cold. Again I searched for a mop – but all I could find were some old rags. Was I supposed to use *them*?

"Nurse Langley!"

I jumped.

"This is *not* how we do the cleaning. Oh dear me, no!" Sister sighed impatiently and opened a tall cupboard. I already knew it was empty, but I didn't dare say so. Sister stared into the empty cupboard in disbelief.

Did she apologize? Oh no! "Run along," was all she said abruptly.

Run *where*?

"Be quick about it," she added. "Medical Officer's round at nine."

The "MO" was the doctor, I knew. I ran.

16

Somehow I managed to scrounge what we needed, and up and down that ward we went again, first one side, then the other, sweeping up the dust and blanket fluff. Then we had to polish the floor using the long-handled thing – it's called a "bumper".

All the time we were doing this the patients egged us on: "That's it, miss, you've got a very good swing there, miss. . . Wish I had muscles like you, miss." My cheeks were flaming now, and it wasn't just the exertion.

Now for the locker tops. After I'd scrubbed the first one thoroughly, I began to put the patient's things back inside.

"Not like that," cried Sister. The army had its own way of doing this, I discovered – even the patients' clothes and wash things have to be laid out in a certain way.

As I carefully folded the clothes in the way I'd been shown, Sister walked by clucking, "Hurry up, Nurse Langley, we don't have all day."

My arms were aching, my back hurt – and I was sure that Sister Rook had it in for me. The patients had gone very quiet but I felt that they were on my side.

We still had the polishing to do. All the brass needed a good shine, apparently – every tiny bit of it – even doorknobs, bed castors and keyholes! Sister says this is very important, but I can't understand why. Neither can Molly, and when Sister was out of earshot (chatting on the wards is *not* allowed) we had a bit of a grumble about it.

It was nine o'clock. Time for the Medical Officer's round. I was standing at the foot of a patient's bed when the MO entered the ward with Sister. He must have walked past me at least twice on his round –

and each time I swear he looked straight through me, as if I didn't exist. Sister was hanging on his every word. It was all "Yes, Major", "No, Major" as they went round the ward together. But he's a *doctor*, I thought, puzzled. Why did Sister address Dr Roberts as "Major" – it wasn't as if he was a soldier? Later, Molly explained. "The doctors and surgeons here are all in the RAMC. They have military ranks, just like soldiers in the army." Honestly, there's just so much to remember!

At ten o'clock my first shift ended and I was sent off for my break. At one I was back on the ward and then I was on duty again until eight. By that time I was so tired that all I wanted to do was crawl out of the ward on my hands and knees.

One of our QA Staff Nurses – Nurse Winter – smiled at me as I left. "You poor kid," she said sympathetically. "Your first day and the worst shift of all."

It *was* the worst shift I thought, as I made my way back along the corridor. We VADs get a three-hour break during the day. Molly was lucky – hers was at five – so she'd already finished for the day. I made my way into the VADs' "mess" for supper.

I slid into my seat. Nurse Mason was there, but I couldn't see Bunty or the twins. As I picked tiredly at my food – corned beef and potatoes again – I wondered where they were. I wanted to find out how they'd got on today – our first day on the wards. I wondered if they felt like me – too tired to know what I felt. Nurse Mason looked tired too. She gave me a tiny smile, but I don't think either of us said a word through the whole meal.

Tuesday 5th September

On Ward B Sister's eye is on us constantly, and if *she's* not hovering, it's Matron. Sister Rook treats us as if we know absolutely nothing. All our Red Cross training – it doesn't seem to count for anything here. It's almost as if we've never even *been* on a ward before.

And then there are the patients. These are sick soldiers who've been sent to us from forces billeted in the area. Sick *officers* are nursed separately in their own block. None of the soldiers have been in action yet. Many of them don't look any older than Peter, and some of them are such teases.

They've already given us nicknames. They're really cheeky. I've not discovered what mine is yet. To my face it's always "miss" – never "nurse".

They like to play jokes on us too. And today it was my turn.

I'd just slapped polish on the floor and was struggling to get the bumper moving when I heard a hoarse voice behind me.

"Miss, I'd like a bedbath."

It was Private Porter. "Now, Private, you know this isn't the time for your bath," I said, trying to sound both firm and sympathetic at the same time.

"Oh, please, miss," he said. "I spilt me tea all down meself."

I had a lot to do before the MO's round and Private Porter's a large man. I did *not* want to stop and give him a bedbath. I did not have *time* to give him a bedbath. But I had no choice.

"I'll just see what the damage is," I said, trying to sound cheerful. Dutifully I marched over to the screens and began to pull one of them over to the Private's bed. The screen was big and heavy, and it wobbled dangerously as I hauled it across the ward. I was just going back for another one, when I heard a second voice call plaintively: "Miss! Miss!"

This patient wanted a bedbath too!

"Me too, miss." I whirled round again.

This patient was sitting, fully dressed, at the ward table. As I looked at him, he shut one brown eye in a long, slow wink. Only then did I realize that they were teasing me! I felt such an idiot.

Unfortunately for me, Sister had heard all the fuss. "What's going on here?" she asked, bustling into the ward. "Well?" she said, looking at Molly, Nurse Mason and me in turn. "Nurse Langley – I should have known," her face seemed to say, as her eyes rested on my scarlet face. I stuttered out an explanation.

"Private Porter wants a bedbath."

"It's not time for his bath," she said, eyebrows raised.

"I . . . I know, Sister," I said feebly. "He says he spilt his tea. I . . . I mean. . ." I didn't know what to say. How could I tell Sister that they'd been teasing me?

"Hmph," she said, and I saw her vanish behind the screen by the Private's bed.

I don't know what went on behind the screen, but Private Porter didn't say anything more about a bedbath after that.

Me, I returned to the bumpering. I seized the handle in both hands. I'll show them, I thought furiously. I'll show them that I can do something well. Ward B's floor was going to get the best polish it had ever had. Slowly I heaved the bumper back and forth, puffing from the effort. Suddenly I found that it was gliding easily over the floor. I turned to find a pair of strong male hands gripping the handle next to mine.

"Sorry about that, miss," the Private murmured. "We didn't mean to get you into trouble with Sister."

Whispering, he told me that his name was Private Barrett and then he asked *my* name. He looked sad when I just said "Nurse Langley". We're not allowed to tell the patients our first names. It's another hospital rule and *not* to be broken. Not ever.

Wednesday 6th September

This morning Nurse Winter showed us how to sterilize the instruments. Dressing bowls, forceps, bandages, scissors – everything has to be sterilized to prevent our patients from picking up infections. We have two sterilizers for this on Ward B. One for all the instruments, the other for dressing bowls. Things like bandages and dressings are sterilized in the autoclave in the operating-theatre suite.

After Nurse Winter had shown us what to do, we all had a go – Nurse Mason, Molly and me.

When it was my turn, I scrubbed my hands thoroughly – our hands have to be spotlessly clean too! – and then I lifted the lid of one of the sterilizers and popped in the instruments. When it had done its job, I lifted the lid again, pulled down the handle and watched the water drain away.

Then we watched as Nurse Winter whisked a pair of forceps out of a jar of disinfectant. "Cheatle forceps," I murmured, looking at the long-handled scissor-like instrument with the curved blades.

Nurse Winter looked at me. "Quite right, Nurse Langley. Can you tell me what we use them for?"

I could!

"To pick up other sterile objects – like swabs or other instruments," I said automatically.

"Would you do that for me now?"

I took the pair of forceps and carefully plucked out each instrument from the sterilizer in turn, tipping the surplus fluid back inside. One by one I placed each item on to the dressing tray.

"Thank you, Nurse Langley," she said when I'd finished. "You did that very well." It was only a little thing but I did feel pleased.

On the notice board this afternoon, BIG warning. Colonel's inspection in the morning. Before we went off duty, Sister told us just how important this is. The Colonel's the most senior-ranking doctor in the hospital. We're all on our toes!

Thursday 7th September

Today was my first Colonel's inspection. What a to-do it is – and to think we get put through this every week!

Everything had to be absolutely spotless. *I* thought we already did a thorough job, but this morning I found out what a clean ward really is. The "up" patients lent us a hand, but even with their help, it was a rush to get everything done in time. Five minutes before the Colonel was due, my reddened hands squeaky clean, fresh apron donned, I scurried back into the ward. In front of me, one of our "up" patients ambled slowly across the room to his bed.

Ash was spilling off the end of his cigarette on to the sparkling linoleum. The Colonel would have our guts for this, I thought, despairingly.

A man with bristly ginger hair hauled himself up in bed.

"What do you think you're doing, Private Barrett?" Corporal Smart wheezed.

"Corporal!" Private Barrett leapt to attention.

"Colonel's inspection, you dozy soldier!"

"Corporal!"

"At eleven!"

"Corporal!"

"So jump to it, soldier!"

Private Barrett stubbed out his cigarette in the tin hat dangling on the locker by his bed. At that Corporal Smart's face turned puce! Private Barrett winked at me, and loped off to clean up the mess, the tin hat swinging in his hand.

At eleven o'clock on the dot the big ward doors swung open and in walked the Colonel, escorted by Matron and what seemed to me to be half the hospital staff. The "up" patients stood stiffly to attention in front of their beds. As the Colonel entered, an order rang out and they clicked their heels smartly together. I felt as if I was on parade – not in a hospital ward at all.

I watched as the Colonel stopped at each patient's bedside; he was listening intently to Matron, but I could tell that he'd miss nothing. I looked round the ward, feeling almost too scared to breathe. The floor shone, but was it really clean? Each bedstead gleamed, but had we polished them thoroughly enough? Each shiny bed castor was lined up with the one next to it. Our sickest patients lay very still under the smoothed-down sheets – they looked almost as scared as me.

The Colonel stopped and ran a white-gloved hand over a locker. We all drew in breath together. The Colonel turned his gloved hand over and inspected it.

My heart began to thump. Almost I felt as if it was *me* who was being inspected.

The glove was spotless, and the Colonel walked on again. It seemed we'd passed – this time.

Friday 8th September

Private Barrett was discharged back to his regiment this morning. I was sent to the store to get his kit and take back his hospital "blues".

"Goodbye, Kitten," he whispered slyly to me as he left. I went beet red. How *did* Private Barrett find out my nickname?

Today we got our first week's pay. For this we all had to line up at Company Office and one by one we were given our wages.

"Langley," barked a voice when it was my turn. I stepped forward and something was pressed into my hand. I looked down. £1 didn't seem a lot for all our hard work, but it was the first money I'd ever earned and I felt quite proud. Not everyone felt the same it seemed, for as we were walking away, I heard a VAD say in a piercing voice, "Oh, I could *never* manage on *this*! *So* lucky that I don't have to." I wished she'd stop banging on about it. Not everyone has parents rich enough to send them an allowance. Nurse Mason was standing nearby. Her face was absolutely stony.

Saturday 9th September

So lucky – my half day off and the others are off too! Slept in – bliss! – and then we cycled into town together – Bunty, me, Molly and Marjorie. I asked Nurse Mason if she'd like to come too, but I was quite relieved when she said no thank you, she had a lot to do. I raced along to the dorm, where the others were waiting for me. It was heaven to get away from the hospital and we sang as we cycled along.

It was very quiet in the town. Because it's on the coast, a lot of the townspeople have left and many of the houses – and a lot of the shops – are boarded up.

After cycling around for a time, we found an ice cream parlour that was still open, and Bunty treated us all to strawberry ice cream. Delish!

We ate our ices sitting on the beach and then I lay back on the warm sand, pillowing my head on my arms.

"So – what's the verdict?" A shadow fell across my face and I opened my eyes to find Bunty peering at me.

I shut my eyes again. I didn't feel like talking.

"Come on, Kitten – tell," Bunty wheedled. "I want to know all about Ward B."

"Ask Molly," I said sleepily.

"Is it true that Sister Rook is the most terrifying QA in the hospital?"

"No," said Marjorie. "That's Sister Brown."

"Who's she?" I asked, eyes still shut.

"She's the Sister on *my* ward," said Marjorie.

We giggled and I sat up, hugging my knees.

"I think I'm lucky then," said Bunty. "Sister Bolton on my ward is sweet."

"How are you getting on with Nurse Mason, Kitty?" asked Marjorie.

"She's all right," I said. "But I wish I was in the dorm with all of you."

"Kitten," said Bunty firmly. "I want to know. Do you like being an army nurse?"

"It's all cleaning, bedbaths and bedpans," I said. "I'd like to do some *real* nursing."

"You and your real nursing," said Bunty. "You're a VAD, not a trained nurse."

"I know, I know," I said, lying back down again. I knew that Bunty was right, but still, I wanted to do more. *Proper* nursing. We cycled slowly back, along the promenade that runs above the beach. While the others rode on ahead I stopped for a moment and stared out to sea. It was another glorious autumn day and the sea looked so calm and peaceful, yet somewhere across that narrow strip of water was our army – the BEF (British Expeditionary Force). Some time soon my brother's unit would be joining them. Today I found that hard to believe. Even seeing those boarded-up houses hadn't made the War any more real to me. It seems so very far away – almost as if it's not really happening at all.

Sunday 10th September

I was in the bath this evening when the alarm bell rang. It was our first air-raid warning.

I leaped out of the bath, pulled on my clothes and hared downstairs. I was terrified – my legs jelly on the stairs, gas mask strapped across my chest, tin hat in my shaking hand. After the Roll had been taken we huddled together in the mess, listening – for what? The drone of an enemy plane flying overhead? A bomb dropping on top of us? We clung on to each other – teeth chattering in chorus.

"Are you frightened?" Bunty whispered to me.

"'Course I am," I said. "Aren't you?"

"Terrified," she said.

It wasn't long before the all-clear went – false alarm. A big sigh went up round the room.

My teeth were still chattering as we went back upstairs. "Are you still scared?" Bunty asked me.

"I'm cold. I was having a bath when the alarm went."

"Honest?"

"Honest!"

Monday 11th September

One of the first things a VAD learns is where the bedpans are kept. This morning, when the cry went up, I dashed as usual into the annexe to fetch one. As fast as I could I pulled screens round my patient's bed. Next I had to slide the thing under the patient's body. This is *never* an easy job – you have the pan in one hand, and have to help hoist the patient up with the other. Afterwards, I carefully remove the pan, cover it with a cloth and slowly walk across the ward to the annexe where the pans are cleaned. Only this morning I forgot to cover it! Sister nearly had a fit when she saw me carry the full pan back across the ward.

After that I felt awfully jumpy, and my fingers were all thumbs. This afternoon I dropped the sterile Cheatle forceps on the floor with a clang. Then it took me ages before I got the water the right temperature for a patient's bath. At that, even nice Nurse Winter lost patience with me. By the time I went off duty I was dog-tired and practically in tears. Out of the corner of my eye I could see Sister smiling – actually smiling! – at Nurse Mason.

I looked back as the ward doors closed behind me. Nurse Mason was wheeling the dressing trolley over to Corporal Smart's bed. I saw her lift the forceps out of the jar. I turned away then. I didn't want to see any more. I just knew that Nurse Mason wouldn't drop them.

Not like me.

Tuesday 12th September

I gave myself a bit of a talking-to last night. I have resolved that:

I must not let Sister Rook upset me. She's right to criticize me when I make mistakes.

I must never forget that I'm here to look after the patients. That's more important than anything else.

The talking-to seemed to have worked. I didn't make a single mistake all morning!

My first shift ended at two today and off I went to have my vaccinations. We all have to have these to protect us from serious diseases like smallpox and typhoid. I was back on duty at five, but my arm felt hot and heavy and by six o'clock I was feeling very wobbly. Sister glanced at me, laid a cool dry hand on my forehead, and jabbed a thermometer in my mouth. 100 degrees! She told me to go to bed and to stay there until my temperature had come down. Her voice was unusually gentle. Most surprising.

My temperature was up again this evening. I'm sure that tossing and turning on those awful army biscuits didn't help.

Something else surprising – Nurse Mason must have brought me a mug of tea. I found it – cold – when I woke up.

Wednesday 13th September

My arm's still rather stiff, but my temperature's down so it was back on duty for me.

Our youngest QA – Nurse Green – was in such a flap this morning. One of our patients – Private Johnson – was due to be discharged back to his regiment today. Suddenly his temperature shot up. 103!

It was very odd. He'd seemed all right at breakfast. And then I saw the mug of tea on his locker. Of course it was obvious then what Private Johnson had done – he'd stuck the thermometer in the mug of hot tea. It's an old, old trick. I went up to Nurse Green.

"Nurse Green," I said shyly, pointing to the mug. "Do you think that . . . maybe. . .?"

She wouldn't even let me finish. "Don't be ridiculous, Nurse Langley," she snapped.

I caught Molly's eye. Her eyes widened when I pointed out the mug. We grinned at each other, and then I turned back to find Nurse Green glaring at me so I hopped off to my duties.

Sister had popped out, so Nurse Green went to fetch a doctor. It wasn't

Major Roberts who came, it was a tall, young doctor I'd not seen before. He strode up to the bed, looking awfully keen. "A real case for me," his face seemed to say. It was such a nice face too, I thought.

Nurse Green explained the problem and the MO nodded seriously. He took Johnson's wrist in his fingers and checked his pulse. Then I watched as he got out his stethoscope to listen to his chest, and then he began to prod and pull Johnson all over the place. He looked very puzzled. He hadn't seen the mug of tea. I wished I could tell him about it, but I was only a VAD and we VADs are *not* supposed to talk to the doctors.

Johnson just lay there, eyes shut, though I saw him wince once or twice.

Then Sister reappeared, and the MO explained his findings. Sister nodded her head. She looked at Johnson.

"Now, Johnson, what's all this?" I heard her ask him briskly.

"Oh, Sister, I come over all bad. Very sudden it was," he said, eyes still firmly shut. Sister nodded grimly and thrust the thermometer back in Johnson's open mouth. After a minute she took it out and examined it.

"Well, it's back to normal now," she said. "You seem to have made an equally sudden recovery." I saw her reach up to the bedside locker. She picked up the mug.

Sister Rook just looked at Nurse Green. She didn't need to say anything. Nurse Green got out a handkerchief and pretended to blow her nose, but we could all see how red her face had gone behind it. I looked down at my feet.

"Thank you, Lieutenant," Sister Rook said, turning to the MO. The expression on her face was clear enough. Major Roberts would never have made a mistake like that. I felt sorry for the MO then.

Sister Rook pursed up her lips in that way of hers and looked at her patient firmly. Johnson just rolled his eyes and shrugged his shoulders. I suppose he'd thought it worth a try.

Nurse Green was on the mat for that, and Sister looked more and more sour as the day went on. It was all "sweep up that fluff!" (there wasn't any) and "why's that patient's sheet not straight?" (it was!). I was very relieved when it was five o'clock and I went off duty.

Bunty and Marjorie were also finishing at five today and they asked me to come into town with them, but my arm was still sore and all I wanted to do was crawl upstairs to bed. It's all I ever want to do when I go off duty. My arms have sprouted muscles I never knew I had from heaving that bumper about. My feet and back ache constantly from standing all day long. As for my hands – already they're rough and red from all the washing and cleaning. Sister's hands are as soft as a baby's. I don't know what her secret is but Bunty reckons it's because she spends more time in the duty room with our MO than on the ward. She says everyone knows that Sister Rook has a soft spot for Major Roberts. That did make us laugh. I even saw Nurse Mason's lips twitch. If you knew Major Roberts you'd understand why.

I *still* don't know Nurse Mason's first name, and wonder if she'll ever tell me it. She's awfully proper. We're all rather in awe of her – even Bunty.

Thursday 14th September

Letter from Anne today! When it was time for my break I settled down to read it.

"Dear Kitten, It's so awful that you're down there and I'm up here in Leeds. I do *not* like it here. The hospital's outside the town, it rains all the time and I don't know a soul. Food's awful. Sister's a little tyrant. We spend most of our time cleaning!

"Are the rest of the St Jude's gang there? Remember me to them.

"Wish I was there – or you here. I miss you so much.

"Are you keeping up your diary? I am! Please write soon. I want lots of gossip. Better stop now – or I'll be late for work and Sister will eat me alive."

I turned the page over. Anne had scribbled a brief PS on the back: "Have you heard from Giles yet? I'll bet he looks dashing in his pilot's uniform."

I *haven't* heard from Giles yet. Giles is sort of my boyfriend. I met him at a village dance earlier this summer and he told me he was joining the RAF. He wants to train as a fighter pilot. Anyway, he asked if he could write to me and would I write back. I felt very flattered – he's awfully handsome – and I liked him too, so I said that I would. I wonder when I'll hear from him. I've been here nearly two weeks now and not a squeak from him. I'm beginning to think he's forgotten me already.

Friday 15th September

I had a bit of a grumble to Molly about Sister today and . . . and . . . well, about *everything*. Like all the silly rules, that clicking of heels, and that to-do about how the patients lay in bed when the Colonel did his inspection. It seemed all wrong to me. "Their comfort should come first," I said to Molly vehemently.

And lastly, I aired my favourite grumble – when when when would I get the chance to do some proper nursing?

"When I can trust you, Nurse Langley," I thought I heard someone say. A moment later I saw Sister sail past us. Was that her voice in my ear, or just a tiny voice inside my head? It's been puzzling me all afternoon, and I just don't know the answer.

Monday 18th September

I got my first-ever letter from Giles today. I was so pleased when I saw it waiting for me – raced off straightaway to read it – but now I just feel miserable.

It was all about the planes he's learning to fly – lots of technical stuff that's too boring to write here. It wasn't what I'd been expecting at all. Then at the end he wrote: "Ripping that you said you'd write to me. Please write back – soon." He sounded a bit lonely – and suddenly I felt sorry for him. But I don't want to feel *sorry* for him – not if he's to be my boyfriend. Oh bother, I don't know what I feel – or what he feels about me! I wish there was someone I could talk to about Giles – someone who really knows him.

I'd been so looking forward to hearing from him. And I know I must write back soon, but now I just don't know what to say to him.

Monday 25th September

Weekly gas drill this morning. For half an hour we had to do the chores with our gas masks and tin hats on. I always want to giggle when I see Sister Rook in hers – today I did, and then my mask misted up and I tripped up over Private Baker's boots. I made a grab for the bedpost and righted myself just in time. Luckily Sister didn't notice, or I'd have been in trouble again.

It's a week now since I had my letter from Giles but I only sat down to answer it today. My first attempt was awfully stilted – all about my work on the wards. It was quite as dull as his. So I tried again. I told myself to forget the awfully unsatisfactory letter I'd got from him and just think about the boy I'd met and how much I'd liked him. That made it much easier and I got on swimmingly. I feel a lot happier now. What does one silly letter matter anyway?

Wednesday 27th September

This evening I saw a bunch of VADs clustered round the notice board in the mess. I couldn't get close enough to see what the fuss was all about, but Molly saw me and called me over.

"We've been asked to a regimental dance," she said excitedly, waving a finger at the board.

I'm thrilled! I've never been to a regimental dance before! Bunty's already planning to go into town first to get her hair done. I don't know how she thinks she'll find the time. Marjorie's going round with a long face. Poor Marjorie. She's just started on night duty and so will miss all the fun.

Friday 29th September

Molly and I are so envious of Nurse Mason! She's won Sister's trust – the first of us three to do so. So now she's being allowed to take the patients' temperature, pulse and respiration – a very responsible job. (Doing the TPRs we call this.) And it's all thanks to Molly's infected hand.

We were in the annexe today, putting away the cleaning things, when I heard Nurse Mason exclaim: "Nurse Smythe – your hand!" She sounded really shocked. Molly looked down at it and tucked it out of sight at once, but Nurse Mason asked if she could have a look. Slowly Molly held out her hand and Nurse Mason took it in hers and turned it over. It was very inflamed and sore-looking. As Nurse Mason was inspecting it, I noticed *her* hands too. I was startled. They look as soft and white as Sister's, yet Nurse Mason spends just as much time cleaning as Molly and me.

"You need to get that treated," she said at last, putting Molly's hand down gently. Then she had a look at Molly's other hand. It, too, was all red and cracked. I clasped my own roughened hands behind my back, feeling rather ashamed of them.

"Make sure you put plenty of cream on that hand," she told Molly firmly. "Germs can get into the cracks. You don't want it to get infected, do you?"

Molly looked awfully sheepish, but before she could say anything Sister's voice cut in.

"Nurse Smythe, Nurse Mason, I'd like a word with you." We all jumped – even Nurse Mason! I wish Sister wouldn't creep up on us like that.

Poor Molly! When Sister Rook saw her hands she gave her such a wigging. Afterwards she shooed her into the treatment room and then she beckoned Nurse Mason over. I thought she was going to get a telling off too – for talking – but Sister Rook was smiling now. I wondered what Sister was saying to her.

Later this morning I found out. Nurse Mason walked up to a patient, a thermometer in her hand. She popped it into his mouth. I thought I'd drop through the floor! Then she put a finger on her patient's pulse to check that that was normal too and looked carefully at him to check his breathing.

Nurse Mason was doing the TPRs! I looked at her face. I thought she'd be thrilled, but she looked just the same as she always does.

As for me, I was still in shock. But I'm not surprised that she's won Sister's trust. Nurse Mason *is* a jolly good VAD.

She's not popular amongst the VADs though. This evening when we left Ward B I heard some VADs giggling about her in the corridor.

"Nurse Mason's nickname's Titch," one of them said.

"Maybe that will bring her down to size," another voice said, giggling.

"Oh, don't be so unkind. She's not that bad," I heard someone burst out suddenly. Me! They looked round, surprised.

"It's Nurse Mason's roommate," I heard one of them whisper as I stalked off.

It's true, I don't dislike Nurse Mason, I just feel I don't know her any better than when we came. She's very reserved. Whenever I try to talk to her all I get is "yes" or "no".

Later I asked Bunty if *she's* got a nickname yet. She went pink, but she won't say.

Sunday 1st October

My first whole day's leave – I spent it at home! I caught the train and Mother met me at the other end. Fell off the train into her arms. I gave her a huge hug – I was so pleased to see her. She held me away from her for a moment.

"Darling, you're so thin!" she said, sounding horrified. I told her I was fine but I ate every morsel at lunch. Seconds too. Roast beef and Yorkshire pud, trifle to follow. Delish! We're not badly fed at the hospital but the food's very dull and I'm always hungry.

The house seemed awfully quiet without Father and Peter. Peter's still training with his unit. And Father?

"He couldn't get any time off," said Mother sadly. She said he's not allowed to tell her anything about his work for the government – it's top secret. Poor Mother. I think she gets pretty lonely, and now Cook's been talking about joining up. So Mother's wondering whether she should join up too.

We listened to Mr Churchill, one of the government ministers, on the wireless. The news is awful. Poland's finally fallen to the enemy.

We British just stood by and watched while our ally, Poland, was invaded. Now the country's being divided up between Germany and Soviet Russia. I think we should be ashamed that we allowed it to happen.

Afterwards, Mother and I went for a brisk walk. We didn't talk any more about the War. She asked me about my work but I quickly changed the subject. For those few precious hours I wanted to forget all about the War – and the hospital.

I felt sad as we drove away from the house. I knew it might be a long time before I could come home again.

When Mother dropped me off at the station, she handed me a bulky package.

"It's a surprise," she smiled. "Open it when you get back."

As soon as I was alone in my room, I opened Mother's parcel. Cake, biscuits, chocolate, fruit tumbled out on to the bed. I felt a bit tearful as I looked at it lying there. Mother's so good to me. Then Nurse Mason walked in and just stared at it all. It did look awful – all that food strewn over my bed – and suddenly I felt very embarrassed. Timidly I asked her to help herself, and eventually she took one biscuit, but she did so very reluctantly. She looked as if she wanted to say something, but she didn't. My roommate is *such* a puzzle still. But at least she's told me her first name now. It's Jean.

Friday 6th October

There are two good things about all the cleaning we have to do. Firstly, it helps keep our patients free of infection. That makes us very proud. And it's when I go round the beds each day, pulling them out, scrubbing and tidying the lockers, polishing the bedsteads, that I can lean over and talk to my patients. For me this is the best thing about being a VAD.

Underneath all their cheek I've come to realize that our patients are just awfully homesick. For most of them it's their first time ever away from home. I want to help them, and I hope that I do, even if it's just little things like this and not the proper nursing I long to do. And as soon as they're well, they're back to their regiments – and danger. I never let myself forget that.

Saturday 7th October

The big day today – and my busiest yet on Ward B. We're short-staffed, as Molly's off sick with her bad hand, and now Nurse Winter's gone

43

down with flu. I don't know how we got all the work done this morning and, to make matters worse, every time I looked up I saw Sister Rook's eyes clamped on me. As the afternoon drew on I was feeling more and more excited. I glanced at the ward clock. Quarter to five. In just fifteen minutes I'd go off duty – so long as Sister didn't want me to do anything else. I tiptoed past her office into the ward kitchen, to make a cup of tea for one of the patients, hoping she wouldn't notice me. I was just tiptoeing back on to the ward again when she shot out of her room. I was so startled that I nearly dropped the cup.

"Nurse Langley, I'd like you to do something for me," she said, as though she was doing me a huge favour.

"Yes, Sister," I said, wondering what she wanted me to do. Was she beginning to trust me at last?

"I need someone to do Private Morris's pressure points. We don't want him to get any bedsores, do we?"

Ugh! Bedsores are one of Sister's Big Things and now I had to listen to her on the subject again. Out of the corner of one eye I saw the hands of the ward clock reach five. Sister was still talking.

"None of my patients ever gets a bedsore!" she said, giving me one of her beady looks.

"Yes, Sister," I said obediently.

It's a horrible job – and it takes ages. When at last I was allowed off duty it was getting on for six and I was dog-tired. I raced off for a bath. I was yearning for a good long soak, but you can't, not in the shallow bath we're allowed here – five inches deep at most. Anyway, I didn't have time now. I leaned back in the tub, watching the steam fill the cubicle, and then I closed my eyes.

Half an hour later I heard someone bang on the bathroom door. I'd nodded off! Still damp from my bath, I belted back to my room. My clothes were laid out ready on the bed, cap freshly made up, but I was in such a hurry by now that I put my heel through my last good pair of stockings. Proper silk ones too! Bunty came to my aid and we did a hasty repair job – dabbing mascara on the pink bits that showed. We raced up to the bus, greatcoats flapping round our shoulders. The driver tooted his horn. We climbed on board just as the bus was pulling out. I had to do my make-up in the back as the bus lurched off down the drive.

The dance was jolly good fun. There was a real band: it was thumping away as we entered – a bit shyly. We VADs were awfully popular, we soon discovered, as there were at least twice the number of men to girls, but after only a couple of dances my feet were killing me and I had to turn down several partners.

Then a Second Lieutenant came up and asked me to dance. I was about to turn him down too, when he blurted out: "We're going to France." He looked excited – and so heartbreakingly young. I felt I *had* to dance with him then.

"My brother's unit will be out there soon too," I told him, trying to stop my voice from wobbling.

"Jolly good show," he said approvingly, and he held out his hand to swing me in to the dance.

As soon as we'd arrived Bunty had vanished into the hot, smoky room, but when my dance was over she suddenly appeared at my shoulder.

"What are you doing?" I said, annoyed, as she hauled me away from the dance floor.

"Your heels," she hissed. I looked down. Great gaping pink bits! In *both* of them!

"Oh, Bunty," I wailed.

"Never mind. We'll soon fix it," she said, fishing mascara out of her handbag.

She looked over my shoulder. "Wait a jif! That officer's coming back." I pulled a face.

"What's wrong?" she said. "He looks nice." Then she smiled. "Of course. Silly me. It's Giles, isn't it?"

"Maybe," I said, blushing.

"You've heard from him, haven't you?" she said, eyes twinkling.

I nodded, face scarlet now.

"I'll get rid of him," she whispered.

The officer had reached us now. Bunty turned and smiled at him. "Would you be very kind and fetch me a drink?" she said, batting her eyelashes at him. Bunty's eyelashes are so long, I sometimes wonder if they're real. The officer swallowed and I saw a tide of colour flood his face. Bunty winked at me as he disappeared back into the throng crowding the bar. Then she slipped into the crowd behind him.

I giggled. Bunty's a real friend.

At the end of the evening the band played "We'll Meet Again" and then someone began to sing "Auld Lang Syne" and one by one we all joined in. I had a lump in my throat and some of the girls were a bit tearful as they said goodbye. The regiment leaves in a week.

I didn't see Bunty again until we were back on the bus. She fell asleep, head on my shoulder. She had a big smile on her face.

Sunday 8th October

Half day this morning. Slept and slept and slept. Jean told me the girls popped by to see me, but she wouldn't let them wake me. There's a kind streak in Jean Mason.

I think one of the patients quite likes me. Anyway, he blushed when I took him his supper this evening. And that made *me* blush. It's that young Private – Private Morris. It's drummed into us that we mustn't have favourites amongst the patients, and I do try to treat them all the same. So when I went back to take away his dirty plate I was a bit brisker with him. He gave me such a sad look and I just felt mean. So I gave him a big smile when I said goodnight and he smiled back, all pink again. Oh dear, I just don't know how to treat him.

As I walked past the dorm this evening, Molly saw me. She pounced. "I want to hear all about the dance – Bunty won't tell me anything!" she cried.

Spent the rest of the evening in the dorm, gossiping. Molly told me she thinks Bunty's got a new flame – *I* think I know who it is!

Tuesday 10th October

Went on the ward today to find that screens have been placed round Private Morris's bed. Private Morris has been here the longest of all our patients now.

Our MO was an awfully long time in there with him this morning and his face looked very grave when he came out again. Matron was with him. He had a long murmured conversation with her as they stood outside the screens.

I took Private Morris his lunch. It's not hard to see why the doctors are so worried about him. He's awfully thin and frail.

I sat down next to his bed. I'd cut up his food into little pieces and now I tried to persuade him to eat it. It was awful – after only one mouthful he was sick. He looked up at me shamefacedly.

"I'm sorry, miss, really sorry," he said.

He was sorry! I was almost in tears as I mopped up. I wish there was something more I could do for him. I wish he'd get better.

Wednesday 11th October

I had a bit of a shock when I reported for duty this morning. Private Morris's bed was empty. He's been transferred to another hospital.

I know it's the right decision. I know that there he'll get the specialist care he needs, but I did feel upset. I'd not even been able to say goodbye.

Molly's hand is better now, and after work I cycled into town with her and Bunty. I cheered up a bit then. We stopped at a hotel for drinks because Bunty said she was hot and needed a long drink before cycling back.

She went very red as she said it, and she blushed each time the hotel doors swung open. I felt sure that she was expecting someone, even though she pretended she wasn't. Anyway, whoever it was, they didn't show, and she was quite grumpy on the way back. I asked her what was wrong. She said it was nothing. Nothing! I cycled on ahead. I felt very put out. Why wouldn't she tell me what was going on? I thought she was my friend! And on top of everything else now we were going to be late for Roll Call. Afterwards, I stomped up to my room on my own and spent the next hour writing letters. I tore up my letter to Giles. I can't write to him again. I've got to wait to hear from him first. Anyway, I don't know *what* to say to him. I got into bed to write my diary, still feeling all cross and bothered.

Sunday 15th October

Yesterday I got a scribbled note from Peter. I turned over the envelope and looked at the date. It was two weeks old.

"This is it, Sis," he'd written hastily in pencil. "The lads are off – by the time you get this I'll be in France. Tell Mater not to worry, won't you? Better still, be a love and pop over to see her if you can." That was the gist of it – Peter's not one for letter-writing.

I felt sure that Mother was worried. *I* was worried – terribly worried – and it was that which drove me to go to church. It was a long time since I'd been, but today I felt I simply had to go.

As I walked up to the church something felt wrong. Slowly it dawned on me what it was. The church bells weren't ringing. And they won't ring again until the War's over, unless it's to warn us that the country's been invaded. *All* the church bells will ring then. Just thinking about that made me feel a whole lot worse.

I don't think I've ever prayed so hard before. I prayed for Peter – and then I prayed for that regiment. They'll be in France too by now. And then I prayed for Giles. I don't know what to think about Giles.

I've still not heard from him. Has something awful happened to him? Or is it simply that he doesn't care any more? I know I shouldn't feel cross – especially not in church – but I did. I just don't know whether I should be worrying about him or not.

Jean was in church too. I saw her, two rows in front of me, when I sat down in my pew again. After the sermon, when we stood for the hymn, she stayed in her seat, head bowed, as though she'd forgotten where she was. And as soon as the service was over she rushed straight out. She looked as if she wanted to be on her own, so I didn't try to catch up with her. I found myself wondering if *she* has someone close – a brother maybe – out in France too.

Spent the evening writing to Anne and Peter and then I went to the VADs' mess to listen to the news on the wireless. Bunty was there. She flushed, and I saw her tuck something hastily away in a pad of paper. She looked up at me and smiled, but it wasn't much of a smile.

I sat down next to her.

"What's wrong, Bunty?" I asked straightaway.

She flushed a deeper shade of pink.

"Come on, Bunty, 'fess," I wheedled.

She looked down at her lap. "Sorry, Kitten, I just – I. . ."

"It's that Lieutenant, isn't it?" I said abruptly. "The Lieutenant we met at the dance. You like him, don't you?"

She nodded. Her hands were clenched tightly in her lap. "Kitten, I meant to tell you, really I did. But . . . oh, Kitten, I do like him, but I don't know what *he* thinks. . . I'd hoped to see him before he left.

I did see him once, and he said he'd try and see me again, but he didn't, and now I don't know what he feels. . . If he feels. . ." her voice trailed away again.

"Oh Bunty, I'm sure he wanted to see you!" I burst out. "He'd have had a lot to do before going out to France." I sort of mumbled the last words, for Bunty's face was crumpling again. She blinked her eyes very fast and I felt my eyes prick too. I can't bear thinking about them all out in France.

"How's Giles?" Bunty asked suddenly.

"I don't know," I said slowly. "He hasn't answered my last letter. Oh Bunty, I don't know what to think any more."

"Maybe he's just very busy too," said Bunty. "Or maybe he never even got your letter."

I hadn't thought of that. "Maybe," I said.

I got up and turned up the wireless and we pulled our chairs up close to the set. Jean came in then. I saw her hesitate when she saw us sitting there so cosily together, so I told her to pull up a chair.

That gloomy newsreader was on again. The news is bad. One of our battleships, *The Royal Oak*, was torpedoed and sunk by a German U-boat in Scapa Flow early yesterday morning. About 700 men drowned – the ship's commander amongst them. I hadn't a clue where Scapa Flow was – neither did Bunty – until Jean told us that it's between the Orkney Islands and the north coast of Scotland. Jean really does know the most extraordinary things.

I think we all felt very down after that, so Jean went down to the kitchen and returned with mugs of steaming cocoa. That cheered us all wonderfully – even Bunty perked up a bit.

Monday 23rd October

Today Sister ordered me to help Nurse Winter with a dressing – a kaolin poultice for one of our patients who's got a bad chest.

I was thrilled. After nearly two months here, they'd learn that I did know something.

"We're a bit short of kaolin," Nurse Winter told me, scrubbing her hands thoroughly as she talked, "so we'll have to heat up the old poultice again."

I watched as she inserted the poultice – a piece of lint wrapped round kaolin clay – between two pan lids over boiling water. She talked me through everything she was doing – step by step. I listened obediently, but I was longing to tell her that I'd done this myself before, during my Red Cross training.

I stood by the gleaming dressing tray and watched as Nurse Winter placed the warm poultice in position. She'd asked me to test it first on the back of my hand to make sure it wasn't too hot for our patient's skin. Then she looked up at me. I smiled – I knew what she was going to ask. I moved eagerly round to the far side of the bed.

"Nurse Langley, I need your help again."

"Yes," I said happily.

"We're going to wrap this bandage back around the Corporal to hold the poultice in place. It's called a many-tail bandage."

I know that! I nearly burst out then.

"You did that very nicely, Nurse Langley," Nurse Winter said when we'd finished. She sounded very pleased. I told myself to try and be content with that.

Monday 30th October

We're going to throw a party for the officers. A bossy VAD's formed a committee to take charge of the arrangements. Bunty's joined it and tonight she dragged me along to a meeting. I discovered that I'd already been allocated a task – to organize the dance music. "It's because you're so musical," I was told.

"What?" I exclaimed. Musical is one thing I'm not! And then, out of the corner of my eye I could see that Bunty was splitting her sides. She's been pulling their legs. Bunty's such a tease! I don't know if she's heard from her Lieutenant yet, but I think she must have, for she seems much more cheerful now.

The meeting had just ended when Molly stomped in, face nearly brushing the floor.

"I'm spending the next two weeks typing up forms and medical notes in the office," she declared crossly.

I'd hate to do that job. Luckily, I won't be. I can't type.

Wednesday 8th November

I got another letter from Giles today. It was another blow-by-blow account of what he's doing at his training school. It was pretty dull, though some of the flying does sound very exciting – spins and rolls and things like that. He's hoping to become a Spitfire pilot.

I don't know why he thinks I'd be interested in all that technical stuff. I'm much more interested in how he feels about *me* – and again there was nothing at all in his letter about that. Honestly, you'd think the wretched planes mattered more to him.

I told Bunty that I'd had another letter from Giles. She told me she was relieved. I could tell what she'd been thinking – that sometimes pilots are killed in training. I know that, of course. I just try not to think about it.

Spent the rest of the evening knitting "comforts" for the troops. Marjorie and Molly are knitting scarves. Molly's is already as big as she is! My effort's no better. It's supposed to be a balaclava "helmet". We've been told to leave only very small holes for the eyes. My holes seem to get bigger by the day and it's all sort of bobbly. I feel sorry for the soldier who gets it. I don't think he'll find it very comforting.

Thursday 9th November

At supper this evening Molly told me that Jean Mason has got herself transferred – to the Surgical ward. Molly said that she went up to Matron – Matron! – and actually asked for the transfer. I gaped at her. I'd never dare to be as bold as that.

"She thinks she needs the experience," Molly added.

Poor Molly! She loathes her new job. Our MO's handwriting is the worst, she said. And practically everything has to be typed in triplicate.

She says the MOs hardly ever say a word to her – even when Matron isn't around to check up on them. Already she's desperate to return to the wards.

Sunday 12th November

There's a stack of books on the box by Jean's bed. I'd always assumed they were nursing manuals, but this evening I took a closer look at them. I hadn't meant to be nosy, but I just couldn't help it – the cover of the one on top had caught my eye. It wasn't a nursing manual, it was a book on anatomy. Old, too. Well-thumbed. The sort of book a medical student would study – not a VAD. I knew I shouldn't, but I had a quick peep inside. It looked very complicated. Why, I wondered, did Jean need to know all this stuff? And then I remembered what Molly had told me – about Jean asking Matron if she could transfer to the Surgical ward. I'd always thought there was a bit of a mystery about Jean Mason – and now I felt sure I was right.

There was a name on the book's inside cover. Alastair Mason. The ink had faded so I knew that it must have been written a long time ago. Who was Alastair Mason? I wondered. Was he her father? Was he a doctor?

Suddenly I felt disgusted with myself. What did I think I was doing – prying into matters that weren't anything to do with me? Already I'd found out more than I had any right to know.

Jean came in later and settled down on her bed. I watched as she leaned across and picked up one of the books off the box. Suddenly out it came: "Do you want to be a doctor?" Just like that.

Jean just looked at me. "Yes," she said at last, quietly.

"That's marvellous," I said. "I'm sure you'll be a very good one," I prattled on, without thinking what I was saying. Jean was silent. Her face looked even paler than usual. "It's all right for *you*," her eyes seemed to say.

I stopped. I felt bewildered.

"My father was a doctor," she said abruptly. "I wanted to be one too – always did – but then he died and. . ." She stopped suddenly and looked away.

Slowly I began to piece it all together. All the little things that hadn't made any sense. Like why she'd been upset about our pay and why she's always so reluctant to take even a biscuit from me. She can't share back. She's poor. And worst of all, there wasn't the money to pay for her training.

I felt so sorry for her. I leaned across and touched her hand. Jean smiled tiredly at me. "It's all right," she said.

It wasn't.

Not everyone is as lucky as me. I can't imagine what it must be like not to be able to do something you really want – just because there's no money. Poor Jean. Sometimes life can be so unfair.

I smiled back at her. I'm going to make a real effort to be a friend to Jean – if she'll let me.

Monday 13th November

Molly reported back to Ward B today.

"Missed this, did you?" I murmured to her while we were doing the bumpering this morning.

"Anything's better than working in the office," she said vehemently, forgetting that we were in the middle of the ward. "Oops," she said, clapping a hand to her mouth and looking around nervously in case Sister had heard. The patients giggled.

After we'd finished bumpering, Nurse Winter talked me though a dressing she was doing. On a medical ward they're usually for chest ailments – no nasty wounds to clean. She told me about the first time she saw a dressing being changed on a surgical ward. "I nearly fainted clean away," she laughed. When she says things like that, I'm so relieved that I don't work on a surgical ward.

Sunday 19th November

Arrangements for our party are going swimmingly. *All* the officers from miles around are coming – so the rumour goes. I hope it's wrong. We've booked the upstairs room at The George. It's a large room, but even there we'd never fit them all in.

Monday 20th November

At breakfast today we learned that three soldiers from the British Expeditionary Force arrived on the ward last night. I was in a huge panic as I pushed open the ward doors. What if one of them was Peter? How would I cope? Visions of horrible illnesses kept flashing through my mind. I told myself I was just being silly. But what awful things *do* our soldiers pick up, squelching about in the French mud?

The men seemed quite cheerful when I took round their milk puddings later on. (And – huge relief! – Peter wasn't one of them.) They told me that they're jolly relieved to be back in Blighty, and to be cared for in a proper hospital. All three of them have bad tummy upsets. I'm not surprised that tummy bugs are rife amongst the men out in France. It can't be easy feeding an army in the field. Our cooks find it hard enough in the hospital kitchen!

Like Peter, these lads are serving in the Infantry but none of them are from his unit. They've quite put our other patients' noses out of joint. We stare at them in awe. They're our first casualties from the Front in France and I think they're enjoying all the fuss. Of course, none of them has seen any action yet.

Tuesday 21st November

Private Abbott, one of our new patients, was awfully sick this morning. His pale face looked up at me as I mopped up around him. "I'm sorry, miss," he said. I smiled brightly at him. I'd only just finished when I noticed that his face was looking a bit green again. Round went the screens, off came the sheets and this time I had to give him a proper wash. As I did this I noticed that he seemed awfully hot. I went to fetch Sister.

"I think Private Abbott's feverish," I told her. She came over to the bed and took out her thermometer. She started to shake it but suddenly she stopped and handed it to me.

"*You* do it, Nurse Langley," she said. I popped the thermometer into the Private's mouth. I was right – he did have a temperature. 100 degrees. I pulled the blanket down to the bottom of the bed to help cool him. When I looked up I saw that Sister was regarding me thoughtfully.

Our poor Private was still unwell this afternoon. He couldn't keep anything down. I'd just finished mopping up again when Sister's head popped round my shoulder.

"Oh, Nurse, could you do the patients' TPRs for me?"

I looked up at her, cloth in hand. I felt dizzy. I was being asked to do the TPRs. Proper nursing at last. And this was only the beginning. . .

Sister's voice broke into my dream. "The TPRs, please, Nurse Langley!" she said, her old irritable self again.

I didn't hesitate any longer. I was terrified she'd change her mind. I went round that ward, thermometer in hand, feeling so proud. After nearly three months here I actually think Sister's beginning to trust me.

Saturday 25th November

I'm writing this tucked under the bedcovers. It's icy in our room. Anne writes that it's unutterably freezing up in Leeds.

It was the VADs' party tonight. Terrific success, so the officers said. And we had gone to a lot of trouble – decorated the room with streamers and danced to music by Henry Hall and Glen Miller.

Jean Mason came too! I'd bullied her into it – and I'm really glad I did. She looked so happy, a huge beam on her face as she was swung round the dance floor. She looked pretty, too – a bit of colour in her clever face.

After we'd got back, Molly went to fetch cocoa and we chewed over the evening together – all of us, even Jean. We squeezed up together on the beds.

"Why are we whispering?" Bunty said suddenly, quite loudly. "We're not keeping anyone awake."

We were in our tiny room.

Suddenly there was a creak outside the door.

"Madam on patrol," Bunty murmured in a loud whisper. We all shut up at once, and then I heard someone giggle as though she couldn't help herself. It was Jean!

"Who were you dancing with?" Bunty said boldly to Jean, when the creaking had stopped. "He looked nice."

I heard another giggle. It was Jean again.

"Which one do you mean?" she managed to get out through her giggles.

I began to giggle too – helplessly.

"You're hopeless, you two," said Bunty. I couldn't see her face in the dark, but I could sense that she was smiling.

It was nice. I wouldn't say that Jean's absolutely one of the gang now, but I do like her and I can tell that the others are warming to her, too.

It was very late when the girls crept back to the dorm. Jean was already fast asleep on top of her bed. I pulled the blankets up over her. As for me, it's a jolly good thing I don't have to get up at six. From tomorrow I'm on nights. No more Sister Rook. Bliss!

Monday 27th November

Night duty on Ward B is hard work because there's just one Sister and two VADs on duty – Molly and me. Between us we have to do everything.

We reported for duty, sharp at eight. The day staff had already put up the blackout boards and only a thin light filtered into the ward from Sister's office.

When I arrived she was still closeted with Sister Rook. After Sister Rook had finished handing over, the Night Sister – that's Sister Adams – called us in. I saw a dark head bent over the desk next to her. As we entered, a chair swivelled round and a man looked up and smiled, stretching out long legs. It was the duty MO. His face looked oddly familiar.

And then I remembered. Of course! Private Johnson and the thermometer! I went pink, but I think the MO had forgotten, because he just smiled at me.

Sister Adams has three wards to look after. "So you'll be on your toes," she told us, nodding at Molly and myself. Our most important job, she said, was to keep a watchful eye on the patients. "After you've done the TPRs, don't disturb them again." If we had a problem, she said, we were to go straight to her. "If you can't find *me*, speak to Lieutenant Venables."

I blushed again, thinking about that thermometer, and looked down at my feet.

Sister Adams went round the ward with us, handing out the medicines, while we did the TPRs. Private Abbott smiled sleepily at me as I popped a thermometer into his mouth. He's much better, and I think he'll be going back to France soon, poor boy.

Then Sister was off to the next ward and we were on our own.

We had a whole pile of dressings to make up. In the next hour I think I must have made enough cotton-wool swabs and gauze dressings to supply a regiment. My fingers grew heavy as one by one I packed the dressings into a dressing drum.

At midnight Sister popped into the ward again and we were allowed a short break. I had a bite to eat in the kitchen. Bliss to sit down and rest my aching feet. Then I got up and toured the ward again.

The hours from two to four were the worst of all. I could feel sleepiness creep up my arms and legs. Up and down I walked, up and down, back and forth, willing myself to stay awake. The patients were all fast asleep. How I wished it was me asleep in bed!

At four one of our patients woke up and asked for a cup of tea. After I'd checked his temperature, I took one over to him. He smiled at me as he drank it.

"Missed this in France," he said, smacking his lips.

Molly got us a mug each and I took one into Lieutenant Venables and Sister in the office. It was truly horrible – bright orange – but by then I think we'd have drunk anything.

At half past seven the day staff came on duty. Was I pleased to see them!

"How do you like working on nights?" Molly asked me as we walked slowly down the corridor and up the stairs.

"Ask me when I've woken up," I told her.

Then I did what I'd been longing to do – fell into bed and slept.

Friday 1st December

It was well into the afternoon when I woke today. I begged some food from the nice VAD cook in the kitchen, and then I wrapped up well and went outside. But as soon as I pushed open the door, an icy wind hurled itself at me, so I quickly went back inside again. Polished the buttons on my greatcoat and then I brushed my shoes ready for Parade on Sunday. At five Jean came in and curled up on her bed with a book. It was one of her medical books, I saw. She looked very studious – head down, bedclothes heaped round her shoulders. I didn't want to disturb her so I crept out again and went down to the games room. Played ping-pong for hours. I was wearing my greatcoat, but I still won all the games!

This evening I heard that the Russian army has bombed Helsinki, the capital of Finland. I don't feel at all like playing ping-pong now and yet I know we must do our best to carry on as normal. It's one way we can stand up to the enemy.

I feel so sorry for the Finns. I can't imagine how we'd feel if London was bombed. The news has come as a shock to all of us here.

Sunday 3rd December

This morning, after only three hours' sleep, I had to get up and go on Parade. A Very Important Person was paying us a visit. Before I went down I got out my measuring tape and made sure that Jean's dress was the regulation 12 inches from the ground and her apron 2 inches from the hem of her skirt. Then she did the same for me. I was very sleepy still, and couldn't help grumbling as I got dressed.

We stood outside the hospital, all neatly lined up in rows, in our nurses' uniforms. A beastly wind whipped up, and even the trees were shivering as it swept through them – and us. The Commandant marched up to inspect us, accompanied by the Very Important Person.

They were both wearing greatcoats, hats on too. It's all right for *them*, I found myself thinking resentfully. By the time they'd passed by me, the smile had practically frozen on my face and my hands were as blue as my dress.

Afterwards, there was a big race for the electric fire in the VADs' mess. Me, I leaped up the stairs as fast as I could, flung off my uniform and crawled back under the bedclothes. I was still fast asleep when Jean woke me again at lunchtime.

Tuesday 5th December

Lieutenant Venables was on duty again last night. He's not like the other doctors I've worked with here. He's friendly and he always smiles at me and Molly, though he's careful not to talk to us when Sister's around. He confided to me that he's never forgotten Private Johnson and the thermometer. It was his first day at the hospital, he said. It was a most valuable lesson. I bet he got well and truly teased for it.

Anyway, I was just thinking how nice he was when Molly whispered, "What do you think of Lieutenant Venables?"

We were having an early morning cup of tea.

"He seems nice," I said.

He looks a bit like Giles, I found myself thinking suddenly. Or does he? I've been finding it harder and harder to remember what Giles looks like.

Suddenly I remembered – I hadn't answered Giles's last letter! When I went off duty I took it out of the cardboard box where I keep all my letters and looked at the date – 1 November! I felt dreadfully guilty so I sat down and wrote to him straightaway. I told him that I'd been awfully busy, but then so, I'm sure, has he. I hope he'll forgive me. I hope it won't stop him writing to me again.

Thursday 7th December

I fell asleep on duty yesterday. This is an awful crime!

I'd taken a cup of tea over to one of our patients and he'd asked me to stop and chat to him. This is one of the few times that you're allowed to sit down on duty. I sat down gratefully, remembering just in time to pull up the sides of my starched apron so that it wouldn't get creased. Actually, the Corporal didn't want to chat, he just wanted someone to listen. What's more, he had plenty to say, and I felt myself growing more and more sleepy listening to his soft voice.

Suddenly I felt a hand shake my shoulder and I practically jumped out of my chair in terror! In the bed next to me my patient was snoring peacefully.

I was in luck. It wasn't Sister, it was Molly.

"Kitty, your cap!" Molly whispered. My relieved sigh turned to a groan as I put my hand to my head.

If rule number one is: Thou must not fall asleep on duty, rule number two is: Never, ever lean back in a chair or thou wilt crease thy cap. Molly shielded me as best she could – eyes darting round the ward in case Sister appeared – while I tried to repair the damage. If Sister *did* notice, she didn't say anything.

As for me, I've found that I like working on nights. It is awfully tiring, but I relish the extra responsibility. I tiptoe round the ward, glancing at our patients, tweaking a blanket back on to a bed here, fetching a cup of tea there, listening – always listening – to make sure that everyone is settled and sleeping. For a time I can even pretend that I'm a proper nurse. . .

Monday 11th December

The town's been battered by frightful storms. I cannot think what it must be like to be on board ship out on the swelling grey sea. I feel sick just looking at it.

All leave's been cancelled so I won't be able to go home. It'll be my first Christmas ever away from home. Felt awfully choked, and then I reminded myself how much worse it is for our patients.

Monday 18th December

I feel really happy today. Mother's written and told me that they're going to drive down and take me out for lunch on Boxing Day. I feel so touched – they'll probably use up every last drop of their petrol ration. Bunty's told me that she's got her ward – Officers' – making streamers for Christmas.

"I doubt Sister Rook will let anyone put streamers up on our ward," I said to her. We were curled up on my bed.

"Get that dishy doctor to ask her."

"Who do you mean?" I asked. I wasn't really listening. I was watching how my breath hung in the air – it was freezing in our room. I burrowed deeper under the blankets.

"Kitten, I despair of you, really I do," Bunty said, grinning and pulling the blankets back off me. "Lieutenant what's-his-name."

"Venables," Marjorie said promptly.

"See, Marjorie knows, and she's not even working on your ward. Don't tell me you haven't noticed?"

I just smiled sweetly at her and pulled the blankets totally over my head.

Monday 25th December

Woke in time for Christmas lunch, which we had in the VADs' mess. The long tables looked so pretty – holly and candles on the starched white tablecloths. Our cooks had done us proud; just like at home we had turkey and all the trimmings; there was even Christmas pudding – about a mouthful each. One of the VADs who'd been on leave had brought back crackers. Someone tried to put a paper hat on, but she couldn't get it on over her white cap.

Soon the whole table was shrieking with laughter – hats toppling off caps. Then Madam came in and we whipped them off. Her face creased into a big smile as her gaze swept the tables. I think she was pleased to see our happy faces.

We'd barely finished our meal when all the lights went out. Pandemonium! A tree had toppled over in the high winds, bringing down one of the lines near the hospital, and all the power failed. Later we found out that in the midst of it all, an emergency appendix was brought in and they had to operate by hurricane lamp. The poor VAD on duty had to sterilize all the surgical instruments on top of primus stoves as the sterilizers weren't working. At least – being Christmas – it was the only operation they had to do today.

After lunch, I popped into the ward to wish our patients a happy Christmas. I gasped when I pushed open the door. It was festooned with greenery and many of the patients had cards by their beds. One of them whipped out a sprig of mistletoe from behind his pillow and asked for a kiss! So embarrassing! Another gave me a bar of chocolate. I felt really pleased and handed round the cards I'd got for everyone.

Lieutenant Venables was there, too. He waved at me across the ward and then he came over to wish me a happy Christmas. Then suddenly I remembered what Bunty had said about him and I felt this huge blush flood my face. I don't know what he must have thought of me.

Tuesday 26th December

Writing this hurriedly before going on duty. Heavenly day. When Mother met me at the hospital she told me there was a surprise waiting for me in the car. She had a big smile on her face but I couldn't guess – so I rushed out ahead of her.

Inside the car, two faces beamed out at me. Father – and Peter!

It was absolutely my bestest Christmas present ever!

Monday 1st January 1940

I'm writing this at home. I finished my first bout of night duty a few days ago and so I have four nights and days off – bliss!

Father's away, and Peter of course has gone back to France. We don't often talk about the War, but on Boxing Day I'd asked him to tell me what it was like across the Channel. Not a lot's been happening, he told me. No one's fired a shot yet, except in training. His unit's been busy digging anti-tank ditches and spreading wire and he's also been working on the roads. He looked awfully tired, but fit. He pretended to be shocked when he saw me and said that my arm muscles were bigger than his! "You'll never get a husband now, Sis," he joked. He told me that he knew what we VADs are nicknamed and when the parents weren't listening he whispered it in my ear. (Unrepeatable!)

Giles has been on leave, too, and yesterday evening he came over and we went to the flicks together. I'd felt very pleased when he rang to ask me out – I hadn't expected him to – he hadn't answered my last letter. He looked awfully handsome in his powder-blue pilot's uniform and flying cap. I was glad I'd dolled up – I spent ages in the bathroom, as it was a special occasion! And I was wearing the lipstick Peter gave me for Christmas. Bright red too!

In the cinema, as soon as the lights had dimmed, Giles took my hand. I thought I'd feel pleased, but I didn't – somehow it felt all wrong. When the lights came on again he snatched away his hand, as if he felt awkward too.

But later he tried a kiss, in the car as he dropped me off. That felt wrong, too. We sat in the car for a minute in silence.

"I nearly didn't call you," he said at last, giving me a sidelong look. "I wasn't sure you wanted to see me." He hesitated. "When you didn't answer my letter for so long I wondered – I wondered if you'd met anyone else. I didn't write again because I didn't know what to say." He turned quickly away and looked out of the window, as if he thought he'd see my answer in my face and was secretly dreading it.

"I haven't—" I began. I was about to explain how I felt, when I saw him smile; he looked hugely relieved. I just couldn't tell him the truth then – that I didn't feel for him the way he felt for me. He promised that he'd write and he gave me a quick peck on the cheek. He was rather subdued, and I felt a bit tearful, and I'm sure he thought it was because of him, but it wasn't, or rather it was, but not in the way he thought. Giles is nice, and he's very good-looking, but all evening I'd felt as if he was a stranger.

At breakfast this morning *I* was very subdued. Mother kept glancing at me across the table, but she didn't say anything. Afterwards, when I went upstairs to pack, she came into my bedroom – to help me, she said – but I knew she wanted to find out how my evening with Giles had gone.

"Well?" she said at last, when I still didn't say anything. She looked worried. Now is not a good time to fall in love – especially with a pilot.

Suddenly I felt a big gush of misery. I flopped down on the bed.

"Oh, Mother, I don't know," I wailed. I told her that I wasn't sure I'd see him again. That I wasn't even sure I wanted to. And . . . and. . . All at once I felt my lips tremble.

"Oh, my poor Kitten," Mother said, hugging me, as if she knew all too well what I was feeling. "It's not easy, is it? Being young." I shook my head, trying to smile, but I felt all choked up inside.

Tuesday 2nd January

There was a letter from Anne waiting for me when I got back. It's been ages since I heard from her. I tore it open eagerly. There was a lot about the awful weather up in Leeds, and that she was trying to get transferred south. That wasn't all.

"Giles sounds such a stick," she said. (I'd told her about my unsatisfactory letters from him.) "Poor Kitten! Don't worry about it. You can do a lot better."

At that I just laid my head down on my arms and cried.

Wednesday 3rd January

It's all round the hospital how plucky the Finns have been. The story goes that they've made a new sort of weapon to hurl at the Russian army's tanks. It's a grenade, nicknamed a "Molotov cocktail" after Molotov, one of the Russian ministers. Anyway, the Russians were very surprised to find that the Finns didn't surrender straightaway, as next to Soviet Russia, Finland's just a small country. Three cheers for the Finns I say! I hope *we* show as much courage when it's our turn to face the enemy.

Here in the hospital *our* worst enemy is the snow. Last night it fell thickly again. When I took down the blackout boards on the ward this morning, I gasped. The world had turned white. Later in the day, I was woken by tyres skidding outside the hospital and a barrage of hooting. Half asleep still, I went to the window and looked out. An ambulance was desperately trying to get through the snow. In front of it, a lorry was stuck fast. There were soldiers swarming all around it, trying to get it moving again. One of them even put his shoulder to it and tried to push it up the drive!

A minute later the ambulance doors opened and a stretcher was carefully passed down. The stretcher bearers walked slowly through the snow to the hospital, eyes fixed on the ground in case they slipped.

77

Sister Adams was looking rather flushed last night and I heard her sneezing when I went past the office. There's been an outbreak of influenza in the hospital. I do hope she's not going to be its next victim.

Wednesday 10th January

Absolute pandemonium!

The hospital's overflowing with cases of influenza – both patients and staff. In our ward first it was Sister Adams, and now poor Molly's sick. The patients have had to be shifted in and out of wards, and forms have to be filled in each time someone's moved. I'm amazed we've not lost anyone yet.

Yesterday we ran out of beds and the stretcher bearers had to dump the stretchers on the floor between the beds, their occupants still in them. When I came on duty last night, Sister took me on one side. She told me that she'd asked for extra help, but that there isn't any. All the other hospitals in the area have been hit hard by flu, too.

Between the two of us we have to do everything: settle the patients down for the night – including all the extra ones, who're still lying on the floor – take round the medicines, give injections and do the TPRs. A lot of this will be down to me now as Sister will be flitting through the other wards in her charge. She told me to call Matron or the duty MO if there were any emergencies. I felt really scared but I knew I just had to knuckle down. I've always wanted responsibility. Well, now I've got it.

Several of our patients have bronchitis and we're afraid that we might have a case of pneumonia on our hands, too. Even our marvellous new drug – M&B693 – cannot always cure pneumonia and the illness requires very careful nursing. And Sister Adams is still a bit weak after her illness. Just how we'd cope I cannot imagine.

Friday 12th January

Thomson developed pneumonia on Wednesday night and we had to move him into a side room. That first night I spent most of my time running in and out of it – and once we had to redo his kaolin poultice, which he'd been given to soothe the pain in his chest. It gets worse when he coughs, which is often. Then every four hours Sister popped by to give him his medicine.

We were so busy! Last night, though, there was another VAD to help us. My word, weren't we pleased to see her! If I hadn't been so busy, I'd have smiled at her nervous, eager expression as she hovered at the ward door – so like me, the day I began. I find it hard to believe that was only a few short months ago. Sister asked her to "special nurse" Thomson, and so she sat down obediently by his bed and glued her eyes to him.

"Any change in his condition must be reported to me at once," Sister told us firmly. "If you can't find me, tell the MO."

Our new VAD nodded, eyes still stuck on Thomson. She looked terrified, so after a while, I went up to check that everything was all right. At about one o'clock she looked as though she was struggling to stay awake so I told her to make us all a mug of Ovaltine. She looked very relieved as she scampered off to the ward kitchen. I sat down in her place. Poor Thomson's breathing still sounded awfully heavy so I propped him up a little on his pillow and gently rubbed his back. Sister had been called to another sick patient and I prayed I wouldn't need to call our MO. We're woefully short of doctors now, as so many of them are down with flu, and poor Lieutenant Venables is rushed off his feet.

At four o'clock I did have to run for the doctor. Our new VAD had told me that Thomson was awake but behaving very strangely. "I think he's hallucinating," she told me anxiously.

Lieutenant Venables looked at Thomson attentively. His breathing sounded better but he was gibbering away. Then he turned and looked full at the doctor.

"Good morning, Sister," he said, smiling brightly.

A broad smile spread over the doctor's face. He told us not to worry that Thomson was talking nonsense. "It's just one of the side effects of the medicine," he whispered. But just to make sure, he gave Thomson a quick check-up before he was called away again, and then I reported to Sister when she came back on to the ward.

I felt a bit of an idiot, but very relieved. Lieutenant Venables is so dependable. It's such a relief to know that I can call on him.

Thomson pulled through the night and I collapsed into bed and slept and slept and slept. Jean looks exhausted and even paler than usual. I do hope she's not going to be ill next.

Sunday 14th January

No more new cases of flu today, but we're still very overstretched on the ward. I'm sure that's why I left an unwashed glass on the ward table when I came off duty early this morning.

I'd been in bed for about an hour when I was woken by a knock on the door. One of our new VADs told me that Sister wanted to see me. Her face looked very apprehensive. What could Sister Rook want? I wondered tiredly, sitting up and rubbing my eyes. I got dressed in my uniform, and made my way sleepily back down to the ward.

It wasn't Sister Rook who was glaring at me in the office – it was a Sister I didn't know, Sister Richardson. Sister Rook's ill, she said shortly, when I asked.

I couldn't think why I'd been summoned, but I was soon to find out. Sister marched me straight into the centre of the ward and pointed at the table.

"What is the meaning of this?" she said.

Every bed in that ward was full, but you could have heard a pin drop. The VAD who'd come to get me stopped what she was doing. Her face was crimson. I didn't know what Sister was talking about. I looked blankly at the table.

"Well, Nurse!" said Sister.

Well, *what*? I thought.

She gave a deep sigh, as if she thought I was really stupid. Then she leaned over the table, picked up a glass and handed it to me.

"This," she said, "was found – unwashed, Nurse – when I came on duty this morning. I was told that you left it there."

I'd forgotten all about that glass.

I began to feel angry. Three months earlier I'd probably have blushed and apologized, but not now. I'd been working nights with very little help for weeks on end, and now I was being hauled in – for this! I knew that glass had been left there to humiliate me – in front of all the patients too. I felt so upset. I wanted to walk out of the ward, down the passage and out of the hospital and never come back. Instead, I took a deep breath, picked up the glass, marched into the annexe, washed it, put it away in its proper place and marched out of the ward again, head held high.

Sister just stood there, watching me. I'd thought Sister Rook was tough. She is, but she isn't petty like Sister Richardson.

Who, I wondered, had told her that I'd left that glass there? Someone who was scared of Sister, a little voice whispered inside my head.

Someone like that new little VAD who'd been sent to get me. I knew who I felt sorry for then.

Back in bed again I pulled the bedclothes up over my head. I've been made to look a fool in front of all my patients. I don't know how I'm going to face them again.

When Jean came in I poured out the whole story.

"I don't think you'll have a problem with the patients," she said. Oh, I pray she's right.

Monday 15th January

Jean *was* right. When I went on duty last night the patients smiled at me and for once they all did exactly as I asked. In a quiet moment, one of them beckoned me over. "This is for you, Nurse," he whispered, holding out some chocolate. I think it was the first time any of my patients had called me nurse. I nearly did burst into tears then.

Monday 5th February

I was transferred to the Surgical ward today. Jean and I are both pleased about this – we're working together again.

My first proper job was to "special" a patient, who'd had his appendix removed and was recovering in a side room.

"His temperature's a little high," Sister told me. "I'd like you to do the 'obs' every half an hour."

"Yes, Sister," I said, and leaned over my patient to pop a thermometer into his mouth. And his temperature *was* high. Sister had told me that he'd had his operation two days ago.

The next "obs" I had to do was check my patient's pulse and breathing.

Later, the surgeon popped round to see our patient. Sister unrolled the bandage from his tummy and the surgeon bent over the wound to examine it. It wasn't red, hot or swollen – the tell-tale signs of infection. He checked his patient's pulse. It wasn't too fast. No clots in the lung to worry about either, then.

After the surgeon had gone, the door to the side room opened again. It was Jean with a cup of tea for me. Was I pleased to see it – and her.

"I'm not sure you deserve this," she said, pretending to be annoyed. "I wish I'd been able to spend my morning sitting in a chair."

By lunch time my patient's temperature had started to come down and he smiled at me for the first time. Sister came in and told me to reduce his obs to two-hourly. She looked awfully pleased. That moment when a patient starts to get better – there's nothing like it.

In the afternoon I had to keep an eye on a patient who'd been sick. After they come round from surgery patients are often sick. Luckily I was to hand when I saw him struggle to sit up. He looked at me. I knew that look.

"Oh, miss, I feel awfully dizzy," he murmured. I thrust a bowl under his mouth just in time, and then I propped him up and Sister told me to give him a little warm water and bicarbonate of soda to sip. Even with that the poor boy was sick again. Three times I had to clean up after him.

Tuesday 13th February

It was tea time and I was doing the TPRs. I was the only nurse on the ward, but I'd done the TPRs many times before. There was nothing to worry about.

Holding the thermometer tightly between thumb and forefinger, I shook it firmly downwards.

I looked down in dismay. My hand was empty. The thermometer had smashed on my starched apron. I needed a new one – fast.

I scrabbled helplessly on the floor, trying to find the broken bits. Without them I'd never be allowed a new one. I couldn't find any of it! The bits had simply vanished – rolled under a floorboard or behind a piece of furniture. Empty-handed I raced up to the Quartermaster's office. I told him what had happened. For a full five minutes I pleaded with him.

"Rules is rules," he said. But at last, grudgingly, he agreed to replace it. He was *not* pleased. Even then I wasn't allowed to take the new thermometer away with me. First I had to fill in a form, saying what had happened to the wretched thing, and then I had to get it signed by an MO. It's another of those mysterious army rules that I find so baffling.

Only then did it dawn on me that the patients were probably still on their own. I tore back to the ward. Ahead of me someone was advancing slowly towards the ward. Matron! I looked at her back in horror. What would she think when she discovered that the patients were on their own? I'll really be on the mat for this, I thought despairingly. I watched as she opened the doors. Legs like jelly, I crept in behind her.

My luck was in. The patients weren't on their own! Jean was back! Later, she explained. "I saw you vanish down the corridor so I came back straightaway."

I was so relieved that I could have hugged her.

"You were lucky," said Bunty, when I told the girls later. "Let me tell you about the time that happened to me."

"Did it really happen to you, too?" Molly asked, wide-eyed.

"Oh yes," she said airily.

"Were you in awful trouble?" Molly asked.

"Oh no. The patients covered for me! They said I was in the annexe –
by the time Matron had searched every corner of it, I'd nipped back
into the ward. Matron didn't know quite what to think. It was a pretty
close shave though."

"Bunty!" gasped Molly.

I gave Bunty a searching look. "Really?" I said.

Bunty's lips were twitching. Suddenly a big laugh burst out of her.
"Oh, you are such sillies! Of course not," she said.

Wednesday 14th February

Just before I went off duty this evening, the stretcher bearers rushed
into the ward. There'd been a motorcycle accident. Its rider skidded on
the wet road and crashed into a tree. As there are no streetlights now
because of the blackout it's very hard to see anything at all outside at
night – and it's especially a problem now the days are so short. Jean says
that there have been several motorcycle crashes since she started work
on the Surgical ward. It reminded me that we're at war. It probably
sounds peculiar, but sometimes I forget that. In this hospital, with no
war casualties to deal with yet, we're cocooned from the worst of it.

I'm in such a spot. I've had a letter from Giles and I don't know what to say to him.

Thursday 15th February

This morning the doors had barely shut behind the Colonel and his party, when the stretcher bearers rushed in again. Another motorcycle accident. Another broken leg.

While we were waiting for our patient to return to the ward – leg swathed in Plaster of Paris – we prepared a special bed for him. It would be twelve or more hours before the plaster set, and we needed to keep the leg absolutely straight, so I held up the mattress while one of our QAs – Nurse Jackson – put boards over the bed's metal frame. Then we lifted the foot of the bed and put blocks underneath to raise it. This would help our patient's blood flow the right way – towards his heart and head. That's important when the patient can't move around in bed.

The plaster was still damp when our patient was put to bed, so we put a mackintosh sheet under him to keep him dry. Then Nurse Jackson put a special cradle over his leg to keep the bedclothes off it while I was sent off to fill up some hot-water bottles.

When I returned with the filled bottles Nurse Jackson told me to place them around our patient's plastered leg.

"Now tell me why we do this, Nurse," she said.

"It helps dry the plaster," I told her promptly.

"And we need to keep the patient warm too, don't we?" Nurse Jackson said, tucking a blanket round him and directing me to put more bottles into the bed.

"Not too close, Nurse, in case you burn him," she said, turning and smiling at our patient.

"Is that all right?" I asked him anxiously.

"That's fine, miss," he said. "But I wish you could do something about this bed. It's awfully hard."

"I'm sorry about that," said Nurse Jackson, "but we must keep your leg straight. We don't want to make it worse, do we?" She turned to smile at me, one eyebrow raised. I smiled back. I like Nurse Jackson. Unlike some of the QAs she doesn't treat me as if I've never been on a ward before.

Just before going off duty I heard a cry behind the screen. "Oh, Nurse, stop. Please, stop!" a voice begged.

What was the matter with that patient? I wondered. He'd lain for several hours on hard boards and I was worried that his back was hurting him. I peeped round the screens. Nurse Jackson was tickling the motorcyclist's bare toes.

"Got to keep the circulation going, my lad," I heard her say to him, chuckling.

Wednesday 21st February

The strangest sound woke me last night – a sort of distant muffled thudding. But when I woke properly, the night was quiet again and I went back to sleep. Much later I woke again. This time I could hear vehicles – lots of them – driving up to the hospital. I padded over to the window, but of course I couldn't see anything because of the blackout shutters. Jean was still fast asleep.

In the morning I'd forgotten all about it. But when I went downstairs I noticed that the corridors were busier than usual, and everyone's faces looked drawn and very grim. Suddenly I remembered the noise that had woken me, and the vehicles I'd heard driving up to the hospital. I felt sure then that something awful must have happened, and I found myself trembling as I walked down the long corridor towards the Surgical ward.

I don't think anything could have prepared me for what I saw there.

The corridor was lined with men, lying, still in uniform, or bits of it, on stretchers. Dozens of them, all with dirty blackened faces and hair. Some of them stared blankly at me as I stepped carefully round them. Others just stared straight ahead unseeingly.

Slowly I pushed open the ward doors. I was dreading what I'd see inside.

If it had been bad in the corridor, this was even worse.

It was chaos. I saw MOs, masks on their faces, khaki sleeves rolled up, striding hastily from bed to bed. On the pillows lay faces black with dirt and oil. Burned arms, hands and legs lay still on the white sheets or under cradles. I saw a QA gently lift a man's burned arm to slip a towel underneath. Stuff oozed out. He didn't complain, though I could tell that it hurt him very much.

For a moment I stood there, swaying. I felt sick. I didn't feel as if I was in a hospital at all. The sight before me – it was what I imagined a field hospital at the Front to be like – except here we weren't being shot at. Then Nurse Jackson saw me. She took off her mask as she hurried up to me. A ship had been blown up by a floating mine in the Channel, she told me quickly. All those men who'd been picked up had been taken to the nearest hospitals. A lot of them had been brought here, I thought. As I looked around the ward, I couldn't see any of the patients I'd nursed yesterday. What was I to do? I thought in a panic. I tried to concentrate on what Nurse Jackson was telling me.

"Heat up some hot-water bottles for me, will you, Nurse?" I heard her say. "We need to get the patients warm. They're in shock," she explained. You can tell that from the look in their eyes – as though they're far away; as though they don't know where they are. I'd read that somewhere in my Red Cross Manual, or had I?

I don't know *anything* I thought humbly. I looked at the QAs. They looked calm and competent as they bent over their patients – and suddenly I felt so relieved that they were there. How dare *I* think of myself as a nurse?

Nurse Jackson's voice interrupted my thoughts.

"The surgeon can't treat them until *we've* treated the shock. We can't wash them – or even undress them. So jump to it, please, Nurse."

Afterwards I went round the ward, holding cups of water and sweet tea up to blistered lips. The ward doors slammed. Another man was being wheeled out to Theatre.

Nurse Jackson was dabbing gentian violet on to a man's badly burned chest. He'd come back from Theatre earlier and it had to be done three times a day. She was wearing a mask and in a whisper told me to put one on too. It protects the men from picking up germs from us – and us from the smell. The smell from our burned patients is terrible. But the look in their eyes – that's far worse.

I watched while she went round the room again, irrigating the men's eyes. Soon she was called to a desperately injured patient. She told me to take over.

"You know what to do now," she said briskly.

My hands were shaking as I held a kidney bowl under a man's cheek to stop liquid running down on to the sheets. I could hardly bear to look at his face. I mustn't funk it, I whispered to myself again and again. *I mustn't.*

I could see Jean, moving from bed to bed. She looked so calm – unlike me.

By the time I'd been round the ward once it was time to begin again. We were so busy that we couldn't stop to think about what was happening there – or anything else.

But when I left the ward it flooded over me. And now – reliving it again as I write my diary – I feel sick again. Jean told me that my face was green when I came off duty. "It's all right now – just a bit pale," she said, smiling tiredly at me and switching off the light. I tried to smile back, but I couldn't.

In just this one day I feel as if I've seen more suffering than most people see in a whole lifetime. The safe little cocoon I've been living in these last few months has been blown away. When I'd got back to my room I'd pulled out Giles's letter. I was thinking about him, but not just him – I was thinking about all the wounded sailors on our ward – and all the others, too. I could do so little for any of them, but somehow – by writing to Giles – I felt as if it was one more – tiny – thing I could do for them. Does that make any sense?

Thursday 22nd February

It seemed only a few hours later that I was again manoeuvring my way down the corridor past the stretchers filled with wounded men. I was exhausted and I hadn't even started work yet. All night, scenes from that nightmare ward had played themselves over and over in my head.

Inside the ward, a QA was giving a patient sips of water from a cup. "Take over, please, Nurse," she said when she saw me. As I got near the bed that awful smell hit me. Trying to ignore it, I turned to smile at the patient. My smile stuck on my face.

It was awful!

His face was all wrong – burnt and twisted out of shape – as though a small child had tried to mould a face out of plasticine. I'd seen plenty of burned men yesterday, but this. . . I forced myself to smile, but it was a pretty feeble one.

"Hello, Nurse," he said to me slowly, his lips stretching painfully into something resembling a smile. His courage made me feel ashamed. I took the cup from the QA and sat down next to him.

I stayed at his side until the QA came back to fetch me. "We need more sterile towels, Nurse," she said briskly. "And then I'd like you to strip and make up the empty beds. Hurry up now!"

"Doesn't he need specialing?" I asked her timidly.

"Look about you, Nurse," she said sadly. "Every one of these boys needs special nursing."

As I was making up the beds, tucking grey blankets over the long, red mackintosh sheets, I wondered who'd been in them last. At that, my mind just shut down.

I feel such rage inside me now when I think about the War. I tell myself to try and live it down. Being angry won't help anyone. But it's awfully hard.

Saturday 24th February

Slept badly again last night. I dread getting up in the morning now. Each time I push open the ward doors I have to screw up all my courage. Some of the things I've seen these last days are too awful even to write in my diary. I haven't been able to talk to *anyone* about it. This morning, lying in bed, I felt worse still. I wanted to run away – leave it all behind. I wanted my life to go back to how it was before this awful war began. I just couldn't cope any more.

I could hear Jean thrashing around in bed, as though she couldn't sleep either.

I got up to open the blackout shutters and poked my head outside. I could see the sea shimmering in the early morning sun. When I turned round Jean was sitting up, rubbing her eyes. She gave me a smile, but I was sure she felt as bad as I did. I was about to say something when she said, "Good morning, Kitty", climbed out of bed and quickly and efficiently pulled out her nurse's uniform. I watched as deftly she made up a fresh cap. I got dressed, too, and hunted for my cap. I found it, lying on a box. I looked at it. I'd worn it for a few days but it would do for another one.

"Kitty, that cap's looking a bit sad. Let me make up another one for you." Jean pinned a fresh white cap on my hair. She handed me her mirror and I peered at it. The face that stared back at me wasn't the sad, drained face I'd expected to see. It looked tired but competent too under the crisply starched white cap. A nurse's face. Suddenly I felt a whole lot better.

Today was just another day for us VADs. I smiled at Jean – a really warm smile this time and we went downstairs together. Once I'd thought she was a cold fish. I couldn't have been more wrong.

Sunday 25th February

At about five o'clock this afternoon, Sister came up to me. She looked harassed.

"Ah, Nurse Langley," she said briskly. "Theatre's just rung and told me they need extra help. Would you go down there, please."

"What – me?" I gulped, looking round wildly for Jean. Surely Sister didn't mean me. I've had precious little Theatre training.

"Yes, you," said Sister briskly. "Run along now."

Jean was just entering the ward as I left. I threw her an anguished glance.

"What's up?" she whispered.

"I've got to go to Theatre!" I told her.

"Good luck!" she whispered.

In a bit of a daze I made my way down to the operating-theatre suite. All down the corridor were men, lying there on stretchers. Some of them looked in a pretty bad way. I tried not to look at their faces. One of them might soon be lying on the operating table in front of me.

Heart thudding in my chest, I marched into the "scrubbing-up" room. I leaned over the sink and began to scrub my hands and arms up to my elbows. I wondered what they'd ask me to do. I was feeling terribly nervous and there was a sick feeling in my tummy.

Theatre Sister told me to get dressed quickly. I got into a theatre gown, and tied a cap on my head, making sure that every hair was tucked securely under it. Then I put on a mask and rubber gloves. My hands were trembling, and I saw Sister look at them.

"Are you all right?" she asked. "The last girl they sent us fainted."

I swallowed. I wished she hadn't said that. Holding my hands clasped in front of me, as we always do after we've washed our hands, so that I wouldn't touch anything that wasn't sterile, I followed her into Theatre.

My job was a simple one – to fetch and carry for the team. I stood by the wall and waited as the long minutes ticked by. I looked anywhere (and everywhere) but at the patient. There was Theatre Sister, standing next to the surgeon. There was another gowned figure nearby – the anaesthetist. My eyes wandered round the room, resting in turn on a lotion bowl in a tall stand, on an instrument table where the surgeon's instruments lay – I tried not to shudder as I looked at them – and then there were dressing trolleys, and a bucket where the dirty swabs were dropped. Every so often I saw the surgeon turn to Sister and ask her to pass him something – a swab or an instrument like a scalpel or probe to examine the wound. I tried not to listen as he bent over the patient. I tried to concentrate on something else – anything but what was happening to our patient. I mustn't faint, I told myself. I mustn't let the team down.

"We need sterile dressing towels, Nurse," a voice interrupted my thoughts. I shot off, heart thudding in my chest, to fetch them. And then suddenly it was all over and our patient was being wheeled out of Theatre. My job now – to rinse out the bloody dressing towels. Then finally it was *my* turn to wash. I looked down at myself. Rivulets of blood were dripping down my front. I really nearly did faint then.

Friday 8th March

We're less busy in Theatre now as most of our ship casualties have been evacuated to hospitals inland. I'd expected to be sent back to Surgical, but I've stayed on here. I thought Jean would be envious that I'm working in Theatre, but she says not.

Anyway, I spend most of my time merely washing stuff in the sluice room. On a busy day, bucket after bucket of dirty towels is dumped at my feet. After they've been rinsed in cold water in the sluice – this helps to get the blood out – there are all the instruments to clean. First they have to be scrubbed and cleaned with metal polish, and only then are they sterilized. Theatre clothing needs to be sterilized too – this goes into the autoclave.

But today, I *was* asked to go into Theatre again. I was awfully pleased. I stood there for about an hour – and then all I had to do was hand the surgeon a towel!

Wednesday 13th March

Our Theatre was crowded this morning. The surgeon was trying out a new technique and the room was full of excited doctors. When I wasn't busy I stopped by to watch too.

One of the surgeons is very nice. He's quite friendly – a bit like nice Lieutenant Venables. When he's not too busy, he even tells me what he's doing. In Theatre, we're like a little family, and I actually miss it when I go off duty.

"You're joking!" Bunty said, shuddering when I told her. We were walking down to the tennis courts together, rackets swinging in our hands.

"There's lots of cleaning too, of course," I said. "That's mostly what I do. I'm not always needed in the operating theatre itself. Sometimes I wish I was back on the wards. I do miss the patients."

"At least your ones can't answer back," said Bunty, grinning.

"Bunty!" exclaimed Molly.

I laughed and lobbed a ball high into the air. "I was back in the operating theatre today," I told her.

"Don't tell me," said Molly shuddering, scurrying down to the far end of the court where Marjorie was waiting. "It was an amputation, I'll bet. I don't want to know."

"It was very interesting," I said, seriously. "The surgeon. . ." I stopped and lunged in vain for the ball, which was soaring high over my head.

"You're putting me off," Bunty said crossly, serving another ball wide of the court. It bounced at Molly's feet. Molly just stood there, looking at it. Even across the court I could see that her face looked odd. It was really green.

Monday 18th March

Early this morning Theatre Sister asked me to help her lay out the instruments for the first operation on the surgeon's list. I muddled through somehow.

"You'll soon learn," Sister said, smiling, as I ran off and came back with the wrong instrument – again. I can't think how she manages to remember it all.

100

After we'd finished the day's operations, she gave me a book to study. "This will help you," she said. "Study it well." I took the book from her. I must have looked awfully anxious, for she laughed. "Don't worry," she said. "I'll check that we have all the right instruments before we go into Theatre."

Feel very flattered that she thinks I'm worth training. On Sunday morning – Sundays are usually quiet as we don't often have any operations – she's going to give me a proper lesson.

Giles has won his pilot's wings! I had a letter from him today in which he told me all about it. He's a fully-fledged fighter pilot with Fighter Command's "11 Group" now. Apparently that's the group that covers south-east England. There are several groups, he told me – each covering a different part of Britain. He'll be flying Spitfires, and he sounds jolly proud. Tomorrow he's going to join his squadron – and is longing to get a shot at the enemy. What is it about men? They spend all their time fighting, and then *we* have to patch them up!

Friday 5th April

Everyone here has been very buoyed up by the Prime Minster's speech. It seems he thinks that the Germans should have attacked us straightaway when the British and French armies weren't ready for them. Now, he believes, the situation's changed – our armies are much stronger now. I hope he's right.

This evening a call was put through from Father. I was thrilled! I haven't spoken to him since Boxing Day. He sounded guarded when I asked him what he thought about the Prime Minister's speech, but I'm going to try not to let his caution worry me.

Wednesday 10th April

The Germans have overrun Denmark and now they've invaded Norway. Norway is a neutral country – not on one side or the other in the conflict. But the Germans don't seem to care about that. It seems incredible but in only two days all the main Norwegian ports have been captured by the Germans.

The whole of Europe is being dragged into this terrible war. Too depressed to write any more.

Monday 15th April

Just as I'm learning to set the instrument table, I've been shifted back to the Surgical ward. Typical!

Today a plane crashed near the hospital. It was so close that all the glass rattled in the window panes. It was very hot in the ward and I'd just gone over to the windows to open one of them when I saw a long tail of black smoke vanish somewhere behind the trees and then suddenly there was a huge explosion. I felt very scared – and a bit sick. How could anyone survive that crash?

For what seemed like an age there was complete silence – then suddenly there was a dash for the windows. From his bed Private Jones swore blind that it was a Jerry plane. Over in his bed Corporal Lister was sceptical. "You couldn't even see the thing," he said. The Private said he just knew, but I could see that his eyes were twinkling. After that there was a lot of argy-bargying back and forth. Some of the men sided with Lister, others with Jones. In the midst of all this, Sister came in to do her round, looking as calm as if nothing had happened.

"What's going on in here?" she asked.

"Nothing, Sister. Sorry, Sister." And off they shuffled, looking sheepish.

Funnily enough, Private Jones was right – it was a Jerry plane. I know because the pilot was brought into the ward just before I went off duty this evening. He's our first prisoner of war. He was very quiet, and seemed rather frightened, and I found myself feeling sorry for him. It must be awful to be shot down in an enemy country and find yourself in a hospital ward surrounded by the very people you're fighting.

None of the aircrew have been brought in, so we think they must have bought it. None of us know what that plane was doing here either.

Later on I had another thought. That plane could so easily have hit the hospital. There's a big red cross painted on the roof so that the enemy will know that we're a hospital and won't target us. But how will *that* protect us if a plane crashes on top of us, or a bomb misses its target and lands on us instead? I feel very scared when I think about that.

Tuesday 16th April

The men don't seem to mind sharing their ward with a German prisoner of war.

"Johannes's all right. . . He's just another poor lad – fighting for his country like the rest of us," one of them told me. I think they feel sorry for him – he's broken both his legs. And he'll be sent off to prisoner-of-war camp as soon as he's recovered.

Johannes seems a bit bewildered by us. He told me that he broke his legs in the fall and when he came round he saw a man pointing a gun at him. "I told him not to shoot. I said I wasn't armed," he said. Then, he said, a woman came out of the house near where he'd landed, a cup of hot, sweet tea in her hand. "She said it was for me." He shook his head. "I do not understand you English," he said.

Wednesday 1st May

I wish I knew what was happening across the Channel. News does reach us in the hospital, but sometimes it's hard to know *what* to believe – the rumours flying round the hospital or the news on the wireless. There've been a lot of angry mutters about how the government is handling the campaign in Norway. Our troops were sent out to help Norway in April – but they were ill-equipped and unprepared for the task they had to do apparently. No match for the Germans or the snow. I am *so* relieved that Peter isn't out there.

Friday 10th May

Jerry's invaded the Low Countries! We're all so shocked – everyone's walking around in a daze. First their airfields, railways and arms depots were bombarded from the air. Then the enemy's tanks rolled across the Dutch, Belgian and Luxembourg borders without warning. German planes are raining bombs down on their cities. Our Allied armies have been taken completely by surprise.

I'm writing this very late, but I had to get this down. Mr Chamberlain, our Prime Minister, has resigned! People haven't been at all happy about the way he's been running the War. Another minister, Mr Winston Churchill, is now our Prime Minister. At nine o'clock this evening we all crowded round the wireless in the VADs' mess to hear Mr Chamberlain's resignation broadcast to the nation. Mr Churchill went to the palace at 6 o'clock this evening to see the King, who's asked him to form a new government. There was a real sense of relief in the room.

"We'll be all right now," I heard someone say after we'd turned off the wireless. Oh, I pray they're right. There's something about Mr Churchill that makes us feel safe. He won't take any nonsense from Jerry, I feel sure, but is there anything anyone can do to help us now?

Thursday 16th May

The German army seems unstoppable. In the last few days they've stormed through neutral Belgium and now their tanks are rolling across France. They entered France through the Ardennes, an area in eastern France. That was another big surprise. The Ardennes region is hilly and forested, and it was thought that their tanks wouldn't be able to cross it. But apparently the Germans have got a new sort of tank, which seems able to cope with all sorts of obstacles – even forests and hills. The French armies are being pushed back under the German onslaught. The British Expeditionary Force is still standing its ground, but how much longer will it be able to do so?

Trying not to think what this means for us, but we're all jolly frightened.

Holland has surrendered to the Germans. As soon as I came off duty, I wrote at once to Peter and Giles. I don't know if my letter will ever reach Peter. I don't know if I will ever see him again. I cannot bear it.

Tuesday 21st May

When I woke up this morning I thought for an instant that I could hear something – guns, or bombs – a sort of distant boom, boom – far away, across the sea. I told myself not to be so silly, we can't possibly hear them here, and anyway, the Germans are still very far away, but I could feel my heart beat a lot faster.

I popped outside on my break. Shielding my eyes in the sun, I looked out to sea. You can't walk on the beach now. It's been mined and there's barbed wire draped everywhere – even on the promenades we used to cycle down.

Mr Churchill says we're in deep trouble. We've nothing to match the Jerry tanks. If the *Prime Minister* says that, then we are indeed in an awful fix.

Bit by bit, the British and French armies are being pushed back towards the sea. Nothing they do seems to be able to stop the German advance. I wish I could stop thinking about that. My brother's out there in that hell.

Wednesday 22nd May

Letter from Mother today. She writes that she's made up her mind and joined ARP (Air Raid Precautions) – as an air-raid warden! She misses having us all to look after, she says, and she needs to feel she's doing something useful. Now it seems she's got a whole village on her hands!

She didn't mention Peter, so I know that she must be very worried about him. I wish I could go and see her but a lot of new patients are expected here soon and more VADs are being drafted in to help. It would be wonderful if Anne was amongst them!

Friday 24th May

On the 20th the Germans captured the French towns of Amiens and Abbeville. Our armies are retreating. At the hospital we're all holding our breath.

I'm trying not to think about the War. It is such a relief to be able to bury myself in work. But as soon as I go off duty, I start to worry again.

I can see worry plain on everyone else's faces, too. It's all anyone can talk about – what's going to happen now? Bunty's going round with a face as white as a sheet. The strain we're all under here is quite awful.

Sunday 26th May

Half day off – I spent it in Surgical. It's all hands to the deck now. All leave's been cancelled. Sister and our MO were kept busy all morning, doing rounds and organizing patients' discharges. For me it was back and forth to the store, returning hospital "blues" and bringing back the soldiers' kits. As I ran back and forth, I saw men in khaki and women, white caps on their heads – doctors and nurses I've never seen before. I don't know what they're doing here.

All those patients well enough to travel are being evacuated to hospitals further inland to make room for the new arrivals. They'll travel by ambulance train, escorted by a team of MOs and nurses. I still don't know who the new patients are, or why so many are expected here. But something's happened. Something big.

Monday 27th May

There are men lying on the floor, all along the corridor and in the ward, and on mattresses between the beds. Sweat pours off their faces, and they're filthy. As I entered I saw a VAD on her knees, cutting off a man's uniform. Her face was white and strained. It was Marjorie! I could see a dirty bandage swathed round the man's leg and there was an identity tag round his neck. It was unreadable – stained with blood and dirt. One of the QAs took me over to another stretcher. Under the blanket the man was fully dressed. She asked me to wash his face. "Do it gently, Nurse," she said. "And be quick about it. There are plenty more here that need washing."

I knelt on the floor by the stretcher, a bowl of warm water to hand. Gently I lifted the soldier's head, pillowing it on my arm, and began to wipe his face. His eyes were bloodshot and sweat was pouring off him.

"Wha. . . a . . . a . . . a . . ." he started to say. Oily stuff dribbled out of his mouth. I laid his head carefully back down on the stretcher. There was something staining my arm where his head had lain. I ran for help.

It was the last thing he said.

I ran into the annexe and leaned over the sink, taking deep breaths.

111

I felt awful – too upset even for tears. Desperately I tried to pull myself together. *I've got to cope – everyone else is. I must cope. I must.*

"Nurse, I need your help," I heard a voice say gently behind me. I dried my face quickly and turned round. The QA had a stack of hot-water bottles in her arms. "Heat these up for me, will you?" she asked.

"The men. . ." I faltered. "I'm supposed to wash them."

"Never mind about that now. Nurse Mason's doing it."

Jean? I thought vaguely. She was working nights. *Was she still on duty?*

As soon as the men are brought in, the QAs and MOs go from mattress to bed, from bed to mattress. They check the men's breathing and pulse. Is that man still in shock? Can we risk removing his uniform? They call me over. "Nurse, I'd like you to wash this man, please." I run over and cut off his uniform as I've been shown. "Be careful how you do it, Nurse. We must try to save all we can." Gently I wash the gritty sand and dirt off him. Under an old bandage there's a wound on his abdomen. Blood is seeping through the bandage. I need a fresh bandage – now! The haemorrhage is staunched, the new bandage wound tightly over the wound.

"His pulse is very weak, Sister." I look up from my patient at Sister's face. Sister's sleeves are rolled up. She looks as if she's been up all night.

An MO takes over and I'm sent to fill up hot-water bottles again. Soon, we've run out. "Nurse, look in the patients' beds – over there, Nurse, over there!" Blankly, I pull out a hot-water bottle from next to a patient's feet. The feet are very cold, I tell the Sister. He's dead, she

112

says briskly. No time for tears here. The body is rolled into a blanket and lifted off the bed. Automatically I wash down the mackintosh sheet, dry it, and then I rip open a package and pull out another blanket, which I lay on top of it. Next to me the stretcher bearers are waiting impatiently. As soon as I've finished, the bed is filled again.

Back and forth I go into the annexe, squeezing out the flannel, watching dirt and blood and sweat swirl away together down the sluice.

QAs run round the ward and the corridors, handing out injections of morphia as though they're cups of tea. There are metal stands between the beds, bottles of blood swinging off them. Rubber tubes connect them to our patients.

A Sister asks me to sort through a pile of bloodstained clothing and get it ready to go off to the store. I'm glad to be able to keep my head down. Glad not to have to look for a time at those exhausted despairing faces, those blank eyes. But I can't shut out the groans, the eternal tramp tramp tramp of the stretcher bearers, bringing more men into the ward, and taking others down to Theatre.

And still the ambulances come. The BEF is being evacuated from Dunkirk. When I first heard the news, I felt strangely relieved. Soon, I hoped, my brother would be home.

Not now.

Each time an ambulance arrives I wonder if he'll be amongst its patients. Each time the doors swing open, I have to force myself not to look up. I'm terrified. I don't want to see Peter here, but even worse is thinking of him left behind in France.

113

A cheerful, smiling nurse can do more to help her patients than a cross and weary one, I suddenly remember from my training. But I cannot laugh, I cannot smile. And oh, I am weary. And this – I feel horribly certain – is only the beginning.

Wednesday 29th May

Dragged myself up to bed at last at *three in the morning* – felt like curling up on the stairs – legs so wobbly and weak. Scribbling this in bed . . . too tired to think. . . That's some little comfort, I suppose. I must write my diary because I promised Anne. But I don't want to. I don't want to *remember* what I've seen today. I want to *forget*. I daren't let myself think – if I stop to think, I'll never get through this.

Thursday 30th May

We've had another blow. The Belgian army have surrendered to the Germans. It happened two days ago, I'm told. In the hospital the wards are overflowing. All our usual routine's gone to the winds, though Sister tries her best to keep order.

Though I'm constantly exhausted, I often wake up when the ambulances drive up to the hospital. It's hot and stuffy in our little room, too, which makes it hard to sleep, but we're not supposed to open the blackout shutters. Tonight, though, I felt I just couldn't breathe. I had to open the window. I crept quietly over to it and managed to prise it open. I gulped in the cool night air.

It was a clear night and I looked up at the stars. Those same stars shine over France, I found myself thinking, and then, without any warning, the tears came. I just stood there, trying not to sob, feeling the tears slide down my cheeks. Oh, please – don't let him be killed. Please.

I heard the door open and a moment later I felt a hand touch my shoulder. Jean had come in.

"What's wrong?" she asked. I couldn't speak. "Is it Peter?" she whispered. I nodded and felt her arm go round my shoulder. "Has anything happened to him?" she asked carefully.

"I don't know," I said. "I just don't know."

Jean stared out into the night. "My brother's out there too," she said.

"Oh, Jean," I said. "I'm so sorry." I put my arm round her shoulders and we stood there, the tears silently pouring down our cheeks.

Friday 31st May

As soon as I arrived on the ward this morning one of the QAs hurried up to me. She took me over to a bed surrounded by screens.

"I'd like you to keep an eye on this boy while I find an MO." She lowered her voice. "He's very sick."

I looked at my charge. His eyes had opened ever so slightly when he heard our voices. Now he closed them again. I saw what an effort even this took. He looked awfully young – younger even than Peter. There was a blanket on the bed and though it was quite warm in the room, he was shivering. I took his hand in mine and rubbed his fingers gently, trying to warm them. They were very cold. I asked him his name, but it was clearly too difficult for him to speak. I talked gently to him. I don't know what I said exactly but soon I forgot everything else – all the chaos and the noise on the other side of the screens. Occasionally I saw him move his lips slightly – they looked awfully dry, so I got up and dampened them with a moistened swab.

My patient's lips were moving again and I leaned over the bed to listen. A smell – that awful stench of dried blood that I know so well now – rose up from the bed and it was all I could do not to retch. "Thank you," I heard him murmur faintly. And then he said something else and I leaned closer to hear. "Billy." His voice sounded as if it were coming from somewhere far away.

"Billy, I'm Kitty," I whispered, close to his ear. I didn't care that it was against the rules to tell him my name. It couldn't matter now. I squeezed his fingers, very gently. Billy's face was very pale and stained with perspiration, and I could see something damp begin to seep through the red army blanket. The wound had begun to bleed again. I stood up urgently. Where was the MO? I needed help – now. And then I heard a sigh and there was a sudden movement under the blanket – a sort of shudder that seemed to pass through Billy's whole body. I was still holding his hand.

A screen was moved aside. The MO was standing there, the QA next to him. The MO leaned over the boy and took his stiffening wrist loosely in his hand. It's too late for that, I thought. I was trying to choke back tears. Quietly I got to my feet and made myself walk across the ward to the annexe. I didn't want anyone to see my tears.

The QA caught up with me a few minutes later. She asked me to wash the bedstead and change the sheets. I didn't need to look back to know that the screens had gone and the body lifted off the bed. How could she ask this of me? I wondered dully. A boy had just died in that bed. Didn't she care? "His name was Billy," I wanted to tell her. I felt angry and upset. And then – fleetingly – I saw the sadness deep in the QA's eyes, and the tiredness, and I felt ashamed.

I made up poor Billy's bed. I don't know how I did it, but I did.

Saturday 1st June

Wounded soldiers are pouring in from the Front in France each day. Here, days and nights run into each other, but I'm thankful that I'm able to do something useful. New VADs arrived again today from outstations – sick bays, first-aid posts and other hospitals. I keep hoping to see Anne's merry face amongst them, but I've heard nothing more about her hoped-for transfer.

Whenever I have time to grab a break, I go outside – stepping through corridors packed with wounded men, all of them waiting to be admitted. I take off my mask and breathe deeply – filling my lungs with fresh air, glad to get rid of the hospital smell. Today I sat down for a time on the warm grass, under the shade of a big sycamore tree. While I was sitting there, a squirrel bounded across the lawn in front of me. It stopped and looked at me and I looked back at it. Then it was off again, running up the tree. That squirrel doesn't know we're at war, I thought suddenly. Its life carries on as it always has. The thought comforted me a little. I looked out to sea again. There was a great ship bobbing up and down in the Channel, nose pointed to port. I wondered if it was a hospital ship, bringing more of the wounded home. It was like a signal to me. Tiredly I got to my feet and made my way back to the ward.

Only the very sickest are brought to coastal hospitals like ours. They're a motley lot – they come from regiments stationed all over the country. Some of them had their wounds dressed in France or on board ship on the way home, but even so, infection can set in. There's not much we can do if it really takes hold. I hate feeling so helpless.

Sunday 2nd June

This morning I was asked to wash a new patient. Like all our new arrivals his face was caked with dirt. He had a shrapnel wound and I knew that he'd soon be going to Theatre. As I washed the dirt off him, I saw his eyes on me, grimacing with pain. I felt distressed. I asked if I was hurting him.

"I'm all right, Nurse," he said shortly. "Don't bother about me," his eyes seemed to be saying. "Don't bother about any of us. We're not worth it." There was such shame on his face.

Gradually I've begun to understand why. Our boys lost the battle and they feel that they've let us down. But to us they're heroes and I cannot begin to imagine what they've had to endure. I hope that they'll understand this soon.

Monday 3rd June

There have been a lot of mutters about the RAF. "Where were the RAF when we needed them?" This is all one poor boy says. Everyone who walks past his bed gets asked the same question. "Where were the RAF?" Just that. Again and again. Sometimes he screams in his sleep. It upsets the other patients, but we can't move him, as there's nowhere for him to go. Another patient told me that they were bombarded by enemy planes as they retreated. They didn't just target soldiers, he said, but refugees as well. Old people, children – it made no difference. Jerry planes strafed the lot. We could do nothing for them, he said. Our planes were nowhere to be seen. I could see that his eyes were swimming as he relived the horror of the memory, and I went to fetch him a cup of tea. My legs were shaking as I walked over to the ward kitchen. I thought I'd heard and seen it all, but the soldier's words sickened me. What kind of person does a thing like that?

It was growing dark, and I put up the blackout boards. I still couldn't put that soldier's words out of my mind. Where had the RAF been, I wondered. I hoped that Giles would be able to tell me.

I don't know what time it was when I went off duty. I hadn't eaten anything since lunch, but I couldn't have touched a morsel.

Jean came in when I was still sitting on the bed, too tired even to get undressed. She had two mugs of Ovaltine in her hands. I looked at her drained face. It seemed to reflect what I was feeling. I took one of the mugs gratefully in my cold and shaking hands. "Nurse Mason," I said to her. "What would I do without you?"

Tuesday 4th June

Mr Winston Churchill, the Prime Minister, has spoken to the nation. It was a wonderful speech. We crowded round the wireless to listen. I managed to scribble down some of what he said.

"We shall fight on the beaches, we shall fight on the landing-grounds, we shall fight in the fields and in the streets, we shall fight in the hills; we shall never surrender."

Feel tearful, proud and full of renewed hope and purpose. Whenever I feel despondent, I will look at these words. I don't merely hope we'll win any more. I *know* we will.

Thursday 6th June

In his speech the Prime Minister also said that the RAF played a big part in helping the British and French armies escape from Dunkirk. I'd heard that German bombers targeted the towns and beaches where the men were waiting and the ships sent to pick up the men. They even bombed hospital ships! And Dunkirk and other French coastal towns nearby have been bombed into blazing ruins. But without the RAF, the Prime Minister says, the situation would have been even worse. There were a few disbelieving snorts amongst our patients when they learnt what he'd said. And today I heard them muttering about it again. I was accompanying some of them down to the station where they were to catch an ambulance train. As we bumped down the drive, a young boy with a bandaged head said: "Our Prime Minister's just covering up for them – RAF cowards."

"Only planes *I* saw had those black-and-white crosses on them," snorted another, who'd lost an eye. "Since when did our planes have black-and-white crosses on them?"

There were more angry snorts. I just sat there silently. I felt sure they were wrong, or were they? After all, they had been there, hadn't they? As I looked at them – at their injuries – I thought they had every right to be bitter. So this evening I sat down at last and wrote to Giles. I know it may be weeks before I hear from him, but I've at least got to try and find out what really happened at Dunkirk.

Monday 10th June

Mother rang today. Peter is home! Not wounded, not dead – he's safe. He's exhausted, Mother said when she finally got put through to me. Otherwise he's all right – and very relieved to be back. Mother says he was picked up in a little boat – that there were hundreds of them helping the soldiers get off the beaches. Whoever picked Peter up saved my brother's life. I don't know who you are but thank you, thank you, thank you.

Tuesday 11th June

All down one side of the ward now are men with arms or legs encased in plaster – bones shattered by gunshot or shrapnel. It's horrible, the smell that comes off them. When I go over to them, I try not to let my face show that I notice it, but they know. Poor boys, it's so much worse for them. We've tried all sorts of things to hide that smell, but nothing works.

Italy declared war on us yesterday.

Monday 17th June

France has surrendered. Now we are really on our own. It may sound odd, but in a way I feel relieved. At least now we know where we stand. Jean's awfully worried. She thinks that her brother's still in France, but she's not had any news of him. She doesn't know if he's been captured, or even if he's still alive.

We sat together in the VADs' mess, aching feet propped up on chairs, mugs of hot tea in our hands. Bunty was looking so pale. I wish I knew if she's heard from her officer, but I feel too scared to ask. Lots of people are going round the hospital with that same look on their faces – people who've lost brothers, husbands or sons at Dunkirk. We didn't talk much – we were all too tired – and I fell asleep in my chair. When I woke up, they'd gone and the half-full mug was still in my hand.

I don't know how I find the energy to keep up my diary, but I don't know what I'd do without it. Sometimes I can't bear to relive my day, and it's only my promise to Anne that makes me write. But at other times it brings me comfort of a sort.

Thursday 20th June

Ambulances full of wounded men arrived here yesterday. The operating theatres are working flat out again and I was told to report there this morning. One after another the men were wheeled in with awful gunshot or shrapnel wounds. Then it's back on to the wards again, a few hours later, often with one bit or another missing. So many shattered or gangrenous limbs that can't be saved.

The last of our forces are being brought back from France. They'd retreated west of Dunkirk to the Cherbourg peninsula. But Jean still has no news of her brother. I feel so grieved for her.

We went out for a walk together this evening. We hadn't gone far when we saw the oddest sight – fields full of old cars. Apparently it's to stop German planes from landing in them. Everyone expects that the Germans will try and invade us soon. All there is to stop them now is a thin stretch of water – and the RAF. But if the worst happens our boys will be ready for them and we are relieved that so many have got safely out of France.

Friday 21st June

I got a letter from Giles today. He did take part in the "battle for France". He says he doesn't think the Germans will risk an invasion until they've destroyed our air force and have control of the air. And there was something else, which made me sit up.

"I'm glad you asked me about Dunkirk," he wrote. "People here seem very angry with the RAF. They don't even try to listen to our side of things and I want to set the record straight. To put it bluntly, if we'd not been there, many of our boys would still be holed up in France, either dead or in a German prisoner-of-war camp. I guess the lads on the ground didn't see us, but we were there all right."

In his letter he said that he'd made many sorties to France. "Once," he said, "I really thought I'd bought it – engine ran out of petrol. I had just enough fuel left to get me back over the Channel but I had to make an emergency landing in a field and find my own way back to base."

I felt very thoughtful as I put the letter away. So my patients had been wrong and the Prime Minister was right. Giles should be very proud of what he did. He sounds different somehow – older, grown up. If only I could feel more for him, but I just can't.

Sunday 23rd June

As soon as I got off duty today I collapsed into bed. I woke up again when Jean came in. She had two mugs of hot tea in her hands, and there was a huge smile on her face. Most unJean-like! Sleepily I sat up in bed.

"All right, tell," I said, patting the bed next to me. She flopped down on the bed at once. I'd guessed what she was going to say, for she looked so happy.

Her brother got out on one of the last ships to leave Cherbourg, she told me, beaming. German tanks harried them all the way to the port. She shivered and I gave her a big hug. I can't begin to imagine what it must have been like – and then I thought about the dirty, exhausted faces of the wounded men pouring into the hospital, and I wondered about those others, the ones who didn't get out.

There are a lot of Poles among our patients now. We all know how brave they were and how they refused to surrender to the enemy when it looked as if it was all up for them. Somehow they managed to reach the French coast and were brought safely across the Channel to Britain. There's a rumour that as many as 20,000 of them have got away!

In spite of everything there's a good atmosphere in the country, and it's rubbing off on us in the hospital. One of the QAs told me that as well as the Poles, Czechs, Canadians, Free French, New Zealanders, Australians and South Africans, and many from other lands too, are flooding into the country to join our forces! *Not* that we needed anything more to stiffen our resolve.

So many acts of heroism and courage. Big ones and little ones. I see them every day in both our patients and staff. This war brings out all that's best in us. It doesn't matter what the enemy does, I *know* that somehow we will come through this. We must.

Friday 28th June

When I went off duty today, the first person I saw was Bunty. She looked very drawn and tired. She smiled at me, but her eyes were sad. She seemed to be making an effort to hold on to herself. She told me she had something to tell me and together we went into the VADs' mess. I felt scared. What was she going to tell me? Had something happened to her officer?

We sat down. I waited.

"It was awful on the ward today," she said at last. Her voice was barely a whisper. "You cannot imagine how awful." Her lips trembled and I was afraid that she was going to break down. I felt shocked. I didn't recognize the Bunty I knew in this sad and shaken girl. So this was what she wanted to tell me. That she couldn't cope. Bunty! Of all people! I put my hands on her shoulders and shook her slightly. She looked surprised. Then I surprised myself.

"Bunty," I said, firmly. "You've got to pull yourself together. It's the same for all of us."

She turned away from me, laying her head on her arm. "You've changed, Kitty. You sound so – so *hard*."

I flinched. "I'm only trying to help," I said. I felt so hurt.

"Oh, Kitten, I can't bear it any more," she burst out suddenly. I looked at her, startled.

She looked up at me, eyes brimming now. "I always used to dread it when the wounded were brought in, in case it was him, but today . . . each time a wounded man came on to the ward, I hoped and prayed it *would* be him, that he's just wounded . . . not . . . not . . ."

She began to sob and suddenly I felt cold all through. "He . . . he's never coming back. Oh, Kitty, he's been killed!"

I stroked her hair until her sobs had died down. "Bunty, I'm so sorry," I whispered. Tears were running down my face now. I wish I'd listened to her when she'd tried to tell me. I wish I hadn't been so hard on her.

Saturday 29th June

As soon as I finished work today I got out my bicycle. Soon I was out in the countryside, pedalling hard.

I was still feeling upset about what I'd said to Bunty – and what she'd said to me. Had I changed? I admired the way professional nurses coped, and somehow I'd also found the strength to cope. But had I become harder too?

I hadn't, had I? I thought desperately.

I cycled until I felt too tired to cycle any more. On the way back to the hospital I saw a radar tower facing out to sea. I remembered what Peter had once told me about them – how they help us track down enemy planes – and I took a good look at it as I cycled past.

Suddenly I hit a stone and my tyre blew. Bother, I thought. I hopped off, and pulled out my repair kit.

I was still fumbling with it rather hopelessly when I heard a voice call out and a bicycle pulled up next to me. It was Lieutenant Venables! Was I relieved to see him! He took my kit from me and I stood by and watched as he deftly fixed the puncture.

When he stood up again, his hands were covered in sticky black oil and there was a smudge on his cheek. I saw that he was about to put his

130

oily hands into his pockets so I quickly fished out a hanky and gave it to him. It was the sort of thing Peter would do, I found myself thinking as, rather sheepishly, he wiped his oily cheek and hands.

Together, we cycled back up to the hospital. I told him I was working in Theatre again and he asked me how I liked it. "I'd rather be on the wards." I told him. He smiled at me as if he understood. By the time we'd got back I was feeling a whole lot happier. I do like Lieutenant Venables. Later I found myself thinking about him again. It'd been such a long time since I'd seen him. And then I remembered Bunty and I felt ashamed that I could have forgotten her troubles so easily, and I went off to find her. Honestly, I'm heartless, I really am.

Thursday 18th July

Letter from Anne today. "It sounds simply awful down there," she wrote. "Poor Kitten, I do feel so worried about you and all our friends. Please write soon and let me know that you're all right.

"You know that transfer I've been trying to get? Well, you'll never guess what the wretched army's gone and done now! It's posting me still further away – to a sick bay attached to a barracks in some deserted spot.

"It's not fair! Here I am, hockey stick at the ready, desperate to come and help you defend our island against the Jerries. Ah well . . . write soon?

"PS: I hope you're writing your diary, as promised. I am! But then, I have precious little else to do in my off-duty time. I don't suppose you've been having much of that."

I feel sad to think that Anne won't be transferring here. I feel a bit guilty, too. I haven't been keeping up my diary as I should. I haven't felt like writing at all. Oh, Anne, I hope you'll forgive me.

Saturday 20th July

I went down to the station this morning. It was my first whole day off in a very long time and I was planning to spend it at home. I was in heaven at the prospect of getting right away from the hospital, even if it was just for a day.

I stood on the platform and waited. At last the train came – a whole hour late! When we chugged into the station at last, I knew I'd have to hurry to catch my connection – and I tore across the platform. As I leaped down the stairs two at a time, I saw the train pull out of the station. There wasn't another train for a very long time, so all I could do was wait and catch the next train back to the hospital. I felt so upset. I'd been looking forward to going home. Mother had written that Peter was home on leave. And for once Father would be at home, too. I haven't seen any of them since New Year.

I scrounged a lift back up to the hospital. Then I went to find the others. Molly was off duty too, and we cycled out into the countryside together. We rode up and down country lanes, and then we stopped at a pub and I blew nearly a whole week's wages on the best meal I'd had since New Year.

It was nearly dark when we climbed back on to our bicycles and we had to cycle really slowly. It's easy to get lost now, as there are no streetlights to guide you, and all the signposts have been taken down to confuse the enemy.

Suddenly Molly clutched my arm and we both wobbled and nearly fell off our bikes. In a loud whisper she told me she'd heard a noise – a sort of rustling in one of the hedges.

"It's probably just a rabbit or a mouse," I told her, sounding braver than I felt. Then Molly started to tell me about the Jerry spies who've been seen parachuting into southern England. Feeling really scared now, I asked her how she knew. Well, then she told me that they've been seen in the town – disguised as nuns! I felt so relieved that I began to laugh. There have been a lot of invasion scares and rumours, but this was just *too* silly. Molly, I think, felt a bit peeved but then she saw the funny side too. Our laughter sounded most peculiar out there in the dark, so we got hastily back on our bikes and cycled on.

It was late when at last we crept up to the hospital, wheeling our bikes. The door was locked but we squeezed in through a ground-floor window that someone had forgotten to close. We couldn't stop giggling as we tiptoed down the darkened corridors and up the stairs. What a day!

Sunday 21st July

Hitler's offered to make peace with Britain! We won't have any of it of course. Peace would mean surrendering all we've been fighting for. We're fighting on.

A trunk call was put through from Mother today. The line was crackling badly, but she managed to ask how I was. I told her I was fine. The crackles got worse. "What did you say?" I asked. I was practically bawling into the phone now. It was something about the enemy bombing the coastal towns. Even through the crackles I could hear the panic in her voice. The town has been hit, but I didn't tell her. Hitler's planes are attacking our shipping, too. I told her not to worry about me, and then I asked how she was, and Father and Peter. It was a while before I realized that the line had gone dead.

Wednesday 24th July

I had the oddest dream yesterday. I dreamed that a plane flew down low – so low that I could even see the pilot's face. It was Giles. I called to him but he couldn't hear me. He could see me though. He smiled and waved. Three times he circled the hospital, each time his plane getting higher and higher. Then off he flew into the clouds, with me still calling vainly after him, the way you do in dreams.

When I woke up I felt very out of sorts. I told myself that it had just been a dream, that probably there'd been planes flying past as I'd slept. But I couldn't stop worrying and I told myself I'd write to Giles as soon as I finished my shift. I didn't though. I was so tired when I came off duty this morning – I'm back on nights again now – that I just collapsed into bed. Tomorrow though I *will* write to Giles. I haven't heard from him since he wrote to me about Dunkirk. I must write back and tell him that I understand better now.

Saturday 27th July

Peter scooted over to see me today. I can't think how he managed to wangle the petrol for the trip. It was wonderful to see him. He told me he felt he had to keep an eye on me – he thought I'd spun a story about the train! We rode out into the countryside, me clinging tightly to his back. It was a bit of a squash. I looked a fright when we arrived at the inn – my hair stuck up all over the place.

After we'd finished our meal he asked me about my work. "You were in the thick of it, weren't you, Sis?"

I doodled with the spoon in my saucer before answering. I knew that he was thinking about Dunkirk but I didn't want to talk about it. "Yes," I said shortly. "But most of the time I was too busy to think about it."

"I know," he said, staring straight ahead of him. "It was a bit like that for me. But now – now I wish I could forget." His eyes looked very far away – as if he was back on the beaches at Dunkirk. Why was I spared? Why me when so many weren't? I could see the thought plain on his face. I tried to bring him back.

"We all have to find our own way through this," I said. "We have to show them we're not beaten. We can't give up, or they've won."

Peter didn't say anything for a long time. He still seemed very far away.

And then he told me how one night they'd made their way down to the beach and waded out to sea. How they'd stood in the icy water, hoping to get picked up by one of the little ships bobbing up and down in the waves – each man for himself. I stopped him then.

"What little ships?" And then dimly I remembered that Mother had said something about the little ships when she told me how Peter had got back to England, and hadn't the Prime Minister also said something about them in his broadcast to us?

Peter looked very surprised. "Didn't you know?" he asked.

"Tell me," I said.

Peter drew in breath. "Everyone who owned a boat on the south-east coast was asked to take it over to France. There were all sorts," he said. "Some quite small – even fishing boats. The troop carriers couldn't get in near enough to pick us up. There was nowhere for them to berth, as all the piers that were any use had been destroyed by Jerry bombers. So the little boats had to ferry us between the beaches and the ships. They made trip after trip." He shook his head wonderingly. "Those chaps were amazing. We'd never have got away without them. Even then, it was a bit of a scramble." His face darkened again.

I imagined the pushing and shoving, as the men fought for a seat in one of the little boats – their only passport to safety. I shuddered.

"All the time there were those silver wings wheeling and diving overhead. They weren't seagulls, Kitty," Peter said, giving a lopsided smile. "They were planes – Jerry planes. We were sitting ducks," he added. "The night I got out – think it was night. Hard to tell – there

137

was a big, black smoky cloud over everything much of the time – we were being bombed all the time, you see. Anyway, when I got out, Dunkirk was blazing so Jerry could see us beautifully, even at night. Picked men out of the sea like fishes. Rat-a-tat-tat," he said, imitating the noise of the planes' guns as they fired on the men. He stopped again, lost in the memory.

"How's Giles?" he said suddenly. There was a touch of bitterness in his voice. RAF pilots, it seemed to say, easy ride *they* had. I remembered what Giles had written in his last letter. I wanted to tell Peter, but there was such anger in his face that I just didn't know if he'd believe me. And I didn't want to row about it and spoil the evening.

"I don't know," I said slowly, answering his question. "I don't really care any more, but I don't know how to tell him."

Peter nodded thoughtfully. "Probably best not to – at least not right now," he said. He stood up. "You're on duty tonight, aren't you? I'd better get you back."

After he'd dropped me off, I hugged him tightly. "Take care of yourself, Pete," I whispered. He had one foot already on the pedal. He flashed a smile up at me.

"You know, we haven't quarrelled this evening – not once," he said. "Must be a record." I felt relieved that I'd not brought up the subject of the RAF's role at Dunkirk.

The twins wanted to know who Peter was. I'd seen them hanging out of the window as we rode back up to the hospital. I told them he was my brother, but I don't think they believed me.

"He's awfully handsome," sighed Mollie.

Handsome? Peter? 'Course, he is. He's my brother.

Wednesday 31st July

The town was bombed again last night. The sky glowed red for hours, like a ghastly wound. Tip-and-run raiders, someone said grimly. The German planes nip across the Channel, drop their fearsome cargo and shoot off back home again before our fighters can catch up with them.

Shelters are being dug in the hospital grounds and there are sandbags piled up around all the buildings. We've got a guard, too. He's only got a stick – as we're a hospital, he's not allowed to have a gun. One man, armed only with a stick! How will that help us? At Dunkirk, the Germans blew up hospital ships in the Channel, so they won't take any notice of this, I feel sure. But then isn't this the *right* thing for us to do – and isn't that what this war is all about? It's no use – I cannot get this straight in my head.

In the afternoon I saw little specks appear in the sky again. I shielded my eyes to see them better, but they were too far away. Even when the drones got louder, I couldn't see the planes properly. I haven't seen a dogfight yet, but here in the hospital we see many of their victims.

Wednesday 7th August

Giles is dead! I feel simply terrible – but I can't cry. I learned what happened in a letter from his best friend at the station. They think that Giles was shot down over the sea. It happened on 23 July – that was the day I had my strange dream. For a long time I just sat and stared at the letter in my hand. I felt sick. In my heart I know it was a coincidence, but that doesn't help. Worse, I feel as if I let Giles down.

His friend said that Giles was a brave and gallant officer and that he knew he'd cared a lot about me. I wished he hadn't written that. Then he apologized for not writing sooner.

He apologized to *me*! I should be apologizing to him – and to Giles. Now I can't even do that. I didn't give Giles the support he needed. I never told him that I was proud of the part he took in rescuing the BEF at Dunkirk. I couldn't even be bothered to write.

Thursday 8th August

Jean found me in the linen store in floods of tears today. I couldn't talk, just waved the letter at her. She sat with me until I'd calmed down, and then we went for a walk together. She thinks I'm upset because I cared about Giles. I couldn't tell her the truth – I can't tell *anyone*. I didn't care about Giles, not in the way they all think. And they're being so sweet to me – especially Bunty. It makes me feel so guilty.

Sometimes I don't know what I'd do without my diary. At least *here* I can confess how I really feel.

Saturday 10th August

A plane was shot down over the town late yesterday afternoon. All the crew managed to bail out. One – the pilot – had gunshot wounds and was rushed into Theatre as soon as he arrived. The rear gunner broke his wrist trying to get out of the plane. No one was badly burned. We've heard terrible things – the enemy has begun bombing our airfields.

Our pilots do their best to get the planes up into the air before they can be destroyed, but they can't always get them up in time, and runways and airbases are being badly damaged. If the enemy manages to do the job well enough, there'll be nothing to stop them from invading.

At night, the stretcher bearers rushed on to the ward again. Another plane had been shot down nearby. While another VAD made up the bed, I went to fill a hot-water bottle. When I came back she was expertly cutting off the pilot's uniform.

It was a German one.

I looked at the man on the stretcher. His face was very pale and he was sweating. He didn't look any different from any other young pilot. I thought I'd hate him, but I didn't.

I wrote to Giles's mother as soon as I came off duty this morning. After I'd sealed up the envelope, I burst into tears. I sat there, head in my arms, and I cried and cried. I thought about Giles – and about that German pilot. So many people's lives are being wrecked by this terrible war. Will it *ever* end?

Thursday 15th August

I was mooching around in the gardens yesterday afternoon when the Assistant Commandant marched up to me. Told me off for not having my tin hat and gas mask with me. "Nurse, what will you do if there's a raid?" She sounded really exasperated and I fled to fetch them. I'd just got to the door when Lieutenant Venables came out, still in his white coat. He didn't see me at first, even though I nearly walked right into him. Then he stopped, looked down at me and smiled. It was such a nice smile – as if he was pleased to see me, and suddenly I felt very pleased to see *him*. It seemed an age since I'd seen him – the day he stopped to mend my puncture.

I watched him lope off down the lawn and then he stopped and stared out to sea, shielding his eyes in the sunlight. I found myself wondering if *he'd* lost anyone close to him.

There was a raid today – a really big one we heard. We saw the planes fly over, so many of them. We heard the guns booming from the ships patrolling the coast.

I've had that dream again – I've had it again and again since Giles was killed. Giles's plane is flying seawards. A German fighter plane is on his tail. Then the pilot opens fire and Giles's plane spirals through the sky and bursts into flames as it hits the sea. All the time I'm screaming after him, "Look behind you! Look behind you!" It's no use. He never hears me. And the ending's always the same. The sea's always on fire.

Friday 30th August

My first day back on day duty – and such an exciting one too. Dr McIndoe was visiting the hospital! Bunty rushed over to tell me. She's working on the Surgical ward now.

I've heard a lot about this surgeon and what he can do for burns patients. We have a new treatment for burns now – our wards are full of men, their legs and arms encased in bags of saline. But this doctor can actually take skin from an unburnt part of a man's body and use it to rebuild the burnt part – their face or hands maybe.

At ten o'clock this morning the great man came. I liked his face at once. He didn't waste any time, but went straight over to the bed of one of our sickest patients, a badly burned airman, who was shot down over the Channel yesterday. Aircraft fuel supposedly burns its victims very rapidly. It's all to the good that he landed in the sea, apparently, as the salt water is good for burns, though you wouldn't think so from looking at this poor boy. We're hoping that the doctor will take him away to be treated at his special burns unit at the Queen Victoria hospital in East Grinstead. The poor airman can hardly move his lips but after Dr McIndoe had left his bedside and gone to speak to Matron, I could see real hope in his eyes for the first time.

Everyone here – even the MOs – talks about Dr McIndoe as if he were God. And I can understand why, if he really can help people like this poor pilot. He gives a burned man his life back – a far better one than he'd have without his help, anyway.

Saturday 14th September

I'm writing this sitting up in bed. I'm in a side room, off the main ward. My hands are still painful but I can write slowly now. Molly smuggled some sheets of writing paper into the ward when she came to see me earlier today. I didn't tell her or the others the reason I wanted them – to write my diary. Sister would have a fit if she saw me. But I must tell how I came to be lying here – a patient – while the memory is still fresh in my mind.

It happened nearly two weeks ago. I didn't feel particularly frightened when the air-raid alert sounded. Just weary. We'd had so many air-raid warnings before – all of them false.

It's always a frantic rush when the alert goes. This day it was no different. Off went our two newest VADs to the shelters, helping those patients able to walk. Sister, Bunty and I stayed behind to look after our other patients. Sister put up the blackout boards. This protects the patients from glass if the windows shatter. Bunty and I pulled the beds away from the walls and windows. We helped our patients put on their gas masks and tin hats, and then we put all those patients we could under their beds. The men always put a brave face on it, but I know that moving hurts them and I always hate doing this.

There were some patients we couldn't move, so we pulled mattresses up near their beds. In an attack these get heaved on top of the beds to protect the men from anything that might fall on them – like falling plaster or shattered glass. Then Bunty was sent off to look after a patient in one of the side rooms. Sister and I pulled on our tin hats and gas masks, too, and crawled under two of the empty beds.

High above us I heard the drone of the planes as they passed by. It sounded as though they were directly overhead. My heart was thumping. Would it be us this time? I was thinking over and over. Then I heard a single drone. It stopped. I saw Sister crawl out from under a bed, and I watched as she struggled to heave a mattress on top of our sickest patient.

In that instant I knew – it wasn't a false alarm.

Everything happened so fast after that. Almost at once there was an awful whistling noise and a huge crump. As soon as I dared I looked up. I gasped. There was an enormous gaping hole where one of the windows had been, and glass and plaster were sprayed all over the place.

It was quiet again. The barrage had stopped – for now. A huge cloud of choking dust billowed through the gaping hole into the room. I began to crawl out from under the bed, knocking my head as I did so. I knew I had to get the patients out.

Suddenly there was a screaming sound and the building shook again. I flung myself to the floor and felt the ground shake under me.

When the plaster and dust had settled I sat up again. There was a strange sort of ringing in my ears. I couldn't see Sister anywhere. I could barely see a thing through the dense dark smoke. And then I did see something – a flash of angry orange.

One of the beds was on fire.

There was a patient in that bed. My heart pounding I staggered to my feet. I grabbed some blankets and ran to the bed. No time to waste. Now I could see it clearly – an orange tongue curling round the foot of the bed. The flames leaped higher, grabbing at the mattress with greedy fingers. I flung the blankets on top of the flames. A sharp, searing pain shot up my hands and arms. I pressed down hard, smothering the flames under my hands, ignoring the groans from the bed and the pain in my hands. I kept doing it, again and again until I was sure that the fire was out. I looked at my patient – tiny smoky tendrils smouldered from the bedding. Hastily I pulled it off and wrapped him gently in another blanket.

I could hear sounds in the room now – as if people were moving around – but I could barely see anything at all as the cloud of dust swirled through the room and up to the doors.

Voices – my patients calling. "Jerry got us that time." Groans from other beds. Who else had been hurt? I had to get help – fast.

I felt my way towards the ward doors, calling to any patients who could to make their way out quickly. I felt pain leap up my hands again as I pushed open the doors. I wanted to cry out but I choked back my tears as I fell forward into the dark. A huge dirty cloud had swallowed up the corridor. I stood there for a minute, helplessly. I didn't know what to do. Then I remembered the side room. Bunty was in there. She'd help me. I felt my way along the corridor and into the little room. Every time I touched anything with my hands it hurt but I pressed on. I could hear voices – but they sounded muffled, as if they were far away.

In the side room, a window had been torn out, but there wasn't any other damage so far as I could tell.

Carefully I made my way over to the bed. I could see that our patient hadn't been hurt. I crouched down and peered underneath the bed. Bunty was still there, her head wrapped in her arms. As I reached in, I could feel her body shaking. I pulled at her arm. She didn't move.

"Bunty," I croaked through my mask. "Are you all right?" She didn't answer. "Bunty," I tried again, desperately. I saw her curl more tightly into herself. "Oh, Bunty," I said sadly.

Leaving her there, I stood up and made my way back into the main corridor. The voices I'd heard earlier were louder now. I leaned back against the wall and called. Through my mask my voice sounded so feeble. They'll *never* hear me, I thought despairingly.

"My patient," I heard my voice say dully, over and over. "Oh, please. Someone . . . . you've got to help him! He's been burnt."

And then there were all the others. Please! I felt someone pull at my arm. It hurt.

"It's all right, I've got you," a voice said gently. The voice sounded very familiar. And then I felt myself lifted up and all at once, like a curtain falling fast, darkness blotted everything out.

It was still dark when I woke, but now I was in bed and my hands and arms were in bags of saline and they hurt. I heard someone cry out – it seemed to be me. A nurse sitting next to my bed leaned close. "Are you all right?" she asked anxiously. I nodded, fighting back the tears that were trying to slide down my cheeks, biting my lips with the pain. I remembered all the burned airmen, and injured soldiers I'd nursed. Their injuries were much more serious than mine. They'd not cried, and neither would I.

Lots of people came to see me while I was in bed. Jean, of course, and Marjorie and Molly – even Sister Rook! The Commandant came too one day. They all made such a fuss of me – you'd think I'd be pleased but actually it was very embarrassing.

Then one day I heard the door open, and I looked up to see who it was this time. I was hoping it would be Bunty. She hadn't been to see me – not once. Marjorie had told me she felt too guilty, but I wanted to see her. I missed her.

It wasn't Bunty.

It was Matron!

"Well done, Nurse Langley," she said crisply. "We're all very proud of you." She told me that my quick response had saved a patient's life – probably several more lives, too. I asked her if Sister was all right.

Matron just looked at me. I felt my lips tremble and for a while I couldn't speak. Then I told her what Sister had done. How she'd put her patients first. She was the heroine – not me.

"You were both very brave," said Matron quietly. "You're a credit to our profession."

She had a great many more things to say, but I can't write them down. I feel embarrassed just thinking about them. I don't think I've been particularly brave. I just happened to be there. Matron asked if I'd thought of training as a professional nurse. "You have the makings of a fine nurse," she said. She told me she'd write in support of any application I made.

I felt my heart swell inside my chest, and after she'd gone I had a bit of a cry – quietly, into my pillow.

I've had plenty of time to think about Matron's words, but I still haven't decided what to do. I don't know what I want – not yet.

Monday 16th September

It's getting easier to write now. Sister says I'll be allowed up tomorrow!

There was a tremendous air battle over southern Britain yesterday. I knew something big was happening – from my bed I could hear the drones of countless planes and then an angry barrage – our anti-aircraft guns answering back. Was I scared! I crossed my fingers and prayed we wouldn't be hit again.

In the evening there was another barrage – shouts and catcalls and cheers from the main ward. Sister popped in to tell me about it – a huge smile on her face. Later, the "up" patients came to tell me, too.

"Nurse, Jerry's on the run. Nurse, the RAF's clipped Jerry's wings. Hundreds and hundreds of Jerry's planes have been shot down." The enemy was bombing London too, of course, but just then all anyone could think about was our victory in the skies.

In the end, Sister came in to shoo them away and the ward grew quiet again.

So much still depends on the RAF. If they carry on fighting like this, maybe the invasion will be delayed. Maybe it will never happen at all. Suddenly I found myself thinking about Giles. Whenever I think about our pilots I remember Giles and I feel so sad. And I know how much he'd have loved to be up there with them.

Saturday 21st September

I'm writing this on the train. I'm on my way home to convalesce – I'll be staying there until my hands and arms are completely better.

Earlier, Jean helped me pack my case. We were chatting and laughing together when I heard a knock on the door.

It was Bunty. Jean slipped out and left us together. It was the first time I'd seen Bunty since the day the bomb dropped.

"Molly told me you're going home today," she said.

I nodded.

"Can I do anything for you?" she asked. I could see she was trying not to look at my hands.

I shook my head. "It's all right, I can manage," I said. I hesitated. "They tell me that they'll soon be as good as new."

Bunty's face crumpled. "In spite of me," she whispered.

"Oh, Bunty, don't," I said, distressed. "It wasn't your fault."

I could see that she was making a big effort to pull herself together. My mind went back to another day, when I'd told her to take courage.

"I'm resigning," she said suddenly.

I was flabbergasted. "Why?" I asked at last.

Bunty turned and looked at me. "I failed you, and not just you, I failed everyone," she said. I was about to say something but she interrupted. "I'm just not cut out to be a nurse," she said. "I knew that long ago."

"Oh, Bunty," I said sadly.

"I . . . I just can't cope." She went over to the window and stared out of it.

"I'll miss you so much," I said miserably.

"Oh, Kitten," she said. "I'm so sorry I let you down." I couldn't see her face, but I knew that she was crying. I went over to her and put my hand on her shoulder. There were tears in my eyes, too. Then suddenly she stopped crying, and I saw the old Bunty in the smile she flashed at me. "What did Matron say?" she asked, almost mischievously.

"Oh, nothing much," I said, embarrassed.

"You're a good nurse," said Bunty. "Stick to it."

She stretched and turned to go, and then she turned back and we hugged each other tight.

I was dashing around later saying my farewells when I saw Lieutenant Venables. Was I better? he asked. In answer, I held out my hands. He looked at them for a long time. He'd been to see me when I was ill – not long after the air raid. I'd still been in shock and all I could remember was how pale his face had looked. Now I remembered something else. It was he who'd carried me away from the fire to safety. I couldn't even remember if I'd thanked him for it. I thanked him now. He looked rather embarrassed.

We walked outside together.

"What are you going to do when your hands are better?" he asked me.

"I don't know," I said.

And then he told me that he was leaving the hospital.

It was a shock. "Why?" I said. I was almost crying. I hoped he couldn't tell.

He said that he was going to work in one of the big London teaching hospitals. "They need all the help they can get now," he said grimly.

Suddenly I felt so frightened. German bombers attack the city nearly every night now.

"Why don't you come too?" he said suddenly. I felt something flutter in my chest. It felt odd but it was nice too.

"Why don't you?" he said again, seriously. "You could train as a nurse – a real one."

The fluttering stopped suddenly.

He didn't understand. To me, I was a real nurse already.

"Oh no," he said hastily, seeing the expression on my face. "You are a real nurse. I mean. . . You . . . you're a marvellous nurse." He swallowed. "I just wondered – why don't you make nursing your career?" His eyes looked very blue.

"I don't know," I said again. I'd seen so much suffering already. Could I bear to make nursing my career?

I told him I'd think about it and then I watched him walk away, hands thrust deep in his pockets, white coat flapping in the warm September breeze. I was smiling. He'd given me his address. It was on a bit of paper in my pocket.

In the afternoon I was driven down to the station. As we left, I looked back at the hospital. The damage to the Surgical wing was being repaired. A lot of the patients had had to be evacuated, of course, but the damage wasn't as bad as had been feared. Soon, I feel sure, the hospital will be as good as new.

I stood on the platform, waiting for the train, my luggage heaped about me. I looked down at it, at the hockey stick and tennis racket propped against my case. I remembered the day I'd arrived. I'd felt like a schoolgirl then. I didn't now.

Just before the train was due a lorry screeched to a halt in the station forecourt. I heard the sound of boots as soldiers jumped down and ran on to the platform. A Sergeant saw me and saluted smartly.

As the train pulled up he was at my side in a jiffy. "We'll help you with that," he said. I wondered if he'd noticed my hands. I watched as the soldiers fought for the right to carry my luggage on to the train.

"Get a move on, lads," the Sergeant barked. He saluted again as I thanked him. "It's nothing, miss," he said. "We'd do anything for you nurses."

He turned quickly away. I looked at him, at the khaki-clad men hoisting themselves up on to the train, and then suddenly I didn't see them any more. I saw all those others – row upon row of wounded men – as clear as if I was still in the hospital. And I knew then what I was going to do. I was staying – here, where I was needed most.

"I'll be back," I promised as I clambered on to the train.

Historical note

In 1859 a Swiss businessman, Henry Dunant, stopped at the small Italian town of Castiglione. What he saw there horrified him. Not far away the Battle of Solferino had been fought, and the wounded lay in houses, and even churches, and on every street corner. French and Italian doctors went from man to man, working tirelessly, but it was clear to Henry Dunant how little they could do – and how much more could be done if things were better organized. So he stepped in to help. He organized the townspeople so that they worked together more efficiently to bring aid to the wounded. Even children were pressed in to help – fetching and carrying water for the thirsty men. And he made sure that *all* the wounded were looked after – even the enemy. And as more doctors were desperately needed he persuaded the authorities to release the Austrian doctors who'd been captured so that they, too, could help treat the wounded.

Henry Dunant never forgot what he saw at Castiglione. After he got home he worked hard to alert governments to the plight of the wounded. He wrote a book – *A Memory of Solferino* – and sent it to national governments and all the important people of the day. It described the awful suffering he'd seen but it also came up with an idea of how to relieve the suffering.

Dunant's idea was a novel one – to set up special relief societies, made up of volunteers, who would be trained in peacetime to care for the wounded in time of war. A committee was set up to look into Dunant's idea. Dunant, of course, was one of its members. The committee would later become the International Committee of the Red Cross.

Dunant knew that it was also very important that the wounded soldiers – and the doctors and nurses caring for them – be considered "neutral" in any conflict and thus protected from harm. Other governments agreed with his ideas, and in 1864 they signed an agreement that became known as the "Convention of Geneva for the amelioration of the condition of the wounded in armies in the field". The "Geneva Convention" was initially signed by 12 nations – Britain signing a year later, in 1865.

In 1863 the first relief society based on Dunant's ideas was founded. Many more relief societies followed – in both Europe and America. The societies adopted a symbol – a red cross on a white background. They would become known as Red Cross societies.

It wasn't until another war broke out – between the French and the Prussians – that there were calls in Britain for a relief society to be established, which would be based on the code of the Geneva Convention. So in 1870 the "British National Society for Aid to the Sick and Wounded in War" was founded. Florence Nightingale – whose work Henri Dunant much admired – lent her support to the new organization. Its first job was to aid wounded combatants – on both sides – in the Franco-Prussian War.

In 1905 the "British National Society for Aid to the Sick and Wounded in War" became the British Red Cross Society (BRCS) – part of the growing international Red Cross movement. Then, in 1908, the Territorial Army (TA) was created. Its job was to provide a military force for home defence in the event of invasion. The following year, the War Office proposed a Voluntary Aid Scheme. Under this scheme, the BRCS, the Order of St John (a much older relief society) and the Territorial Force Association were asked to provide trained personnel to supplement the TA's medical service. They did this by raising "Voluntary Aid Detachments" of men and women through their county branches. After training in first aid, members of the detachments – later to become known as "VADs" – worked in hospitals and dispensaries and at public events, developing the skills they would later need in wartime. As well as training in first aid, VAD nursing members had to do a course in home nursing. VADs could also choose to train in cookery, sanitation and hygiene.

Within a year of the start of the scheme there were more than 6,000 trained VADs. With the outbreak of war in 1914, many more flocked to join the relief organizations – about 57,000 men and women in nearly 2,000 Red Cross detachments. The BRCS and Order of St John decided to join forces for the duration of the War. They formed a Joint War Committee, enabling them to provide relief more efficiently to those who most needed it.

When the War began, many VADs worked in private homes that had been turned into auxiliary hospitals and convalescent homes. Then in

1915, owing to the shortage of nurses, the War Office allowed VADs to work in military hospitals. They were supervised by trained military nurses and worked under the hospital's Matron and Commanding Officer. At first VADs served in home hospitals, but as the War progressed more VADs were sent to serve abroad.

They worked in the newly established hospitals and hospital trains, rest centres and hostels for relatives of the wounded. But not all VADs were nurses. Some worked as ambulance drivers. Many VADs had enrolled as "general service" members, working as hospital wardmaids, storekeepers, telephonists, cooks, drivers, dispensers, X-ray assistants and clerks.

After the War ended in 1918 the League of Red Cross Societies was formed. Its object was to extend the role of Red Cross societies to other areas – like improving public health, preventing disease, and providing aid to people suffering from emergencies other than war – such as earthquakes and floods. The BRCS also established branches of the society in its overseas territories. The Junior Red Cross was founded for younger members. Welfare became an increasingly important aspect of Red Cross work.

VADs continued to be trained to serve in army hospitals, but now regulations were brought into force so that in future they could be mobilized to serve in naval and air-force hospitals as well, in conflicts anywhere in the world.

With the outbreak of the Second World War in 1939, the BRCS and Order of St John again came together to make the best use of their resources. Private homes were again opened as auxiliary hospitals and convalescent homes for the less seriously wounded in the forces. Initially just for officers, after the evacuation of Dunkirk many more were opened for "other ranks", and Rest Homes were established for foreign soldiers serving alongside the British. As well as serving in these hospitals and military hospitals, VADs also staffed first-aid posts, worked in emergency shelters, ambulance trains, hostels and nurseries. And a number served in military hospitals abroad.

When the War ended in 1945, the work of the BRCS and other Red Cross societies carried on. There was still a great deal for them to do. One consequence of the War was the huge number of refugees and "displaced" people – all of whom needed help. So in 1949 the Fourth Geneva Convention was signed so that all these innocent victims of war were also entitled to receive aid from the relief societies.

But what of the VADs? After the War ended most VADs returned to their ordinary lives. But there was still a need for nursing members – even after the NHS was formed in 1948. In hospitals, Red Cross nursing auxiliaries worked alongside trained nurses, while other Red Cross volunteers took on other duties, like transporting convalescent patients home, or helping out at the National Blood Transfusion Service.

There are no VADs now, but their values live on in the work carried out today by organizations like the British Red Cross and the Order of St John. Over its long history the Red Cross has found many ways to provide voluntary relief to the sick and suffering worldwide. Its work continues to evolve. There are Red Cross branches all over Britain.

Today you will find Red Cross volunteers doing all sorts of jobs – from fundraising and providing relief for victims of conflicts, emergencies and natural disasters – both at home and overseas – to tracing displaced persons and helping out at public events. If – at one of these events – you were to go up and ask one of these volunteers about their work, you may perhaps find that she was once a VAD. Maybe she will have a story or two to tell you about her work as a VAD when – as a young girl – she nursed the sick in the Second World War.

Timeline

1859   Swiss businessman Henry Dunant witnesses the suffering of wounded soldiers at the Battle of Solferino in Italy.

1862   Dunant publishes *A Memory of Solferino*.

1863   The Geneva committee set up to investigate the relief of the sick and wounded in war leads to the founding of the first Red Cross society.

1864   The first Geneva Convention is signed by 12 nations.

1865   Britain signs the Geneva Convention.

1870   The British National Society for Aid to the Sick and Wounded in War is founded.

1875   The Geneva Committee becomes the International Committee (of the Red Cross).

1882   The USA signs the Geneva Convention.

1905   The British National Society for Aid to the Sick and Wounded in War becomes the British Red Cross Society (BRCS) and receives its founding Charter in 1908. Its first president is Queen Alexandra.

1909   The War Office in Britain draws up a Voluntary Aid Scheme. As a result of this, "Voluntary Aid Detachments" are created by the BRCS and Order of St John. Detachment members – later to become known simply as "VADs" – train in peacetime in first aid and other skills so that they can help supplement the work of the medical services of the TA in war.

1910   The Voluntary Aid Scheme is introduced in Scotland. (Branches of the Red Cross are also gradually established in all parts of the United Kingdom and Northern Ireland.)

1912   A party of 12 VADs – the first to serve abroad – is sent to aid the wounded in the Balkan War.

1914   The First World War begins. The BRCS and the Christian-based Order of St John form a Joint War Committee.

1918   The First World War ends.

1919   The League of Red Cross Societies (now called the International Federation of Red Cross and Red Crescent Societies) is formed. One of its new aims is to relieve suffering from causes other than war. The BRCS establishes branches in British territories abroad.

1921   The BRCS creates the first United Kingdom blood-transfusion service.

1924   British Junior Red Cross is formed.

1929   The Third Geneva Convention provides rules for fair treatment of prisoners of war.

1939   The Second World War begins. In Britain a "Civil Nursing Reserve" is organized by the government to staff Emergency Medical Service (EMS) hospitals that would treat the large numbers of civilian casualties that were expected in the event of war. Owing to the shortage of available professional nurses, VADs are released to serve in the Reserve.

1945 The Second World War ends.

1949 The Fourth Geneva Convention allows for the relief of civilians in war, especially those in enemy territories or those living under an occupying power.

Acknowledgments

A number of people and organizations have helped me with my research for this book. In particular I'd like to thank: the staff and volunteers of the British Red Cross Society and the Museum and Archive, Tate Greenhalgh (Thackray Museum), the Imperial War Museum Sound and Document archives, Kate Mason (Royal College of Nursing Archives), Tom Snowball, Captain Starling (AMS Museum).

My thanks also go to Jill Sawyer and Lisa Edwards at Scholastic for all their help and fine editing.

And to Jerry Crewe, Sheila Reid, Angela Sinclair and especially Madge Dobinson (Dobbie) – serving VADS in WWII – my most grateful thanks for sharing their knowledge and so many memories with me.

SOPHIE'S SECRET WAR

Jill Atkins

Normandy, France 1939

Sunday 25th June

Mama gave me this book last Christmas, and today is exactly six months since then so I think it's about time I wrote in it! First of all, I was going to use it to practise my English. I suspect that's why Mama bought it for me. I've been learning English for a couple of years and I love it. But then I changed my mind. I've decided to write a diary. I'll keep it secret. I don't want anybody reading my private thoughts – not even Yvette Bertrand. I really like Yvette. She's been my best friend all my life. We do everything together and share everything, but I'm not sharing this diary. I won't even tell her I'm writing it.

How shall I begin? My name is Sophie Ridel. I was thirteen on 25th February. I've got long, dark hair and I'm quite small for my age. Not like my brother, Sebastien. He's fifteen and he's tall and blond. We're always arguing, and Mama's always moaning that she's sick of hearing us. It's Sebastien's fault. He insists on annoying me.

We live in a little village in the middle of the countryside. Papa works at Mr Masson's farm, which is close by, just across the railway tracks. Our house is quite small. We've got a kitchen and a living room downstairs and three bedrooms upstairs. You have to climb a ladder from the kitchen to get upstairs. My room is really tiny, but I like it.

I'm lying on my bed now, writing this. It's so peaceful living here. I don't want it ever to change.

Monday 26th June

I hate Sebastien! He always has to be one up on me. Today, he challenged me to a race home from school. He didn't have his bicycle with him so I thought it would be easy, but as I pedalled round the last corner, there he stood, right in the middle of the road. I braked and skidded and landed in a patch of nettles. I yelled at him then I spat on the palm of my hand and patted my legs. The white lumps of the stinging nettles were already beginning to show. Olivier Masson was there, too. The pair of them stood towering above me, laughing. I was so mad, especially when I noticed a scratch in the red paint on my bicycle. Then I found out how Sebastien had managed to get home so quickly. He had a lift across the fields on Mr Masson's tractor. The cheat!

Tuesday 27th June

I feel a lot better today. When I had relaxed a bit yesterday, I went down the garden to the hen house. I let myself in and the hens clucked and fussed around me like they always do. I sat down on the end of the feeding trough, listening to their chattering and watching them scratching and pecking in the dirt.

I told them about Sebastien, about Mama moaning and about Papa always being busy out in the fields. As usual, the hens made sympathetic noises. They always understand. That's what I love about them. Some people say they're stupid creatures, but I know better.

After a while, I looked towards the house. Mama was swinging the level-crossing barriers across the road. That's her job. She has to open and close the gates every time a train goes through. Mr Masson had driven up on his tractor and was waiting on the other side of the tracks.

I heard the whining of the rails then the rumble of the engine as the train came round the bend. I closed my eyes. Soon I felt the earth trembling, and I was surrounded by a cloud of grey smoke. I love that smell of coal smoke and oil. Then the train whistle squealed. It made me jump, even though I hear it every day. I opened my eyes and watched the trucks rattle by on their way to the sugar-beet factory on the other side of the village.

A few of the hens chattered nervously and one hid under the nesting boxes, but most of them ignored the train. They are used to it. Mama opened the gates and the tractor chugged across. I stood up and opened the nesting boxes. There were ten brown eggs. I carefully lifted them out and put them in my basket, thanked the hens and let myself out of the run, making sure I fastened the door. I don't want a fox to get in among my beautiful hens!

Wednesday 28th June

The news is always bad lately. It's all the fault of a man called Adolf Hitler. I don't know much about him except that he lives in Germany and everyone says he's doing some dreadful things. I don't like the sound of Adolf Hitler.

Thursday 29th June

When I got home from school today, I climbed up to my bedroom and did my English homework. After a while, Mama called up and asked me to take Grandma some eggs. I love going to Grandma's. Mama said she's a bit worried about her and told me to check up on her. I put three eggs in my cycle basket and pedalled off. Sebastien yelled at me and tried to make me fall off my bicycle, but I ignored him. I haven't forgiven him yet.

In five minutes, I had passed the church and was leaning my bicycle against Grandma's hedge. I ran inside and kissed her on both cheeks then put the eggs on the table and drank the home-made apple juice she gave me. I told her that Mama was worried about her. She laughed and said Mama fusses too much. She's probably right! Then she asked me what I've been doing lately. When I told her about my English she went on and on about it. She can't understand why I want to learn it. That's old people for you. She's always telling me she was ready to leave school when she was thirteen like me and how she was working up at the chateau by the time she was fourteen.

She asked me if I've got a boyfriend. Well, I really like Georges Dubois. He's so handsome and all the girls are in love with him, including me, but I wasn't going to tell her that. I felt myself go red and she noticed. She held up her hands and teased me about being in love!

Friday 30th June

Last day of school! We've got two months off. Yvette and I are going to do lots of things together and I'm going to keep away from Sebastien as much as possible. Maybe I'll get to see Georges Dubois a few times!

Saturday 1st July

All the adults seem to be talking about Adolf Hitler. I wonder why he's so important. He doesn't come from around here so why do they keep talking about him?

Monday 3rd July

Today, Yvette and I cycled to Veules les Roses. It's a village right on the coast with a steep white cliff at each end of the bay. It's only a few kilometres away so we go there a lot. We swam in the sea, messed about on the beach, laughed a lot, sunbathed and helped the fishermen when they arrived on the incoming tide. Then we climbed up the cliff path and lay on our fronts on the edge of the cliff. We looked down at the rocks and pebbles below and watched the waves as they came in and out, listening to the crash and the hiss as the water sifted through the stones. I feel peaceful when I hear the sounds of the sea. I've always loved it.

Later on we went to see Aunty Régine. She's Mama's sister. She lives with Uncle Thierry and their little boy, Charles. Uncle Thierry wasn't there. He was at work. I wish I could live in their house, right there near the cliffs. It must be so much fun to be able to see and hear the sea all the time. Yvette and I played with Charles. I love having a little two-year-old cousin. I think he adores me. He cried when we left.

Tuesday 4th July

They're at it again. War, war, war is all I hear. People seem obsessed by it. This morning it was Mr Masson and Mama. Mr Masson has been listening to the news broadcast on the wireless. He doesn't like the sound of what he's heard. Adolf Hitler is planning all sorts of things – he's building up his troops – he's threatening other countries. Why does he need to do that?

Mama wanted to know if Mr Hitler will invade France and Mr Masson said he hopes not. (So do I.) Mr Masson said he's thankful the boys aren't old enough to go to war, but he reckons that the government will be calling our people up to fight soon.

I ran to the hen house. I sat among my friends and told them how scared I am. Who is Adolf Hitler and what is he doing? I just hope he doesn't decide to come here.

Monday 10th July

Yvette and I went to Veules les Roses several times last week. On Saturday, Uncle Thierry was at home. We all went to the beach and had a picnic. We met some of Aunty Régine's friends. They started on about Hitler and what he was up to. All the adults seem to think that he's a real threat. Uncle Thierry said he will go into the navy if they call him up to fight because he's an engineer. I hope they don't, and I bet Aunty Régine wouldn't want him to either.

Mama has started listening to the wireless (such a huge ugly wooden thing there on the dresser). She sits with her ear close to it and keeps telling us news about what Adolf Hitler is doing. I'm sick of hearing his name!

Tuesday 1st August

I've been really busy. I've had a great month away from school, cycling around and seeing friends. I've seen Georges a few times, too, but I get tongue-tied when I see him. He's so good-looking he takes my breath away. I feel all silly and weak when we meet. I'm sure he thinks I'm pathetic.

Sebastien and I have been arguing a lot and Mama keeps warning us, so I've been trying to keep away from him, but it's not easy in such a small house. Yvette's mama is nice and she lets me go there often. I've been chatting to my hens, of course, and I visit Grandma nearly every day. Sebastien spends a lot of time over at the farm. Olivier Masson is his best friend. Olivier is fifteen, too, and he has two little sisters and a baby brother.

Sunday 6th August

Today, we went to St Valery en Caux for a family outing. It's a bit further along the coast and it's a bigger town than Veules les Roses. It's got a port full of fishing boats and a few private yachts. We watched the boats going in and out of the port. Papa promised that one day soon we can go out on one of those yachts, but then Mama went and spoiled it by saying, "Not if Adolf Hitler has anything to do with it." For once, Sebastien and I were thinking the same. We both told Mama not to be such an old misery!

Friday 11th August

Papa says the wheat is almost ripe. It will soon be harvest time. We'll all help. I'm looking forward to that.

Wednesday 16th August

The harvest started today. Everyone went, except Mama who had to stay and open and close the level-crossing gates. I couldn't believe it when she said she didn't mind. I suppose she thinks she can stay near the wireless and listen for news of Hitler!

I've had such a great day and now I'm so tired I can hardly keep my eyes open to write this. It was so hot and dusty, especially when Mr Masson and Papa and the other farm workers cut the wheat and threshed it. We all helped after that. Yvette and I got into a tangle trying to tie the stalks into bundles. We laughed so much we kept falling over each other. At lunchtime, we sat on the bundles of straw and ate bread and Camembert and salad and drank Grandma's apple juice.

Georges was there. He sat near me and smiled at me several times. It made me feel like I was floating on air. Is this what Grandma called being "in love"?

Wednesday 30th August

I can't believe the holidays are over so soon. The summer has flashed by. I've enjoyed it so much I want it to go on for ever, but lately things have been different in the village. Everyone looks worried, not full of the friendly smiles I'm used to. It's Adolf Hitler's fault.

I ran in from Yvette's this afternoon. Mama was listening to the wireless as usual. She put her finger to her lips, leaning closer to it. I knew it would be about Hitler. At last, she turned off the wireless and sighed. She told me he's built up a massive army in Germany. I think I knew that too, but it must be getting worse. Apparently, Hitler has ordered the German army to invade some other countries already. What a revolting man! He makes me sick. I feel a horrible tightness in my chest when I think about what he's doing. I wonder why Mr Daladier, our Prime Minister, doesn't do something to stop such a madman!

Sunday 3rd September

It's happened – what we all dreaded. I don't know quite what to think – it doesn't seem possible. It's now evening and the news still hasn't sunk in. It's been one of those days I'll never forget.

I spent the afternoon at Yvette's house, but as I cycled towards our house on my way home, I noticed Papa standing by the crossing gates. He was talking to a group of men, including Mr Masson. I wondered what was going on. I called to them as I arrived at our gateway. Several of them turned towards me, but none of them smiled, not even Papa. I thought somebody must have died. Papa hurried towards me. I could see tears in his eyes.

Then he told me. Adolf Hitler has invaded Poland. I asked what difference that makes and Mr Masson told me about an agreement that France and Great Britain have with Poland. If anyone attacks Poland, we have to stand up for them. So this morning, Mr Chamberlain, the British Prime Minister, declared war on Germany. And this afternoon, Mr Daladier did, too.

We're at war! The news made me feel so cold even though it was a warm day. I folded my arms across my chest and hunched my shoulders against it. I shuddered. I'm still shivering now as I write about it. War!

Up to now it has been all talk, but this is real. It's horrible. I'm scared about what's going to happen to us. Will people get killed, like in the last war? I don't really know much about the last war except that two of my uncles were killed. Their names are engraved on the memorial in the cemetery at the top of the hill.

I put my bicycle away and hurried to the hen house. I crouched down amongst the hens and told them about the terrible news. It didn't worry them. They're acting normally, as if nothing has changed.

Monday 4th September

Sebastien ran over from the farm this afternoon when I was in the hen house. His face was flushed and his eyes were wild. He gripped the wire of the hen run and peered through at me. Then he said that he and Olivier had been talking about the war. He sounded excited, not scared like me. What he said next really shocked me. They're going to volunteer to go and fight.

I pretended to laugh. I told him not to be so silly. He's not old enough, but he reckons he could lie. He is tall for his age and his voice has broken. He thinks they will take him in the army. I burst into tears. I couldn't help it. Sebastien is my brother, after all. He might be the most aggravating and frustrating brother on this earth, but he's the only one I've got!

I whispered that I couldn't bear it if he got himself killed like Papa's brothers that we never knew. I don't think Sebastien has ever wondered how Papa felt when his big brothers went away to fight and never came back. He stared at me. Then he made a joke about it, but I could see he was shaken. I stood up and gripped his fingers fiercely. I felt my brain spinning. I wanted to scream and shout, "Adolf Hitler's got to be stopped!"

Then we made a pact. I can't believe that this was me and Sebastien talking like this. We agreed that if anything happens here, we'll do everything we can together. We won't tell our parents because they'd say we're too young and they'd watch us like hawks. It will be our secret.

From now on, I'll have to keep this diary hidden. If Mama finds it, there'll be trouble. I think it will be a good idea to offer to clean my own room from now on. Then she won't ever be in here to find it. She'll be pleased with that. She's always complaining about how difficult it is to even get in here, let alone move around.

Monday 9th October

No news, except more about the German army, of course. It seems to be always on the move, threatening every country it can think of. Life goes on here as before (thank goodness). I go to school, learn English

– which I still enjoy – see Yvette and Grandma and my hens. Sebastien and I are getting on fine. Mama can't believe it. I think she almost preferred it when we were rowing all the time. At least it gave her an excuse to moan at us.

I met Georges face to face outside school today and actually managed to say something. I can't remember what! I was so embarrassed that it took me half an hour to recover. I wish I wasn't so stupid. It's not as if I had never seen a boy before. We always have Sebastien's friends round. Apart from Olivier, there's Marcel Cariat and a couple of others. It's just that I'm not in love with any of them – only Georges.

Sunday 12th November

It's really strange. More than two months have passed since that day Britain and France declared war on Germany and sometimes I almost forget we're at war. Of course, I know about the fighting far away. How could I ever forget that? Mama always listens to the wireless.

Then, last night, we had a party in the village for the young men who are going into the army. Quite a few have signed up. I had a great time, dancing with Yvette. We were useless, tripping over each other's feet and giggling so much we almost fell over, like at the harvest. I know Georges was watching me. I sensed his eyes on me though

I dared not look in his direction. I felt rather giddy and I couldn't help giggling even more.

But this morning we went to the Mayor's office to wave the young soldiers off. I didn't feel like laughing then. I had to bite my lip very hard to stop myself from bursting into tears. I kept thinking of Papa. As soon as he came in from work, I rushed over and gave him an enormous hug. He squeezed me tight and asked what he had done to deserve it. I felt embarrassed then, but I managed to whisper that I was glad he didn't have to go to war. He chuckled and kissed the top of my head. He said he's too old and that they only want to kill off the young ones. I heard a kind of bitterness in his voice. I snuggled against him. He has never said much about losing his brothers, but he must hurt deep down. I asked him if he thinks the fighting will reach here. He doesn't know. He thinks maybe Adolf Hitler will stop at nothing. I suppose he was being honest, but I don't like it – not one little bit.

Sunday 19th November

I'm miserable today. Uncle Thierry is going to join the navy. He doesn't want a farewell party, but I cycled over to Veules les Roses to see him. He said he'll be working in an engine room on a warship.

187

I gulped. I hate the sound of that. It must be dark and noisy and smelly. And dangerous!

I looked at Aunty Régine. I could tell she'd been crying. Her eyes were red and her nose was swollen. She looked so miserable that it brought a lump to my throat. I kissed and hugged Uncle Thierry then I hurried outside to my bicycle and cried all the way home.

Monday 25th December 1939

Christmas Day has been very quiet! No one's in the mood for it. We all miss Uncle Thierry, especially Aunty Régine. He had been hoping to get home, but his fleet is always on stand-by, he said in his letter (he's not allowed to say where). There has been more fighting in other countries, but luckily there's no sign of it here. I hope it never reaches our region, I really do. I wonder if the soldiers have called a ceasefire today, like they did in the trenches of the last war.

Monday 1st January 1940

Happy New Year! I hope it will be a happy year, but I hate to think it probably won't be.

Thursday 11th January

The weather has turned bitterly cold. Everything is covered in a thick white blanket of snow. I haven't been to school this week. The water pipes have burst.

I woke up this morning and poked my nose out from under the covers. It was absolutely freezing – the worst day so far! I yanked the covers higher and peeped out over the top of them. Even though the shutters had been closed overnight I could make out leafy patterns of ice on my window.

Mama called up the ladder – time to get up and do my chores. I heard the back door slam then the clunk of the gates. I snuggled lower. Soon, the

189

house shook as the train trundled by. I could tell it was a passenger train. Carriages don't clank as much as trucks! I heard Mama open the gates and come back indoors. She called again. I sighed and climbed out of bed, slipping quickly into my freezing clothes and shinning down the ladder. It was slightly warmer downstairs. I made myself some chocolate and sat by the stove, sipping the hot drink until I felt warmer. A few minutes later, I was dressed in my thick coat, hat, gloves, scarf and boots. As I opened the door to go out, I almost bumped into Olivier. His papa needed help with the animals. Mama said I could go when I had done my chores.

I took the eggs in then fetched a basket of logs for the stove. After that, Sebastien and I ran across the tracks. We found Papa and Olivier with Mr Masson in the barn. We were just in time to help deliver a lamb. It was so sweet. It gave me such a warm feeling inside.

Friday 26th January

Aunty Régine has had a letter from Uncle Thierry. It took three weeks to reach her and she has no idea where he is. She thinks he might be somewhere out in the Atlantic Ocean. That's such a long way away and so dangerous. She's very worried. I keep thinking of him stuck down in a warship's engine room. Poor Uncle Thierry – I hope there are no enemy submarines in that part of the ocean.

Monday 19th February

Something really thrilling happened today – to do with Sebastien and me. This morning, we listened to the wireless with Mama. It was all about the German army forcing its way across Europe. It made my whole body feel tensed up. I needed to get out. I hurried outside, grabbed my bicycle and pedalled off along the lane. The snow has gone at last, but it's still pretty cold. I rode fast, pushing my legs hard. I didn't notice where I was going, but slowly I felt more relaxed.

When I got back, Sebastien was out. He came in later, looking really excited. He told me he's joined a secret group with Marcel Cariat, who feels like we do about the German threat. Marcel's older brother, Patrice, formed the group and he's recruiting people they know feel the same. We've been hoping something like this would happen!

But Sebastien suddenly looked embarrassed. The Cariat brothers say I'm not old enough to join. I almost hit the ceiling. I am nearly fourteen! Sebastien agrees I should be in. There's going to be a meeting tomorrow night, and he's promised to take me with him, whatever they say. I'm so elated! I'm sworn to secrecy, of course!

Tuesday 20th February

I'm a girl of importance! I wish I could tell Yvette. Normally, I would have dashed straight round to her house, but I know that if I breathe a single word to her, it will prove to the Cariat brothers that I am too young after all.

I couldn't eat my dinner this evening. I guess it was nerves. I was relieved when at last Sebastien and I set off for the Cariats' house. Patrice frowned when he opened the door. He asked what I was doing there. He was rude about little sisters who blabbed. I was really proud of Sebastien. He stood up to Patrice. Marcel made a joke about me only blabbing to my chickens. I suppose he must have seen me in the hen house. In the end, Patrice shrugged and agreed I could join as long as I swore to secrecy. Of course, I did. So Patrice told us about the group – it's made up of people from Veules les Roses and our village and other villages around the area.

Then suddenly he turned to me. He actually smiled and said I might be useful, after all. Nobody in our village has a telephone so the group will need a messenger – and it's me! It's because of my bicycle. Patrice says everyone is used to seeing me cycling around so no one will suspect me. I can't wait to start. Mind you, it's scary too. It might be very dangerous.

Sunday 25th February

It's my birthday today! I had a new pen from Mama and Papa, which I am writing with now. It's good – no scratches or blots! Grandma gave me some lovely soft red gloves and a red scarf to match – very useful as it's still cold. Yvette came to dinner and we played some games. For once, we all forgot our thoughts of war.

Tuesday 19th March

There hasn't been a lot to write. It's exactly a month since I got excited about being a messenger and what have I done so far? Nothing! All I've done is go to school, as usual, learn English, as usual, feed my hens, as usual, visit Grandma, as usual, muck around with Yvette, as usual. It's so frustrating that I haven't had to do a single thing. No messages, nothing. (One good thing is that I've spoken to gorgeous Georges a few times – three, to be exact. I think he might like me.)

It's so hard not being allowed to tell Yvette about our group, but what is there to tell anyway? The war is still going on, but how can I be expected to stay interested if I'm not doing anything? Mama still tells us the news, but it all seems so far away. At least spring is coming and it's a lot warmer.

Friday 22nd March

Two days ago Mr Daladier resigned. I suppose he couldn't stand the strain of what's happening in Europe. Our new Prime Minister is Mr Reynaud. I hope he is strong enough to keep out the enemy.

Sunday 21st April

Another month has gone by. Hitler's armies are still marching all over the place and killing loads of people. Why can't someone stop him? I suppose he's too powerful. How can people get so much power?

The British are fighting against Hitler. Thousands of their soldiers are somewhere in Europe, but I'm not sure where. I don't talk about the war with any of my friends, only at home with Sebastien.

Friday 10th May

We've had a shock this evening. We were listening to the news broadcast on the wireless. The Germans have invaded Holland and Belgium. Belgium is next to France. That's such a frightening thought I couldn't help gripping Mama's arm. The French and British armies are fighting against them, but Hitler's army is so enormous, it seems as if it will never be defeated. Papa made it worse. He said, "If they've managed to invade our neighbours, what will stop him trying us?" It made my stomach turn over. The threat is growing nearer.

Saturday 11th May

Britain has a new Prime Minister, too. He's called Winston Churchill. Papa is pleased. He says he's a much stronger leader than Mr Chamberlain. Perhaps Mr Churchill will be able to stop Hitler doing any more damage.

Wednesday 15th May

I feel so sorry for the Dutch and Belgian people. I can't imagine how terrible it must be for them. They've had heavy bombing of their cities and there has been such fierce fighting. Today, we heard that Holland has surrendered to the Germans. I suppose they didn't have much choice.

I still haven't heard anything from Patrice. I'm feeling so frustrated. I want to be the one to stop Adolf Hitler! Sebastien says he hasn't heard anything either, but I'm suspicious. I think he's having secret meetings with Marcel and Patrice, but he won't admit it.

Today I cycled over to Yvette's house after school, but it's getting more and more difficult not being able to share my secret. I wish Yvette could be in our group, but I daren't mention it. I must keep quiet. Anyway, she never talks about the war or fighting or anything like that. That's where we seem to be different. She doesn't seem as worried as I am. She's more interested in homely things like cooking. She even enjoys helping her mama do the housework. I can't understand that. Yvette has been my friend since we were babies and we still sometimes cycle to Veules les Roses at the weekends and do all the usual things, but it almost seems like I've got more in common with my brother!

I'm finding it difficult to concentrate on my homework. The only subject I still like is English. I practise useful phrases on the hens. Then I try them on the family. Papa doesn't take me seriously and laughs at me. He sounds like Grandma. At least my teacher says I'm good! I want to become as good at English as her.

Thursday 23rd May

The news is dreadful! The German army has fought through the lines of French and British troops. The enemy has fought its way over the border from Belgium and is now in northeast France. Just think. They're in my country. I hoped they would never get here, but it's happened. Perhaps they will be defeated soon and the German army won't come this way. At the moment, they are battling their way towards the Channel near a place called Dunkerque. The British and French soldiers are being forced back towards the coast. They are heading into a dead end.

I asked Papa how far that is from here. It's only two or three hundred kilometres! Sebastien says the Germans might try to invade England. Perhaps if they do that, they won't bother to come along here.

Monday 27th May

This evening we heard some awful news on the wireless. Thousands of British and French soldiers are trapped on the beaches at Dunkerque. The German army is closing in on them. What will happen to them, poor things?

Tuesday 28th May

Belgium surrendered today, like the Dutch. I don't blame them. I suppose they couldn't stand being bullied by the German army any longer. I wonder what it's like to have the enemy taking over everything. I hope our government doesn't give in to the enemy! It's almost nine months since they declared war on Germany. Thank goodness there still hasn't been any fighting in our region.

Wednesday 29th May

I've waited and waited for messages from Patrice. Perhaps he only said I could be a messenger to keep me happy. Perhaps he never intended to use me. I'll try to find other ways to help without him.

The fighting is slowly creeping nearer. The German army has reached Abbeville. That's not far away at all!

Thursday 30th May

I'm finding it almost impossible to swallow my food. I'm so worried about what might happen to us. The news is that the German army is marching closer and closer. I wish this would all go away. I wish I could wake up and find it is all a nasty dream.

I just wish we could stop this war. I hate it! Why do people have to fight? Why do maniacs like Adolf Hitler have to try to take over the world?

Friday 31st May

At last – some action! This evening, Marcel Cariat knocked on the door. He pretended he wanted to borrow a book from Sebastien, but I sensed it was something else. Mama was in the room so he didn't say anything, but he kept glancing at me. My stomach began doing somersaults. I went out to the hen house and prowled around the pen, telling my hens about Marcel. They listened with their heads on one side.

I had only been there for a few minutes when Marcel and Sebastien strolled out into the garden. Marcel laughed when he saw where I was. I hurried out of the hen house. I felt so edgy, I thought I would burst. But I was right. Early tomorrow morning, I have to take a message from Patrice to Veules les Roses!

Marcel has given me instructions. I've got to go to the Rue Victor Hugo. I know it. It's quite near Aunty Régine's house. I have to find number 12 – it's a little cottage quite close to the sea and has a black front door. I have to knock once and wait. A person called Hélène will come to the door. The message is for her alone.

Now for the even more exciting bit – I've got a coded message to say first! I have to say, "How are the flowers in your garden?" and she will reply, "The red ones are the most beautiful." Then I have to give her the message.

Marcel handed me a small envelope and I tucked it in the pocket of my skirt. It's under my pillow now, waiting till tomorrow. Marcel asked me if I was up to the job, but when he saw the expression on my face, he didn't want an answer!

I've got this kind of thrill running through me. It won't go away. How will I ever sleep tonight? This is what I've been waiting for ever since we knew we were at war. It's the real thing!

Saturday 1st June
Morning

I hardly slept. I've got up and dressed very early. I'm so nervous. If I creep down the ladder, perhaps they won't notice me going out. Then I can get to Veules les Roses and back before they wonder where I am.

Midday

I've done it! I crept down the ladder and hurried to fetch my bicycle. I was wheeling it round the side of the house when Mama came out of the door. She made me jump and I was sure she could tell there was a letter in my pocket. She wanted to know where I was going. I almost panicked. An idea popped into my head. I said I thought I'd go and see Aunty Régine because she must miss Uncle Thierry. I asked if I could take her a few eggs. Mama thought that was a good idea. But that was an awkward moment.

Mama wrapped four eggs in paper and I placed them in my cycle basket. Then I rode away up the slope. I met nobody as I sped along the lanes towards Veules les Roses. I delved into my pocket loads of times to check that the letter was still there. My hand was shaking. As I approached Veules les Roses, I realized my legs were shaking too. Supposing Hélène wasn't there?

I pedalled along the main street, the Rue Victor Hugo. I rode slowly, looking for number 12, the house that Marcel had described. I was almost at the sea when, at last, I found the little run-down cottage with the black front door. Trembling all over, I leant my bicycle against the wall and walked up to the door. Before I could knock, the door opened a few centimetres. Quickly, I stepped back. Then I heard a very quiet shaky voice and the face of an old woman appeared in the narrow opening.

She asked if I had come to see her. I was suspicious. I didn't think this could be Hélène. I was expecting a younger woman. I could hardly stand there for shaking. My mouth felt incredibly dry, but I licked my lips and whispered, "How are the flowers in your garden?"

She didn't hear me at first and I had to repeat it. I held my breath, waiting to see if she was the right person. She gave me the answer I needed, and I felt the air rushing out of my lungs like the steam from a train. I felt a bit dizzy. My brain was spinning, but I was delighted. The coded message had worked!

A shrivelled, rather knobbly hand reached out towards me. I was really amazed that this old woman was Hélène. She asked me if I had a message from Patrice. I put my hand in my pocket, but she told me to wait. She opened the door a little wider. I wasn't sure if I should step into the old lady's house. You never know who to trust, but then I remembered that she had said the password so she must be all right, and I took a step forward. She grabbed my arm. Her fingers reminded me of birds' claws. She pulled me into the dark cottage. When I took out the letter, she snatched it immediately.

She opened the envelope and peered at the letter. She smiled at me and told me it was a dummy run just to see if I could do the job. She said I'd done well, and she wrote me a quick note to take back to Patrice. Then she told me she thought they might need me again soon.

I was still shaking a few minutes later as I climbed the hill to my aunt's house, high above the village, with a new letter in my pocket. But I forgot everything else when I saw Aunty Régine's face. She'd been crying. I put the eggs on the kitchen table, then kissed Aunty Régine and picked up Charles and gave him a big hug. She stood at the window, staring out to sea. She misses Uncle Thierry so much. She showed me another letter she has had from him.

I stood beside her. The sea looked so calm and harmless and peaceful. It's difficult to believe that there are many warships out there, trying to defend France. I thought about Uncle Thierry. He's such great fun and I've missed seeing him since he went into the navy. I swallowed hard and said I hoped the war would be over very soon, and I expect the ships are solid. I don't know if that helped. Aunty Régine says she tries to be strong for little Charles's sake.

I couldn't relax. My hand kept straying to the letter inside my pocket. At last, I left her house and cycled away from the sea. I hurried straight home, as I was instructed. Now I'm waiting for Marcel to come.

Afternoon

I saw Marcel coming down the lane just after I had finished writing in my diary. He was holding Sebastien's book. I went out to meet him. I nodded and grinned, but said nothing. He nodded back and held the book out to me. I took it and quickly slipped the letter into his hand. I went indoors, feeling pleased with myself. My first official mission has been a success.

Sunday 2nd June

What a day! I'm feeling really good about everything. Well, except one thing, but more about that later.

I was cycling home today when I met an old man from the village. He started chatting about my red bicycle. He always sees me speeding around, he said. I'm famous! I was pleased. That was exactly what Patrice Cariat said all those months ago. Then the old man said he had seen refugees on the main road towards Veules les Roses. They've had to flee because the Germans have taken over their towns.

It was so hot and the sky was quite dark, but I headed towards Veules les Roses. I wanted to see for myself. As I came to the brow of the hill and looked down on the road I saw a long column of women and children and old people. There seemed to be hundreds of them. Some were dragging handcarts piled high with their belongings, but most of them had nothing but what they were carrying. Some were limping and I could hear children crying. They all looked so miserable that I wanted to cry, too.

I bit my lip and pedalled down amongst them. I spoke to a girl who looked about the same age as me. I told her my name as I dropped my bicycle at the roadside. The girl burst into tears. I put my arm round her then she managed to tell me what had happened. She's called Anais Leclerc and she lives north of Abbeville. Two days ago, the Germans came with tanks and now their house is in ruins. They ran away, but they have no idea where they are going. I can't imagine how terrible that must be.

Anais told me they've slept rough for the past two nights. They've had no food and they've been drinking any water they could find. I met her mama, who was carrying a little boy. She looked exhausted and her eyes were so sad.

There was a flash of lightning. It must have been the lightning that sprang me into action. Never mind Patrice. I decided to do this on my own. I leapt on my bicycle, telling them to wait here. I would see what I could do. I'd had an idea.

I raced along the lanes, back to the village. Mama was at the level-crossing gate. A train had just gone through. I shouted, and Mama looked up. I stood astride my bicycle as there was another flash. I was out of breath, but I had to tell Mama everything as fast as I could. Mama frowned. She said, "You can't make a feast appear like magic!"

Sebastien and Olivier came out of the house. I repeated my story even faster. I finished by suggesting that the people could sleep in Mr Masson's barn while we went round the village collecting food. Sebastien smiled at me and I smiled back. That felt good.

The boys set off at once to ask Olivier's papa. I hoped that the two of them would manage to persuade Mr Masson. Mama wanted to know how many people there were. Then she said, "We can't let fellow human beings suffer." I hugged her quickly then followed the boys to the farm. The sky was jet black. Flashes of lightning streaked across the dark clouds and thunder rumbled noisily. Sebastien and Olivier had found Mr Masson in the barn. Mrs Masson was there, too, with Olivier's little brother and two little sisters.

Mrs Masson is marvellous! She persuaded Mr Masson to say "yes", but he's only allowing them to stay for one night. I thanked him as I whizzed off again on my bicycle. By the time I reached the main road, big spots of rain had begun to fall. I found that a lot of the people had moved on, but Anais and about forty others were sheltering under the trees that lined the road.

I waved and shouted the good news against the noise of the wind that was whirling through the trees. We stayed under the trees while the worst of the storm passed. We were all very bedraggled as we set off along the lane to the village.

They are safely in Mr Masson's barn now.

Later

I'm so tired I don't know how I climbed the ladder tonight. It's late and I've had the busiest evening of my life! But I'll have to stay awake. There's so much more to write. When I had left the refugees in the barn, I hurried to Yvette's house. I knew that she would want to help collect food for the refugees. As soon as she heard about them she rushed out to fetch her bicycle. Then Olivier and Sebastien covered one half of the village while Yvette and I did the other. At each house, I explained what we wanted and smiled in my most pleasing way so that most people gave me something.

My heart was fluttering as I rode up to Georges Dubois's house. I felt myself blush when Georges opened the door. I muttered and shuffled my feet. I couldn't look him in the eye. My mouth felt dry and I had difficulty thinking what to say. In the end I mumbled something about refugees and about them being hungry. I don't know what I was expecting from him, but not the sharp voice telling me that the people were only gypsies, out to see what they could get.

I was stunned. I glanced up. An ugly sneer transformed his handsome face as he told me how much he admired the Germans because they are such a strong nation. He even said we should be strong like them.

He didn't believe all the "lies" about their cruelty. He had the nerve to tell me I didn't understand and that I'm just a weak sentimental female!

I was disgusted. How could he think like that? How could I ever have imagined I was in love with him? I turned away and cycled madly along to the next house, seething. I had to call on quite a few friendly villagers before I could get rid of my anger and put thoughts of Georges right out of my head. Soon my cycle basket was full of cheese and bread, fruit and salad. It was growing dark, and I was beginning to feel tired, but I kept going. I made several deliveries to the barn.

News had got round. When I arrived at Grandma's house, I could smell soup cooking. I looked at the huge pan on the stove and hugged Grandma. She's a marvel! She told me what a good girl I am to help the refugees. She agreed how terrible it must be to lose your home like that! The pot of soup was so big she said I was to send Papa to fetch it. After another hug, I was on my way again, collecting food and delivering it to the barn. Some villagers gave me clothes, too.

On my final visit to the barn, I shared some of Grandma's delicious soup with Anais and her mama. Mrs Leclerc had tears in her eyes as she told me that her husband is in the army. They don't know where he is, or even if he's still alive. I didn't know what to say so I finished my soup in silence. I couldn't help a guilty feeling creeping into my mind. Why have they lost so much, while I still have everything?

Monday 3rd June

They've gone! The train whistle woke me up this morning. The sun was shining brightly through the slats in the shutters. My first thought was about Georges. I hadn't got over the shock of his words. I hate him now instead of thinking I loved him! Then I remembered the refugees. I dressed quickly, snatched a hunk of bread from the kitchen and ran across the railway line towards the farm. But when I arrived at the barn it was empty. I sat down on a bale of straw and cried. They hadn't even said goodbye. After a few moments, I hurried to the farmhouse.

Mrs Masson was in the kitchen. She told me that they had gone at first light. She said some nice things about how kind I had been, but that didn't help much. I felt so disappointed. But then she handed me a sheet of paper. It was a note from Anais. I felt better immediately as I unfolded the paper and read. It said:

Dear Sophie,

You will be my friend for life, even though we may never meet again. We all feel so much better for the food and shelter you arranged for us. We are heading west, in the hope that we might find somewhere to stay, away from the fighting. Please thank your brother and your

friends and all those people who gave us food, especially the old lady
who made that delicious soup!

    I hope the war is soon over so that we can all start to build our lives
again. Pray for my papa, wherever he is.

    Grosses bises,

    Anais Leclerc

I hope they'll be all right. I wonder if I'll ever hear from Anais again.

Tuesday 4th June

There are more refugees on the main road every day. I'd love to help
them all, but know that's impossible. Mama says we can't feed the whole
of France. I suppose she's right. We ought to save as much food as we
can in case we need it ourselves.

Wednesday 5th June

Those British and French soldiers we heard about last week – the ones that were trapped on the beaches at Dunkerque – well, we've heard that loads have been rescued by warships and hundreds of little boats that made the journey over the sea from England, but thousands more soldiers have been killed or taken prisoner. I asked Papa what happens to the captured ones. He said they'll be kept in prisoner-of-war camps until the end of the war and there will be many more casualties and prisoners before it's all over.

War is so ghastly!

Patrice says that some British soldiers are moving this way. Perhaps they'll be able to look after us. I think Mama is trying to put on a brave face for my sake. I'm sure she's really as scared as I am. If both sides keep on coming, we might be stuck right in the middle! They'll be fighting right here in our village!

Thursday 6th June

It's been such a hectic and exciting day! How will I ever forget such surprising events? It's lunchtime now and I've snatched a few minutes to run home and write in my diary. We haven't been to school, for obvious reasons! We had just eaten our breakfast this morning when we heard a strange sound in the distance. It was like a wailing animal mixed with a deep miserable groan. I had no idea what it could be. Sebastien and I dashed out and raced up the lane to the corner.

I couldn't believe my eyes. A long line of soldiers in khaki uniforms was marching into the village, but at their head was a man wearing a skirt. That man was holding a strange instrument in front of him. He had some kind of bag under his arm and he was blowing into a pipe, which was making the terrible sound. I've never seen or heard anything so weird in all my life!

Sebastien ran towards the soldiers. He called over his shoulder that they were British. I ran behind him and joined the group of people watching from the grassy bank at the corner. Grandma was there. I stood next to her, panting hard. Grandma was thrilled. She thought my English would be useful after all. Then Yvette ran over to join us. She held her hands over her ears and laughed. She dared me to go and speak to the soldiers as I'm best in the class. I grinned at her and nodded. I began to tingle all over. It was so exciting! This seemed like a chance to show them all how well I can speak English!

Suddenly, the strange instrument gave a loud whine then a gasp. Then it shuddered and was silent. I stared at the man with the instrument and asked Sebastien why an Englishman would wear a skirt like that. He laughed and told me it isn't a skirt. It's called a kilt. He said they're not English, they're Scottish. And the strange instrument is called a bagpipe. He's so clever, my brother!

I took a closer look at the soldiers. Some had bandages round their heads, some had arms in slings and others had crutches to help them along. They all looked bedraggled and many looked utterly miserable.

Their officer stepped forward and shouted to the crowd, "*Parlez-vous anglais?*" He had a weird accent and it sounded really funny. I held back for a moment, though my heart was racing. I felt Yvette nudging me. Suddenly, Grandma waved to the soldiers. She pointed at me and called, "*Oui, ma petite-fille, Sophie, parle anglais.*" I felt my face redden. I was furious with Grandma, but I was secretly pleased, too.

I felt Sebastien's hand on my back and suddenly, I was running down the bank and standing facing the officer. I tried really hard and told him I speak a little English, but my face was burning like a forest fire. He asked me my name and I told him – "My name is Sophie Ridel." I was really pleased that I had understood his question. I said, "I am fourteen years old."

He told me that he's called Captain Mackenzie. After that he spoke so fast I had no idea what he said. I shrugged my shoulders and shook my head. The officer rubbed his stomach then pointed into his mouth. They were hungry. He pretended to yawn. They were tired, too.

I beamed at him. I remembered how easy it had been to feed the refugees and find them somewhere to sleep. Somehow or other I managed to tell him that we would help. I asked Sebastien if he thought Mr Masson would let them stay in the barn. Sebastien ran to the farm to find out.

There's so much to write. I'll try and carry on tonight.

Evening

I tried my hardest to explain to Captain Mackenzie about the barn and the food that we would collect. I can see now that my English isn't very good at all, but I did my best. Luckily, Sebastien wasn't long in coming back. Olivier was with him and I could see old Mr Duval, the Mayor, a short way behind, hobbling along with his walking stick. Sebastien brought good news. Mr Masson said yes. So the next thing was to persuade everyone to donate food again. Yvette promised to fetch some from her mama. Grandma hurried away to make some more soup. She made us all laugh when she asked if we thought the foreigners would like French soup.

Mr Duval was hot and bothered. His face was red and he leant on his stick while he got his breath back. I felt very important as I introduced him to Captain Mackenzie. The officer saluted and Mr Duval bowed and apologized for not being there sooner. They didn't understand a word of what each other said so I was kept busy trying to translate. It wasn't easy! The Captain asked if there was a doctor in the village. He looked sad when he told us his army doctor had been killed by the Germans.

Mr Duval sent Yvette to fetch Dr Lambert. Then Marcel walked over to me. He told me there would be another message to take to Hélène tomorrow. It didn't seem fair. Instead of no action at all, now I was needed in two places at once.

Suddenly, I noticed Georges Dubois standing watching us. I coughed. Luckily, Marcel took the hint and walked over to his friends. A few moments later he strolled casually towards Georges. I heard what they said. Marcel talked about the soldiers. He asked Georges if he was excited to see them. I know he was sounding Georges out to find out whose side he was on. Georges scowled at Marcel as he told him he didn't like the British soldiers. He doesn't want them here. When Marcel pointed out that the German army is getting closer, Georges turned and walked away. When Georges was out of earshot I warned Marcel about him. Then the soldiers went to the barn.

We've worked so hard today and now it's late. All I want to do now is sleep.

Friday 7th June
8 am

Marcel has just arrived. I heard his voice downstairs. I guess it's time to go to Veules les Roses. We had a message last night that school has been cancelled for the time being. I don't know whether I'm happy or sad about that. I like school, but I think I'm going to be kept busy here.

Midday

This morning I thought I was going to die! My writing is rather wobbly because I'm still shaking now. If this is war, I wish it had never started and I hope it finishes very soon. This is what happened.

I climbed down the ladder and said hello to Marcel. When we were sure Mama wasn't looking, he gave me another letter. I shoved it into my pocket. I promised to be as quick as I could, fetched my bicycle and set off. Veules les Roses is only a few kilometres away, so I hoped I wouldn't be long.

In no time at all, I was knocking on the old door in Rue Victor Hugo. As soon as the door opened a crack, I slipped inside. Hélène slit open the envelope and read the letter. She told me it said that the British are here and that the enemy is closing in. She said she would make preparations there in Veules les Roses, in case the soldiers can't stop them. Then she thanked me and said there was no reply.

I didn't have time to visit Aunty Régine. I knew I would be needed in the village. Even if they didn't need me to translate, there was food to collect.

I'm all of a quiver as I write this – I can hardly bear to recall it. I was halfway home when I heard the sound of aircraft. I stopped and looked behind me. There were two low-flying planes heading straight towards me. For a few seconds, I watched them as they came nearer and nearer. Why were they flying so low? Were they French planes? Or British? Or were they German?

Just in time, I threw myself into the ditch at the side of the road. There was a sudden deafening burst of gunfire. I heard a rain of bullets hit the road where I had been only a few seconds before. The planes roared overhead, skimming the bushes, but I had seen the black cross on the wings. They must be German.

The shock of what had happened hit me like a punch in the stomach. They had tried to kill me! I had to fight for breath. It felt as if someone had tied a belt round my body and was pulling it tight. I couldn't move for several minutes. Then all I wanted was to be back in the village. I made myself move.

Feeling very shaky, I climbed out of the ditch and picked up my bicycle. A really scary thought kept going round and round in my head. *They were trying to kill me!* But what were those planes doing around here? I guess there's only one answer. They were on the look-out for British or French soldiers.

I had to get back to the village to warn everyone, but I had no energy in my legs. The wind seemed against me and the journey that was usually so easy felt like climbing a mountain peak. And I had to stay alert, looking and listening in case those planes came back.

It felt like ages before I was free-wheeling down the hill into the village. All the streets were empty and silent.

Instead of rushing to the barn, I've climbed up here, into the safety of my bedroom. I think I might stay at home for the rest of the day. I'll go and see my hens. They'll help me to get over my first real experience of war.

Evening

I feel a bit better now. I didn't stay at home, after all. I've been over to the barn. It was bursting with soldiers and people helping them. I couldn't see anyone I knew at first. Then I saw Yvette with Dr Lambert. She was bandaging a soldier's head and she waved to me, so I pushed through the crowds of men to reach her. I know what she wants to do when she leaves school. She's going to be a nurse, and I'm sure she'll be an excellent one. As I talked to her I could hear a quaking in my voice – I still haven't fully recovered – but Yvette didn't seem to notice. She was already moving on to the next patient.

I saw Captain Mackenzie over in the far corner. He was trying to talk to Mr Duval, but they were both shrugging their shoulders and waving their hands. It was obvious they didn't understand each other. I managed to reach them. I asked Mr Duval if two planes flew low over here this morning and he said they had. They were German Stukas. Luckily, everyone was inside the barn when they flew over so they can't have seen the soldiers. That's a relief, anyway.

I told him about my narrow escape then I tried to tell my story to Captain Mackenzie, in English. A frown spread across his face. Apparently some of his men had been killed by Stukas a few days ago. I asked him why he had come to this part of France, but I couldn't understand any of his reply. It's becoming more and more obvious how little English I know. I felt tearful and turned away. Mr Duval must have noticed. He patted my arm and told me I was doing very well. I don't think he realized quite how shaken I felt. I wished Mrs Ferrand, my English teacher, was there.

At that moment, my wish was granted. I saw Mrs Ferrand pushing through the crowds. Someone must have gone to fetch her. I felt stronger as I introduced her to the Scottish Captain. It helped me recover a little. Mrs Ferrand listened to the Captain then translated everything for

Mr Duval. She learned that the Scottish soldiers are part of the 51st Highland Division. They were at Dunkerque, but instead of being evacuated like many of the other British soldiers they were ordered to move on to this region. They've been fighting in the Somme valley. Now they're here to guard the railway – to make sure the Germans don't take it over – and also to protect the sugar factory.

At that moment, I caught sight of Marcel. He was heading my way. As he passed by, I whispered, "No message." I smiled to myself. No one had noticed. I felt like a real spy! But I had no time to think about that. I joined the others who were collecting food. Then I headed home. Mama was by the crossing gates. She says she doesn't mind missing all the action. (I wouldn't have minded missing a certain part of it!) I didn't tell her about my trip to Veules les Roses or the Stukas.

Late

This evening, I saw a single line of soldiers marching over from the barn. They reached the railway line and began to take up positions along the track. One soldier remained at the barriers. I noticed his dark brown hair, pale freckly face and bright blue eyes. I thought he looked very young.

Mama went back indoors, but I decided to visit the chickens. I fed them with grain and collected several eggs. I felt the young soldier's eyes watching me. As I took the eggs to the house, I smiled at him. I told him my name and asked him for his. He's called Angus Brown. Then I told him my age. He's eighteen.

I can't help thinking about Sebastien. He's sixteen now, only two years younger than Angus. In only two years' time, Sebastien might have to go and fight! I hope the war will be over by then.

I watched Angus for a moment as he walked up and down with his rifle over his shoulder. The grey circles round his eyes made him look tired and ill. I wonder what he's experienced since he's been in France. So far, I thought I was doing quite well speaking English with him, but when I asked him if he was hungry, I had a bit of a problem. He said, "Aye." I didn't understand. Then he told me it's a Scottish word for "Yes" – it's all too complicated.

He flashed me a smile and his eyes twinkled. When he did that I realized he's rather good-looking. I ran indoors, cut a chunk of bread and a piece of cheese, and ran back outside with the food for Angus.

Saturday 8th June
Midday

This morning, I've been fetching more food from the villagers. They weren't as generous as when we fed the refugees. They say they might need the food for themselves if things get worse. Then I went to the barn and helped as much as I could with the wounded soldiers. Several times, I heard German aircraft flying low over the village.

I'm shaking again as I write this. Why? Well, a little while ago, I thought I heard a rumble of thunder. Papa said it isn't thunder. It's gunfire! It's in the distance, but I keep imagining it's getting nearer. I'm keeping my fingers crossed that it isn't. Oh dear! What will we do?

I was really pleased to see Angus on duty again. I went to talk to him. I wanted to try out my English and find out more about him. I discovered that he speaks a bit of French. Between us, we managed to communicate. He lives in Scotland, in the mountains, in a town called Inverness – I think that's how you spell it. He told me he misses his home terribly. His eyes looked very sad when he said that. Then he told me about his parents and his sister. Her name is Morag and she's fourteen years old, too.

Angus thinks I ask a lot of questions, but he doesn't seem to mind.

He's right. I'm inquisitive. I want to know everything about him. He doesn't like being a soldier and he doesn't want to fight, but he had no choice. All the boys of his age had to go to war. Just like our boys, I suppose. He asked me about my family. I told him about my hens, too, and how much I love them. And he didn't laugh. He seemed to understand. I'm beginning to realize that I like Angus! He's gone off duty now.

I'm feeling very restless. I'm lying on my bed listening to the heavy guns in the distance. How far away are they? Not many kilometres, I guess.

Afternoon

The trains that have rumbled in today are full of British and French soldiers. Other troops are arriving by lorry or on foot. Why are they all coming here? I went into the village. I just had to see what was going on. I'll admit it was also an excuse to see Angus again. I cycled around the village, looking for him, but there was no sign of him anywhere. I stopped by a group of Scottish soldiers and asked them. I wish I hadn't. They all laughed. I understood enough of what they said to know that they were joking about Angus finding a French girlfriend already. I hurried away, blushing scarlet.

I wonder where Angus is.

I watched other soldiers preparing their guns. I'm sure I got in everyone's way. Soldiers filled the village. Apart from their rifles, they had machine guns, which they set up on the southern side of the village.

Then a French motorcycle messenger sped into the village. Quickly, news spread that the Germans are not far away. They're flattening everything in their path. They've got tanks and other heavy weapons. Can nothing stop the German war machine?

Suddenly, I was scared. I wanted to be with Mama, but I was nearly back at the house when I heard a shout behind me. It was Marcel. I'd got to take a message. Patrice hadn't had time to write a note so I had to memorize it. I repeated the message several times to make sure I had got it right.

When Marcel had gone, I found myself speeding along the road to Veules les Roses. The wind blew my fear away. It was so exciting to be delivering such an urgent message. I recited the message to myself in time with my knees as they pumped up and down. I arrived breathless at Hélène's house.

I was panting heavily as I recited the message. Hélène was to hide all her papers, burn evidence and warn other friends, then she must prepare for the worst as the enemy is not far off.

I couldn't believe I was saying this. It didn't feel real, more like acting in a play. I think that's what helped me cope with it.

The old lady was so calm. She thanked me. I was to tell Patrice that all the secrets are safe with her. She'll give nothing away, even under torture.

She's sure the Germans will not suspect her. They'll think she's too old. Then she told me to go.

I didn't need telling a second time! My legs worked up and down like pistons. I desperately wanted to get back home before there was any fighting in the village. I thought about Hélène's words, "even under torture". It made shivers shoot up and down my spine. I had learned in history lessons about torture that took place a long time ago. Surely that doesn't still happen nowadays?

I was nearly home. I could hear sounds of guns firing over in Mr Masson's fields on the other side of the village. I saw French and Scottish soldiers everywhere, hidden in ditches, in position at corners, manning machine guns, but there was no sign of the enemy. I dodged between the jeeps and trucks and soldiers and weapons that clogged the road and sped directly to Patrice's house, dropped my bicycle at the gate and ran up the path. Patrice must have seen me coming. He opened a window and leaned out. I repeated Hélène's message, almost word for word, then before Patrice could reply, I had turned and was running for the gate.

I arrived home just as the first shell whistled through the air. I dived in through the doorway as the explosion rocked the house. I ran to the window and saw a huge cloud of smoke rising into the sky. The shell had landed only a couple of hundred metres away. Mama looked deathly white and she was shaking all over. I found that I was shaking, too. I can hardly hold my pen to write this.

Later

I'm still shaking. I'm so scared I can hardly keep still, let alone write. It's been going on for hours.

I'm glad Papa and Sebastien got back safely from the farm just after that first shell. It had landed quite near Yvette's house. I'm so desperately worried. Yvette, dear kind Yvette. Please let her be all right. Please don't let anyone get hurt or killed. As I huddled in a corner I thought about poor Grandma, all on her own in her house near the church. She must be frightened out of her wits!

A second shell whistled and exploded somewhere near the first one. Mama and I clung to each other as the deafening sound of gunfire sounded across the village. Then we heard another shell whistling through the air. This one sounded nearer. We all flattened ourselves on the cold stone floor. The windows rattled loudly as the shell exploded.

Mama shrieked, "We have to close the shutters!" She started clambering up the ladder. I followed her. Before closing my bedroom shutters I stared out across the farmyard to the village. Black smoke and flames billowed out from one of the houses and an old shed, but it looked as if Grandma's and Yvette's houses were undamaged.

Suddenly, I saw a huge German tank trundling into the village. I screamed. Mama hurried over and stood beside me at the window. She put her hands to her mouth as I pointed. There were German soldiers, too, running beside the tank, firing their rifles. It was horrible. I was terrified. Yet it seemed so unreal, almost as if I was watching a film like the one I had seen once at the Picture Palace in Rouen. But it was also so real, here, in my own village.

We quickly closed the shutters and climbed back down the ladder. No one spoke after that. We all sat in the living room, waiting, listening to the booms and bangs and the constant rat-a-tat of the machine guns. The room was almost dark with the shutters closed and when the next shell landed, the house shook as much as before, but the windows didn't rattle so loudly. Then we heard the aircraft.

Sebastien said it sounded heavier than the ones that came over yesterday. It did. It was a very loud drone. Papa said it was a bomber! A bomber? I thought I was scared before. But now – I was petrified. We were all going to be killed! I moved closer to Papa. I could feel the tension in his body as he pulled me into his arms. Suddenly, there was a different kind of noise, like a rush of wind. We all threw ourselves on the floor. It was a bomb! I held my breath. A second later, there was a massive explosion. The shutters rattled noisily and the ground shook. The enemy had dropped a bomb on our village!

Papa gripped me so tightly I felt crushed, but I didn't want to move. I was totally tensed up, waiting for more bombs to fall. But the drone of the aircraft faded, leaving the everlasting noise of machine guns, rifles and tanks. After a while, Papa gently pushed me away from him and stood up.

My body began to relax a little, but so many questions rushed into my brain. Where had the bomb landed? We had survived it, but how many people had it killed? I was terrified for Grandma, all alone in her house. I prayed the bomb hadn't landed anywhere near her, but it was impossible to find out if she was all right. Nobody could go outside while bullets were flying.

For ages, we all had to stay in the house. I felt twitchy and restless. I hated being cooped up like this. Besides worrying about the people of the village, I was desperately anxious about the hens. They were cooped up, too. The poor things must be petrified out there with all the noise and no shutters to close. I wished I could go and comfort them. But I knew there was nothing I could do. We just had to wait until this was over.

Very late

It's getting dark. They're still fighting outside. I think it's going to keep on forever. I'm lying on my bed, using a torch to write by. Mama and Papa don't know I'm writing this, of course. They told me and Sebastien to try and sleep. As if we could! Every so often, I peep through cracks in the shutters, but I can't see much. I hold my breath each time I hear a shell and hope that no one in the village will be hurt. I listen to the gunfire and keep thinking about Grandma and Yvette and the soldiers out there fighting, especially Angus Brown. How many of the soldiers will be killed? Will we all survive?

Sunday 9th June
6 am

I don't know what time it stopped. I must have fallen asleep eventually with my diary and pencil in my hands because when I woke up that was the first thing I noticed. The second thing was the quiet. I listened. Silence!

I've just climbed out of bed and opened the shutter a little way. There's no sign of the tanks. The soldiers have all gone, but I'm sure I can see some bodies lying on the ground. Are they dead? I'm going to wake the others up.

10 am

After I had hidden my diary, I called Mama and Papa and Sebastien. We all dressed very quickly, shinned down the ladder and hurried outside. First, we had to go and see if Grandma was all right.

I was stunned by what I saw as we ran through the village. It had been such a quiet peaceful place until a few hours ago. Now it was torn to pieces. Burnt-out vehicles littered the road and several houses had been flattened and many damaged.

And the bodies! My stomach felt as if it had been gripped by a giant claw. I covered my eyes as we passed through. I couldn't bear to look. There were quite a lot of people around – people carrying the dead and wounded, Dr Lambert walking amongst the bodies, Mr Duval hobbling about, muttering, his old face as grey as stone. I heard that they had set up a temporary hospital for the wounded in the village hall. The dead were being taken to the Mayor's office.

I wondered about Angus. What had happened to him?

We reached Yvette's house. Some of the shutters were damaged and a few slates were missing from the roof, but I was so relieved when she ran out to the gate as we went by. I hugged her. She was very pale and she didn't smile. She looked absolutely terrified.

But we didn't stop. We had to check that Grandma was all right. I sprinted ahead. As I came round the bend near her house, I screamed. Grandma's house had several broken windows and there was a hole in one corner of the wall, but it was the church I was staring at – or the space where the church had been. It was just a pile of rubble. That bomb – it must have been a direct hit. It was terrible, but at least it had missed Grandma!

We all ran towards her house. Grandma opened the door as we hurried up the path. She was covered in dust and bits of plaster, but otherwise she was unharmed. I burst into tears. I was so relieved. I brushed away some of the dirt on her clothes and she gently told me not to fuss. She smiled and said that she was fine. She told us that when the tanks came she just lay on the floor underneath the kitchen table and prayed. She said it would take more than a few Germans to put an end to her! She spat on the ground in disgust.

I hugged her. Good old Grandma!

As soon as I knew that she was safe, I hurried back home. I wanted to know how the chickens were. I opened the pen and went in. I was amazed. They met me in the normal way, as if nothing unusual had happened. They fussed around me as I threw them a few handfuls of grain, and muttered away as they scratched in the soil. I do love the way they manage to cope with everything. They're so brilliant and ridiculous!

I started to giggle and that turned into a laugh. Then I was sobbing. I couldn't stop. I must have been there for quite a while, but eventually I sat down on the edge of the feeding trough and wiped my eyes.

Several hens stopped to look up at me then carried on as before. They seemed to have coped better than the humans! They had even managed to lay some eggs!

After a few more minutes with the hens, I ran back to Grandma's. The others had already set about clearing up the mess. I took Grandma's mat outside and began to shake it. We swept and cleaned for about an hour then we came home. I always seem to feel tired lately. The whole world is turned upside down.

Midday

I can't believe it. Marcel has just been here. I've got to go to Veules les Roses. I don't know if I'm brave enough to go.

Afternoon

I did go. I made myself. We're at war. Sebastien and I promised we'd do what we can, so this is what I have to do.

It's a warm, sunny Sunday. Papa was over at Mr Masson's farm and

Mama was on duty at the level-crossing gates so it was easy for me to sneak to the shed to fetch my bicycle. I found Sebastien pumping up his tyres. I told him where I was going then I instructed him to cover for me. If Mama or Papa asked where I'd gone, he had to say I was visiting Aunty Régine. And if I got into any difficulties, I told him I'd go there anyway.

I was amazed at his reaction. He actually told me to take care. Then I was bowled over by what he said next. He thinks I'm very brave. His words gave me a warm feeling inside. I smiled and gently pushed his arm. I told him he's brave, too. I let on that I know he's been out and about with Marcel and Patrice. He opened his mouth to speak, but I stopped him. It's best I know as little as possible.

I met nobody as I pedalled along the lanes, although I could hear gunfire in the distance. The fighting had moved towards the west. I had Patrice's message safely in my head again. This time I felt more confident about it and I wasn't worried about forgetting it before I reached Hélène. The message was about the soldiers who had fought in the village the day before, including Angus Brown, of course.

In spite of what Sebastien had said, I didn't feel brave as I approached Veules les Roses. Once again, I had to control shaking arms and legs and a permanently aching stomach. But I wasn't going to let a little thing like that stop me.

I paused for a moment on the brow of the hill by the main road to make sure it was safe to carry on. Thankfully, there was no sign of the enemy, but I was shocked to see that now there were thousands and thousands of refugees. They blocked the road. Where would they all end up?

Then I looked towards the west. A huge cloud of black smoke filled the sky. At that moment, I realized that a choking smell had caught the back of my throat. What could it be?

I pushed my way across the road and sped into Veules les Roses. The main street was full of people, rushing about, looking nervously around. They were preparing to leave. Suddenly, I heard a roar overhead. I glanced up. German aircraft! I leapt off my bicycle and dodged into a doorway, my heart pounding. I didn't want to be shot at again. But they didn't fire and soon they were gone. I waited a while for my heart to slow down then I tore along the road and slipped into Hélène's little house.

I recited the message – that the German army is much too strong for our soldiers, the enemy have much bigger, better weapons, the British and French troops have had to withdraw and they've received orders to head for Le Havre where they'll be picked up by warships and taken to England.

Hélène gasped. "Not Le Havre!" she cried. She told me that the German army has already taken over the city. She asked me if I'd seen the black smoke in the west. I nodded. Then what she told me made me terrified for the soldiers who had gone that way. The smoke is from the oil refineries in the port. They've been bombed, destroyed by the German army and air force. She made me promise to tell Patrice to send word to the British and French soldiers. They must not go there. They'll run into a trap.

Her next piece of news was even worse. Apparently, General Rommel and the German army are surging this way from Le Havre. Our men and the British must head for St Valery en Caux. Perhaps the ships will take them off from there. I repeated the message to check I had got it right.

When I delivered Hélène's message a short while later, Patrice looked shattered. He had deep worry lines across his forehead. Perhaps he was wondering who could take this message to the soldiers. It would be a very difficult and dangerous task. He glanced at me and opened his mouth to speak. Then he shut it again. He seemed undecided. Did he think I could do it? Then he thanked me and sent me home. I had to admit to myself as I left Patrice that I was secretly relieved I didn't have to go. The mission is too dangerous for a young girl, even a brave one!

Evening

Just now, I popped round to Yvette's. She seemed quiet. When I asked her if she was all right she nodded then shook her head. She was on the verge of tears as she admitted she's scared – of all that fighting in the village and the church and the German tanks and that bomb. It was so close she thought she was going to die.

She wanted to talk about everything and I was happy to listen. Suddenly, she became very agitated. Her eyes were fiery with anger as she told me she can't believe how much she hates the enemy. She said she'd do anything to get them out of our country. I stared at her. I've never seen my kind, gentle friend so mad. That got me thinking. Perhaps Yvette will be able to join our group after all! I'm going to ask Patrice.

When I got home, I came upstairs to write my diary, but a short while ago, I heard loud voices outside. A man was shouting, giving orders – in German! I shinned down the ladder and stepped outside. I saw a group of German soldiers near the level-crossing gates. I stared, frozen, unable to believe what I was witnessing. One by one the soldiers marched off along the railway line, just as the Scottish soldiers had done just a little while before. They were taking over the railway!

Mama stood in the doorway. She folded her arms and declared that she was *not* going to work for them. The German officer who had been giving orders marched over to me and Mama. He halted very stiffly, clicking his heels together and saluting. I took several steps back and stood close beside Mama. The officer began to speak. He spoke in French, but he had a very strong accent and he made lots of mistakes. Mama turned away from him. The officer told us he is in charge now. Mama didn't reply.

I watched the officer closely. At first, his face was calm. I think he was trying to be pleasant, but when Mama refused to speak or even turn back towards him his face began to twitch. Then he began giving orders. I winced at the harshness of his voice. Mama swung round towards him with a look of defiance on her face. She snapped at him – he may have won a small battle here, but the war is not over yet, not by a long way!

I held my breath, dreading his reaction. But at that moment, I heard a train coming. I looked along the railway. German soldiers had taken up their positions along the line. The train had reached the bend so the gates needed closing, but Mama did not move. The officer waited for a moment then he scowled at Mama and closed the gates himself.

The train trundled noisily through. It was full of German soldiers. I shuddered at the sight of them. Whatever Mama had said, the Germans had definitely taken charge. I heard the train stop at the station. Doors slammed. Men shouted. Soldiers swarmed everywhere. They think they own the place! This is *our* country.

The officer marched stiffly towards us and I clutched Mama's arm tightly. *Go away and leave us alone!* I shouted in my head. I desperately needed to yell it out loud, but I didn't want the German soldiers suspecting me of acting against them. I swallowed my anger and asked about the wounded soldiers in the village hall. He said they're prisoners of war and will be taken to camps in Germany. He had such a superior attitude. I wanted to go and punch him on the nose or scream in his ear, but I bit my lip and clenched my fists hard by my sides. I came back up here to write in my diary.

Monday 10th June
8 am

I'm so miserable. The page is blotchy with my tears. I hate the Germans with every part of me. I want to kick and punch and hit and bite and... Why? Because they're murderers, that's why!

I had a bad night. I was hot. I tossed and turned. I hated having those German soldiers outside and my brain was overflowing with questions again.

What's going to happen to us? Will they hurt us? Will the Scottish soldiers fall into the trap? Or will they escape?

I must have slept some of the time, but eventually, at first light, I decided to get up and go and see my hens. They always calm my nerves with their muttering and chattering and their heads on one side.

Quietly, I dressed and slipped down the ladder. I opened the back door and crept out into the garden, heading straight for the hen house. But as I came to the outer wire, I stopped. The door stood wide open. I ran to the doorway and stared in disbelief. I saw a few feathers lying among the uneaten grains of corn, but that was all that was left. My hands flew to my mouth and I smothered a scream. Then I sank on to my knees and I began to shudder with sobs.

My hens have gone!

10 am

When Mama came to find me, I had stopped crying, but was still huddled in the doorway of the hen house. I heard her gasp, and when I looked up I saw how pale she had become. Her mouth was clamped shut in a hard line, and I could tell she was almost as angry and upset as I was. "This isn't the work of the fox," she said.

There was a sound from the railway. A soldier was approaching. Mama stepped out and stood directly in his path. She went for him. She pointed towards the empty hen house and demanded to know how he dared to do this. The soldier held up his hand and shook his head. But Mama's eyes were flashing with anger as she demanded to speak with his officer. I couldn't bear to look at him; I was so full of disgust. He marched off towards the farm.

Mama put her arm round me – she knows how much I loved my lovely hens. She almost made me cry again, but at that moment, we saw the officer marching towards us. Mama's anger burst out again and she yelled at him for ages, accusing him of all sorts of horrible crimes. The officer might not have understood every word, but he had understood the gist. His face was twitching again. I cringed. I didn't want Mama to get us into trouble. She told him he had no right to take the hens. He stepped menacingly towards us and shouted that he had every right now they're in charge.

That did it! I burst into tears again. Of course, we have always lived by our traditional French way of life and I accept it. The hens gave us eggs, but we would have eaten them eventually. That's how we live, here in the country, but not all at once. That's cold-blooded murder. The soldier bowed his head sharply and clicked his heels. Then he swivelled round and marched away.

I'll never get over it. I'm still crying now. I can't help it. It's not fair.

Midday

I've just been to Yvette's. It was creepy, cycling through the village, knowing that enemy soldiers had taken over, and I was glad I didn't see many of them, except a few standing on guard. But now I hate them with all my heart. I'll never forgive what they've done. I'll work harder from now on, to defeat them.

I was almost at her house when I saw something that made me wobble so violently that I nearly fell off my bicycle. Georges Dubois was talking to a German soldier! He was smiling, looking up at the soldier with admiration in his eyes. Georges is definitely a traitor to France.

He's worse than the enemy! I wanted to spit, just like Grandma had done, but I gritted my teeth instead and managed to cycle on.

I told Yvette about my hens. She's very sympathetic. She says the soldiers are brutes! I came home the other way, to avoid having to see Georges again, but as I was passing the Cariat's house, Marcel came out of his front gate and I slowed down. There's a message to take. Marcel will be here shortly.

Sebastien came out to meet me when I reached home. He gave me a hug and muttered something about the hens. I stared at him, utterly amazed. Sebastien never hugs anyone, least of all me. It must be the war. It's turning us all into different people.

Thursday 13th June

I'm writing this now because I've been away from home and therefore I couldn't write in my diary. I might not get it all down in one go. Such a lot has happened over the past three days. I'll try and remember everything. Where have I been? Well, I'll begin where I left off, with Sebastien hugging me. I like to think about that. He's not such a bad brother, is he?

This is what happened on Monday afternoon

Half an hour after the "hug", I was on my way, carrying a letter for Hélène and a bag of home-made biscuits in my basket. I could hear distant sounds of gunfire as I pedalled along the lane. It was coming from the west. I wondered what was happening. Was it the Scottish regiment? Had they fallen into the German trap, as Hélène had warned? Or had Patrice managed to get a message to them? Perhaps even now, they were heading for St Valery en Caux to be rescued by ship.

As I rounded a bend, a column of German soldiers appeared, marching towards me. I gripped the handlebars hard and pedalled on. What should I do? If I stopped or turned round, they might be suspicious. So I decided to carry on, right past them. My heart pounded rapidly as I cycled by, but I needn't have worried. They kept their eyes firmly ahead and marched on. They didn't seem to notice me. I'm glad I look young for my age. None of them suspected a little French girl.

I crossed the main road safely, but I was just approaching Veules les Roses when I came across another group of German soldiers. They were all heavily armed and looked as if they were waiting for something. One of them held up his hand. This time I had to stop. I felt

243

weak as I braked and jumped off my bicycle. My knees almost gave way as I stood shakily before him.

One of them asked where I was going and I answered, "To my aunt's house." I showed him the biscuits and said they were for her and my baby cousin. The soldier helped himself to a biscuit and took a bite. He nodded, finished the biscuit and passed the bag around. Soon all the biscuits were gone. One of the soldiers laughed and then they all joined in. I was seething. They had stolen my country and killed my hens. Now they were stealing everything else in sight and they thought it was funny! I don't know how I managed to control my temper this time, but I did. I bit my tongue and said nothing. I couldn't afford to annoy them.

Suddenly, the mood changed. I was told to empty my pockets. Slowly, I took my handkerchief, a piece of string and a pencil from my skirt pocket. The soldiers peered into the pocket, inspected my basket and stared at me with cold eyes, but they wouldn't find the note from Patrice to Hélène. As I left our village, I'd pushed it into my knickers, just in case!

Eventually, they waved me on, but I dared not relax until I was pedalling as innocently as I could away from them. I felt many pairs of eyes boring into my back as I went. At last, I gasped in air and tried to calm myself. It was getting really bad. The enemy was everywhere.

There was nobody on the street as I approached Hélène's house so I quickly left my bicycle in the usual place and knocked on the door. I slipped inside as soon as it was opened, but Hélène didn't even read the letter. She just snatched it from my hand, pushed me outside, told me to dash home and closed the door behind me. I was shocked by her hurry to get rid of me. Was the danger that close? Did she know something I didn't?

Suddenly, I heard the sound of gunfire. It didn't seem to be very far away. I wondered if the soldiers I had just met had received the orders they were waiting for. I dreaded that they might enter Veules les Roses at any minute. My legs were too shaky to ride my bicycle, but I was not going to leave it behind. The streets were still deserted as I pushed it up the hill towards Aunty Régine's house.

Keeping my head down and panting hard, I finally arrived at the house near the top of the cliff and ran round the back. Aunty Régine pulled me inside. She looked very scared and Charles was crying.

We went to the window. Across the little cove I could see the flashes of gunfire along the cliffs, from the port of St Valery en Caux. Then I stared out to sea. There was an oily black fog hanging over the water, but if I screwed up my eyes, I could just make out the shapes of quite a few large ships off the coast.

I thought they must have come to rescue the Scottish soldiers, but I didn't realize that I was thinking aloud until too late. I put my hand over my mouth. I'd let out a secret. Aunty Régine looked at me. She asked me how I knew that so I grinned and shrugged and tapped the side of my nose with my finger.

She's guessed I'm a... What am I? A spy?

I put my finger to my lips. I didn't want to lie to her, but I didn't deny anything either. It doesn't matter if she suspects what I'm up to. I trust her. She won't give my secret away.

This is what happened on Monday evening

The fighting seemed to be in and around St Valery en Caux, but I couldn't tell exactly where. If I stared really hard out of the window, I could see flashes of the guns along the cliffs.

I desperately wanted to get home. Mama would be out of her mind with worry. Several times I made up my mind to try, but each time I fetched my bicycle from behind the house, we imagined the fighting was coming nearer and I had to dash back inside. Aunty Régine wouldn't let me leave. She said it was much too dangerous. Maybe the Germans were fighting on the main road. My way would be blocked and I might be killed. That convinced me! I realized I'd have to wait there until it was safe to leave. Anyway, Sebastien knew where I was.

So I played with Charles for a while, but then I went to stand at the window. I found Uncle Thierry's binoculars and focused them along the coast. I became hypnotised! I had difficulty taking my eyes off the sight of the battle that was raging in the distance. It was like watching a film again, as if it wasn't really happening. I couldn't move away. Yet, just like in our village, I knew how real it was.

By supper time, I was still trapped. The battle at St Valery en Caux was really fierce. I heard massive explosions resounding along the coast. I saw German aircraft shoot overhead and dive-bomb the town. Off the coast, I noticed that the ships had come nearer to the shore. My brain was packed with questions I could not answer. Were they trying to evacuate our soldiers? Were the Scots fighting there? Was Angus still alive? Would he escape?

Was Uncle Thierry on one of those ships? I was sure Aunty Régine must be wondering the same thing, but she said nothing. After that first glimpse, she stayed away from the window. I don't think she could bear to look any longer.

Then the aircraft began to attack the warships, too, and I could see flashes from the anti-aircraft guns on the ships. All at once, I saw a great splash of water close to a ship. I gasped. The German tanks were firing out to sea. Several more shells landed near the ships. The ships returned fire. I couldn't believe it! The French ships were firing shells at their own land. I had a horrible thought – they might kill their own people.

Suddenly, through the binoculars, I picked out a smaller boat heading out to sea from the port of St Valery. It was full of people. It seemed to be making for one of the warships. But at that moment, a shell landed on the boat. It exploded in a ball of flames. I covered my eyes. They must all be dead, blown to pieces! I sat down, feeling sick.

After a few minutes, I couldn't resist looking again. More small boats were heading out to sea. Several reached the ships. Some soldiers were managing to escape!

By then, I thought I could see flames above St Valery en Caux. Huge plumes of smoke rose above the town. The fighting must be very fierce. How could the British and French soldiers defend it any longer? Would they surrender? Or would they, and all the people of St Valery, be killed?

This is what happened on Monday night

I stayed at Aunty Régine's window all evening. I didn't want to sleep although I ached all over, shattered by what I had witnessed along the coast. It was almost dark when Aunty Régine insisted. She more or less carried me to bed.

Even though I was exhausted, I was too restless to sleep well. I dozed a few times, but I kept snapping awake. I don't think Aunty Régine slept any more than I did. I could hear her walking about and I am sure I heard her crying.

The night was just as noisy as the day had been. The fighting raged on. I could hear gunfire and explosions. I got out of bed several times, but it seemed foggy and I couldn't see a thing except a glow from along the coast. Then I realized – the sounds were becoming louder. I found my way to my aunt's room and snuggled up to her. I felt safer there.

This is what happened on Tuesday 11th June

It gets harder and harder to write about these things. There are so many ghastly memories. But I want to write everything down as it happened if I can, so here goes.

As it began to grow light, I crept to the window. My eyes ached as I peered through the binoculars. Through the fog and drizzle, I could make out a ship that had come in close to the cliffs. The other ships were nearer than they had been the night before and some had come along into the little bay off Veules les Roses. Rowing boats and motor boats full of soldiers were trying to reach the ships. Some were succeeding, but German aircraft kept dive-bombing and there was heavy firing from the shore. Then I noticed things floating on the water, bobbing up and down on the waves. Bodies! I rushed away from the window and threw myself down on the bed, burying my head in the pillows. It was too horrible!

I couldn't eat any breakfast, not even when I saw Charles tucking in as usual. But after a while, I was drawn once again back to the window. Keeping my eyes off the sea below us, I focused the binoculars along the cliffs. The fire was raging fiercely in St Valery en Caux and now I could see thousands of soldiers swarming along the cliffs.

Aunty Régine joined me at the window, with Charles held tightly in her arms. She had deep worry lines across her forehead. She said we were in terrible danger if we stayed where we were. But how could we leave? The fighting was moving in our direction. Soon the place would be swarming with soldiers and their weapons. Worst of all, I could see a giant tank creeping along the opposite cliff. We could be shot or blown to pieces. I wished we had left when I first arrived. It might have been safer then. Poor Aunty Régine! She felt so guilty. She said she would never forgive herself if anything happened to me. She would never be able to face my parents again.

I bit my lip to stop myself crying, thinking Mama and Papa must be worried out of their minds. Aunty Régine put her arm round me and we moved away from the window. I swallowed hard. I had to try and convince myself that the tanks wouldn't fire in our direction. It wasn't that easy. Charles began to whimper, so I found his cuddly blanket and gave it to him.

At that moment, without any warning, there was an enormous explosion, louder than I had ever heard before. The door crashed off its hinges and the window blew in. Glass splintered on to the floor. I think I screamed, but the next few moments were so confusing, I'm not sure what happened. I found myself cowering, with Aunty Régine and Charles, under the big oak table in the kitchen, absolutely petrified, too scared to cry.

We lay there on the floor for hours, with me gripping the table leg so hard my shoulders ached. I flinched at each explosion as the fighting went on and on outside. Aunty Régine's face was as pale as the cliffs below us. She just lay there, staring blindly at nothing. Charles was clinging to his mama and whimpering. Poor little boy! He didn't know what was going on. After a while, I started singing to him. It helped me cope with the noise and my fear. I began to feel a bit calmer. But all the while, I had one ghastly thought going round and round in my head. It only needed one of those shells to fly in our direction then it would be "Goodbye, Sophie". I didn't want to die.

The noise was deafening – the metallic rumbling of the tanks as they came nearer, the boom of the ships' guns, the whistle of the shells followed by the earth-shaking explosion as each one landed, the whining of the aircraft as they zipped overhead, the ack-ack-ack of their guns, the constant firing of machine guns, the sudden crack of rifles, the shouts and screams of men.

I wasn't thinking of the soldiers out there at that moment: how many were dying or wounded. All I could think of was: would we come out of this alive?

This is what happened on
Wednesday 12th June, midday

The fighting carried on well into the night, but I must have gone to sleep eventually, even with all that noise. Suddenly, I was wide awake. I opened my eyes and listened. It was broad daylight though I've no idea what time it was. Everything had gone quiet. Aunty Régine and Charles were snuggled together, still fast asleep, so I slowly dragged myself out from under the table and stood up. I felt incredibly stiff in all my joints. Then I heard voices.

I hurried to the living room, treading carefully across the broken glass, and peered out of the window. I gasped. There were hundreds of soldiers quite close by. I couldn't tell which nationality most of them were, but I recognized the Germans that stood guard over them. (They wear dome-shaped helmets.) A few ships were still out there on the water, in the distance, except for one that seemed to be lying at a slight angle in the shallow water, pretty close to the beach. It was on fire.

I ran back to the kitchen and gently nudged Aunty Régine. She opened her eyes. For a moment, she didn't seem to realize where she was, then she blinked. I told her that the fighting had stopped. She said she guessed our soldiers must have surrendered. I couldn't help wondering: what's going to happen now? Are the Germans going to take over the whole of France?

It was time to escape. We grabbed all the food we could find and quickly collected together a few clothes and other essentials, bundled them up and headed out through the open doorway. I ran round the back of the house and found, to my relief, that my bicycle didn't seem to have been damaged. I pushed it round the front and loaded my basket with our things. Then we set off. Keeping our heads down, we ran down the road into the centre of the village. I don't know if the soldiers noticed us, but none of them called out and we weren't stopped.

My hand aches. I seem to have been writing for hours. More later.

This is what happened on Wednesday afternoon

The village of Veules les Roses was devastated. I was horrified at what we saw as we wove our way past deep holes in the road, burnt-out vehicles, weapons and piles of rubble that were the remains of some of the houses. I couldn't bear to look at the bodies lying there. There were so many! It was hideous!

We reached the Rue Victor Hugo. Suddenly, I stopped. I felt faint. I had to sit down on a low wall and put my head between my knees for a moment. I couldn't speak. I just pointed to a large mound of bricks where number 12 had been. Where was Hélène? A young lady appeared from behind the house next door, which was damaged but still standing. She must have seen us there. She told us what had happened. It was a direct hit. Hélène must have been killed instantly. I gasped and covered my mouth with my hands.

Aunty Régine was giving me a strange look. She asked if I had known Hélène. I nodded then shook my head. I wasn't supposed to let out these secrets, even to my own family. But it wouldn't matter so much now, would it? Now she was dead?

Then suddenly, I went cold all over. The thought still sends shivers cascading down my back. I'd been with her in that house. If Hélène had not sent me away … that would have been the end of me! All I wanted was to get home.

The journey took us ages, because of the number of obstacles on the road and the number of other people like us who were escaping from their damaged or ruined homes. Anyway, I had no energy left and it was a struggle even to walk. But at last, we were there, on the edge of my village.

Suddenly, we were surrounded. Everyone was shouting and crowding round us as if we were film stars. They were all thanking God that I was safe. They had thought I must be dead.

Someone must have run ahead of us. At that moment, Sebastien raced from the direction of our house. He flung himself at me, nearly knocking me over. It was the second hug I had had from him in a very short time, and if I hadn't been ready for tears again, I might have thought up something rude to say to him! But I felt too emotional for that, especially when I saw Mama and Papa not far behind him.

Mama shouted at me and asked me what I thought I was doing, going off like that! I could have got myself killed. She didn't realize how true that was! Then she burst into tears and flung her arms round me. Papa didn't say anything. He just gave me a giant squeeze and kissed the top of my head.

This is what happened late on Wednesday night

I felt quite depressed as we all made our way home. After the fear and excitement of the fighting and the shock of Hélène and all those bodies, I just wanted to bury my head somewhere and be left alone. I climbed the ladder and lay down on my bed, shutting out the sound of voices from downstairs. I didn't even have the energy to write in my diary.

After a while, I went downstairs. Mama was trying to arrange the furniture to fit a small bed in to a corner of the room. I'm going to sleep downstairs for a while so Aunty Régine and Charles can have my room. I don't mind. Why should I mind about something like that when there's a war going on only a few kilometres away? Mind you, I'll have to find a new hiding place for my diary.

Thursday 13th June 11 am
This is now today!

I slept fairly well in my new "bedroom". Early this morning, I heard someone calling me. Then Yvette came in. I felt better for seeing her. I even managed to joke that I didn't need a nurse! Then I told her what had happened. She asked me why I had been to Veules les Roses – I must have known it would be dangerous. I lied that I wanted to see my aunt. She laughed. You can't fool Yvette – not when you've been her best friend all your life. She knows there's another reason. And I haven't had a chance to ask Patrice yet.

I admitted that I was doing something else, but I still couldn't tell her what. I almost did. I wanted to share my feelings about Hélène. I've promised her that I'll talk to someone first and that if he agrees, I'll tell her.

I walked into the village with Yvette. I left her at her house and hurried to Patrice's place. I ran quickly up the path and round the back. I knocked on the kitchen door and it was immediately opened. Patrice looked so relieved to see me. He apologized. He's been feeling bad about sending me with that message. He doesn't know how the news got round that I had gone to Veules les Roses, but the whole village has been talking about me.

I told him the sad news about Hélène. It was really odd. Perhaps war has made some people hard and unfeeling, but when he asked me how she died and I told him about the house being flattened and that she would have died instantly and not suffered, I couldn't believe his reaction. He was just glad that she hadn't been able to give away any secrets! Nothing else. Sometimes I just don't understand how other people's minds work.

Then I told him about Yvette. I said I was sure she would be trustworthy, and he's promised to think about it. I'm not convinced he's really going to think very hard about her because he changed the subject immediately. He says we need a new contact in Veules les Roses.

I called in on Grandma on the way home and told her all about my adventure in Veules les Roses.

6 pm

I've found a new hidey-hole for this diary. It's not as convenient as my own room, of course, but I think it's a very good place – under the nesting boxes in the hen house!

Also, for the first time in ages I've got something happy to write in my diary. Well, I hope it's happy because I'm extremely worried as well. I'll write about how my good news happened.

There's still no school. I've been feeling really restless and I can't settle down to anything. My brain is so full of everything that happened in Veules les Roses so I cycled over to Yvette's this afternoon. She's itching to hear Patrice's answer.

I told her I had other things on my mind. I needed to find out what was going on. What's happened to all those soldiers? Did their leaders surrender? Are they all prisoners? I suggested to her that we could go up to the main road and see if there's anything happening. She was scared that it would be dangerous. I told her we'd be fine because the fighting had stopped, although I was a bit apprehensive, too.

As we sped along the lane, I told her about when I had first seen the refugees. I thought we could go to the same spot because we would get the best view from there.

Before we reached the brow of the hill, we could hear the rhythmic crunch of marching feet. Then we saw them. A long column of soldiers stretched in both directions as far as we could see; thousands and thousands of them, French, English and Scottish, I guessed, marching away from Veules les Roses. They were all prisoners of war.

German guards marched on both sides of the road. From the way the prisoners were moving, I thought they looked dejected and tired. Lots of them were bandaged, many were limping and some were being carried on stretchers. I felt so sorry for them. They must feel miserable. How far would they have to walk? Where would they end up? Was Angus among them?

Suddenly, a familiar sound carried up towards us and an enormous smile spread over my face. It was the weird howl and groan of the bagpipe. It was the Scottish soldiers. We could see the piper striding proudly along in his kilt. At least he was still alive! Quite near the piper, I noticed a soldier with a massive bandage round his head. He was limping badly. At that moment, the soldier fell down. Yvette must have been watching him, too, because we both gasped.

Then the soldier neatly rolled over and dropped into the ditch at the side of the road. None of the German guards had noticed! I couldn't be sure whether he was so badly wounded that he couldn't go on or whether he had done it on purpose. Was he trying to escape?

But there was no way we could find out. We couldn't go down there to investigate. We just had to wait. The crocodile of prisoners kept coming and coming and I couldn't believe how many there were, but at last they had all gone. The road was empty.

I was expecting the soldier to climb out of the ditch, but nothing happened. I looked at Yvette and I'm sure she was thinking exactly the same thing. Perhaps he was really badly wounded. Perhaps he hadn't rolled over on purpose. Perhaps he needed our help.

Keeping an eye out for any remaining German soldiers, we crept down the slope towards the road. As we approached the ditch, I thought I heard a sound and I dodged down, pulling Yvette down with me. We waited and listened. There it was again – a low moaning noise. Yvette's eyes lit up with excitement. We both knew it was the soldier.

I crept slowly forward, feeling tense, ready to spring back and run for it. I don't know why, but I was half expecting him to leap up like a Jack-in-a-box at any moment. But we reached the ditch and peered down into it. There, at the bottom, lying in a few centimetres of water, was the soldier. The bandage round his head was dirty and covered in splashes of blood. He was groaning and his muddy face was twisted in pain. But I instantly noticed the brilliant blue eyes that were staring up at us. There was something familiar about those eyes.

Suddenly, I gasped. Angus? I jumped down into the ditch. I showered questions on him, which I'm sure he didn't understand. What had happened to him? Was he badly hurt? Where were they being taken? Were the German soldiers good to them? I wiped some of the mud from his face and could see how deathly pale he was underneath. He must have lost a lot of blood. He was shivering, too, so I thought he might have a fever. He looked very ill and I felt his forehead. It was hot. Then I glanced up at Yvette, who was staring down with a look of disbelief on her face.

She wanted to know how I knew his name, but I said I'd tell her later. Angus needed a doctor, but when I suggested that to him, he certainly understood and I saw fear in his eyes. He tried to get up. He made me promise that I wouldn't fetch a doctor. I guessed he couldn't trust anyone. A doctor might give him away. He's an escaped prisoner of war. If he's caught now, he'll be shot. But if I didn't fetch a doctor, was Angus going to die? I tried to lift him, but I couldn't budge him. He seemed to be stuck in the mud at the bottom of the ditch.

After heaving and pushing for ages, I helped him shift to one side, so he wasn't lying in the water, then climbed back up to Yvette. I'd had an idea. I leaned over the ditch and told Angus to stay where he was (as if he could do anything else) and said we'd be back as soon as we could.

I'm at the house now. Yvette went home, but she's coming back soon, and I've sneaked down the garden. I'm trying to ignore the German guard at the level crossing and I'm sitting on the hens' feeding trough writing this! I've been trying to organize some help, but it's been difficult and now I'm waiting for Sebastien to get the next part sorted out. I'm feeling so impatient. We need to get back to Angus as quickly as we can. I couldn't bear it if he died. It has done me good to write it all down.

Evening

Phew! What a hectic, terrifying, exciting time we've had!

On the way home, I had told Yvette how I knew Angus and revealed my idea for his rescue, which ended with him hiding up in our house. I was sure we could make it work, but when I told Mama, she went into a panic and told me we'd all get shot. Also she reminded me that we didn't have any room now Aunty Régine and Charles are here.

Anyway, we soon got round that. Grandma came into the kitchen. She had overheard our conversation and offered to look after Angus herself.

She repeated that it would take more than a few Germans to finish her off! In the end, it was Aunty Régine who came up with the answer. She is going to stay at Grandma's with Charles so that leaves room for Angus.

At that moment, Sebastien arrived home with Marcel and Olivier. I looked at Grandma and put my finger to my lips. Of course, we knew we could trust Marcel and Sebastien, but Olivier wasn't in our group. You can never be sure! I took Sebastien out into the garden to explain what Yvette and I had been doing. He was really impressed with me. He beckoned to Marcel and they had a private conversation. A few minutes later, Olivier went home to the farm.

That was when I went to the hen house to write about everything. Then Yvette came back and we stood by the front gate, waiting. Sebastien and Marcel were nowhere to be seen. We had to get back to Angus. Suppose the Germans found him before we got back. Suppose he died before we could save him. My life seemed to me to be one waiting game after another.

But I was totally amazed ten minutes later, when Olivier Masson crossed over the railway line and stopped outside our gate. He was sitting high up on his papa's cart, which was being drawn by an old bay mare. On the back of the cart was a large pile of straw. Sebastien was running behind the cart. Olivier grinned. He's one of us and I didn't even realize it.

Yvette and I scrambled up on to the cart behind Olivier. Sebastien rode up front. It was a very bumpy ride and Yvette and I had to hang on tightly, but I didn't care. It had been my idea, to borrow Mr Masson's cart, but I had been wondering how I could explain it to Mr Masson without giving anything away. It had been easier than I thought. I was really pleased that Olivier was one of us! As we rode we concocted a story about where we were going and what we were doing, in case we were questioned.

We reached the brow of the hill overlooking the main road and Olivier stopped the cart. We all glanced around us. After all the activity of the past few days, it was uncannily quiet. I slipped down and ran to the ditch while Oliver took the cart down on to the main road. I knelt at the side of the ditch and peered down. I told Angus we'd come to rescue him.

His eyes were closed and my heart lurched. Was he dead? To my relief, his eyes fluttered open and he tried to smile, then he winced. He was obviously in dreadful pain, but at least he was alive! I beckoned to the others. I'm glad we had the two boys with us. They may not be equal to us girls in many ways, but I have to admit their superior strength was very useful!

Gently, Sebastien and Olivier pushed a wide plank of wood underneath Angus. He cried out as they moved him. Yvette and I kept a look-out. Then the boys carefully raised him out of the ditch and on to the cart. We covered him in straw then quickly climbed up ourselves. Olivier flicked the reins and clicked out of the side of his mouth to set the horse in motion. The whole operation had only taken us about five minutes.

The journey back to the village seemed to last forever. No one spoke. We were all feeling too tense. My brain was racing. Supposing we met a

German patrol? Would our made-up story convince them? Would they search the cart and find Angus?

We had almost reached the village when I heard the sound of a motorbike heading our way. As it came towards us I could see the dome-shaped helmet I recognized so well. I felt disgust in the pit of my stomach. A German!

I whispered to Angus to keep still and stay quiet. I just hoped he understood me. I crossed my fingers and everything else I could think of and held my breath as the German approached. Would he speed right by? Then my worst nightmare was happening. He was slowing down.

As he came alongside the cart, he stopped. He held up his hand and Olivier pulled on the reins. The horse obeyed and the cart came to a standstill. I prayed that Angus would not give us away. The German sat astride his motorbike, keeping the engine running, and indicated with a wave that we should all get down. He spoke quite good French. He asked where we were going. Olivier said we were going home to the farm. He looked the German in the eye, but I could hear a slight tremor in his voice. The German nodded. He pointed at the straw and asked what it was. I put on my best appealing expression as I told him it was straw for the animals, but I desperately hoped he wouldn't notice my entire body shaking.

The German frowned and said that it's summer so the animals are in the fields and don't need straw. Luckily, we had thought of this! Olivier was ready with the answer: that he has two sick horses that need fresh straw every day.

I couldn't make out whether the German had understood, but his frown didn't go away. He pointed at the straw, which was piled in an untidy heap on the cart. Then he formed a bundle with his hands. I almost panicked. We hadn't anticipated this question. Why wasn't the straw in a bundle? I dare not look at the others in case we gave ourselves away. I had to think fast. Suddenly, I had a brainwave.

I smiled and lowered my eyes. Then I tried to look highly embarrassed, pointed at Olivier and said that he was my boyfriend. Yvette caught on. She pointed at Sebastien and told the German that they were in love. I don't know how she managed it, but she actually blushed! Both the boys looked stunned for a second then they nudged each other and grinned sheepishly at the soldier.

The German looked from one to another of us. I could see the cogs of his brain working it all out. Two boys, two girls, the girls' clothes covered in bits of straw, one of the girls blushing, the other one seeming shy, the boys looking pleased with themselves... He was coming to the conclusion I had hoped for – that we had all been rolling in the straw!

After a moment, a slow smile replaced the frown on the German's face. The engine roared and he accelerated away. We stood there for ages, unable to move. It was Olivier who broke the silence. He patted the top of my head and said he didn't know I cared! I grinned, the relief flooding into me now the immediate danger was over. Then I noticed Sebastien staring at Yvette as if he was seeing her for the first time. She was still blushing. Maybe it hadn't all been an act! Is she really in love with my brother? Is he in love with her, too? I'm totally amazed!

We climbed back on to the cart and trundled into the village. When Olivier halted the cart close to our gateway, I jumped down, crept to the corner of the house and peered along the railway. There were two German soldiers about 25 metres away. They were smoking and talking and not looking in our direction. Luckily, there was no one on guard at the crossing gates. I kept watch while Olivier and Sebastien carefully lifted the wooden stretcher down. It took less than a minute to carry Angus inside.

Just as the German soldier returned to his post at the gates, Olivier leapt back on to the cart and flicked the reins. The horse began to walk and Olivier drove the cart across the track, waving to the soldier as he went. Yvette and I hurried indoors. Angus was lying on my bed in the corner and Mama was bending over him. She looked worried. Then she looked up and her eyes were angry. "We'll show those German soldiers," she whispered.

Late

We're waiting for the doctor to come.

A little while ago, Angus stirred in his sleep, but he didn't wake up. He looked dreadful. I wanted to start cleaning him up straight away, but Mama thought we should get him upstairs first. My room is empty because Aunty Régine and Charles have already gone to Grandma's. Sebastien argued that Angus is too ill to move and, anyway, too heavy to lift up the ladder.

Yvette felt Angus's pulse. Seeing her do that made me feel incredibly jealous of her. He's *my* soldier. I'm the one who befriended him at the crossing barrier. I'm the one who recognized him in the ditch. I'm the one who thought up the plan for his rescue. I don't want Yvette taking over! I'm the one to care for Angus.

So I persuaded Mama to fill a bowl with warm water mixed with disinfectant. She found an old sheet and ripped it into strips then she dipped a strip into the water. I took it from her and squeezed the liquid from the cloth, gently wiping more dirt and dried blood from Angus's face. Then I took some little scissors and began to cut at the bandage. I had to grit my teeth. I dreaded what I might find underneath. As I unwound the lengths of cloth, I revealed his tangled hair, matted with sweat, mud and blood. Then I saw the wound.

I gasped and turned my eyes away, feeling dizzy. The gash is deep and long. It stretches from his forehead right across the crown of his head, like a parting drawn by a deadly comb. I wonder how it had happened. If it had been two centimetres lower, he would have been killed!

When I made myself look back, I found Angus's eyes on me. He began mumbling and muttering, but I didn't understand what he was trying to say. So I began to bathe the wound as gently as I could. He was so brave. He winced a few times, but didn't cry out although it must have been dreadfully painful. Yvette was watching closely.

The more I washed the wound, the more I realized how deep it is. He needs stitches. All around the cut, Angus's head is red and looks very sore. It must be infected. That must be why he has a fever. Even Yvette, who was such a good nurse to the other Scottish soldiers, hasn't the skill to heal this or to bring his temperature down.

Sebastien ran round to Patrice Cariat's house. He is sure there must be a doctor in the network. I carried on washing away all the dirt in the wound and Mama fetched several changes of water. Angus began tossing and turning on the little bed. He was awake one minute and in a deep sleep the next. He seemed to be getting worse. Sometimes, he groaned and his face was screwed up in pain. His head felt so hot. I was really worried. I knew he desperately needed the doctor. I wished Sebastien wasn't taking so long.

Papa came home from working late at the farm a few minutes ago. He wanted to know what on earth we were doing, getting ourselves in danger for the sake of this young Scotsman, but I'm sure he didn't mean anything. He soon recovered from the shock of seeing Angus and he's on our side, of course.

We were all going mad with impatience by the time Sebastien came back. (He smiled at Yvette. She blushed again. Yuck! Fancy being in love with my brother!) Then he told us about a doctor in Luneray who can be trusted. Patrice has gone to fetch him now. Sebastien has a coded message to say when he arrives. The doctor has to reply then we'll know it's really him.

I feel that same shiver of excitement as when I took that first message to poor Hélène. We're really involved – the fighting, the enemy outside, an escaped prisoner and now another coded message. Then I look down at the pale thin face and my worry returns. I wish the doctor would hurry up and come.

Very late

At last, he's been.

I heard the noise of a bicycle being leant against the wall outside. I held my breath, praying it was the doctor, not an enemy soldier. There was a sharp knock on the door and I felt my stomach tighten. We all looked at each other in silence as Sebastien went to the door. I heard him speak, "It'll be a full moon tonight." I held my breath, waiting for the reply. A deep voice replied, "But there are storms heading our way." Was it the right answer?

It must have been, because Sebastien let him in. I let out a loud sigh. Yvette did the same. She was obviously feeling as tense as I was. The doctor said his name is Dr Boulais. He's quite young with dark hair and deep brown eyes. He went straight over to Angus and felt his pulse. Then he peered closely at the wound. Angus opened his eyes. He tried to sit up and push the doctor away, but I told him it was all right and that this doctor is a friend.

Angus relaxed back on to the bed and closed his eyes again. Dr Boulais washed his hands then began working on the wound. He said I'd done a good job of cleaning it up. His praise made me feel warm inside. I smiled at him and stayed close by as he found a needle and thread in his bag and began to stitch. Yvette watched closely, but Sebastien went up to his room. He's a bit squeamish.

The doctor was almost finished when there was another knock at the door. Everyone froze. We all stared at each other with wide eyes, not daring to move or make a sound. Who could it be? Mama went to the door. I heard her open it. Then I heard her talking and another female voice answering. It was only Yvette's mama. What a relief!

Yvette headed for the door. She said she'd better go home with her mama now and she'd see us tomorrow. I said something to her that I regret. I warned her not to tell her mama about Angus. She glared at me as if she would like to see me taken away by the enemy. Of course she won't, any more than I will and I know I'd be offended if anyone said that to me, but I couldn't help saying it. I've upset her. I hope she'll forgive me.

When the doctor had finished, he said how dangerous it is here with the German guards outside. He didn't need to remind us that one of the soldiers could glance through the window and see Angus. He thought we should try and get him upstairs. So Sebastien and Papa pulled from above and Dr Boulais pushed from below and they managed to lift Angus up the ladder. Now he's sleeping peacefully in my bed.

Dr Boulais is very worried about Angus. He's coming back tomorrow. I hope Angus won't die in the night – especially in my bed.

Friday 14th June

He didn't die in the night, but he's still desperately ill. I've spent all day sitting beside him. I've bathed his forehead and given him sips of water. He's slept most of the time, so I've been reading my English book and practising some phrases.

Dr Boulais came this morning. He told us he left his bicycle behind a hedge and came across the fields to our house. He wants to avoid being stopped by the German guards. He thinks Angus will pull through, as he puts it. I hope that means he's going to get better.

Mama says she heard on the wireless that many people have fled from Paris because they fear the Germans are going to attack.

Evening

About seven o'clock this evening, I heard a tap on the door. I crept to the top of the ladder and listened as Mama opened it. I'm sure my heart stopped beating for a moment and I almost overbalanced and fell headfirst down the ladder when I heard who it was – Georges Dubois! What did he want? Not me, for certain. I know well what he thinks of me! So I thought it must be about Angus, but it couldn't be. No one knows about him, except for my family, plus Olivier, Marcel, Patrice, Dr Boulais and Yvette. And they wouldn't give him away, would they?

Mama asked him what he wanted and he asked if Sebastien was in. Mama said he was over at the farm. I was dying to warn Mama about Georges, but I had to stay silent and still and I just hoped she wouldn't invite him in. Luckily, Georges just said it didn't matter and it wasn't important, then he left.

Mama closed the door and came to the bottom of the ladder. She looked worried. She told me that there's something about Georges that she can't quite put her finger on and I said I knew what it was. Then I told her that he likes the Germans being here! And I added that he knows what I think.

That scares me. And I don't reckon he came to see Sebastien at all.

It was just an excuse to come here, I'm sure. We're going to have to be extra careful from now on, if he's going to be snooping around.

Saturday 15th June

Today we heard some terrible news on the wireless. The Germans have taken over Paris:

"There has been fighting in the streets. German swastika flags are flying from all the important buildings. Thousands of people are streaming out of the city, some in cars, but most of them on foot. They are fleeing in every direction. As they escape, many of these refugees are being attacked from the air. Enemy planes have dive-bombed or cut through the crowds with machine-gun fire. Hundreds are being killed or wounded."

I shuddered, remembering the way those aircraft had attacked me. Those German airmen are cowards. Our capital city is in the hands of the enemy. What will happen now?

Evening

Angus is still sleeping most of the time. He tosses and turns, and I've been sitting with him, bathing his head with cold water to try to lower his temperature. I don't feel jealous of Yvette now. She's been round and I let her spend some time by his bedside. She seems to have forgiven me for what I said. She was bursting with excitement when she arrived. Patrice has allowed her to join the group. Well, he couldn't really refuse after she helped rescue Angus, could he? I gave her a big hug. I'm really pleased, too. It's like old times. I don't have to keep secrets from my best friend now.

Dr Boulais came again. He thinks there is some sign of improvement, and Angus's temperature is down so the cold water must be doing some good. When the bandages were changed, I could see that the wound isn't so infected. It's healing well.

Sunday 16th June

Angus is definitely improving. Today, I managed to persuade him to drink some soup. He opens his eyes quite often. They're so blue. He smiles a lot, too, and keeps thanking me. Dr Boulais says he's so pleased with Angus that he won't come tomorrow unless we call him. He'll come back the next day to take out the stitches.

This evening, after the doctor had gone, Georges came round again. Sebastien saw him cycling down the lane and went out to meet him. I watched from the window. They talked for a few minutes then Georges went away. When Sebastien came inside he was seething. He called Georges a German-loving moron. Neither of us can stand him. I asked Sebastien what Georges wanted. He apparently asked to borrow a bicycle pump. I couldn't believe it. What a feeble excuse!

We understand his game. We're sure he doesn't know about Angus or we would have had a visit from the enemy by now, but he suspects we're up to something. He also asked Sebastien why he is suddenly much friendlier with Marcel than he used to be. We know Georges is dangerous. We'll have to be even more careful and warn the others. He just needs to pick up one piece of evidence and we'll have real problems.

Monday 17th June

Shocking news! We all listened to the wireless this evening. Our Prime Minister is a traitor. He's asked the Nazis (these are the real nasty Germans who are true followers of Hitler) for an armistice (a kind of peace treaty) where our leaders would sign an agreement that says we don't mind the Germans taking over France. What a lie! Of course we mind – very much. This is terrible. We're all devastated. I'm also extremely angry.

Angus is getting stronger. If I help him to sit up he manages to eat a bit.

Evening

The postman came today, which is really surprising considering what's been going on. He had a letter for me. I felt so excited as I took the envelope. I had recognized the writing. It's from Anais. I quickly ripped it open and pulled out a single sheet of paper. I could hardly read it through my tears:

Dear Sophie,

I hope this reaches you without any trouble. After we left your lovely village we walked for several more days. We had to hide from the German army three times along the route, but eventually we came to the River Seine. We had difficulty getting across. We were stopped by German sentries on the bridge and I thought they were going to take Mama prisoner because she had lost one of her papers.

Then we walked and walked and walked. I thought we would never stop. At last we were picked up by a very kind farmer and he took us to his farmhouse. We are settled well here, but we have to work from sunrise to sunset as all the men have gone to war. It is hard, but at least we have a roof over our heads and we are not hungry.

I hope the war does not reach you. Please write if you can and tell me how you and your family are doing. You can reach me at the farm (the address is at the top of the letter).

We still have no news of my Papa, but we still pray all the time.

Grosses bises,

Anais

I'm so relieved she's found somewhere safe, but it must be so sad not knowing where your papa is or whether he is alive or dead. I've decided to write back to her. Mama's warned me not to tell her any details about what's been happening here. She said my letter could fall into enemy hands. I shall be very careful. After the cruelty I've seen lately, I don't want to risk anything.

Tuesday 18th June

Yesterday, our most important military leader, General de Gaulle, fled to England. He's spoken out against our government and so he's an enemy to them as well as the Germans. He's going to live over there, in exile. Some people are calling him a coward, running away from France when we're in trouble, but Papa thinks it's the best place for him to be to try and help the French people. If he stayed in France he could be captured and imprisoned or executed and then he wouldn't be any help to our country.

We managed to pick up a wireless broadcast from London. This is what General de Gaulle said:

"Frenchmen, Frenchwomen. Be strong. Keep fighting. The War will be won. Whatever happens, the flame of French Resistance must not and will not be extinguished."

That's exactly what we believe in! It makes me even more determined to go on fighting.

Angus had his stitches out today. He looked very pale and winced a lot as Dr Boulais pulled them out one by one. I feel proud of myself. I didn't mind watching – not like Sebastien. I thought he was going to faint.

Wednesday 19th June

I'm all of a flutter. It's Angus. I think I'm in love with him! This evening, I was sitting beside him, reading my English book as the light began to fade. Suddenly, he whispered my name. It made me jump and I felt a blush spread over my face. I spoke to him in English and asked how he was feeling. He told me he's much better. He smiled. He's really good-looking when he does that! And his eyes – they're so brilliant blue and sparkly. Then he started talking much too quickly. I held up my hand to stop him. From then on we spoke half English, half French. We coped quite well.

He asked me where he was and how he got here. Of course, I told him about Sebastien, Yvette and Olivier and the ditch and the cart and even the German motorcyclist. He listened in silence then he thanked me. We're gradually beginning to understand each other more and more. He's sitting up most of the time now although he sometimes feels dizzy.

Mama came upstairs with some food for him. She says he needs to build up his strength. He smiled at Mama and thanked her for everything. He knows he's putting us all in danger and that he can't stay here much longer. I don't want him to go. I told him he's too ill to be moved.

The door opened downstairs. It was Sebastien. He had been at the Cariats' house all evening. He came up the ladder. Apparently, Patrice says we must move Angus as soon as possible. He knows a safe house where Angus can stay until he is strong enough to travel. I wanted to argue that he's safe here, but I know that's not true, especially since Sebastien told us some bad news. He's worried about the guards outside, but worse than that, Georges and a couple of his friends have been asking more questions. Even worse than that, Sebastien is sure he was followed this evening.

I bit my lip. I was too full of emotion to speak. I have to admit it really is becoming too dangerous to keep Angus in our house. What would happen to all of us if he was discovered? Anyway, there's a plan. We just have to hope no one finds him before tomorrow. Tomorrow, after dark, Angus will leave.

I've just closed the shutters. A guard was watching me from his post at the barrier. I instantly froze inside, but I tried to act normally. Does he suspect anything? Is he about to come knocking on our door and arrest us all?

Thursday 20th June

This morning, Sebastien brought Angus a bundle of his clothes and told him to put them on. Angus nodded. Sebastien told him to try and practise walking, but to stay out of sight of the windows. He also said that Marcel will be coming round this afternoon with instructions. I'll have several jobs to do. Then we all have to be ready when the signal comes.

I've felt twitchy all morning, listening for the guard outside, dreading the sharp rap on the door and thinking of what we had to do later on. I came downstairs so that Angus could get changed in private. I could hear him moving about in my room above. His footsteps sounded unsteady and slow. Later, I climbed the ladder and went to join him. Angus was sitting on the bed, dressed in Sebastien's clothes. He looked so different. Really French! I giggled, but then I saw he had such a sad expression on his face. He told me he kept having flashbacks of the battle in St Valery en Caux. Many of his friends died, he told me.

He seemed to want to talk about it so I sat down beside him. Half in English, half in French, he told me all about it. He began with the strong German attack as his regiment tried to defend the port. I understood some of what he said and guessed a lot more. Some of it I knew already. The soldiers had been ordered to fight as long as possible to protect

St Valery, then there was the promise of warships coming to rescue them. They fought like dogs, but there were German tanks and planes. The Scottish and French soldiers only had their smaller weapons.

They had to go down into the town, which was on fire by then. (I knew about this – I saw it from Aunty Régine's window.) He saw people running in terror. Then after hours of fighting, the French General surrendered. Angus was shocked. Scotsmen don't like to give in. They always fight to the end. So they fought on. His best friend, Jock, was killed right in the centre of St Valery en Caux.

Angus had tears in his eyes. I felt choked, too, so I held his hand and we sat in silence for a while. Then he was ready to go on. He remembered rain and black fog over the sea. He saw that the ships had arrived so they went to the port, but the enemy aircraft were dive-bombing and they couldn't leave. So they went along the cliffs. It was then that something hit his head. Next thing he knew, his head was bandaged and he discovered that they had surrendered. Straight away, he knew he had to escape.

He lay down and turned his face to the wall. I guess it was all too much for him, telling me about something so dreadful that had happened to him such a short time ago. I left him for a while, and when I returned with some hot chocolate and some warm bread from the baker, he rolled over and looked up at me.

I'm blushing as I write this! He told me how kind I am and that he likes me. The blood rushed to my face and there was an ache in my chest. It was so different from the feelings I had for Georges. How can I have imagined that I was in love with him? It's Angus I'm in love with! I kissed his cheek and he blushed, too. Is he in love with me?

He took my hand and reminded me (as if I wanted to be reminded) that he has to leave tonight. I nodded. I didn't dare speak for fear of bursting into tears.

Later

Marcel came around lunchtime with the plans for Angus's escape. By the time he had finished, I realized I had an important part to play. I've been extremely busy this afternoon. I've had a list of jobs to do and an enormous amount to memorize. I was itching to begin, even though I knew that this meant Angus would be leaving us. Just before Marcel left, he gave me a coded message and two written ones. He told me not to let anyone get their hands on these messages. He warned me that it's not only the German soldiers we have to watch, but there are several French people like Georges who are befriending the enemy. They wouldn't hesitate to betray us.

I promised him that the messages would be safe. I'll hide them in my knickers – not that I'd tell him that!

So off I went, always remembering Marcel's warning to be careful. First, I called at a house in Luneray and delivered the coded message.

I said, "The wheat is ready to be harvested," to the young woman who opened the door. I waited nervously for her answer. She smiled then replied, "And everyone is ready to harvest it." It was the right answer. Then I told her the full message. I was pleased that my first job had gone well.

Next I cycled to a little village a few kilometres away. As I entered the village, I had a creeping sensation on the back of my neck. I was convinced I was being followed, but every time I looked round, there was no one there. Just to be sure, I dodged round a few corners and doubled back. I'm pretty quick on my bicycle and I must have shaken off my follower, if there was one.

I felt very tense all the while as I left the two written messages, one under a flowerpot and the other behind a loose brick in a wall. I didn't relax until I was safely home again.

Papa was working over at the farm as usual and Sebastien was not at home. It seemed very quiet in the house. I could tell Mama was not in a good mood. All her movements were hurried and jerky. She snapped at me when I got in her way. She's had a letter from her bosses ordering her to obey the Germans. She's livid, but if she refuses she'll lose her job – apart from making the soldiers angry – and she doesn't want that.

Angus was in the living room, walking slowly around, but keeping well away from the window, as instructed. He kept clutching his hands together and frowning and taking deep breaths. I stayed there with him. I think he feels the same as me. He doesn't really want to leave, but at the same time, he can't wait for it all to be over.

Late

He's gone! I'm heartbroken!

It was quite dark. We were waiting for Sebastien, Marcel and Olivier to arrive and the escape plan would begin. Mama had just come in from opening the crossing gates for the final train of the day when we heard voices outside. It didn't sound like any of the boys or Papa. It must have been instinct, but I had this horrible feeing that we were in deadly danger.

I hissed at Angus and beckoned for him to follow me. I dashed to the back window, opened it, checked that there was no one around and jumped out. I had to help Angus climb over the sill then, keeping low, we ran through the garden to the empty hen house. I opened the door and shoved him in, pushing him down behind the nesting boxes, close to where I hide this diary.

There was no time to pause there. As I dashed back to the house and climbed back in through the window, I could hear raised voices in the kitchen. Mama was shouting, "How dare you?" It was Georges Dubois she was shouting at. It seemed he had walked into the house uninvited. Mama told him Sebastien wasn't at home, but he said they hadn't come to see Sebastien. They had come to see what he called "our visitor".

I stayed where I was, listening. There was someone else in the kitchen. Who was with Georges? Then I heard a second voice. He was speaking French, but with a strong accent – a German accent! He said he believed we had a guest staying here. Mama's so good at thinking on her feet. She laughed and pretended she thought they meant Aunty Régine and little Charles. She rattled on about how their house in Veules les Roses was badly damaged by the German attack.

But the German interrupted. He said it was not Mama's sister or her infant they wanted to see, but a male. I stepped into the kitchen at that moment. I went up to Georges and smiled at him although my guts were churning uncontrollably. I mentioned Sebastien, but Georges snapped back. He said he already knew he's not here. So I quizzed him. So why was he here? Then I put on my very best act (while feeling sick). I stepped closer and asked him if the truth was that he's in love with *me*!

Mama and the German looked astonished, but the expression on Georges's face was grotesque. It was so ugly. He stepped back from me and told me angrily not to be so ridiculous. I don't know where this would have led if Sebastien had not arrived at that moment with Olivier and Marcel. Georges went for them, saying he knew we had someone staying here. I have to admire my coolness, even though everyone must have noticed my shaking limbs. I told him the truth – that there was no one in this house except us, and that if he would like to search, that was fine by everyone here.

I saw a startled look in Marcel's eyes, but Sebastien and Olivier have seen my acting before. They didn't look too worried.

Georges and the soldier searched the whole house. Georges seemed confident at first, talking loudly and laughing. He was so certain of himself, but gradually he grew quieter and then silent. A frown developed across his forehead and I could see he was becoming angry. He had been so sure he was right.

I was beginning to feel confident that Angus was safe, but suddenly, Georges reached the living-room window. He stood still and grimaced at me. Then he began laughing loudly as he pointed through the darkness. He was convinced that he knew where our visitor was – "in Sophie's precious hen house!"

He shot out of the back door, turned on a powerful torch and raced across the grass with all of us close behind him. I felt sick and so scared I could hardly force my legs to carry me, but when Georges rushed through the enclosure and burst into the little wooden building, I thought I would die of relief. It was empty!

Georges was furious. He shouted at us all – we had won this time, but he knows there's something going on and he'll get us next time. He stormed back up the garden with the German soldier on his tail, leaving us quaking and quivering in the darkness. I burst into tears. I had no idea where Angus was.

Suddenly, Angus emerged out of the darkness and came and stood close to me. Luckily, he had guessed his hideout might be found. I hugged him, but Marcel was pulling him away. He said Angus must go immediately, while Georges is out of the way and before he decides to come back.

There was no time to say goodbye. Sebastien fetched the small suitcase of clothes for Angus and a cap, which he would have to wear to cover his injury. Then they were leaving, four "French" boys walking close together, talking only in whispers. I felt totally deflated and disappointed. I had imagined kissing Angus and both of us whispering that we would never forget each other, but there had been nothing.

I was just about to turn away and go back indoors, when Angus lifted his arm and waved. I waved back and blew a kiss.

Friday 21st June

I've moved back up into my bedroom. Sebastien says that they rendezvoused with Patrice last night. He had papers prepared and took Angus to meet one of the contacts who had received a message earlier, thanks to me. Poor Angus! I bet he's feeling exhausted. I don't know where he'll go from there. The network spreads a long way. Somehow they are trying to get Angus out of France, but it will be a long hard journey for him. Eventually, I hope he'll get back to Scotland. I miss him. Will I ever hear from him again? I do hope so.

Saturday 22nd June

I keep thinking about Angus. Where is he now?

Aunty Régine came round to see us. She wants to go home. Mama tried to persuade her to stay in the village for a while. She'll be safer here. But Aunty Régine won't change her mind. She wants to be at home in case there's news from Uncle Thierry.

So Papa, Sebastien and I went to Veules les Roses to see how badly her house has been damaged. As we passed along the streets, we found that many of the people of the village have returned home already. There was lots of hammering and sawing as people repaired broken roofs and replaced doors. There were a few German soldiers keeping guard on the edge of the village, but they ignored us. Other soldiers were removing burnt-out vehicles. Thankfully, there was no sign of the bodies that had littered the streets.

As we passed number 12 Rue Victor Hugo, I glanced sadly at the pile of rubble. I whispered to Sebastien that it was where Hélène lived. I had already told him about her horrible death. We climbed the steep road up to Aunty Régine's house. I was surprised to see that, apart from the door that had blown in and the panes of glass shattered on the front of the house, it didn't look too bad. Papa and Sebastien began working on the repairs. I left them to it. I needed to explore. I couldn't help the vivid flashes of memory of the battle that had raged around us. I was thinking about Angus's story.

I walked to the edge of the cliff where Yvette and I had often peered over at the sea. I found our usual spot and lay down on my front. I felt rather shaky. Only a few days ago, there were thousands of soldiers on this cliff.

I looked straight out towards the sea. I blinked and stared again. It was incredible! There, right below me, in the shallows of the low tide, sat an enormous ship. I knew it had gone aground that night, but my first close sighting of it still shook me. It's lying there, leaning slightly to one side, with several large shell holes ripped into its body. Its deck is a complete wreck of blackened and twisted metal. But, there's something even more peculiar. It's a gun, one of the large anti-aircraft guns from the deck of the ship. It's standing like an out-of-place statue in the middle of the pale sandy beach.

After a while, I looked to my left, along the beach. I could see the ruins of armoured cars, and weapons left where they had been dropped. I imagined the hundreds of soldiers still lying where they had fallen, some on the pebbles at the foot of the cliff and many others floating in the sea. The thought turned my stomach over. I've seen so many bodies in the past few days. I just wish that the killing would stop.

I turned away and closed my eyes. Suddenly, I heard a sound. I opened my eyes. A man was walking towards me along the cliff path. I stood up, embarrassed at being caught viewing the scene. He pointed at the wreck of the ship. He thought it was a terrible tragedy that such a fine ship should end like that. He told me it's called the *Cérons* and that there were hundreds of lives lost on these cliffs. I nodded, but didn't tell him that I had been so close.

Sunday 23rd June

It makes me so angry! We heard on the news last night that our Prime Minister has signed the armistice. Everyone was hoping he would be braver than that. He shouldn't have given in so easily. Adolf Hitler came to Paris to sign it. That means Germany rules France. I hate it!

Our neighbour has been along to St Valery en Caux. He says we wouldn't believe the total devastation he found there after the battle. The whole of the town centre is either flattened by shells or bombs or burnt out. I told him I had witnessed some of the fighting through binoculars from Aunty Régine's house. The fire looked so fierce, but his news shocked me, all the same. St Valery is such a nice little town. He says the best thing to do will be to demolish the lot and start again, but that won't be possible at the moment, not with the Germans having taken it over.

Monday 24th June

Aunty Régine and Charles went home this afternoon. Mama and I went with them. Aunty Régine was silent all the way. She seems to have no energy at the moment. I think it's because she hasn't heard from Uncle Thierry for a while. She's on edge, waiting for news. Grandma and Mama had tried to persuade her to stay in our village, but she refused.

Tuesday 25th June

I cycled over to Veules les Roses after school today. Aunty Régine looks better than yesterday. I think she is glad to be home. She's still very pale, but her eyes were shining. She had a letter from Uncle Thierry this morning. Mind you, she still doesn't know where he is.

But there was something else. She said she wanted to talk to me. She reminded me that I had let slip about some kind of secret work. I nodded, but I didn't know how to answer. I still can't tell her about our secret organization. Then she mentioned the house in the Rue Victor

Hugo that was demolished and the old lady that was killed. She also knows what we did for Angus. It's getting very difficult. I know I can trust her, but a promise is a promise, after all, and I gave nothing away.

In the end, I asked her what she was getting at. I was amazed at her answer. She said she can't just sit here and let the enemy tread all over us. She needs to do something. She more or less pleaded with me to help her find something to do.

I remembered what Patrice had said. We need a new contact in Veules les Roses. She would be perfect. But would she be willing to do it? I promised her I'd ask around and let her know.

Wednesday 26th June

It makes me furious. We've had news that Adolf Hitler has been sightseeing in Paris. He went to the Eiffel Tower and other famous monuments. They say he likes our capital city very much. So if this is true, why couldn't he leave it alone?

Thursday 27th June

I've asked Patrice and he's agreed to meet up with Aunty Régine. It'll be really great if she joins the network and it'll be an excuse for me to go and visit her often.

Every day, I think about Angus. I wonder if he got out of France. Perhaps he's already home. I wonder if he'll remember me.

Friday 28th June

Aunty Régine is one of us! She's our agent in Veules les Roses. I'm so excited. I cycled over to see her. Now we don't have to pretend any more and I don't have to hold my tongue when I really want to tell her everything. She's going to be needed even more, too, because Veules les Roses has become a base for German soldiers. They've taken over all the big buildings. The town hall is their headquarters with a *Kommandant* in charge. I haven't seen him yet, but whenever I go to Veules les Roses, I see soldiers everywhere. They're too busy building concrete gun posts

294

overlooking the sea to bother with me. Perhaps they think there'll be an invasion. I wonder if the British will come to our rescue. I hope so.

Saturday 29th June

School has finished for the summer – not that we've been able to learn much in the past few weeks, not since the 51st Highland Division arrived in our village. I somehow think Yvette and I won't be doing the same kind of summer activities as we did last year. There are too many enemy soldiers around. They often stop and search people, but so far they haven't bothered with me.

Tuesday 9th July

I just had to rush upstairs and find my diary – not in the hen house now I have my bedroom back. I have to write what happened straight away. It can't wait. I'm so ecstatically happy. I met the postman outside the house a few minutes ago. He held out a letter and asked if I was Sophie Ridel. I told him I was and he gave me the letter. I studied the envelope.

I thought at first it was from Anais, but the postmark was not from the area where she's living now. My heart started pounding double-time. I suddenly realized it had a Spanish stamp on it. Who do I know in Spain? Nobody – and yet…?

I dashed indoors and I ripped it open. My fingers were shaking so much I could hardly get it open. At last I pulled out a scrap of paper with a message on, written in very good French:

> *Dear Sophie,*
> *I like Spain very much. The journey was long, but I am happy to be here. I will stay for a few days then I will continue my journey. Thanks to everyone, especially to you. I will never forget you.*
> *Love AB*

Angus Brown! He's safely out of France. I feel a warm glow spread right through me. He's remembered me. He says he'll never forget me. And he's sent his love! Maybe I'll see him again when the war is over. I really hope so!

Wednesday 31st July

We're busy from day to day, fighting the enemy. France has been divided into two, sort of diagonally across the middle. Marshal Pétain is in charge of the south and east, but Papa says he's a friend of the Germans anyway. That half is called Vichy France. Our half (north and west) is governed by the Germans, worse luck, so they have control of all the ports along the Channel and the Atlantic. This is why we have to keep fighting against them. They might have taken over our country, but one thing is certain. We'll never be defeated!

General de Gaulle often broadcasts from Britain. He helps raise our spirits. We remember what he said to us when he made that broadcast on the day France surrendered, that all French people should keep on fighting for our freedom. I shall always do that, right until this horrible war is over.

Historical note

In May 1940, the war in Europe started in earnest. When Hitler invaded Holland and Belgium, many thousands of British troops were sent to fight, but soon the German army fought its way into northern France and the soldiers were forced back towards the sea at Dunkerque. It seemed as if they had little chance of escape.

However, the British government put out an appeal to anyone in southern England who owned a boat to travel across the English Channel to help with the rescue of these troops. Many people responded to this appeal and a total of around 700 vessels, including hundreds of tiny craft, bigger boats and warships, came to the rescue. From 26 May to 4 June, they managed to evacuate over 338,000 soldiers from the beaches. This was codenamed Operation Dynamo.

Sadly, several thousand soldiers were killed by German firepower from the ground and from the air. Many thousands were captured and taken away to prisoner-of-war camps in Germany.

Meanwhile, thousands of soldiers of the 51st Highland Division were ordered to remain in France. They were to go to the valley of the River Somme and to defend that area under the command of the French generals.

When they arrived, they found that the French army was in disarray and that the German army was well equipped and too strong. There was much fighting, but it was obvious that the Scottish Division could not win against the might of the German command. The 51st Highlanders were then ordered to withdraw and head in the direction of Rouen and Le Havre to see if they could defend that area and keep the Germans back from the coast. The plan was that, if that failed, it might be possible for the Highlanders to embark for England from there.

However, General Rommel and the 7th German Panzer Division arrived at Rouen and Le Havre first and cut off the escape route. General Fortune, of the 51st Highland Division, chose St Valery en Caux, a small fishing port to the east of Le Havre, for the attempted embarkation.

As the Scottish soldiers approached St Valery en Caux, they were attacked by Rommel's army and the town was heavily bombarded by the German tanks and aircraft and then by the ships that were waiting off-shore to embark the soldiers. The Highlanders fought bravely. The battle raged from 10 to 12 June 1940. Some soldiers were evacuated by small boats from the port to the warships waiting off the coast, but many were killed.

The warships moved along the coast towards Veules les Roses and the soldiers swarmed along the cliffs. Many were killed by the German tanks, machine guns and aircraft. Others were killed falling down the cliffs as they tried to escape. Many men were drowned.

Around 1,300 British and 900 French soldiers managed to escape. One French warship, the *Cérons*, came in too close to the cliffs at Veules les Roses and as the tide went out, it was stuck on the sand. The men on board had to be transferred to another ship.

In the early morning of 12 June 1940, the French general surrendered to Rommel, but the Scots, not willing to give in so easily, fought on. Finally, a few hours later, General Fortune was forced to surrender under the might of the German army. Eight thousand men of the 51st Highland Division were taken prisoner and marched away to German prisoner-of-war camps. A few lucky soldiers managed to escape and, helped by the French people, returned to Britain. Those who were taken prisoner were held in the camps until they were released in 1945, five years later.

The centre of St Valery en Caux was so badly damaged that, after the war, it was totally demolished and rebuilt.

The 51st Highland Division was almost wiped out and had to be built up again with thousands more soldiers. After the Normandy landings on 6 June 1944, they were sent to liberate St Valery en Caux and the surrounding area. They arrived on 2 September 1944.

The French and Scottish soldiers who died between 9 and 12 June 1940 in that area are buried in a war cemetery on the edge of St Valery en Caux. There is also a memorial on the cliffs to the soldiers who died.

High on the east cliff above Veules les Roses is a memorial in the form of a large anti-aircraft gun from the ship, the *Cérons*. Beside the gun are three flagpoles. From the first flutters the Union Flag of Great Britain, from the second, the French *Tricolore* and from the third, the diagonal cross of St Andrew of Scotland. This memorial is directly above the wreck of the *Cérons*. When there is a very low tide, the remains of the *Cérons* can sometimes still be seen, almost 70 years on.

Timeline

1889 Adolf Hitler is born in Austria.

1919 Hitler joins the German Workers' Party.

1920 The German Workers' Party changes its name to The National Socialist Party (Nazis). Hitler chooses the symbol we know as the swastika for the party's emblem.

1921 Hitler becomes leader of the Nazi Party.

1925 Hitler publishes his book, *Mein Kampf*. Germany is going through difficult times and most of the people are poor and hungry. They begin to listen to Hitler's promises of a better life; promises he never fulfils.

1933
30 January Hitler becomes Chancellor of Germany.
26 April The Gestapo is formed and many people who disagree with Hitler are rounded up and imprisoned, tortured or killed.
1933–39 Hitler becomes more and more powerful. He builds up the strength of the German army, navy and air force.

1939

15 March Germany invades Czechoslovakia.

1 September Germany invades Poland.

3 September Britain, France, Australia and New Zealand declare war on Germany.

10 September Canada declares war on Germany.

September 1939–March 1940 is called the "Phoney War" in Britain because there is no fighting in Northern Europe. It almost seems as if there is no war.

1940

20 March Paul Reynaud becomes the new French Prime Minister.

9 April Germany invades Norway and Denmark.

10 May Germany invades Holland, Belgium and Luxembourg.

10 May The British Prime Minister, Neville Chamberlain, resigns and Winston Churchill becomes the new British Prime Minister.

13 May The German army enters France, and the British and French troops are pushed back.

15 May Holland surrenders to the Germans.

26 May The evacuation of British troops begins from Dunkerque.

28 May Belgium surrenders to the Germans.

14 June The German army enters Paris.

16 June Marshal Philippe Pétain takes over as French Prime Minister.

22 June Marshal Pétain signs an armistice with the Nazis. France is split in two. One half, to the north and west, is run by the Germans, who occupy the territory; the other half is run by Marshal Pétain, but he is working under German orders. This second area of France is called Vichy France.

16 July Hitler orders the German military to plan an invasion of Britain – Operation Sealion.

5 August The Battle of Britain begins with heavy bombing raids by German planes.

7 September The London Blitz begins.

12 October Hitler cancels Operation Sealion and turns his attention towards Russia.

1941

22 June Hitler invades Russia.

7 December Japanese planes attack the United States navy in Pearl Harbor on Hawaii in the Pacific Ocean.

8 December America declares war on Japan.

11 December Germany declares war on America.

1942 The conflict has now become a World War, with many countries joining in on both sides. There is fighting in Europe, North Africa, Burma, Hong Kong, Singapore and other areas of the Far East.

1943

Italy, who joined in the War on the side of Germany, is invaded by the Allies.

2 February After a long time of fighting Russia, Germany at last surrenders at Stalingrad.

8 September Italy surrenders.

1944

6 June D-Day: The Allied forces invade the Normandy coast of France, to the west of the River Seine.
The Allies begin to move through France, liberating towns as they go. The German army is in retreat.

25 August Paris is liberated.
There is still much fighting in Europe and in the East. This continues well into the following year.

1945

1 May Germany announces that Hitler is dead.

7 May Germany signs an unconditional surrender.

8 May is celebrated in Europe as VE Day – Victory in Europe Day. There is still fighting in the Far East.

6 August America drops an atomic bomb on Hiroshima, Japan.

9 August America drops an atomic bomb on Nagasaki, Japan.

15 August is celebrated as VJ Day – Victory in Japan Day.

2 September Japan signs an unconditional surrender.
The war is over almost six years to the day after it began.

BLITZ

Vince Cross

Lewisham, London
1940

Saturday 20th July 1940

I jumped out of my skin when the air-raid siren started wailing last evening. I was in the garden picking sweet peas for Mum and the whole bunch nearly went on the ground. It was very hot, even at seven o'clock, and there wasn't a breath of wind, the kind of weather that always makes you feel something's about to happen.

At tea Mum had been saying how rattled everyone seemed. That morning there'd been chatter at the shops. Someone knew for certain the Germans were going to invade this weekend, and they'd be in London by Monday unless our boys looked sharp. There are always rumours doing the rounds. It's difficult to know who to believe.

Anyway, Mum shouted from the kitchen for me to come in at once, sounding panicky. I wasn't going to argue. I couldn't see or hear any German bombers, but I've never been in an air raid. How much time do you have between hearing a bomber fly over your house, and a bomb dropping and blowing you to bits?

As I went up the steps to go inside, I could see old Mrs Andrews from next door. She was walking in circles around her patch of lawn, looking up at the sky and wagging her finger, just like she was giving someone a good telling-off. God or the Germans? Who knows?

From inside our kitchen we could still hear her, the muttering turning into shouting.

"She'll get herself killed, she will," said Mum, sounding anxious and exasperated. "Barmy woman! Whatever's she doing?" Mum wafted me towards the hall. "You, go and get yourself under the stairs quick, while I try to sort Bessie out. As if life wasn't difficult enough!"

We're waiting for a proper air-raid shelter to be put in the garden. The Council's going to deliver one this week. In the meantime we're making do by sitting under the stairs or the kitchen table. It seems daft to me, but Mum says it's better than nothing.

I didn't do what Mum asked. I wanted to see what happened. I watched as she ran down the garden, out the back gate, and into Bessie Andrews's wilderness.

Old Bessie was drifting around in a world of her own. Mum might as well not have been there. Mum tried talking to her softly and when that didn't work she caught Bessie by the shoulders and shook her gently. The mad old woman pulled away and stared in complete amazement as if it was Mum who was off her head. I held my breath, wondering what I'd do if Bessie started hitting out. But she broke away in a sudden flood of tears and scuttled inside to her thirteen cats. Like Mum says, completely barmy!

Because it was Friday evening, and Dad was doing an extra shift at the Fire Station, no one else was at home, so Mum and I crouched together under the stairs listening to the wireless until, fifteen minutes later, the all-clear sounded. Just another false alarm!

Monday 22nd July

When my sister Shirl crept out to go off to work this morning, I lay in bed for an extra half-hour. While the birds chirruped away merrily in the tree outside our window, all I could feel was miserable. It seems so muddled that there can be a beautiful blue sky and thrushes singing their heads off while there's a war with Germany going on, ships being sunk and people shooting at each other.

There's no one left to talk to, now that Maggie's gone. Alison left first, back in the panic last September. Lots of the children from my class at school were evacuated then, to Bexhill in Sussex. Mum says she can't think why they think it's safer there. If the Germans invade, it's the first place they'll arrive. Then, in May, Betty's parents got all nervous and packed her off to her Aunt Sally's in Devon.

Maggie's my best friend. She'd always said her family would never send her away, until last Friday she suddenly mentions casually she's off to Northampton till I don't know when. She might as well be going to the moon, as far as I'm concerned. So here I am all on my own-i-o, and feeling really fed-up and lonely, even if the sky is a wonderful clear blue.

That's why for the first time ever I've decided I'll keep a diary. I'm going to write down my real feelings about the awful, frightening war in this old exercise book. If I haven't got Mags, Alison or Betty to talk to, at least I'll have some way of giving vent to my thoughts and feelings.

Tuesday 23rd July

So I'd better tell you about my family and where we live, hadn't I? I'll make a start with the house, and we'll get on to the people in a minute.

Summerfield Road runs beside a steep railway embankment about three-quarters of a mile from the town centre in Lewisham, and we live at number 47. It's all terraced houses round here, and I suppose our street is just the same as lots of others, except I like ours best. There are trees along the road, and you know you've arrived at our house because the front gate's painted bright green, Dad's favourite colour. Out the back there are lots of flowers and vegetables in a garden which goes down about 30 yards past the shed to the foot of the embankment. Every quarter of an hour during the day there's the long, loud rattle of an electric train on its way to Charing Cross. That's a big station right in the middle of London, eight miles away. Shirl and I are lucky to have a front bedroom. In the boys' room at the back it's far too noisy because of the constant clatter from the trains.

I often wonder what it was like when there really was a "summer field" where our house is now. It's funny to think of cows and sheep in our nice back garden. Perhaps that's why things grow so well. All that manure!

Anyway, now you know I've got a sister called Shirl, short for Shirley. She's much older than me. Seventeen and a bit full of herself, but she can be a good laugh. Considering we have to share, she doesn't get on my nerves *too* much. She works on the linen counter at Chiesman's department store in the centre of Lewisham, which is useful for us Bensons.

Tom's my little brother. He's ten, so he's very nearly two years younger than me. Tom can't keep still. There's always a streak of dirt showing on him somewhere. Unlike me, he doesn't read books unless he's forced to. What more can I say? He's a boy!

When Frank and Maureen were here, I had to share with Tom, which was horrible with a capital H. Even so, I'd rather have Frank back. We all miss him terribly. I worry about him all the time and so do Mum and Dad. Frank is one of the ground crew at a Royal Air Force station called Biggin Hill. Everyone says he'll be safe and it's quite a cushy number, but how do they know? I'm sure the Germans are going to try to bomb the runways and planes Frank looks after. RAF pilots are killed every day now.

Frank's the oldest of us Benson children. Maureen's next and she's 21, but we don't hear from her much. She's with the army up north at some training camp. When she comes home, which is only once in a blue moon, she looks really smart in her khaki uniform, but I don't really know what she does. We've never got on, you see. Frank always brings me a present when he visits, even if it's just an old comic, but Mo just ignores me. Always has done!

My dad is Mr Albert Benson and he's wonderful. Nearly everyone calls him Bert. I think I told you he's a fireman, and he's as big and strong as you'd expect a fireman to be. He doesn't get cross very often (and never with me) though Mum makes up for it. She's nice underneath, but she hides it well by shouting a lot. I think she does the worrying for too many people, though maybe it's just her red hair. Mum's name is Beatrice, which sounds a bit old-fashioned to me. Don't tell her I said so!

So there you are! Now you know all about us. Oh, I nearly forgot. I'm Edie, short for Edith (ugh!). Pleased to meet you, I'm sure.

PS I mustn't leave out Chamberlain, our fox terrier! I know it's a funny name, but Dad says it's because he's always hopeful, just like the old Prime Minister. That was Mr Neville Chamberlain who thought he could make peace with the Germans. He was the one who came before Mr Churchill. Our Chamberlain's usually disappointed too! I suppose if we ever had a bulldog, he'd be called Churchill. You can tell from looking at his face Mr Churchill won't take any nonsense from Jerry.

Thursday 25th July

You know that lovely back garden I was telling you about? Well, it doesn't look half as neat and tidy as it did a day or two ago.

Frank came home on leave yesterday afternoon. He's got a motorbike down at Biggin Hill, and he managed to wangle some petrol, even though it's not really allowed because of the rationing. He looks just *so* wonderful and romantic in his uniform, though Dad didn't let him keep it on two minutes. No sooner was Frank through the front door than the two of them were in the garden digging the hole for our new air-raid shelter. Now we'll be safe no matter what Hitler tells his bombers to do!

Mind you, Dad was a bit fed-up when he found out he'd have to buy our safety. He had to shell out seven quid for the shelter, and apparently all because he earns *too much*. First I've heard! Most people in the street have got theirs free. It's called an *Anderson* shelter after the man who thought it up, and the first thing you have to do is dig this hole.

You should have seen the size of it. I said it looked as if they were tunnelling to Australia, and Frank said it felt as if they were. The hole's three feet deep, and of course it's got to be long and wide enough for us all to sit inside. Dad and Frank bolted together the corrugated iron sheets to make the roof and sides, and finally they piled all the earth back on to the top, deep enough that you could grow rhubarb. Dad says that's what we're going to do. Fancy spending the night under a clump of rhubarb! Anyone would think we were a family of rabbits – still, at least we'll be safe rabbits! When they'd finished, Tom and I lit a candle, and crept inside. It felt really cold and spooky, but I suppose when we're all in there together it won't be so bad.

I'm a woodenhead. I told you my name the other day, but afterwards I realized you don't know anything else about me. Well, I'm tall for my age (about five-foot-three), and I'm skinny, and in summer I get awful freckles all round my face. Mum says I'd be clever if I put my mind to it, but I don't know about that. I look a lot like Shirl, but I don't think I'll ever be as pretty. (Mind you, she spends long enough doing her face!) I like going to the pictures, I like books, and I'm good at netball. I'm as good as Tom at football too, but you'd better not tell him. Oh, and I *hate* rice pudding, which is a pity because Mum makes one every Sunday dinnertime. All that sloppy milk with bits in. Ugh!

Saturday 27th July

Mum's been like a cat on hot bricks since Frank's visit. I caught her moping in the kitchen after he'd roared off down the road towards Bromley. She said Frank had told her bad things.

318

Apparently there's German aircraft in the skies over Kent every day now, trying to take pictures, and Frank says it's only a matter of time before they try to shoot up the airfields. After that he thinks they really will start bombing London.

Building the Anderson has made it all seem so much more real. Dad's taking it more seriously too. He checked all our gas masks last night and made Tom and me practise putting them on, in case Hitler puts poison gas in the bombs. When you look in the mirror, it's like there's a monster or a creature from outer space looking back at you.

Then after dark we tried out the shelter. Dad's made it as comfortable as possible with a bit of old carpet laid across the planks, but it's cold and clammy even on a nice warm and dry July evening. Whatever's it going to be like when it rains and it's the middle of winter? As soon as we got in there, Tom decided he wanted to go to the toilet. Mum tutted and said he should have thought of that earlier. That's all very well, but what if we're in the shelter for hours, and the bombs are falling? What do we do then? Run inside the house and go as quickly as possible, I suppose. Dad won't have time to read the newspaper like he usually does!

Tuesday 30th July

What a cheek! I know Mr Churchill, the Prime Minister, says we've got to "dig for victory", because Britain needs to grow more food, but digging up the Lewisham municipal park's going a bit far! Where am I going to walk Chamberlain now?

I said to Dad I couldn't see the point, what with it being July. There wasn't anything they could plant. Dad said he reckoned they'd put in allotments and everyone would grow cabbages. Wonderful! So not only is the park going to look horrible, it's going to smell awful too. Not fair!

Shirl's got herself a boyfriend at last. I'm sure she has. If not, who was the bloke who walked her home after work last night?

Friday 2nd August

The strangest thing happened yesterday, really frightening. It's getting dark slightly earlier again now, and when I went up to bed at about nine o'clock there wasn't enough light to read. Shirl needed to take off her warpaint and we had two candles lit in the room so we could both just about see without having the electric on. Anyway, we mustn't have drawn the curtains properly, because five minutes later there's a huge knock on the door like the world's coming to an end and when Mum answers it she finds a policeman on the doorstep making a fuss. Then he elbows his way past her into the house, saying someone's signalling to the Germans.

Mum tells him as politely as she can that he must be off his rocker, but he demands to see our room and waltzes upstairs to give us a right bawling out, shouting didn't we know there was a blackout and were we on Jerry's side? Shirl was completely shocked and embarrassed, and I cowered under the eiderdown. Good job Shirl still had most of her clothes on!

When he'd finally gone Mum went completely mad. She didn't know whether to be more annoyed with us for showing her up, or with him for being so rude and barging in like that. Shirl and I ended up in tears and all in all it was a horrible end to the evening. When Dad came home at the end of his shift this morning, Mum packed him off down the police station to tell the desk sergeant what he thought, but I don't see what good that'll do.

I suppose the blackout's necessary. It makes sense that we shouldn't give the Jerry bombers any idea of what's on the ground, but it doesn't half cause problems. Dad said it was a good thing it was only a beat copper and not one of the ARP wardens who usually go round telling people to put lights out, because they really *are* little dictators. Then Mum shocked us all by saying that if you can't beat 'em you should join 'em, and that she thought she'd apply to be a warden, because none of them had two grains of sense to rub together and if things got really nasty we couldn't afford to leave it to morons. So that'll be four of the family with uniforms, five if you include what Shirl has to wear for Chiesman's. Shirl said I could always join the Girl Guides if I was so desperate. I told her she must be joking. No uniform was worth that!

Tuesday 6th August

You've got to hand it to Mum. If she says she's going to do something there's no stopping her. Yesterday she went down and signed up as an ARP warden, just like she'd said. No uniform, though. Just an arm-band with ARP (for "Air Raid Precautions") written on it in big white letters.

Dad laughed when he saw her. "We're all in trouble now, Beattie," he said. "Signed up just like that! How do they know you aren't a German spy?"

"Sid Bazeley's running the show down there," Mum answered, unpinning her hat. "If he doesn't know I'm not a spy, there's something wrong. We were kids together in Madras Terrace. There's a few stories I could tell you about Sid!"

Ever since Shirl and I had our spot of bother last week, Mum's been flapping about the blackout. She checks our room every evening, and makes us pin up spare blankets round the window.

"Now it won't matter what you two monkeys get up to," she says.

I suppose if she's going to be a warden and boss other people about, she's got to keep things tight at home.

The warden's post is in our old school, down Hengist Road. They moved in as soon as the kids were evacuated last year. There hasn't been any proper school since, because all the teachers were evacuated as well, and it's funny to think of the wardens sitting in our old classrooms drinking tea. Mum says it's about time the ARP did something more for people than just shouting at them. She's got ideas about running concerts, and parties for the kids and all that. We'll see. From what I remember of Sid Bazeley, it's not the kind of thing he'd go for. He keeps a fruit and veg shop up towards Catford and he's always been as miserable as sin with us kids.

As far as the blackout goes, there's good news and bad news. You'd be surprised at the number of accidents that happen because no one can see anything in the dark. Last week in Dad's local paper I read that someone was killed falling off a railway platform over near Bromley. And just down the road old Annie Makins toppled off the kerb one night and broke her ankle, poor thing! In some places they're painting the kerbs white, and even putting a white band round postboxes so that you don't walk into them, but they haven't got to Summerfield Road yet.

The good news? You should just see the stars! In the old days before the war they were always hidden by the street lights. Now on clear evenings the sky's jet-black and covered with millions of sparkly diamonds. You can even see the Milky Way stretching across like a sort of gauzy scarf.

Wednesday 7th August

I'm really bored. It's raining and it doesn't feel like the summer holidays one bit. But then since there's no school terms now, what's a holiday and what isn't?

When everyone was evacuated last year, it was great at first. As I said, all the teachers went off with the kids, and there wasn't anyone left to run the schools so we had to stop at home. But I really didn't want to be packed off to Sussex or Devon or somewhere where we wouldn't know anybody, and I could see Tom was scared stiff too. I got myself in a right state worrying till finally Mum said they'd send Tom and me away over her dead body.

Mrs Chambers from the school paid us a visit to try to make her change her mind. I was listening outside the front parlour door and there was quite a row. Mrs Chambers said Mum was setting a bad example. She ought to do what the government said was best. Mum said she didn't like anyone telling her what to do when it came to her children. Mrs Chambers snapped: what would Mum feel like if a bomb dropped and Tom and me were killed?

Mum didn't say anything for a moment. I put my ear right to the keyhole and heard her whisper that if we were, she hoped we'd all go together, and she wasn't going to give in to threats from Hitler or Mrs Chambers, thank you. And that was that.

So, most of this year, Tom and me have spent three mornings each week with Mrs Riley. She used to be a teacher until she retired. Mrs Riley's very nice, but it's not like school. For starters she has trouble staying awake a whole morning, and though she's all right at reading and writing, I know more about geography than she does. Tom isn't interested at all. It's all Mrs Riley can do to keep him in his seat for ten minutes at a time, he's such a shufflebottom. I read with him a bit each day and give him a few sums to do. The rest of the time I help Mum, and do as many paper rounds as I can for Mr Lineham. He owns the corner shop.

So you see I miss school, and my friends. Especially when it's raining like it is today!

The same bloke walked Shirl home again last evening. Looks a bit old for her, if you ask me! And he's got a moustache. I won't ask Shirl if it tickles!

Saturday 10th August

Yesterday was my birthday. I can't quite believe I'm twelve. I keep saying, "Edie Benson is twelve years old!" to myself. I think it sounds much better than eleven, don't you?

Mind you, it was a funny start to a birthday. We were all in the Anderson half of Thursday night. The sirens went at nine in the evening and then again somewhere around midnight, so we were all a bit bleary-eyed by the morning. There's still no bombs, leastways not that we've heard. I wonder what it's going to be like when they do start falling?

In Mum's *Woman's Own* the "Doctor's Note" column says if you want to sleep at night you should eat lots of lettuce and nothing at all in the evenings. Oh, and cotton wool ear plugs are supposed to help too. I bet the Doctor doesn't spend his nights with four other people in a hole the size of a rabbit hutch! Is that why rabbits eat lettuce? To help them sleep?

There was a lovely surprise at tea-time. Maureen had got some leave and turned up on the doorstep with a big bunch of flowers for Mum, and a really nice hair-band for me. Fancy that! I'd been secretly hoping Frank would get home too, but at least he remembered to send a card to his "favourite not-so-little sister".

In the evening we all went off to the Lewisham Hippodrome to see *Over the Rainbow*, with me feeling very grown up about going out to the theatre of an evening. Even Dad managed to wangle out of a shift to come with us. *Over the Rainbow* is the Wizard of Oz story, just like the film with Judy Garland that everyone's talking about. It was so funny and sad and beautiful, and even though we were sitting right up at the back it was a wonderful treat for a special day. Best of all, we got right through the evening without an air-raid warning, so well done Frank and the lads in the RAF. They must have scared the bombers away just for me. By the time we'd walked back to Summerfield Road we were all properly done for, what with the lack of sleep from the previous night.

One of the things I miss about school is not being in plays. I'd really, really like to be Dorothy in the *Wizard of Oz*. Last night I just wanted to jump up on stage and sing along.

Sunday 11th August

Today was Civil Defence Day in Lewisham, and of course Mum had to be on duty along with all the other wardens. Dad was working, and went out grumbling. They'd all been told to turn up with their shoes shined and their uniforms smartly pressed. "Someone important" was coming to inspect them. "Don't they know there's a war on?" he muttered. "We've got more than enough work to do, without standing around waiting for la-di-da rubberneckers."

Shirl had gone off to Chiesman's at about half past seven, so when Tom and I'd done the breakfast dishes and got the house more or less straight (well I had!) we sneaked out to see what was going on.

Until we talked about it the other evening, I hadn't cottoned on that Mum's going to be right in the thick of things if the bombs do start falling. When a factory or a house gets hit the wardens are supposed to get there as quick as they can. They take a quick shufti and then they've got to telephone the Town Hall to tell the ARP centre what's happened. How many people have been hurt or killed? Is anyone still trapped in the rubble? Then they do what's necessary, rescuing people and giving first aid until proper help arrives.

Mum's very brave. It made me shudder to think about finding dead bodies and things. I don't think I could do it.

Down by Finch's Builders' Yard there was a crowd gawping at something, but we couldn't get close enough to see. Tom amazes me, really he does. He knows the alleys and back doubles much better than me, and eventually he found a wall we could sit on with a view out over the yard.

Everyone was pretending a bomb had just fallen. We couldn't see Mum but various wardens were running around like scalded cats. There were people lying on the ground. They were groaning loudly and waving their arms and legs to show they were injured until nurses came and bandaged them up. None of them would have won any prizes for acting. Then they were stretchered off into a couple of ambulances. After five minutes of this Tom was already saying, "I've had enough," so we jumped down from the wall and walked on into Lewisham. Occasionally we could hear the bells on the fire engines ringing, so we headed for the Fire Station, me trying to keep up with Tom.

"Just make sure Dad doesn't see us," I shouted at his heels. "We'll catch it if he does, especially today!" Dad doesn't like us hanging around the Station. "Work and home?" he says. "Oil and water!"

The crowd around the Fire Station was huge, so this time there was nothing for it but to push to the front. There was a lot of excited chatter.

"Let the littl'uns through," said a big lady wearing a pink and yellow headscarf who was looming behind us. "They'll want to see royalty." As the crowd parted, she shoved us forward, using us as the excuse for her to get a better view too.

I turned my head and asked her, "What royalty?" and over the crowd's cheering she shouted, "It's the King and Queen, ducks! Come to see how the other half lives!"

In front of us we could see a line of firemen standing against a gleaming fire engine, while with their backs to us a man in smart military uniform moved slowly down the line accompanied by a lady in a blue feathered hat. We were just in time to see them pass Dad. The King stopped and seemed to say something, and Dad bowed his head slightly, smiling a reply.

"It's not the King!" said Tom a bit too loudly. "Where's his crown?"

"Don't be so daft," I said. "You don't think he carries it with him everywhere, do you?" Tom tutted. "You're the end, you are," I said. "Here's your dad meeting the King, and all you care is that he's not wearing the Crown Jewels on his head."

A few minutes later, the King and Queen shook the mayor's hand and sped off in shiny black cars towards Blackheath. Then there were some rescue demonstrations with people jumping off the Fire Station tower into sheets, and firemen showing how to put out pretend incendiary bombs – the little ones that don't blow you up, but just burn you to death by starting fires. Apparently you don't throw water over them like everyone thinks. That only makes things worse. You have to use sand. I think Tom enjoyed that more than seeing the King.

"Funny thing about that inspection, Beat. . ." Dad said to Mum later at tea.

"I know," she said. "I heard. Didn't come to see us workers, did they?" She sounded miffed, but she was only joking. Proud really.

"Spoke to me, he did," said Dad, looking round at us all. "Our King spoke . . . to *me*."

Dad had us in the palm of his hand. We were holding our breath waiting to hear details of this great conversation.

"Do you want to know what he said, then?"

We all nodded our heads. Dad pulled his mouth wide, showed his teeth and put on a high-class accent, "*Isn't it a laavely day*'."

"Bert!" said Mum.

"He did!" said Dad. "Come to Lewisham to cheer us up, and talks about the weather. I ask you! I feel so much better now!" He shook his head.

"At least he came!" said Mum. "They could just hide away in a bunker, you know!"

Monday 12th August

Mum sprung something on us today. She's taking Tom and me to see Auntie Mavis down near Tonbridge tomorrow. Yippee! And we're staying till Friday. It's a holiday, or at least something like it.

No beach, but at least we'll be out of smelly Lewisham. (And getting smellier all the time! Now they're letting people keep *pigs* in their back garden and they've put waste bins on the street corners. The idea is we should put all our old food scraps in them to feed the wretched porkers. And when it's as hot as it was yesterday, you don't want to go nearer than half a mile to those bins. They stink to high heaven!)

Shirl's in a right sulk about Tonbridge. She scarcely spoke to me all evening. I think she fancied a few days in the country.

When we were getting ready for bed, I asked her about the bloke who walks her home. She blushed red to her roots. Very satisfactory!

"What's his name?" I asked.

"Mind your own business!" Shirl snapped. Then, because she was clearly dying to tell someone, she gave in. "Oh go on! It's Alec, if you must know. I think he's a bit sweet on me."

"And you?" I pushed.

"Mind your own business!" she said again. And this time the shutters were down. For the time being. . .

Tuesday 13th August

We caught a bus down to Hither Green and didn't have to wait long for the electric train to Sevenoaks. That was where the fun and games started.

When you get to your destination these days, you have to hope you hear the porter shout "Sevenoaks" or whatever the station is because there aren't any signs. They've all been taken down. Dad says the idea is that if the Germans ever do invade, they won't know where they are. It's the same with road signs.

Luckily that wasn't a worry because our train was only going as far as Sevenoaks. Then we sat and waited for ages for the steam train to take us on to Tonbridge. Tom didn't mind. I can't think why, but he actually likes standing on station platforms watching engines shunting backwards and forwards.

"Flippin' war!" said a man standing next to us. "Gives them all the excuse they need, don't it? Blessed trains don't never run to time now."

Eventually a train puffed into a platform on the far side of the station. We ran over the footbridge in a panic. No one seemed to know if it was the Tonbridge train, and even when we finally set off, Mum was still a bit nervous, asking the other passengers if we were all going to end up in Hastings.

Inside the trains now there are blinds on every window so it's really dark. It's the blackout again. A brightly lit train would be a sitting target at night I suppose. There are strange blue lamps in all the compartments so that you can just about see, though only so as not to fall over each other.

We were two hours late arriving in Tonbridge, but little Uncle Fred – red cheeks polished and shining under a cheeky hat – was still there waiting for us. With his car.

"We could have caught the bus," said Mum. "Think of the petrol. You don't want to waste your rations."

Uncle Fred tapped his nose. "No names, no pack-drill," he said. "Never a problem with a bit of extra petrol, if you know where to ask."

Mum pretended to look shocked. Then: "How's Mavis?" she asked. I glanced over at Tom. The way she asked the question, it wasn't just a polite enquiry, she was really concerned. But Tom hadn't noticed anything.

"The old girl's not so well. Not at all," Uncle Fred answered, and I could have sworn he blinked rather more than he should've.

Of course as soon as we actually saw Auntie Mavis I knew why we'd come to Tonbridge all of a sudden. She seems half the size I remember, and her skin's a sickly kind of yellow colour. This might be a holiday for us, but I'm afraid Mum's visiting her sister for quite another reason.

Wednesday 14th August

When we got a moment to ourselves this morning, I asked Mum about Auntie Mavis. She looked me straight in the eye.

"She's very ill, Edith," Mum said softly. I always know something's up when she calls me by my full name like that. "We've just got to look after her as much as we can. And Fred. I don't know what he'd do without Mavis." And she turned away rather too quickly.

In the afternoon Tom and me walked out through the houses into the fields. We climbed up steadily towards a wood, the corn as high as Tom's shoulders on both sides of the path. We were almost level with the trees when we heard the first planes, high and distant. We turned and looked, shading our eyes against the sun.

"There," said Tom, pointing into the sky. It took me a couple of moments but then I saw them too, a formation of dots dodging the clouds.

"Germans," Tom added.

"Do you think so? How do you know?" I asked.

"Heinkels! You can tell by the shape, can't you?" he said, like I was just a stupid girl and knew nothing. But he was right, because then there was the sound of more planes coming from behind us over the wood, and as the German bombers came nearly overhead, suddenly the sky above us was full of aircraft zooming up and down, and we began to hear gunfire.

I don't know about Tom, but I was rooted to the spot. I'd never seen or heard anything like it, and it was all so sudden and unexpected. I didn't know whether to run for home, or take shelter in the woods.

"What do we do, Tom?" I asked, though I should have been making the decision myself.

He just shrugged his shoulders. "Stay and watch?" he suggested.

So we did. It seemed like the dogfight went on for hours, but it was probably more like ten minutes. We saw one plane start to smoke as it wheeled away from the pack. Then it seemed to hang and pitch forward, before tumbling over itself into a dive that took it out of sight to the side of a hill. It must have fallen miles away, because there was no sound of its landing, no explosion.

"I hope it was one of theirs," said Tom, almost enjoying the moment.

"The pilot might be dead," I replied, not sure what to think.

"Good!" said Tom. "The only good German is a dead. . ."

"Shut up," I said. "You mustn't say that."

"Why not?" he asked crossly. "It's true."

Tom and I don't fall out very often, but after that we walked in silence for a bit. As we crossed the road towards Auntie Mavis and Uncle Fred's house there was shiny metal lying on the concrete.

"Bullets," said Tom, eyes wide with excitement. He went to pick one of them up.

"Don't you dare," I shouted. "You might blow your hand off. Stop, Tom. Now!"

He gave me a dirty look, but he did as he was told.

So that's it. Now the war's real. It's happening to us, not just to other people.

Thursday 15th August

The first thing you notice about living in Tonbridge is how quiet it is. So when the telephone rang in the middle of last night, I almost jumped out of my skin. There's no telephone at Summerfield Road. It's a call box for us if we ever want to talk to Auntie Mavis or Uncle Fred. Telephones in houses are posh, I reckon.

Uncle Fred works near Sevenoaks at somewhere called Fort Halstead. I know he works for the Government, but that's all I know, and Mum says it's probably best not to ask. Uncle Fred's definitely clever. You only have to play him at chess to know that. Dad says he's a boffin, whatever that is.

The telephone hadn't wakened Tom. He was breathing deeply, still fast asleep. I pulled a jumper over my nightie and gently opened the bedroom door. I could hear Uncle Fred talking into the phone down in the hall. I tiptoed across the landing as he said goodbye to whoever was on the other end of the line. As he put the phone down, he turned and saw me at the top of the stairs and it was his turn to jump. There was a strange look on his face, half amused, half worried.

"What's the matter, Uncle Fred?" I whispered, coming down the stairs and sitting on the bottom step.

He looked at me as if he couldn't decide what to say. "It's probably nothing," he stalled.

"It can't be nothing," I insisted. "Not in the middle of the night!"

He gave in. "All right. I'm a member of the Home Guard, Edie love," he whispered back. "And people are always seeing things. Somebody reckons the Germans have landed out Paddock Wood way. It's a load of baloney, of course. It's probably just a poacher, but I'll have to go and make sure. Look, it's more likely to be Martians than Germans, so go back to bed and don't worry."

I hadn't seen the rifle hidden behind the hat-stand in the hall until then.

Back upstairs, I heard his car drive off, and for the next two hours I lay and shivered, half-expecting a brigade of stormtroopers to smash their way in though the front door. But when he came back, he shut the door behind him so gently and carefully I knew we hadn't been invaded by either Martians or Germans, and I rolled over and went to sleep.

This morning we caught a bus into Tonbridge, and went shopping for Auntie Mavis. When she makes tea it normally comes out a thick dark brown colour. "Strong enough to stand a spoon up in," Mum says. She must use about five teaspoonfuls. But now they're rationing tea just like they do butter and meat. To get your ration you have to hand in coupons from your ration book. So if we come down again, maybe Auntie Mavis's tea will be drinkable!

If we come down again! According to Mum what poor Auntie's got is cancer, and the doctors don't give her much chance. What does *that* mean? Months? Weeks?

Poor Mavis. Poor Mum. Whatever does it feel like to know your sister is dying of cancer? It could be me and Shirl!

Friday 16th August

At breakfast, while Mum was helping Auntie Mavis make the porridge, I asked my uncle, "What's it like in the Home Guard, Uncle Fred?"

He twinkled at me. "It's all right. Makes me feel young again."

"Why's that?" I asked.

"Everybody else is older than me, that's why," he laughed. "And don't look so amazed!" He pulled a face. "All right, maybe I'm exaggerating but there *are* a fair few old codgers in our company. George Chapman must be 65 if he's a day. But we've all got to do our bit, haven't we?"

"What *do* you actually do, then?" piped up Tom.

"Well, they're training us to guard anything strategically important – gun batteries, railways, main roads, all that kind of thing. If Hitler was daft enough to invade, we'd do our best to make life difficult for him."

"Is it true you've only got broomsticks and pitchforks to fight with?" Tom asked. He hadn't spotted the gun either. I don't think Tom meant to be rude, but that's the way it sounded, and I kicked him hard. I needn't have worried though. Uncle Fred was laughing.

"Not quite. When we first enrolled about four months ago, it's true there weren't many weapons available. But they're working us hard now. We'll even have a machine gun soon!"

"How do you find the time?" I said.

"Oh, it's not so bad. There's plenty of evenings and weekends." He looked me straight in the eye, and dropped his voice. "Takes my mind off things, to be honest."

"Have you ever thrown a grenade?" asked Tom enthusiastically.

"Only pretend ones," said Uncle Fred. "Hope I never have to throw one for real. Still, I was a good cricketer at school! I expect it'd be all right."

"Do you think it's true the Germans would use poison gas?" I asked. I have bad dreams about the gas. In them I'm always trying to escape from Summerfield Road. However hard I struggle, my legs won't carry me out of the house. I can't see anything and I can't breathe.

"Depends how you look at it," said Uncle Fred, leaning back in his chair. "On the one hand it's against the rules of war. And on the other hand I wouldn't put anything past that dreadful little man if he found himself in a tight spot."

Then Mum and Auntie Mavis came into the dining room. Uncle Fred stopped talking, like turning off a tap, and turned and smiled at Auntie as if there wasn't anything to worry about in the whole world.

Saturday 17th August

Until we got home, I hadn't realized how much I'd missed Summerfield Road. Lewisham isn't so smelly after all! (Well it is, but no worse than Tonbridge. Pigs in the one, cows in the other!)

And it seems ages since we went away, although it's really only five days. It's funny the things you notice for the first time. A pile of sandbags on a street corner here, a roll of barbed wire there. You can't be sure, but you don't think they were there a few days ago. It's as if, week by week, water's building up pressure behind a dam and sooner or later it's going to burst. Does that make sense?

Dad seemed to have survived Shirl looking after him. But the big wide grin on his face when we walked through the front door showed how pleased he was to have us back. He almost swung my mum off her feet and gave her a great big kiss.

"Put me down, Bert," she said. "Go on with you. Everybody knows it's only the apple pie you miss."

It's funny to see them like that, and it made me extra sad to think about Auntie Mavis and Uncle Fred.

Chamberlain was glad to have us back too. I hope they've been feeding him properly.

Tuesday 20th August

I was reading Dad's *Kentish Mercury*, catching up on last week's news, and there's something I don't understand.

If Hitler and the Nazis are so bad, like most people say, why are there some people who don't agree?

Apparently there was a Communist demonstration against the war down in Catford on Wednesday. I asked Dad about it and he said the police actually stopped some men who wanted to give the Communists a bloody nose.

"I don't see why," I said. "They're traitors."

Dad looked serious for a minute. I thought I'd made him cross, though I didn't know the reason.

"It's what we're fighting for, girl," he said. "There's no free speech in Germany. If your face doesn't fit, you're for the high jump. That's why our Frank's spending the best years of his life in a dirty God-forsaken hut down at Westerham. And our Maureen, wherever she is up north.

Don't ever forget, it doesn't matter what someone's opinions are, they've a right to speak their mind."

I still don't get it.

Wednesday 21st August

And here's something else from the paper. Every week there's a sort of court called a tribunal where conscientious objectors have to go to explain why they don't want to fight. This time it was someone who said he was a Christian pacifist, and he was about to go to Bible College.

From what I can see they let him get away with it. They've put him on "non-combatant duties only", and I reckon he was just spinning a yarn. Mum agrees and says in the Great War the girls used to hand out white feathers to men who wouldn't fight to show them they thought they were cowards. But Mum said she thought "non-combatant" only meant he wouldn't have to fire a gun. He might still end up in the front line carrying stretchers.

Then later I started thinking about what it would feel like to be "called up", and how frightened I'd be if it was me.

But they've still got to do their duty, haven't they? Frank and Maureen are! I just wish they didn't have to.

Meanwhile Shirl is having a high old time. She was out with Alec again last night. Up at the Palais, dancing till gone 10.30. I saw the looks Mum and Dad exchanged when she went out done up to the nines – lipstick, stockings and all.

"Is that our daughter, Beat?" said my father. "Pretty as a picture, isn't she?"

"If you say so," Mum answered, lips pursed and hand on hip. "I hope she knows what she's doing!"

Interesting!

Tuesday 27th August

There I was queuing for bananas at the greengrocer's, when suddenly there was a tremendous kerfuffle on the other side of the road, and everyone in the queue turned to look. Two men were holding another one in an armlock. They seemed to be trying to frog-march him down towards the clock tower, till a copper came up and stopped them. Then there was a lot of shouting and fingerpointing, and the one man kept trying to throw punches at the other two. The policeman's helmet went on the skew over his eyes, and people started sniggering.

Rosa Jacobsen, who used to go to my school, was trailing down the pavement watching what was going on.

"Watch'er Rosa," I said. "What's that all about?"

"They think he's a fifth columnist or something," Rosa answered.

That was a new one on me. "And what's that when it's at home?"

"Like a German spy who's been living here and doing sabotage. Blowing things up and that!"

"So how come they're so sure?" I asked Rosa.

She shrugged her shoulders. "I dunno," she said, disappointed now no one was hitting anyone else. "Spoke with an accent, I expect."

That rang bells. The *third* thing I'd read in the *Kentish Mercury* was about a priest called Schwabacher (or something like that). Till last week he'd been working up at a church in Blackheath for years, but now he's been sent off to an internment camp, like a prison, just because his dad was German.

Surely a priest wouldn't be a spy, would he? The world's getting more confusing every day.

I expect you're wondering about the bananas. It's funny, but no one in our house would touch a banana before the war. Now a rumour goes around that Harrold's had a few boxes of them come in, and we all queue like mad to get our share. Strike while the iron's hot, Mum says, but war or no war, they still taste yucky to me!

I asked Shirl about her night out with Alec, but she won't tell.

Friday 30th August

Last night was very still and clear. As Dad went out for the evening shift, he looked up and said grimly, "If they're ever going to come, it'll be on a night like this."

And sure enough, the first air-raid warning came at a few minutes past nine. Mum was out at the ARP post, and Shirl, Tom and I were huddled together in the shelter with Chamberlain. Because it was clear, it was chilly too, and we needed the blankets and coats we'd taken down the garden with us.

Shirl's teeth were chattering already. "Cor blimey!" she said. "What's it going to be like in the middle of winter? I've got no feeling in my toes at all."

I could see Tom about to open his mouth to say something clever when we heard the first explosion, and then two more following close on the first one. The sound was heavy and sharp at the same time. Chamberlain's ears were pricked. He gave a long growl, and started towards the door of the Anderson. I held him back.

"Gawd, what was that?" gasped Shirl.

Tom's face was white in the candlelight, his eyes big and scared.

"It's started," I found myself saying.

We'd heard the bombs drop before we picked up the rumbling sound of the aircraft, but they weren't overhead and I selfishly said thank you to God because they weren't coming any nearer. Then we heard our gun batteries open up, rattling bullets towards the bombers.

"How close are they?" asked Tom shakily.

"Miles away," said Shirl, recovering herself and trying to sound confident. But as soon as she spoke, as if to put her in her place, there were two more explosions, this time much nearer. Chamberlain barked loudly. Now we could hear the bells of the fire engines too, and more frantic gunfire.

Then the drone of the aircraft faded, and we held our breath wondering if the planes were going to come back and what would happen if they did. But though the gun batteries kept chattering away, in a quarter of an hour or so the single long wail of the all-clear sounded, and we went inside to make ourselves a cup of tea and get warm.

"I hope Mum and Dad are all right," I croaked.

Shirl drummed her fingers on the kitchen table and looked at me. "Yeah. I hope so too," she said.

Saturday 31st August

Dad told us at tea-time that the bombs had landed by a housing estate over near Downham. That really is miles away! The Lewisham Station had been called down there, but there was nothing to do. No one hurt, he said, and just a few big holes in the playing fields. Hitler'll have to do better than that, he laughed. But I could see he was putting a brave face on it for Mum, and she was wondering if she'd done the right thing taking on a job, and leaving us to cope.

"It's all right, Mum," I said, and I put my hand on hers across the table.

Wednesday 4th September

One of the good things about my paper rounds is that if I get a quiet moment in the shop I can sneak a quick look at all the papers and magazines we don't get at home. I have to be careful not to put any creases or tears in them, mind, or I'd catch an earful from Mr Lineham.

Anyway, I can't remember where I read it, but apparently it's awful in the public shelters because of all the snoring. Stands to reason, I suppose.

In our family, Mum whistles a bit through her false teeth and Shirl makes a sort of piggy snorting sound. It's her adenoids, Mum says. But Dad takes the biscuit. He sounds like the band of the Royal Marines all on his own. So there's not much chance of sleep in *our* dugout, if we're all at home.

Can you imagine what it'd be like in an underground station full of people you didn't know, and trying to get some sleep? And if you wanted to go to the toilet, having to nip behind some piece of canvas on the platform and go in a bucket? Well, there's hundreds doing it every night. As Mum says, there's always someone worse off than yourself.

Sunday 8th September

I'm trying to write this in the Anderson. There isn't much light and I'm all scrunched up in a corner so who knows whether I'll be able to make sense of it later on. It's half past six in the evening, but we've been here an hour or so already.

I feel small and scared, and dog-tired. None of us got much sleep last night. In fact, I think yesterday was the worst day of my life.

Everything was fine until the afternoon. The weather's been brilliant the whole of last week – not too hot, but clear and fresh. Dad had been given a day's leave so he went off, whistling a happy tune, to play cricket with his mates at Crofton Park. He doesn't get much chance these days.

In the morning, Mum had organized some games for the little kids over at the Hengist Road school, so I went along to give her a hand. Then Tom and me went down the market in the afternoon. Even if you don't buy anything, it's fun to listen to the traders. Each one's got his own patter, just like the comedians you get at the Hippodrome. One of them tells jokes about his mother-in-law all day long. The more you listen, the funnier it gets. Sometimes there's 50 standing around, laughing their heads off. Mind you, I wouldn't trust any of the stall-holders further than I could throw 'em.

It took everyone completely by surprise when the siren went. It must have been just after half past four.

There've been so many false alarms, people were getting fed up with it, so all you could hear was a sort of annoyed muttering in the crowd and among the traders. Of course, there's always some people who panic and rush for cover straight away, but this time because it was so close to the end of the afternoon and the weather was so nice, most people were reluctant to pack up and go home.

I'd just said to Tom, "Come on then. We'd better go..." when a couple of people pointed up into the eastern sky over Eltham.

Glinting in the sun was a V-formation of silver crosses. There must have been twenty planes flying steadily over London.

"Where's the blinking RAF when you need them?" shouted someone.

People were running for cover now, and the market traders began to shove plates and pans into boxes and suitcases, then ripping the metal poles of the stands apart and throwing them on to the ground with a clatter.

We ran all the way back to Summerfield Road, and even before we reached number 47, we could faintly hear the distant sound of the first explosions. Mum was waiting at the door to scold us down the garden and into the Anderson, where for the next hour and a half we worried about Dad and Shirley.

At half past six, the all-clear sounded and we crawled outside, rubbing our eyes against the light.

Across the gardens beside the railway, the land lies fairly flat to the River Thames between Blackheath on one side and Lewisham Hill on the other. Rising into the sky from the direction of the river was a huge tower of evil, sinister, billowing smoke, slowly rolling over on itself, black at the bottom and turning grey at its height.

"Oh my word," Mum exclaimed. "It's the docks! Must be." And then, as if personally he could have done something about the massive fire, she said crossly, "Wherever's your dad got to? Blow the blooming cricket. . ."

In fact, as we trooped into the house one way, he was coming in at the front door, red-faced and breathing heavily, throwing off his cricket whites as he came.

"Better . . . go into . . . work. . ." he said between gulps of air. "They're going to need . . . all hands . . . on deck."

But even before he'd got out of the front door, the siren was screaming at us again and, carrying books, crossword puzzles, toys and blankets, we scurried back down to the Anderson.

We were there until *five o'clock in the morning*, more or less, and not a moment's sleep. There was a break in the middle of the evening just after it had got dark. Shirl had joined us by then, having scampered out of the public shelter down by Chiesman's.

"It don't half pong in there," she said, shaking the smell out of her hair, her nose shrivelling up in disgust. "I don't think half of Lewisham ever has a wash." She drew in a sharp breath. "Would you just look at that!"

We were standing in the garden, looking towards the river again. The evening was still now, and though we could hear the occasional car and the bells of fire engines ringing their way across to Deptford, it was quiet enough to hear an animal rustle through the bushes on the railway embankment to our left. You get foxes up there sometimes.

But now where the smoke had been, the whole sky was an angry wound of red. We might be three or four miles away from the flames but with the amount of light they were making I could have easily read the paper Mum held.

"It's like the end of the world," Mum said slowly.

"Poor beggars," said Shirl.

"Is Dad over there?" asked Tom in a small voice.

"Him and every fireman in London, I shouldn't wonder," Mum answered, giving Tom a reassuring cuddle. "But then the whole city might be up in flames, for all we know. What a waste!"

Later in the evening, when Mum had gone off on duty, we could hear the drone of planes overhead more or less all the time. It's horrible. You feel the butterflies building up in your stomach till it almost becomes painful. I could see Shirl's fingers. The nails were bitten back hard, and her two hands were gripped together, the fingers sliding backwards and forwards over each other. It was about three o'clock when a stick of three bombs dropped closer than we'd ever heard before. They came through the air with a sound like the tearing of a curtain, and the explosions shook the ground. Chamberlain was beside himself with fear, past barking now, just trembling uncontrollably and whining pitifully.

We were all still white and shaking at breakfast. Mum wouldn't talk about the previous night. She fidgeted about the house, making a stew, dusting things that didn't need dusting, worrying about Dad.

Outside it was weird. If you looked down the street one way, it was a normal sunny Sunday morning, except everyone was more talkative than usual, leaning over fences and gates. Just over the road I could see Mrs Maclennan and Mrs Nott chatting to each other like they were old friends. This was strange, because everyone knew they hadn't got on for years. If you glanced the other way the pall of smoke hanging over the river reminded you of the nightmare you'd just been through.

Dad arrived home at noon, exhausted. He shook his head in despair. "I ain't ever seen anything remotely like it, Beattie," he said clasping a cup of tea in his hands. "It's a regular blinking inferno. All that oil, you see. I don't think we'll ever put it out."

Thursday 12th September

It's the same every night now. Bombs and more bombs, and they're getting closer. A house got hit in Sandringham Road last night. That's one over from Summerfield. Sometimes I feel frightened and sometimes it makes me angry. The Germans don't seem to care who they might kill. What's going through the minds of the pilots when they drop their bombs? Haven't they got wives and families? So how can they try to kill other people's children?

I mean, I understand why they might want to bomb a factory that's making guns. I can even understand why they might try to hit a power station. But what difference does it make to the war if they kill Mum, or Tom? Or me?

Eventually they *did* put out most of the fire in the docks, despite what Dad said, but it took them a few days. According to Dad, it pretty much had to burn itself out.

Life's gone a bit funny. Sort of upside down. The best time to sleep is in the early morning, and because Mum and Dad both have to be out quite often at night, they try to catch a bit of kip during the daytime. So I seem to end up doing even more dishes and tidying up than normal. *And* most of the shopping too! Even Tom lends a hand from time to time. Mum says it's our bit towards the war effort, and put that way we can't grumble, can we?

Monday 16th September

Mum came in on Friday night looking shaken up, eyes red as if she'd been crying. They'd been a bit short of wardens over at New Cross so she'd cycled up there to help out. There'd been a raid in the early evening, and a row of terraced houses had been hit – blasted to bits, Mum said.

"Sit down, Mum. I'll make you a cup of something," I said helplessly. As she took the cup of tea, her hands had a life of their own. They couldn't keep still.

"I think I'm a bit shocked, that's all love," she said. "Thanks for the tea, though. You're a good girl." And she burst into tears.

I just sat and watched. Mum wasn't *ever* like this. She got cross, but she never cried. When they went to the pictures together, it was the family's standing joke that Dad was more likely to cry than Mum.

After a minute or two she said, "I shouldn't be telling you, Edie, but I've got to talk to someone or I'll burst." She swallowed hard. "It was kids, you see. They were pulling kids out of the houses."

Now I understood. It was as if it could have been Tom or me.

"Poor things. I hope to God they never knew what hit them." She was crying again now. "We could hear a baby crying inside the rubble where a door had been. There was still a hole to get through but the blokes were too big. They said they couldn't ask me, but I knew what they wanted. I squeezed in all right, but she died in my arms. Poor little mite."

"Oh, Mum," I said and cuddled her. I didn't know what else to do. After a while she came to and asked, "Where's Tom?"

"I don't know," I said. He went out to play with Jim Simmonds about an hour ago.

Mum went spare. "*Why* don't you know?" she shouted. "What do you think you're here for? You're old enough to take some responsibility. You can't just let him wander off on his own. Anyone would think you were born stupid. Go and find him. And if he's not back in a quarter of an hour you'll both have your dad to answer to."

I didn't argue. Mum and I both knew what was going on. She'd been through a lot that day and she was taking some of it out on me, and that was all right this once. Tom was in the alley where I thought he'd be, kicking a ball around with Jim. He looked a bit surprised to see me, though – almost guilty – and Jim stuffed something deeper into his pocket so I couldn't see.

Something's going on between those two. Jim isn't a good influence on Tom.

Thursday 19th September

Mum's been pretty quiet since the weekend, not saying a word more than she has to. But then the lack of sleep's getting us all down, lying in the shelter each night wondering whether it'll be "our turn". That's the way people are starting to talk, like it's inevitable we'll all catch it in the long run.

Dad's trying to keep us all cheerful, but you can see in his eyes he's just so tired from working shift after shift. He's always kept himself fit and strong, but now he's so stiff and sore from all the work, he can scarcely lever himself out of his chair in the mornings.

In his time Dad must have seen some awful things. I shouldn't think you can avoid it if your job's putting out fires. He's never talked about it, and I shouldn't think he's going to now, but I wonder how much more even he can take.

Shirl isn't helping. She got in well after midnight on Wednesday evening. A party with friends from Chiesman's, she said. One *particular* friend, I reckon. It's that Alec, isn't it?

Dad gave her what for the next morning and told her not to do that again while she was living under his roof.

Shirl was very off-hand. "We might all be dead tomorrow," she said.

"Eat, drink and be merry, I say. What's the problem as long as no one gets hurt?"

"There's lots of ways of getting hurt, girl," Dad said abruptly. "You're old enough to know that."

Saturday 21st September

Right from the word go Mum was different this morning. She was back to her old self, brisk and organizing, as if this was a bright shiny new day, rather than the wet and windy one we'd actually got.

"Life must go on," she said. "It's what Hitler's after, isn't it – to have us moping around and thinking we can't cope. We've got to cope! 'Don't let the beggars grind you down.' That's my motto for the week."

And she took herself and the Mansion House polish outside to do the front step in the drizzle. Shirl, who has a late start at Chiesman's most Saturdays, raised a pencilled eyebrow at me.

There was a letter on the mantelpiece, tucked behind Mum's favourite china dog.

Shirl flicked it with a fingernail as she passed. "It's from Uncle Fred," she muttered. "Not good news, I shouldn't think."

But if it isn't, how come Mum's pulled herself together?

Tuesday 24th September

Today Mum got me organized helping serve lunch down at the church hall to people who've been bombed out. The WVS (that stands for Women's Voluntary Service, in case you didn't know) are in charge, and don't they let you know it! They're a right bunch of old battle-axes, but I suppose their hearts are in the right place.

A lot of the people there have only got left what they're stood up in. No more house, no more furniture, no more clothes. Everything smashed and burnt. You'd think they'd be miserable, but they were yakking away over their dumplings like nobody's business. They get bread and jam in the mornings and evenings and a hot meal at midday. All free. When they've finished eating in the evenings, they stretch out on camp beds to try and get some sleep in between the raids.

In a spare moment, I sidled up to Mum and asked her about the letter on the mantelpiece. Her face fell for just a moment, and then she said quickly, "Shirl saw me open it, didn't she? Doesn't miss anything, that girl." She paused. "I won't kid you, Edie. It *is* bad news. Your Auntie Mavis died last Thursday. She went very quickly in the end. "

"That's very sad," I gulped. "Are *you* all right?"

"I knew it was coming," Mum answered. "I'd pushed it to the back of my mind, what with everything else. Then when the letter came I thought, Well we've got to get on with things while we can, haven't we? It made me cheer up, in a funny sort of way. Do you understand?"

I told her I thought I did.

Thursday 26th September

When Shirl arrived for work at Chiesman's yesterday morning, she found one corner of the store missing, blown away the previous night by a bomb. All the windows were out and there was broken glass where you wouldn't think glass could get. Chiesman's weren't going to sell any china today or any ladies' hats and shoes, because they didn't have any, at least not in one piece.

"What did you do?" we asked Shirl.

"It's like you said, Mum. Don't let the beggars grind you down," she grinned. "We cleaned up the best we could. They told us the building wouldn't come down round our ears, but we shouldn't let the customers in yet. So while the chippies put up wooden partitions, me and the other girls carried some tables on to the pavement. Then we wrote a big sign saying, 'CHIESMAN'S: EVEN MORE OPEN THAN USUAL.' It got a few laughs, I can tell you! And we took a few quid, too!"

We laughed along with Shirl, but it's not so funny when you think about it.

Tuesday 1st October

It was Auntie Mavis's funeral yesterday, but only Mum made the trip down to Tonbridge. I wanted to go too, but Mum said with Dad working someone had to look after Tom. So that was me, wasn't it!

There'd been a heavy raid on Sunday night. The big bombs are bad enough, but the incendiaries are almost worse. They look like thin tin cans about eighteen inches long and they don't cause damage simply by blowing up, although I shouldn't think it'd do you much good if one landed on you from 10,000 feet. They just start fires everywhere, and the Fire Service can't keep up, Dad says. On bad nights, they don't know where to start. The Germans drop hundreds at a time.

There are delayed-action bombs too. They're really nasty, because they cause a mess when they land and then when people come to inspect the damage, the bomb goes off properly, taking anybody close-by with it. Every time Mum or Dad goes out I panic they're not going to come back.

When Mum had gone off to the station, looking sad and beautiful in her black dress, Tom hung around the house for a while, bored out of his skin, not helping with the cleaning. Then, about eleven o'clock, Jim Simmonds knocked on the door for Tom to go out and play. The two of them said they'd be up the alley as usual, pretending to be Charlton Athletic versus the Arsenal. I told Tom he should be back for lunchtime, and no messing about. If there was a siren, he was to come home at once.

Well, at 12.30 there wasn't a sign of them and after last time I started to worry.

Mum wasn't going to be back for hours, but if she ever knew Tom had been absent without leave she'd go off her rocker. At me as much as him!

I put Chamberlain on his lead and we walked up to the alley. It was empty.

"Tom, you little varmint," I said to myself. "Why am I always getting you out of trouble?"

They could have gone anywhere. I counted off Tom's favourite nooks and crannies in my head. The trouble was, the bombs were changing the geography of Lewisham every day. The Germans kept making new and exciting places for boys like Tom to be. It even interested me the way that if you dodged the officials you could see familiar things from different angles.

It was a risk either way. If Tom arrived at number 47 now, and found it deserted, *he* might panic. On the other hand I couldn't *not* search for them, could I?

I half-walked, half-ran down towards Catford Bridge, across the main road and along the edge of the slight hill on the far side. They weren't at the recreation ground, or behind the church. I cut through an alley where you could slip into the overgrown garden of a boarded-up house. There were trees there we all liked to climb. No Tom or Jim! It was one o'clock now and reluctantly I thought I'd better make for home.

We crossed the dirty old stream at the bottom of Mount Pleasant Road, where some sheds along the bank had been laid flat by a blast. Wood and rubble were strewn everywhere. From the far side, out of sight, I heard a shout that sounded suspiciously like Tom. Chamberlain's ears pricked and he woofed in the direction of the shout. I climbed down carefully and picked my way across. Everywhere smelled horrible. Drains, with a whiff of gas thrown in! The remains of a wall blocked my view. I pulled myself up on the crumbling bricks to see, and sure enough there were Tom and Jim. On the ground in front of them was a crumpled metal canister like a large tin-can. They looked like they might be about to use it as a football.

I bawled at the two boys, "Get away from that! Now! It might be a bomb, you stupid little blighters!"

Tom looked startled out of his wits, and the horrified look on my face must have convinced them. They backed off from the canister at a rate of knots.

I told Jim he could come back and have some chips and rice pudding with us, and that kept them quiet for half an hour or so, before they were running up and down the back garden path again, pretending to be Hurricanes and Spitfires shooting down German aircraft over Kent. I didn't let on to Mum about what had happened. It didn't seem fair.

Was it a bomb? I don't know, but I hope it taught my idiot little brother a lesson!

Yes, I know! Rice pudding! I'll make it, but I won't eat it.

Friday 4th October

I don't know what's got into Tom. He was brought home by a policeman yesterday, of all things, and got a good hiding from Mum into the bargain. He and Jim and some other kids had been messing about on the running boards of what they thought was a disused van. Afterwards Tom said it was so covered with dust and dirt you couldn't see a thing through the windscreen. As if that made everything all right!

Well, the owner caught them, didn't he, and Tom was the one who couldn't run fast enough.

After she'd walloped him, Mum sent him upstairs and told him he couldn't go out for a week. She said she'd just about had enough of him running wild on the streets and she was getting to the end of her tether. She didn't want the neighbours thinking the Bensons were criminals. How dare he ruin the good name of the family!

I tried talking to him later up in his bedroom but he went all sulky on me, and in the end I gave up.

Last night Mum was still so upset she told the wardens she couldn't go in to work. She stayed in the Anderson with us, cuddling Tom through the raid and letting him know she loves him even though he is a complete donkey. We've made sleeping bags now, and with four of us in there it gets quite cosy. The one thing I like about it is the smell. It's a mixture of the paraffin lamp, and the grassy, damp earth.

Sometimes, in the odd moment when it's quiet – no guns, no bombs, no fire-bells, no planes – I can almost think we're having fun camping in the garden like we did before the War when I was a little girl. But the feeling never lasts long.

Saturday 5th October

An awful thing happened near Lewisham station yesterday afternoon. A train was just rattling in from New Cross, and a German aircraft coming back from a raid over the river deliberately opened up its machine guns.

The pilot must have known exactly what he was doing. It's a miracle nobody in the train was killed. I hope his plane crashed on the way back to Germany. Or that Frank's boys shot him down. He doesn't deserve to live, if you ask me.

Shirl looked dreadful this morning. Huge circles under her eyes, and I couldn't get a peep out of her, no matter how much I tried to make her laugh. When she'd gone out I asked Mum if she knew what was wrong.

"It's that Alec fellow," she sighed. "Don't let on to Shirl I told you, but it turns out he's married. Never told Shirl of course, did he? Just been stringing her along these past couple of months. One of the other girls shopped him! I've a good mind to go into Chiesman's and tell him what I think of him, right there in the store!"

I didn't know whether she was serious or not, and she must have caught the look in my eye.

"No, well of course I won't!" she exploded. "But it'd make me feel better if I could. Why does Shirley always have to learn the hard way?"

Thursday 10th October

They got the Hengist Road school last night, the one where Mum works. The wardens were all out looking after other people, thank goodness, so no one was hurt – but according to Mum it's a right mess. The building's three storeys high, with the hall on the ground floor and the classrooms on the two floors above, but now all the ceilings have gone and some of the walls are a bit dodgy, so Mum thinks it'll have to come down.

There've been raids every night now since September 7th. It's become a routine, like going to school or having breakfast. Sometimes it feels as if we're small furry animals, staying in our burrows during the night and popping out for a few hours during the day to eat and scavenge among the mess.

And the mess can be unbelievable. Imagine. A bomb lands on the pavement in front of a house. Even if it doesn't kill or injure anyone, it makes a huge hole in the road and scatters rubble and rubbish all over it, so the road's useless until it's cleared. All the windows of the house are blown out and maybe the front wall is unsafe, so the house may end up being pulled down. Of course the electric gets cut off and the water and gas mains may be broken, so everyone in the street ends up having to carry buckets up to stand-pipes at the end of the road just so they can clean their teeth. If you want to make tea, you'll have to do it on a primus stove!

And this happens a few times every day in Lewisham! And in most other parts of London too, from what Mum and Dad say.

Day by day, it's getting harder to have fun. The cinemas are closing down one by one. What's the point in staying open, if there's going to be an air-raid warning five minutes into the programme? We used to have sing-songs and games for the kids down at the school, but now that's history. There's still the wireless, of course, and we all listen in for programmes like *It's That Man Again*. Tuesdays at 9.30, bombs permitting. I think Tommy Handley is *so* funny. Mum tries to look disapproving and says I'm not old enough, but there's not much to laugh at in the world, is there? It's really strange how we all keep so cheerful.

Tuesday 15th October

Tom's really gone and done it now. I thought he looked a bit sheepish when he came home for his tea last evening. Normally he bursts in, hair all over the place, making a noise, wanting something to eat, telling everyone what he's been doing, asking questions and telling daft jokes. Yesterday he sort of slunk in, and curled up in a corner looking at an old cartoon book he's had for years.

Later on we found out why. There was an unfriendly knock on the door and it was Mr Lineham from the corner shop, demanding to see Mr or Mrs Benson please. He didn't look very comfortable. His eye twitches a bit when there's something not right, and now it was going nineteen to the dozen. Mum was late to go out and already looking a bit harassed, but she dried her hands on the dishcloth she was holding and took Mr Lineham, still twitching, into the front parlour.

I was a bit scared. I thought *I* must have done something wrong. Maybe he'd come to complain about me being too slow delivering the papers, or putting them through the wrong doors. But it wasn't me he was after. It was Tom.

After a bit Mum came out of the front parlour very quietly and asked me, "Where's Tom? I want him."

She was so calm, I knew something was up.

But Tom wasn't there. He must have slipped out of the back door when he'd seen Mr Lineham arrive.

"Go and find him," Mum said firmly. "We've given that boy enough chances. We've got to put a stop to this once and for all!"

So off I went again, trailing the streets after Tom in the drizzle, this time knowing it was about to get dark, and there might be a siren any minute.

You remember that back garden I told you about, the one that's all overgrown? Well, I reckoned that's where he'd be. We'd made a sort of camp there last spring, and he'd know it would at least keep him dry for an hour or so. When I found him huddled under the dripping trees, he looked small, frightened and pathetic. He cowered away from me, shaking so much the words wouldn't come out properly.

"What's . . . going . . . to . . . happen?" he sobbed. "I don't . . . want . . . to go . . . to prison."

I wasn't going to let him off the hook yet. I didn't know what he'd done at that point, but it obviously wasn't very clever. "Well, you should have thought of that sooner," I said, hauling him to his feet. "What on earth have you been up to?"

"It . . . was . . . Jim's idea," he wailed.

"Oh yes," I said, "and whatever it was, you had no part in it I suppose?"

I expected Mum to go up the wall when we got back to number 47, but she stayed very calm. She took Tom into the parlour to apologize to Mr Lineham. I expect for a few minutes she also had visions of Tom languishing in a prison cell.

Eventually the parlour door opened and Mr Lineham stepped on to the street, raising his little black hat to Mum one last time and saying twitchily, "I'm sorry to have troubled you, Mrs Benson, but, ehmm, it's for the best in the long run. . ."

It turned out Tom and Jim had been in the shop yesterday afternoon. While Jim was buying some ha'penny chews, Tom had pocketed a couple of toy soldiers from the other end of the counter.

I could have told him old Lineham doesn't miss a trick. He's had that shop for years, and he knows enough to keep eyes in the back of his head when two small boys come in together.

Mum was her usual self the rest of the evening, apart from the fact she had to send Shirl down to give her apologies to the ARP again, but it's left me with an uncomfortable feeling in the stomach. I just know we haven't heard the last of this.

Friday 18th October

So now I know the worst, and it's just about as bad as it could be. Mum took me on one side after breakfast this morning. Her face was lined with worry. She didn't look as if she'd slept a wink.

"Edie," she said, taking my hands in hers. "I've arranged for you and Tom to go away for a while. I know I said I never would, but this is no good, is it?"

I was shocked rigid. "No, Mum," I said. "You can't do it. Where would we go? Who would we stay with?" Although I desperately didn't want to, I started to cry, and then she joined in and for a few minutes I just held on to her, sobbing my guts out.

"It's not just that business with Tom and Mr Lineham, love," she said eventually, when we'd both calmed down a bit. "Though I'm at my wits' end with him, really I am. It's not even as though you can say it's Tom's fault. This isn't proper living, is it? He needs a break, and so do you. I've been to see the authorities down at the Town Hall and they've found you a place in the country. South Wales, near Brecon. On a farm I think. It'll be safe there. I had to pull a few strings to get you out of Lewisham quick."

I knew there wasn't a hope of changing her mind, but I was appalled.

"How long for?" I croaked hopelessly.

Mum looked me straight in the eye. "You're a big girl now, Edie, so I'm going to treat you like one. I honestly can't say for how long. But there's people moving out of Lewisham every day now. You must have cottoned on to that. Who knows how long Hitler can keep throwing the kitchen-sink at us? There doesn't seem to be any sign of a let-up. And it worries me things might be much, much worse this winter."

"I don't want to leave you and Dad," I wept. "I couldn't bear it if anything happened."

"Your dad agrees with me," she said firmly. "Turn it on its head! How do you think we could live with ourselves if we kept you here and either of you got hurt? In the end Mrs Chambers was right, though I hate to admit it. You've got to go."

And the way she argues it, in the end I suppose I agree with her.

Monday 21st October

When they told Tom, it was terrible. He just howled and howled for what seemed like hours. They must have heard it up the other end of the street. At about tea-time, I went out with him down to the one set of swings in Lewisham they haven't melted down for the war effort. I tried really hard to be as enthusiastic as I knew how. I told him what fun we were going to have.

"Just think," I said, "no more sleeping in a crummy old shelter. No more dodging the bombs."

"But what is there to do in Wales?" he said despondently.

"Don't know till we get there, do we?" I answered brightly.

I can see his point. And I bet I know the other thing that's worrying him. It worries me slightly too. School!

Sunday 27th October

The air-raid warnings came late last night, so at least we got an hour or two in bed before we decamped to the shelter.

As we were turning in, Shirl fished around in her handbag and pulled out two large, white, five pound notes. She pushed them into my hand.

"For a rainy day," she said, with a shy grin. I was astonished. Ten pounds is a *lot* of money. I've never held so much in my hand at one time.

"What are you doing, Shirl?" I asked. "You can't afford this. It must have taken you weeks and weeks to save!"

"Look after it then," she said. "I'm not going to complain if you bring it back with you, am I? But, like I say, you might need it."

I hugged and hugged her. When it's mattered, Shirl's always been there for me.

Monday 28th October

Our train was supposed to leave Paddington station in West London at eight this morning. Dad's boss – Mr Abbott – was a star and took us there in his Austin.

"You didn't need to do this, Reg," my dad said as Mr Abbott stood on the doorstep, stifling a yawn. Like Reg Abbott's, Dad's face was raw and red from working the previous night. There was a cut on his cheek and his right sleeve was rolled back to stop it rubbing on a painful burn that ran a good four or five inches up towards the elbow.

"'Course I did, Bert," said Mr Abbott. "At least you'll know the nippers have done one bit of the journey safely. Are you fit?"

We hugged Mum and Shirl tearfully and I smoothed Chamberlain's beautiful ears back one last time.

"Be good," said Mum pointedly to Tom, looking him deep in the eyes. "Do what Edie tells you. I'll be thinking of you every other minute, I shouldn't wonder." And before she lost control, she bundled us into the back of the car with a final kiss. Only Shirl stayed on the pavement to wave us goodbye.

"Don't get too used to having the room to yourself," I shouted at her through the window. "We're not going to be that long."

She grinned. "I promise," she said. "What am I going to do with no one to moan at?"

The excitement of being in the car kept Tom's mind occupied. Somewhere near Vauxhall we had to steer our way cautiously round a tram that was leaning over crazily, its front half down a crater in the road.

Dad let out a low whistle as we drove past. "Nasty," he said. "I hope that wasn't as bad as it looked!"

It was a misty, damp morning. In one street you'd think there wasn't a war on at all. People were beginning to make their way smartly to work, carrying bags and newspapers. And in the next grey and mournful street, where a bomb had fallen or there'd been a recent fire, the inhabitants were either standing on their doorsteps looking dazed at the destruction around them or disconsolately setting to work with brooms and shovels to put a bit of order and normality back in their lives.

Under the curved metal roof of Paddington station where the smoke from the locomotives hung greasily in the girders, we said our second lot of goodbyes.

Tom and I found ourselves seats, and pulled down the window in the compartment, squeezing our heads round the blackout blind.

"We're not going to hang around," Dad shouted. "Going home to get some shut-eye." And suddenly we were on our own.

When the little slow train from Cardiff at last pulled into Llantrisant station it was five o'clock, and even Tom had had enough of trains for

374

one day. The platform was eerily quiet apart from the hissing of steam and the birds tweeting. Bushes hung over the fences looking badly in need of a haircut. We were the only passengers getting off, but as if there was any danger of missing us, a scowling man stood by the station building holding a piece of cardboard high in the air. On it was scrawled the one word: "BENSON". The writing was worse than Tom's. The man was overweight and bald. A pair of leather braces barely kept his stomach and his dirty trousers from falling apart.

"That's got to be Mr James," I said, pulling our battered old suitcase out of the carriage on to the gravelled platform.

"He doesn't look very pleased to see us," Tom muttered.

We must have looked odd, standing there with our gas masks around our necks in their cardboard boxes, and our old school satchels (full of the few home comforts we could bring with us) falling off our shoulders. Suddenly the gas masks seemed completely unnecessary. There was nothing to tell you there was a war on in Llantrisant. Even the station name stood out defiantly on the board beside us. The paint looked new.

"You've got here, then," was all Mr James could say in welcome, his voice a sing-song Welsh. "This way. You'd better hurry up or you'll miss tea." And leaving us to struggle with the luggage, he lumbered through the building to the drive outside the station where a tractor and a wagon were parked.

He jerked a thumb at the wagon where high up there were a couple of rough seats facing back up the road. "That's for you up there, see!"

he said. "You can climb up," he went on, though it sounded more like an order than a request.

Tom was riveted to the spot. He just stood there gawping.

"Didn't you 'ear me?" said Mr James rudely. "In the wagon. Quick now."

Whether it was lack of food after a day's travelling or just the bucking and swaying of the cart, I don't know, but I felt sick after a few yards, so it was a good job the station and the small village of Llantrisant were only a couple of miles from the farmhouse. Throwing up all over Mr James's wagon wouldn't have got us off to a good start, would it?

Tuesday 29th October

I've got to be positive, and I've got to be strong. I told myself before we left home that this was going to be hard. I just didn't know quite *how* hard. I'm missing Mum and Dad and number 47 like mad. There's a gnawing pain in my stomach, and I find I keep wanting to cry. Last night when we were all in bed, I couldn't help myself, and I really did weep buckets. I hope Tom didn't hear me. Most of all, I've got to be brave for his sake.

So, what are the good points of Llantrisant? Well, to start with, obviously we're safe. Not even the Jerries would think it was worthwhile bombing this place. There's nothing much here except us and the cows.

Then, except for the strange musty smell, I suppose the James's farmhouse is nice. We've got a room each and they're so big we're rattling around in them. Big and cold!

The furniture's a bit rickety, but it's not as though my clothes even a quarter-fill the drawers and wardrobe in the room. I put Freddie my mascot bear on the chest of drawers facing the bed so that I can always see him. He's been with me as long as I can remember. Then I arranged the five books I've brought with me on the shelf. I took Shirl's money, and carefully slipped one five pound note inside the dust jacket of *Diary of a Nobody*, by George and Weedon Grossmith, and one inside the cover of *Winnie the Pooh*. I think the money should stay a secret between me and Shirl for now.

My bed's a bit odd. It's really high off the ground and the mattress sags badly at the sides, so it's rather like sleeping on top of a roof. I feel as if I'm going to fall off at any moment.

Looking out of the bedroom window this morning, I can see that the countryside's very pretty. The fields all around us are a bright, beautiful green, and in the distance I can see hazy, furry, flat-topped hills with shadows passing over the purple. They remind me of the cushions on the settee in the front parlour at home. But I mustn't think too much about that.

On the other hand, there's not much good to say about Mr and Mrs James. From the photographs on the mantelpiece in the dining room, Tom and I reckon they must have three grown-up children. If they treated them like they treated us last night, I should think the kids must have left home as soon as they could. Why did they take us in, if they hate us so much? During tea and then before we went to bed, Mr James scarcely said a word and if he did it was rude or cross. On the other hand, Mrs James never let up. She seemed to have it in for me more than Tom. "*Don't put your elbows on the table! Don't gobble your food! Don't scrape your chair on the floor!*" (The floor in the dining room's made of stone, and the chairs make a noise on it.) "*Don't talk with your mouth full!*" (When she'd just asked me a question!)

Then there were the personal comments about my hair (*scruffy!*) and my dress (*too short and too many patterns!*).

Thursday 31st October

I couldn't face writing yesterday. It would have come out all miserable and depressed. Just like the weather.

Shirl said it rained a lot in Wales, and now I believe her. It started on Tuesday afternoon, and it's poured down more or less ever since.

To keep us from getting bored, the Dragon's had us working for our living. (Well, I'm right that the dragon's a Welsh national emblem, aren't I? It seems to suit Mrs James rather well.) She's had the two of us cleaning her silver and helping with the washing. It hasn't taken us long to find out that nothing's ever good enough.

But we had two letters from home today, one from Mum and Dad and the other from Shirl, and that made us feel better and worse all at the same time. I'm so mixed up, but underneath everything else, I really wish we could go home.

The food here's just about all right, but Tom can't cope with the Dragon's soup, all watery cabbage. Yesterday he ended up having nothing but chewy bread and yucky jam for tea, because he couldn't finish his bowl of gruel! There's plenty of vegetables from the farm, so we won't be short of beetroot sandwiches, but boy, are we going to miss our fish and chips!

Saturday 2nd November

Yesterday's chore was gathering kindling for the James's fire. The Dragon packed us off with baskets over the fields behind the farm to a small copse. And one journey wasn't enough. Oh no! She had us backwards and forwards at least five times. Now we've got enough wood to keep a fire going all winter, if we have to!

It was an easy enough job because the way the wind's been blowing up these last few days it's brought down loads of small branches and twigs from the trees. I don't mind having something to do. It's just the way she seems to think we're here for her personal convenience, like we're servants or something. There's never a please or thank you, it's simply "Do this!" or "Do that!" Or just as often: "*Don't* do that!"

In the afternoon, she sent us off to the stores in Llantrisant to buy some bread and tea. I've been carrying an emergency supply of coppers in the pocket of my skirt and I was feeling so down, I thought I'd try and phone Dad from the call box by the crossroads in the middle of the village.

I just wanted to hear a friendly voice, but when I got through to the fire station in Lewisham, Dad was out on a "shout", and all I could do was leave a message with the duty desk. This time I couldn't help it. When I'd put the phone down I cried my eyes out in sheer frustration as Tom looked on pathetically. It can't be nice to see your big sister properly upset. In the end he put a sticky hand on my arm and I came to.

"I'll be all right now," I sniffed. "Don't mind me. I shouldn't have done it. I shouldn't have phoned. It won't change anything, will it?"

Sunday 3rd November

Today must rank as one of the most boring ever. It was a sort of Chapel sandwich. We had to walk to Chapel with Mr and Mrs James for the eleven o'clock morning service, then walk back to the farm for lunch, then back to Sunday School (at the Chapel) in the afternoon, and then (would you believe it?) there was another lot of Chapel in the evening! And the James's call Sunday a "day of rest"!

The Chapel is an angry red brick building in the middle of Llantrisant, with "BETHESDA 1888" carved into a large piece of stone high on the front. As you stand in the street it feels like the three big arched windows are like eyes following you as you go, and inside it felt pretty much the same. Everyone turned to look at us when we walked in. Did we each have two heads, I asked myself?

Morning and evening the Reverend Gwynfor Evans – he's the pastor at Bethesda – preached a sermon that must have lasted 45 minutes. In the evening I had to keep kicking Tom on the ankle so he wouldn't fall asleep. And scary stuff it was too, all about sin, hell-fire and damnation. The gist of it was that if we didn't do what we were told (and I'm sure he kept looking at Tom and me) we were going to burn for certain. Which, given that we've come to Wales to escape just that, seems a bit funny really.

But I tell you what, they can certainly sing round here. I've never heard anything like it. A hundred and fifty people in that chapel, and they were making more noise than the crowd do down at The Valley when Charlton are playing at home.

Sunday school was just awful. The other kids gawped at us, and in between singing and praying we had to kneel on the grubby floor of the chapel hall and use our chairs as a sort of table to colour in some silly pictures of Moses in the bulrushes. I ask you, how old do they think we are? Tom gave up in disgust, so I expect we're both marked down as members of the awkward squad now.

Monday 4th November

Today we went to a real school for the first time in a year. Well, at least it's something to do, and gets us away from the smell of the pigs. There's only the one class in the village school and Miss Williams the teacher seems sweet. She's quite young and friendly, with beautiful long brown hair done in ringlets. I think she feels sorry for us. In the afternoon, she made us tell the rest of the children about life in Lewisham. You should have seen their eyes when we told them about the bombing. They were standing out on stalks.

I'm one of the oldest, so I don't think they'll give me any bother, but I'll have to look out for Tom. There's one ginger kid who might be trouble.

Tuesday 5th November

Firework night! But there won't be any fireworks in Llantrisant this evening. I don't think the Welsh would have cared if Guy Fawkes had got away with blowing up the Houses of Parliament. London seems a very long way away.

And thinking of Mum and Dad and dear Shirl (and Frank and Maureen too), I hope there aren't too many fireworks over their way either!

School's difficult, though the work's really easy-peasy. But I know I can't keep putting my hand up to answer questions or I'll look a right little show-off.

And every time my back's turned, I catch that ginger kid giving Tom the eye. His name's Philip Morgan, and he's obviously used to being cock of the walk round here. Two things I don't understand about boys. One is why they're dirty so much of the time. The other is why they're always fighting.

Wednesday 6th November

A bad day. The Dragon's getting worse. She picks me up on everything I do. According to her I'm the most impolite, selfish person there's ever been. I'm trying really hard, and all she can do is tell me how dreadful I am.

And then there's Tom. I thought he was beginning to cope. He's smiled a bit more in the last day or so, but then I turned my back on him for no more than five minutes at lunchtime, and suddenly there he was, hunched up in a corner with a bloody nose. You've guessed it. Philip Morgan!

Tom's never been bullied in his life, so I asked him, "Why did you let him do it? I hope you gave him a fourpenny one in return!"

Tom shook his head miserably.

"Why not?" I said in amazement.

"He said they'd all come and get me," he snivelled.

Well I saw red, didn't I? I wasn't having my little brother being pushed around. "We'll see about that," I said, and before school started again after lunch I collared the Morgan kid and shoved him up against a wall. He was very surprised. I don't think a girl had ever spoken to him like that before.

"Look," I said, "do that again, and you'll need a hospital. Understand?" I hope he didn't see me shaking, as he crept away to find a stone to hide under. And there's me complaining about *boys* fighting all the time. Well isn't the message of the war that we have to stand up to bullies?

Anyway, then he went and told on me to "nice" Miss Williams, who turned into not-so-nice Miss Williams. And somehow by the end of the afternoon word had got back to the Dragon her London kids were ruffians and thugs and that it wouldn't do.

So neither of us had anything to eat tonight, and Tom's beside himself with homesickness and anger. I tiptoed out of my room into his to try and hold him together.

"Stick it out," I whispered. "It'll get better, you'll see!"

"It won't," he moaned, miserably. "I want to go home. I hate this place and I hate school. I want my mum. I've had enough!"

"Tom," I said, starting to wonder if he might do something stupid, "listen to me. Give it a week. If it isn't better by then, we might have to think again. But give it a week. Trust me. All right?"

In the end, he nodded his head.

Thursday 7th November

We had a letter from Mum today, but I had to more or less prise it out of the Dragon's grasp.

If she hadn't dropped the pile of newspapers she was carrying, I don't think we'd ever have seen it. She looked really annoyed as the letter fluttered from between the newsprint down on to the floor and I helpfully picked it up for her, but she covered her tracks quickly.

"I was just going to give you that," she said without a hint of a blush. "Is it from your mum and dad?" As if it was from anyone else!

Still, they all seem fine, and say not to worry about anything. No mention of my telephone call. Perhaps the message was never passed on?

Friday 8th November

Things are going from bad to worse. Now Tom's ill!

He said he didn't feel too clever on Thursday evening, but then he woke me in the middle of the night to tell me in a very small weak

386

voice that he'd been sick all over his bed. Only the sheets actually, so that wasn't too bad.

I tiptoed around trying not to wake anyone, cleaning poor Tom up, pulling the soiled sheets off his bed and replacing them with mine, and finding him a glass of water and a bowl so that if he was sick again the same thing wouldn't happen. Finally I found an extra moth-eaten blanket in the cupboard and wrapped it around myself till the morning.

In the morning I got to the Dragon as early as I could. I knew she'd give someone a rollicking, and I wanted it to be me, not Tom. She raged and banged around for a bit, saying that she didn't have the time to be bothered with stupid children, but in the end she gave me some spare sheets with the threat that they'd have to stay on "for a fortnight at least".

Sunday 10th November

Tom's still not completely better. He's up and about now, but he's still complaining of a dreadful headache, and it's obvious he's got absolutely no energy. I don't think he'll make it to school tomorrow. Still, at least we got out of Chapel and Sunday School – Tom because he was ill, and me because I had to look after him, didn't I?

Before the Dragons came home in the evening I took my chance and used their tin bath in front of the living room fire for half an hour, boiling up half a dozen kettles on the stove to get the water hot enough.

I got everything put away in the nick of time before they came in. But it's very hard not to leave any wet marks behind when you're trying to wash yourself in a tin bath, and I prayed they wouldn't see the damp patch I'd left on the rug.

Monday 11th November

The Dragon more or less forced Tom to go to school this morning, accusing him of being a malingerer. I had to explain to Tom she wasn't saying he'd got a dreadful disease, just that he was lazy! The poor boy sat and shivered by the stove in the schoolroom all day, and even Miss Williams and the other children could see he wasn't up to working and left him alone.

In the evening the Dragon came up to my room to call me for dinner, and sort of hung about as if she was trying to find the words to say something important to me. Maybe she'd decided she actually wanted a conversation after two weeks of shouting. I'd been reading my *Jane Eyre* and she eyed my little row of books suspiciously, up and down, up and down. For a moment I was afraid she was going to tell me reading was a waste of time (which was obviously what she was thinking) and confiscate the books and their hidden hoard of treasure. But she contented herself with a tetchy shake of the head, as if she pitied me, and turned on her heels.

Wednesday 13th November

I've never done anything really bad in my life before, but I think I might be about to, and I feel all tied up in knots about it.

When I think about it, even in the mornings when I'm at my most cheerful, the last fortnight's been horrible. After that bother with Philip Morgan, the other kids at school have just ignored us. I'd say they've sent us to Coventry, but since we're in Wales that doesn't seem quite right, does it? Maybe they've sent us to Cardiff then! (You can see I haven't completely lost my sense of humour!)

After the first day or so, we just stopped bothering about it, talked to each other, and got on with what Miss Williams gave us to do. She's gone all stand-offish too, but perhaps that's just in my imagination. That's the trouble, you see: keeping things in proportion.

The final straw came today. It's a week since I said to Tom I was sure things would improve, and I was wondering what I was going to say to him after school today because I knew they hadn't. Anyway, that's when it happened. I wasn't there, mind. I only saw the results.

For the last couple of days now, Mr and Mrs Dragon have been pushing Tom outside to help with small things on the farm, even though he's not really better – pulling up vegetables for supper, piling silage on to the wagon, watching how the cows are milked and so on. That's all right, I suppose. The fresh air's probably good for him, and it's better than him hanging round the house getting bullied along with me.

Anyway, Mr James had Tom in his workshop this afternoon, supposedly teaching him some woodwork. Tom told me he'd been practising knocking nails into a bit of wood with one of Mr James's hammers when he missed the nail and hit his thumb hard.

I don't know what Tom said because he won't tell me, and I can't think it can have been too awful, because I don't think he knows many really bad words, but whatever it was shocked old James. I don't think Chapel folk swear very much, though it doesn't prevent them being as rude as they like.

So Mr James comes back in the house literally holding Tom by the ear, and tells the Dragon what he's said. Now once or twice I've heard Mum use the expression "*Wash your mouth out with soap and water*" when someone's said a rude word, but I never dreamed anyone would really do it. But that's exactly what they did. Mr James held Tom down, and she applied the soap. None too gently either.

I was shocked. As Tom began to howl I started to say they should leave him alone, but the Dragon roughly told me to be quiet or I'd be next for the high jump.

When they'd finished it was the usual thing. Tom was sent upstairs and told not to come down till he was called. I went with him and dared them to stop me.

Anyway, I've made my mind up. We can't stay here. Not after that! We've given it our best shot, and things aren't going to get any better.

Thursday 14th November

I've thought about this very carefully, and we're not going to get two chances. We've got to make our escape work first time.

Thank heavens for the money Shirl gave me. If ever there was a "rainy day" this has got to be it!

After school today, Tom and I went to spy out the land at Llantrisant station. The timetable on the platform says there's just two trains a day to Cardiff, but the good news is one of them's at 8.25.

If we say we're going down to school ten minutes early tomorrow morning we can be on that train. Most of our luggage will have to stay here: all we can carry is our school bags.

I said a special prayer tonight for the train not to be cancelled. What'll happen when we get home I've got no idea, but the only way to convince Mum and Dad about this is face to face. A letter won't do.

Friday 15th November

The man in the ticket office peered over his glasses very suspiciously when we bought two singles for Paddington. It was exactly 8.22 and down the platform the little tank engine was already champing at the bit in front of the three carriages that made up the 8.25 for Cardiff.

We had the money, didn't we? I looked him straight in the eye when I handed it over, as if this was what we did every day of the week.

He stared right back, knowing he'd seen us before, but not quite able to make the right connection. I held my breath and waited for him to say something, but then he dropped his gaze and slowly, oh so slowly, gave me the change. This time there were some other passengers on the train so he couldn't keep them waiting just because we looked a bit dodgy, could he?

All the way to Cardiff I think we both expected the train to creak to a halt any minute, and a copper to come and haul us off. But it rumbled on into the grey stone suburbs, and just after ten we were standing scanning the destination board inside the station canopy.

There was an express for Paddington at 10.45. If we made that, we were safe. Once in London, even if by chance they rounded us up, I reasoned they'd have to take us home and not back to Llantrisant.

Every time a ticket collector banged his way down the corridor on the express, every time the door of our compartment slid back, every time someone in uniform passed down the train, I thought the game was up. Now I know what it must feel like to be a spy behind enemy lines.

Whenever the train pulled up at a signal, our hearts began to beat faster. At Swindon, wherever that is, it stopped for a full fifteen minutes though it wasn't meant to, and I thought we'd had it. But no one came, and eventually the train wheezed back into life.

Every chance I got I talked quietly to Tom, encouraging him, telling him why we were doing what we were doing and how well we were getting on. He was as scared as I was. *I* knew he didn't normally look that pale and wan, but nobody else did so that was all right. As the day went on, hunger made us even more edgy, but I didn't want to spend any of our precious cash till we were safely in London. Food could wait. We weren't going to die of starvation.

Finally, after hours of sitting on the edge of our seats, the train drew slowly into Paddington. As we handed our tickets in at the barrier I felt like doing a dance, but of course the worst bit was still to come. Facing the music at number 47!

Tom must have been reading my mind.

"Food?" I said. "Or home first?"

"Home," he said decisively.

Saturday 16th November

I was dog tired last night, and almost fell asleep over the diary. And there was a miracle! No air-raid sirens. No bombs! I slept through till nine in the morning, and I don't remember a thing.

Now where was I in the story?

Well, we caught the tube to Charing Cross, and then the Southern Electric to Lewisham. It was easier than working out which buses were running. I haven't been in the tube for months. The Circle line runs only just underground, not like the Northern where you have to go down hundreds of stairs, so it isn't great as a shelter. Even so, tonnes of people move in every night from the look of things. They're supposed to clean up every morning, but there's still lots of stuff left around. And the disgusting smell hits you in the face the minute you walk inside. I don't know how the people who camp out there don't catch dreadful diseases.

When we walked in the back door of number 47, Mum was doing the washing. When she saw us her face was a picture. In an instant the colour bleached out of her, and I thought she was going to faint. She caught hold of the mangle for support, and then without a word the three of us hugged till we cried.

She knew. Just from the fact we were there, she knew. "You're a truthful girl, Edie," she said later in the evening, when I'd stopped explaining. "I know you wouldn't have done it unless you had to." Finally, she relaxed and leaned back slightly in her chair. Pursing her lips in a half-smile, she said, "So what are we going to say to Mr and Mrs Dragon, then?"

Tom had been subdued and serious all through the evening, but as he caught the twinkle in Mum's eye, he laughed and laughed with relief until his sides ached. I'd forgotten the smell of home, of cosiness and baking and polish, and now I want to stay here for ever.

As I was falling asleep last night, Shirl came and put her arms around me and planted a kiss on my forehead "Good on you, girl," she said. "I hope I'd have done exactly the same."

Tuesday 19th November

We came back at the right time. Jerry's leaving London alone now, but from what I read in the paper yesterday, that means other people are having it even worse than we did. Last weekend they say Coventry was badly hit, and pretty well burned to a cinder. And today they've sent all the Lewisham regular firemen and a lot of the auxiliaries up to Birmingham. The fires there are burning right out of control. Who knows when Dad'll be home!

Mum says perhaps Hitler's seeing sense. He thought he could bomb the spirit out of the British people, but now he knows he can't. It makes me feel sort of proud. Back in September, when the RAF won the "Battle of Britain" by seeing off the German bombers, Mr Churchill said never had so much been owed by so many to so few, and I thought of how our Frank was one of those few. Well someone has to keep the planes flying, don't they! Not everyone can get the glory of shooting down Messerschmitts.

And now we've all done our bit by not giving in. Maybe even Tom and me, by not staying in Wales.

The fact the bombing's stopped made it easier for Mum and Dad not to send us back to the Dragons, though we've had some old-fashioned looks from a few people who knew we'd gone. Mr Lineham, for one. He didn't mind having me back to help with the papers, though. (By the way, newspapers are shrinking every week. The government wants all the paper it can lay its hands on for the war effort.)

On the other hand, I've heard they're opening the elementary schools again next month. I'm too old now, but Tom'll have to go. I think Mum's relieved. Now at least she'll know where Tom is every day.

Wednesday 20th November

Dad's still in Birmingham and there's been no news. I'm not used to Dad being away, and when I think about it the hairs on the back of my neck go all hot with worry.

One of the main reasons I'm glad to be back at number 47 is the food. I didn't realize till I went away how good a cook Mum is, and Shirl too come to that.

What with the shortages and the rationing, it's getting harder to make do, but Mum says that's where a good cook can really shine. Bacon's rationed, and so is butter and margarine of course, and now tea. I suppose that's obvious since it comes to England in ships, and the German U-boats are blowing up so many of them. There's not much chance of proper meat anymore, so we have to put up with liver and kidneys. And ox tongue. Actually, I'm starting to really like that. Tinned salmon's nice, too. We eat a lot more veg than we used to, and Mum makes us keep up our vitamins by drinking tomato juice, which I can't say I like. It's far too slimy!

We can still get fresh eggs, but Mum reckons we'll be lucky if they're not rationed too before long. She wants us to keep chickens, so at least we'll have the eggs from them.

It's Mum's puddings I like best: jam roly-poly and honey-and-walnut cake are my favourites. If *I* try to make them they just aren't the same.

The queues at shops are getting longer now that people are starting to think about Christmas, so I expect I'll be doing a lot of hanging around in the cold. Everyone tries it on to get more than their fair share. When the War started you heard some dreadful stories about rich people turning up in their chauffeur-driven cars and cleaning out shops far away from where they lived. That's why rationing was brought in, and why we can only get rationed goods from the shop where we're registered – in our case, Nuttall's for the meat, and Harrold's for the groceries.

You can't always trust shopkeepers either. They might seem as nice as pie, but a bloke in Deptford was had up for watering down his milk the other day and selling eggs that were smaller than they were supposed to be.

Of course, if you're in with the shopkeepers there's always the chance you can get something "under the counter", on the black market. It's funny how some people always seem to have cigarettes, and other people can't get them for love nor money. Not that I want them, only Shirl!

Saturday 23rd November

It's rained cats and dogs for the last 24 hours, and the River Ravensbourne's flooded. Half a mile away there's mud and rubbish all over people's houses, as if things haven't been bad enough.

Dad's back from the Midlands, and I've never seen him like this. Even when the Blitz here was at its worst, he usually came up smiling, but this is different. He came home and went to bed without saying a word. He must have slept twelve hours solid.

Sunday 24th November

It was just Dad and me this morning. He'd been tidying up the garden and I caught him when he was putting his tools away in the garden shed. I asked him what was wrong.

"It was awful, love," he answered in a low voice. "I've seen some things, but this was like nothing else. . ." And his voice trailed off into nothing. I could see he was close to tears. He pulled himself together, and this time when he spoke it was with anger, even hatred.

"They hit a school where there were kids having a party," he said eventually. "There were maybe 40 inside. We got there too late. It was just one great wall of flame. Choking fumes and smoke everywhere. We tried our best to get in, time after time, but it was no good. Do you know what they say it was, Edie? An oil bomb! I ask you, what kind of perverted minds drop bombs that spray burning oil on five-year-old kids? And I couldn't do a damn thing to help." He was openly crying now with the memory of the horrors he'd seen. I went and put my arms round him, but there was nothing I could do. There were terrifying pictures in his mind and nothing I said would ever wipe them out.

Tuesday 26th November

With winter coming on, everyone's talking about getting ill. What's worrying is all those folk crowded together in the big public shelters. The bombs may have stopped for a bit, but everyone's sure Hitler'll come back to London one day soon, and most people don't want to take a chance. It's cold and dirty in the tube stations. People even go down to the caves in Chislehurst every night, because they think they'll be safe. But what if there's an epidemic of flu? Apparently, in 1918, it killed tens of thousands of people just after the Great War, and maybe the same thing will happen again this time. Except it might be diphtheria, or the plague. It just doesn't bear thinking about. With all those people coughing over each other, any illness could spread like wildfire.

I've started cycling over to help out at a Red Cross centre for bombed-out people in Deptford, and that's opened my eyes I can tell you!

At night there's only buckets for toilets, and not even enough of those. I won't go into it too closely, but sometimes in the morning there's stuff leaking all over the floor. The smell's unbelievable. And people are sleeping and eating in there. So now you see what I mean!

Saturday 30th November

Yesterday evening Shirl told me that one day, when we were in Wales, the Germans dropped a delayed-action bomb down towards Catford. They cordoned off the area, but before the Bomb Disposal team could arrive, it exploded and demolished a row of terraced houses. (No one hurt, luckily.) Back in Lewisham half an hour later, it was raining feathers in the town centre. The rumour started to go round that a chicken factory had caught it, but really it was only bedding from the terrace up in Catford! Any excuse to laugh, these days!

Wednesday 4th December

Mum tipped me the wink that Dad's boss wants to put him in for a commendation after what happened in Birmingham. It sounds like Dad was a bit of a hero on the quiet. It's just typical that to have heard him you'd have thought he did nothing at all.

Frank's written to say that he won't be able to get leave at Christmas, but he can spend the weekend after next with us. Hooray! So we'll just have to celebrate Christmas *twice*, won't we?

Friday 6th December

I went window shopping at Chiesman's yesterday. I haven't a clue what to buy anyone for Christmas, mostly because I haven't the money to buy anything nice.

And the way it is in England right now, you feel bad about spending anything on frivolous things anyway. There's posters everywhere telling you about the "Squander Bug", making you feel guilty if you're not giving your money to help buy another new bomber, or putting it in the bank so the government can use it.

I saw a brilliant green bus conductor's set in the toy department. Two years ago, Tom would have loved it, but he's grown up too fast. Anyway, five shillings and eleven pence is too much for me. Even a new football's three and six, and I can't afford that.

If Shirl can get me the wool, I've still got the time to knit Mum something warm, and I'll work on old Lineham to see if I can wangle some of Dad's favourite pipe tobacco out of him. Mum's given me the OK to make a collage of family photos for Frank. I'll mount them and overlay them so he'll have something he can put beside his bed to remember us by.

Thursday 12th December

Mr Lineham's a funny old stick. I asked him about the tobacco for Dad's Christmas box yesterday and he tapped his nose and said, "No problems, young Edie. We'll see Mr Benson all right for Christmas, you and me. Man like Mr Benson deserves a little respect and recognition." Then he turned and asked, as if it was an afterthought, "What are you giving young Thomas?"

I shrugged, and said honestly that I didn't know if I could afford much.

Then blow me if he didn't fetch a few soldiers from the back of the shop, similar to the ones Tom had nicked, wrap them in tissue paper, put them carefully in an old shoebox, and give it to me.

I didn't know what to say, and stuttered an inadequate thank you.

"Don't mention it," he said. "You're a bright girl, and a good worker. It's just a little something to show my appreciation."

Well I never!

Saturday 14th December

Frank's home! And he looks so well. I'd swear he looks tanned even though it's December and near freezing. All that fresh air must be doing him good. Over tea he announced that he's going to apply to train as a pilot, and I saw Mum's face fall. Dad asked calmly if he thought he stood much chance, and Frank said what with all the pilot losses there'd been during the Battle of Britain, he thought there was *every* chance. He says he's been thinking about flying every day for the past eighteen months – eating, drinking and sleeping it. It's just that he hasn't actually been *doing* any.

I don't know what to think. On the one hand I can see the glamour of it all. There's this idea that it's very dashing to be a pilot, and all the girls will think you're wonderful. On the other hand, Frank's nice and safe if he stays as ground crew. I read somewhere that once you're trained as a fighter pilot, your life expectancy's three weeks. I just hope and pray Frank's either very sensible or very lucky.

He brought me a very beautiful, very grown-up blue and green silk scarf. It's daft really, because I haven't got anything to wear it with. He just looked at me and smiled and said, "It's your colours. You'll find something." Then he gave me a big hug. I think he was really touched with my collage of photographs, and I know he meant it when he said he thought of us every day.

Monday 23rd December

For a few days now Tom and I have been out collecting. There's a party for the homeless kids in the Red Cross Centre out at Deptford tonight, and we've been after toys that we could wrap up to make some sort of Christmas presents for them. We've not done too badly, and Dad's knocked up some trucks and boats out of the spare wood he keeps in the shed. They look all right once they're painted up.

Mum was home this afternoon, and she and I made a huge cracker from paper Shirl conned out of the management up at Chiesman's. It's about four foot long, and we've put lots of the smaller toys inside. The Red Cross van's coming round to collect the cracker and us in a few minutes!

I know they've decorated the hall so that it looks quite festive, even if it still smells a bit "off". We'll have some singing and dancing, and I think they've got a Charlie Chaplin film and some cartoons to keep the kids amused. The Christmas tea might not be all that wonderful, but I think they've managed a cake of sorts. When those kids get hold of it, and there are about 40 of them, you can bet it won't last long! Happy Christmas, Deptford!

Wednesday 25th December

Last night we went to the midnight service at St Matthew's. As we walked down to the church the air was crisp and cold, and the sky was clear and starry. There was a bomber's moon, but everything was quiet. Even Germans celebrate Christmas! When the bells rang out, and the vicar was talking about "Peace on earth, goodwill to all men", it was very odd to think of people in Germany doing exactly the same thing.

If they say they're Christians like us, how come they've been bombing us to pieces these last few months? I thought of everything we've been through, and I said thank you to whoever it is up there that we're still in number 47, and not homeless like those kids out in Deptford. And I made a big wish that Hitler would get the message and be happy with what he's got and leave us alone.

Before we sang "Hark the Herald Angels Sing", the vicar made a point of saying it was a German tune, and that we had to pray there could be peace with justice soon. As I looked around the church it was obvious not everyone was singing. Mum and I weren't the only ones with tears in our eyes.

Monday 30th December

Uncle Bob keeps the Lord Wellington pub in Webber Street near London Bridge. He's Dad's older brother and we don't see him very often. He joined the Auxiliary Fire Service early in the war. Dad says Bob saw which way the wind was blowing and thought that if he was called up Auntie Doris would never be able to run the pub on her own. This way Uncle Bob can keep an eye on things. Dad and Bob get on well, but generally there's a funny relationship between regular firemen and auxiliaries, like the regulars think the auxiliaries aren't proper somehow.

Anyway, yesterday Dad piled us on to the bus to spend the day with them. There haven't been any air raids in a while, and we took our night things and toothbrushes thinking we'd stay over.

They're both big, jolly people. Uncle Bob always wears a bow tie, quite often a spotted one, and just to look at her, you'd *know* Auntie Doris worked behind a bar, all bosom and behind. Uncle Bob is the *only* person I know who calls my dad "Albert".

We'd had a lovely day in their living room, high above the chatter of the bars, talking and playing board games (mostly Tom and me) but then the siren caught us unawares when it went off half an hour or so after blackout. Dad and Bob looked at each other, put down their glasses of Guinness, and resignedly went off to do their duty.

Bob and Doris have done the cellar up quite nicely, and I shouldn't think there are many places safer in the whole of London, but we were down there hours and hours and bored silly by the time the all-clear went. We heard, or rather felt, the occasional dull explosion, but nothing to indicate what had really been going on outside. The walls of the Lord Wellington must be very thick.

When we went upstairs about midnight, Doris went to the window and cried out softly, "Oh my Gawd!"

From the big picture-windows of their lounge, you can see across the railway and the River Thames to the City of London. St Paul's sits in the middle, surrounded by all the great buildings belonging to the newspapers and the banks. It's a wonderful view, so good you feel you should be paying to look at it.

But now the light thrown back from the fires raging across the beautiful city was as strong as the electric light in Bob and Doris's lounge could have been. The shells of at least two of Sir Christopher Wren's churches stood out clearly against the black sky, lit from inside like torches as the flames burnt away 300 years of history. Even at that distance you could see sparks shooting into the air, so powerful was the force of the blaze. The whole panorama was silhouetted in red, like a mad sunset. It made you understand the terror Dad and Bob must face every time they go out to work. The city was being destroyed before our eyes, a second Great Fire of London.

This afternoon, before we left for home and Bob had dragged himself back to the Lord Wellington (blackened and bruised after a twelve-hour shift), the fires were still burning. And you can be sure the bombers will come back for the kill tonight.

Thursday 2nd January 1941

I don't know quite know how to write my diary today. I'm so full up I could burst. Words won't do any more. I thought I could get rid of my fear and unhappiness by putting it on paper. Now I know that, when it comes down to it, there are some things you can never tell.

Frank's dead. We had a letter this morning saying so. It must have been the same raids we'd seen from Uncle Bob and Aunt Doris's flat.

I suppose the Germans were softening up the RAF stations to keep our fighters out of the air. Then they'd have had a free run at the city. As if it matters. Everyone knows our boys are no good after dark anyway. They just can't see the bombers well enough, despite the searchlights.

Anyway, according to Frank's commanding officer, some German planes got through to Biggin Hill and strafed the runways. Frank and two other men were out there, desperately trying to get some Hurricanes ready to fly. A petrol tank went up. And that was it.

I thought he'd be safe if he stayed on the ground. I thought death was something that happened to other families. I thought this year would be better than last. God, I don't believe in you, not if you take away the life of someone like Frank who never did anybody any harm. It's not fair. It's so awful, sometimes I catch myself thinking it hasn't really happened at all. How on earth will we ever recover?

Saturday 4th January

Mum had to go to the undertaker's this morning to make arrangements for the funeral. I went with her. It was a bitingly cold morning under a steely grey sky, so our bodies were as numb as our minds, despite being wrapped up as much as possible in scarves and gloves.

It was a fair walk right up towards New Cross, and I don't know why but on the way home we wandered down through Crofton Park. We were walking along a row of terraces when this woman with her hair in curlers rushes out of her house.

"You've got to help," she says. "She's started. What are we going to do?

I can't believe it. How can she have started now? She's not due for another month."

Mum calmed her down, and we went inside. The house was in a right state. I should think it hadn't been cleaned in a month of Sundays. On the sofa in the front room was a girl who didn't look much older than me, groaning and screaming by turns – having a baby. I mean, I've never seen anyone give birth before, but I didn't need telling.

To spare the gory details, it was all over in about half an hour. I didn't know it could be that quick! By the time the doctor arrived he'd missed the arrival of a beautiful new little baby boy. Well, as ugly as a shrivelled prune actually, but who's going to tell a new mother and grandmother that?

And then I made the connection between a birth and a death, and for the first time since we had that letter three days ago I couldn't help myself and I was in floods and floods of tears that just wouldn't stop coming. Soon I was shaking and I couldn't have spoken even if there'd been anything to say.

Friday 18th April

I know I've been bad and I haven't kept this diary going, but in the weeks after Frank's funeral I just couldn't find the energy. I couldn't see the point in much at all to be honest. The people who'd left Lewisham during the back end of last year have begun to drift back, and I've started to go to a school that's running (mornings only) near Lee Green, so I suppose, what with everything else, my time's been pretty well occupied.

And (until Wednesday) life had been what passes for normal these days. On the whole it's been quiet these last few weeks. The sirens go pretty regularly but compared with before Christmas, there's not been much damage.

On Wednesday the warnings went in the mid-evening, about eight o'clock, and we settled down in the Anderson as usual. It's all right in there now. There's even electric light, though you have to be careful you don't trip over the cables.

You don't often hear the droning of the planes like we did that day. They seemed unusually low and concentrated. Then suddenly out of the blue, there were two almighty explosions. The Anderson and the earth around us seemed to bend and change shape almost before we felt the hollow whoosh of noise that surrounded us and caught us up. Earth was flying everywhere, the lights went out, and then there was the sound of splintering wood and glass. For one awful moment I thought we were going to be buried alive.

Mum was in there with us. Dad was on duty. In the ominous quiet that followed the explosions, she asked anxiously, "Everyone all right?" and though we were all shivering we all said we were.

"What do we do, Mum?" squeaked Tom in panic.

"Hold still," she said. "Who knows if Jerry's finished? Until we know he has, we're safer here."

In fact the all-clear sounded quite soon, but when we crawled out of the shelter and looked back towards the house, number 47 wasn't there any more, and neither was Bessie Andrews's house next door. As we stood there we could already hear the fire bells ringing down the road and, by the time we'd picked our dazed way across the rubble to the street, a fire tender (with Dad clinging on to the side) was dodging the bricks towards where the front gate had been. Mum ran to the tender and she and Dad clung to each other, while we kids looked on not knowing what to do.

In the cold light of day, there wasn't any good news. Bessie must have been in the house next door when the bomb struck. The only consolation is she wouldn't have known anything about it. We'd never been able to persuade her to let the council put in a shelter of her own, or to come and share ours.

When they told us it was safe to go on the site, we wandered about sifting through the remains of our old life. It's funny the way the bomb has utterly destroyed some things, and left others almost undamaged. Take the kitchen for instance. The furniture in there just seems to have vanished, but I found a cup and a saucer covered in dust but otherwise completely untouched – not a chip, not a scratch.

And then there was my diary. By the new year it had filled three exercise books, which I'd kept in a square biscuit tin in my room. Now, as I wandered about on the bricks and fallen beams, I almost fell over the tin, dented but in one piece.

413

It's a miracle! I don't know why but clearly it was meant to survive along with us. So having made this last entry, I'll keep the diary with me to bring us good luck in whatever comes next. We might need it!

Postscript
April 1946

Five years on, and I've been re-reading what I wrote in that terrible autumn and winter, a time that now seems so very far away.

We *didn't* find ourselves living in the Red Cross Centre after the collapse of the house in Summerfield Road, as I remember being afraid we might. We were luckier than most. Dad's friends at the Fire Station saw us all right, and though we were cramped up together in a poky flat for about a year afterwards, at least we didn't have to leave Lewisham.

Shirl moved straight in with Margaret, a friend from Chiesman's, which was sensible but a bit of a shock for me at the time. As of last October she's become Mrs Goodfellow, and her husband, Christopher, works for Wray's in Downham. They manufacture lenses for the cameras that go in reconnaissance aircraft. He's very clever, and obviously thinks the world of Shirl.

Maureen's still in the forces and says she might make a career out of it. We saw less and less of her during the last couple of years of the war, but she seems happy. To be honest, we don't have much in common.

Tom's a nice lad now. He's taller than me and still growing fast. I don't know where he gets it from. He's got himself a first job down the river at Vickers, near Erith. It's a bit of a bus ride, but I think he thrives on the independence. Somehow I don't think he'll be at home for long. Good thing, too: he takes up too much room! When I look at him he sometimes reminds me of Frank.

Dad didn't come out of the War well. All the years of inhaling smoke and soot have gone to his chest, and he's been invalided out of the Fire Service. These days even gardening's a struggle, which for a man of 51 is ridiculous. For what he did in Birmingham he received a George Medal, a distinction very few firemen in London achieved during the war. To this day he's never talked about the exact details. So he got to meet the King a second time, and reminded His Majesty that the previous time they'd talked about the weather.

"Did we?" said the King. "And what was it like that day?"

My mum goes from strength to strength. Dad says there's no stopping her. In a funny way the war gave Mum an opportunity she didn't have before. If there'd been no war, maybe she'd have spent the next ten years being a housewife, looking after us kids, cooking and cleaning. Being an ARP warden gave her a taste of how good she is at organizing people. She works for Lewisham Council now, and she's on her second new job in a year.

Chamberlain still lives with us in our new house just off Lee High Road. He suffers badly with his nerves after all the bombing, and I shouldn't think he'll ever really be right again. But I'm so glad we didn't have him put down, even though we'd thought about it long and hard during the Blitz. He's far too precious.

Me? I'm a real bookworm these days. I want to go to university to study history, and then maybe politics. This Second World War we've lived through has left most of Europe ruined. We've got to rebuild it, and make it better than it was before. And somehow we've got to ensure there's never a third war, because now we know that if ever there *is*, no diary and no person is likely to survive it.

Historical note

The First World War (or Great War) ended in 1918. By the 1919 Treaty of Versailles, Germany was prevented from re-arming, and made to accept responsibility for all the damage caused by the war. Germany's pride was badly dented, but more than that, the Treaty of Versailles meant a lot of hardship for her people over the next ten years.

Hitler seemed to be a man who could give Germany back her pride, and as he came to power in the 1930s he promised to make her wealthy again. His National Socialist Party, the Nazis, were concerned to make Germany great. They weren't too worried about the morality of the means used to achieve this.

In Britain, the governments of the 1930s watched what was happening in Germany with anxiety. On the whole they thought that a strong Germany would make for a safer Europe. They admired German spirit and technology: they didn't *want* to see the violence that Hitler was unleashing. So they stood by while Germany re-armed and created a powerful air force, and then as it swallowed up Austria and Czechoslovakia. This became known as the policy of "appeasement".

Gradually it was realized that even at home Hitler was using extreme force against groups and nationalities he believed were making trouble.

Later, Hitler's bizarre ideas about the superiority of the German people were to lead to the deaths of millions of Jews and others in concentration camps.

In 1939, the British government, led by Prime Minister Neville Chamberlain, eventually decided that a line had to be drawn. They told Germany that if Poland were invaded, a state of war would exist between Britain and Germany. On September 1st, German troops entered Poland, and two days later Britain declared war.

German air tactics were well-known by now. They used dive bombers to terrify ordinary civilian populations, to weaken morale and create panic, making ground operations by their army more effective. So when war was declared, the British people expected German bombers overhead immediately, and indeed on that very first day of the war the air-raid warnings sounded in London. But no bombers came. Not yet.

It was also expected that the Germans would use poison gas, so everyone was equipped with a gas mask, even the very youngest children. In the event no poison gas was used anywhere in the Second World War.

Neville Chamberlain was never going to be the strong war leader Britain needed, because he was seen as one of those who had appeased Hitler. Winston Churchill had always opposed concessions to Germany. He wasn't without his faults because he was hot-blooded and always likely to make errors of judgement, but he was a daring and inspirational leader with great vision and a gift for public speaking. He became Prime Minister in May 1940 at a point when Germany had just overrun Holland

and Belgium and was about to defeat France. Now, with the United States shying away from declaring war, Britain stood alone.

Invasion by Germany seemed inevitable, and in May 1940, with many able-bodied young men "called-up" into the armed forces, the Local Defence Volunteers or "Home Guard" was formed to help defend Britain.

In July Hitler began to lay his plans. His air force, the Luftwaffe, had always been so successful in the past that most of his military actions on the ground had gone more or less unopposed. He believed the same might be true this time. At first he attacked shipping in the English Channel with great success, halting all convoys through the Straits of Dover. Then, during August, he started to attack the British fighter bases in southern England. The losses of aircraft and men on both sides were great, and if he'd continued with this tactic Hitler might have destroyed British air power completely. But he was distracted into retaliating for the first British night bombing-raids against Germany. He called his planes away from the airfields, and told them to bomb London. He hoped to win complete air superiority, and crush Britain's morale. In the event he achieved neither objective.

For 57 consecutive nights from September 7th 1940, Hitler's planes raided London. Londoners called this the **Blitz** after the German expression **Blitzkrieg**, which means "lightning war". Given the length of time the bombing went on, perhaps this wasn't quite the right word! After London, most other British cities came in for similar bombardment during the period up to May 1941, some – like the centre of Coventry – being almost completely devastated.

More than three and a half million homes were destroyed, often by incendiary or fire bombs. The House of Commons was left in ruins and even Buckingham Palace was damaged. Ordinary life stopped almost completely. About 30,000 people were killed in the Blitz, half of them in London. Up to September 1941, Hitler had killed more British civilians than fighting men. In Lewisham there were over 2,000 fires between September 1940 and May 1941. More than 20,000 incendiary bombs fell in Lewisham, and a further 2,000 packed with high explosive. Nearly 1,000 people were killed here alone. To put it another way, about one in fifty of the average war-time population of the borough was killed or seriously injured.

But the spirit of the British people in Lewisham and elsewhere wasn't crushed, and having failed to find an opportunity to invade in September 1940, Hitler never got another chance. The tide of the war slowly turned against him, although it took until 1945 for the allied armies to reach Berlin and the bunker where he committed suicide.

The story of Edie Benson and her family may read like a fairy tale, but Edie might have been your grandma. These things are not so far away as they seem. . .

Timeline

1939

3 September Britain declares war on Germany.

1940

9 May Winston Churchill becomes Prime Minister.

27 May British troops are evacuated from Dunkirk, France.

22 June Most of France is under German occupation.

10 July "Battle of Britain" begins.

16 July Hitler makes plans to invade Britain.

25 August British planes bomb German towns including Berlin.

7 September First "big raid" on London by German bombers.

17 September Hitler abandons invasion "until further notice".

12 October Hitler cancels invasion for winter.

2 November Last of 57 consecutive night raids on London.

14 November Major raid on Coventry leaves city in ruins.

November 1940–April 1941 Raids on most major British cities.

29–31 December Devastating air raids on the City of London.

1941

16–19 April Some of the worst raids of the war in Lewisham.

May Hitler turns his attention to Russia. The Blitz is over.

7 December Japanese aircraft attack the American fleet in Pearl Harbor, on the Hawaiian island of Oahu. The US enters the war.

1944

6 June D-day. Allied troops land in Normandy.

1944–early 1945 V-1 "doodle-bug" and V-2 rocket attacks on London.

1945

14 February As many civilians killed in a single British air-raid on Dresden as in the entire German "Blitz".

7 May Germans unconditionally surrender on all fronts.

6–9 August Atomic bombs are dropped on Hiroshima and Nagasaki. The world enters the nuclear age.

2 September Official celebration of victory over Japan.

Experience history first-hand with My Story –
a series of vividly imagined accounts of life in the past.

MY STORY
POMPEII
SUE REID